City of Shards

Steve Rodgers

DEDICATION

To my wife Lori, for putting up with my crazy habit.

Table of Contents

Praise for City of Shards vi

City of Aldive Map viii

Empire of Tanbar Map ix

Chronos xi

I 1

II 10

III 18

IV 22

V 32

VI 43

VII 51

VIII 60

IX 66

X 75

XI 87

XII 99

XIII 113

XIV 126

XV 137

XVI 148

XVII 162

XVIII 174

XIX 185

XX 199

XXI 209

XXII 223

XXIII 228

XXIV..234

XXV...238

Newsletter Signup and Reviews 249

Books by Steve Rodgers...250

Acknowledgements 251

About the Author..252

Praise for City of Shards

"Rodgers creates an intricate world of fabulous creatures, diverse deities, colorful locales, and spectacular battles. His characters, whether human or Lidathi, are empathetic, realistic individuals. The author's writing style is spot-on for this fantastic tale, never straying into the type of heroic language that can often turn into a parody of itself. Rather, the prose is crisp and image-filled.... An exhilarating tale for fans of sword and sorcery, fantasy, and rich worldbuilding."
—**Kirkus Reviews**
Review link: https://www.kirkusreviews.com/book-reviews/steve-rodgers/city-of-shards/

"....Larin's hero's journey features familiar fantasy elements: kings, monsters, magic and mysticism. Yet Rodgers manages to weave a stunningly refreshing take on traditional genre tropes. Plot developments are highly unpredictable, and the story is admirably nuanced, with Larin forced to choose between allegiances that each carry dark consequences. With a sharp, incisive narrative style, Rodgers delivers a colorful cast of fully developed characters and believably flawed heroes... the author has created a fictional world that shines with a rare degree of immediacy and realism—even with its wizards, monsters and six-legged gods. Readers will savor the journey."
—**Blue Ink Review**
Review link: https://www.blueinkreview.com/book-reviews/city-of-shards/

"In Steve Rodgers's fantasy City of Shards, a boy learns that the hero's journey is never a straight path; sometimes, the only way forward is to plunge into darkness....City of Shards is an engaging and immersive story, mainly because its world building is so detailed...These characters come to life through crisp, action-filled prose....City of Shards is a dazzling and captivating introduction to a new fantasy adventure series. Larin may not seem like the hero to save the world, but he proves to be one who can lead the way through the darkness."
—**Foreword Reviews**
Review link: https://www.forewordreviews.com/reviews/city-of-shards/

"...City of Shards by Steve Rodgers is a unique and exciting dark fantasy...City of Shards starts slowly as Rodgers immerses the reader in the rich and unique world before pushing Larin towards an impossible choice between future slavery and human sacrifice under the six-legged gods, or annihilation at the hands of the demons. Rodgers removes any truly good outcome from the premise and the effect is amazing."
—**Readers' Favorite**
Review link: https://readersfavorite.com/book-review/city-of-shards

"Drop whatever fantasy you're reading and pick up this book right now. And I know this is a long review, by hear me out. This is one of the best epic fantasy series in existence."...
—**Netgalley Review (from Goodreads)**
Review link: https://www.goodreads.com/book/show/38119693-city-of-shards

To sign up for Steve Rodgers' mailing list, go here:

https://www.steverodgersauthor.com/

City of Aldive Map

Empire of Tanbar Map

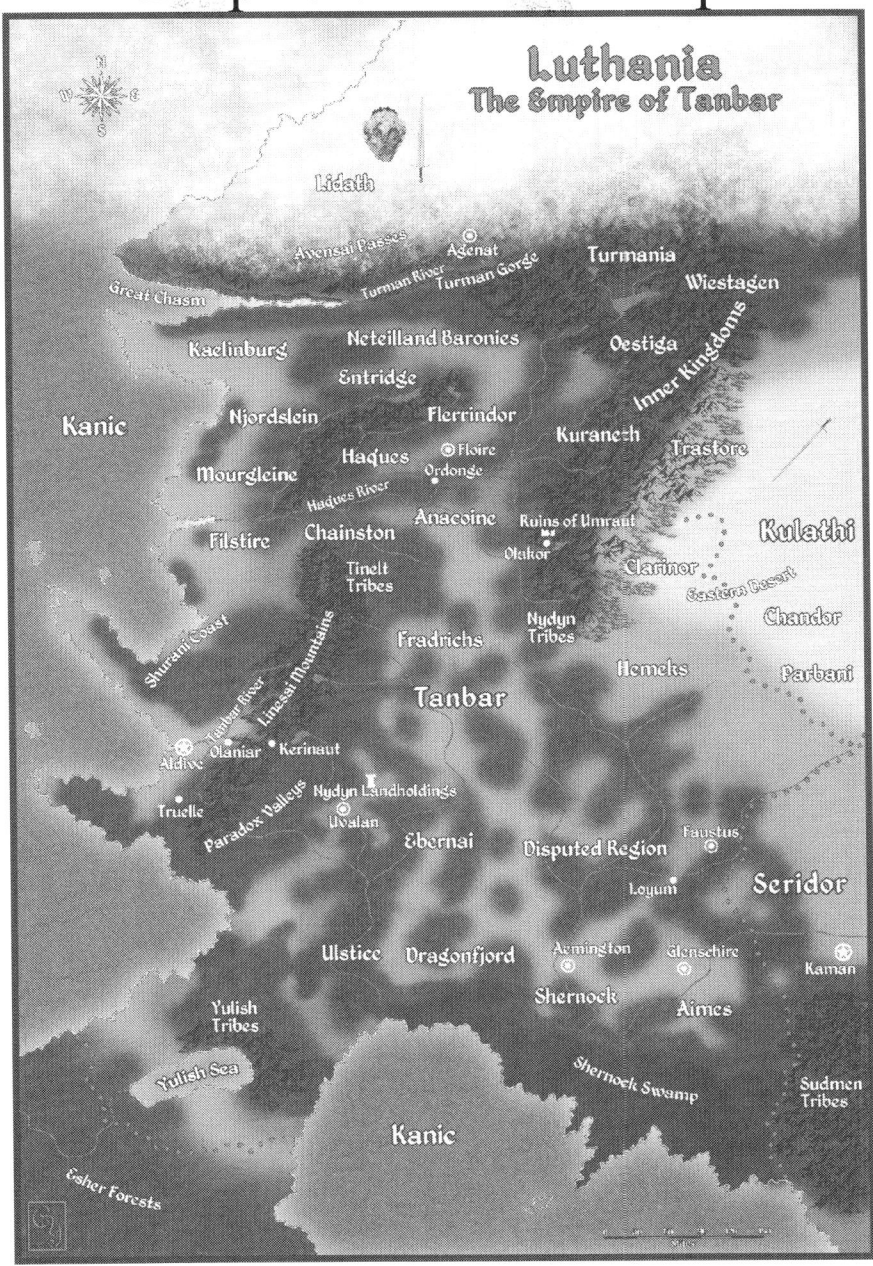

Chronos

- **~-20000 CH**: Old Gods (Eldegod) are first described by Lidathi legends
- **~-19,000 CH**: Eldegod win against Avillan (Demons). Demons cast to gray lands
- **Unknown → ~-18000 CH**: Age of Carvers
- **~-18,000 CH**: Carvers disappear, beginning Age of Indigen
- **-18,000 → -1 CH**: Age of the Indigen
- **0 CH**: Creation of Humanity (CH), birth of both New Gods, revival of Eldegod.
- **2,150 CH**: Humanity arrives on continent of Luthania, beginning first Lidathi wars
- **2865 CH**: First Carver ruins found on Luthania
- **3980 CH**: Yulish tribes found, build first City of Aldive
- **4105 CH**: Tanbari tribes defeat Yuls, sack, and gut Aldive
- **4115 CH**: Largest trove of Carver ruins found, magical disciplines of lightbending and transmutation born
- **4129 CH**: Tanbars finish building second City of Aldive.
- **4145 CH**: Lidathi defeat Tanbars, City of Aldive partially burned.
- **4304 → 4345 CH**: Second Lidathi war, Tanbars push Lidathi north
- **4210 CH**: Serida tribes form kingdom of Seridor
- **4346 CH**: Jathan the Great gouges the Great Chasm, trapping Lidathi in northern mountains.
- **4346 → 5450 CH**: Age of expansion, Tanbars push outward from Aldive, forming Empire of Tanbar
- **5451 CH**: Tanbari emperor Chithienne II demarcates borders of provinces
- **5780 → 5900 CH**: Seridor wars. Tanbar, Seridor fight for the southern provinces
- **5920 CH**: Chandor/Parbani tribes from Eastern deserts invade weakened Seridor.
- **5980 CH**: Seridor officially embraces the Old Gods (Eldegod), refutes New Gods
- **6250 CH**: Tanbar Emperor Fasivio III dies without heir, empire split among generals
- **6250 → 7025 CH**: Internecine wars. Four remnants of Tanbar Empire fight amongst themselves
- **7020 CH**: Lidath briefly descend from Northern Mountains onto a weakened Tanbar
- **7025 CH**: Seridor invades Aimes and Shernock
- **7030 CH**: Four Tanbari kingdoms unite, push Lidath back to northern mountains
- **7165 CH**: King Gedarme II of Aldive defeats other Tanbari kingdoms, restores Empire of Tanbar
- **7167 CH**: King Gedarme II drafts legions of wizards to begin hardening palace walls against magic
- **7180 CH**: Northern provinces (previously in northern Tanbari kingdom) revolt
- **7195 CH**: King Gedarme III destroys provincial army, places garrisons throughout the empire
- **7205 CH**: Nydyn tribes from Northeast invade a weakened Tanbar, depose King Gedarme III

- **7206 CH**: Maldovin I becomes emperor of Tanbar, first Nydyn king
- **7236 CH**: Maldovin I reclaims provinces of Aimes and Shernock from Seridor.

- **7237 CH**: Ongoing effort to harden Imperial Compound walls against magic fully complete
- **7240 CH**: Duchies of Aimes and Shernock formed, Dukes installed by Maldovin I
- **7248 CH**: Maldovin I expands Tanbar Empire to edge of Eastern Deserts
- **7249 CH**: Emperor Maldovin I dies, Maldovin II takes throne
- **7252 CH**: Emperor Maldovin II enacts provincial levy laws, increases taxes
- **7264 CH**: Revolt of the provinces, Tanbar Empire thrown into disarray
- **7268 CH**: Revolt ends in stalemate, treaty of Gifain
- **7270 CH**: Maldovin II dies, Maldovin III takes throne
- **7288 CH**: Beginning of Tanbar/Seridor wars over disputed regions
- **7295 CH**: Maldovin III incorporates kingdom of Clarinor into Tanbar by marriage of his son
- **7298 CH**: Maldovin III dies, Maldovin IV takes throne
- **7301 CH**: Swamp wars—Seridor begins full invasion of Aimes, Shernock, and other southern reaches
- **7303➔7311 CH**: Commander Lukas (under Maldovin IV) smashes Seridor army 4 times
- **7311 CH**: Seridor sues for peace, ending swamp wars
- **7312 CH**: Lidathi commander Kemharak unites tribes, begins harassing Tanbari northern legions
- **7314 CH**: Commander Lukas (under Maldovin IV) defeats Kemharak, restores quiet to the north
- **7315➔7317 CH**: Turmanian revolt against Tanbar, revolt defeated in 7317 CH
- **7335 CH**: Present day

City of Shards

Steve Rodgers

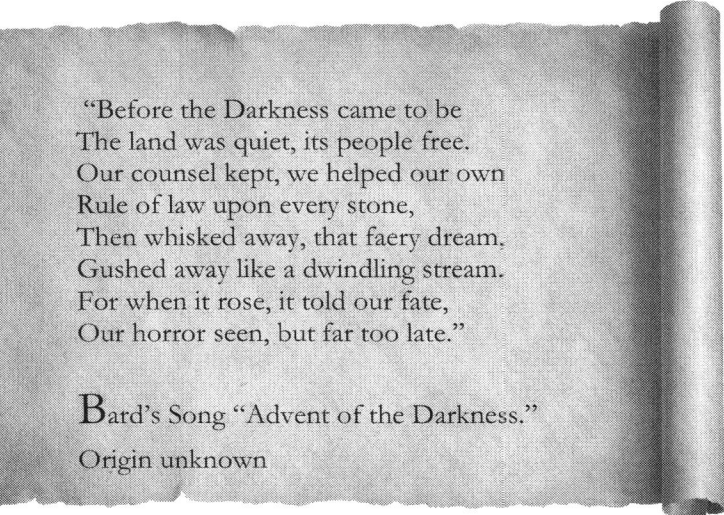

"Before the Darkness came to be
The land was quiet, its people free.
Our counsel kept, we helped our own
Rule of law upon every stone,
Then whisked away, that faery dream,
Gushed away like a dwindling stream.
For when it rose, it told our fate,
Our horror seen, but far too late."

Bard's Song "Advent of the Darkness."

Origin unknown

I

The day Larin first exploded was one of flint skies and a fog that mercifully shrouded the Wormpile's trash-filled alleys. A dark layer of soot and vaporized goose fat laced the mists as they settled over the district's balconies, proving that nothing touching the Wormpile could ever remain pure. Fortunately, this gloom was barely visible from behind arched temple windows, as Larin's uncle and Priest Kedrick held their usual standoff over how much premium ale to order for the night.

"Only eight flagons?" Akul sputtered, his incredulous expression a tired act. Akul's smooth dome was shiny with sweat, adding a sheen to the fat rolls at the back of his neck. The scar running from ear to nose was bright red, and he towered over Kedrick in false menace. "Remind me again—when you refer to your flock, do you mean an *actual* flock of birds?"

"Save your indignation for the man who last shaved your melon," Kedrick said, scratching both stubbly chins. He rested a hand on the ample belly beneath his robe. "Do you know how much Blueflower ale costs to make?"

"They *pay* for Blueflower, unlike the other swill you serve!"

"Not enough, as you know. The barley has to be imported from—"

"*Kinech!*" Larin yelled.

Both men whirled around and stared.

Larin shuffled his feet, stepped forward, and pumped a clenched fist into the air.

"*Aklad Vahrusen!*"

Akul blinked. He rubbed the back of his head. "What say you, little one?"

Larin stared wide-eyed at his uncle's vast baldness, still shaken by the seizure that had just roared through him. Scalding liquid ran through his veins, its hot rush threatening to burst through his forehead. At four years old, he had no idea what had just happened, and the shocked looks of the two men only made it worse.

A deathly quiet hung in the oak hallway, marred only by the muffled sound of prayers from another room. Floor-to-ceiling murals depicted the God Emja astride his chariot, his red mustache flowing in the wind, his eyes glowering down at Larin.

"By Emja's name, those words sound familiar," Kedrick said finally, bending down to envelope Larin in a cloud of alcohol vapor. Larin held his breath, watching with fascination as the priest's pupils dilated until they seemed to occupy his whole grizzled face. After a moment in which he almost toppled over, Kedrick blinked and straightened up.

"Feh. I'm late for lunch prayers."

With that, he shuffled away, leaving them alone beneath Emja's red eyebrows and furious glare. Larin moved closer to Akul, who squinted at the priest's retreating back.

"Sprite," Akul said, "I have a feeling we just got very lucky today."

So it was that Larin narrowly avoided a very different childhood.

It took some time before he understood why his outbursts made Akul so nervous. In those early years, all he knew was that the activities of other temple children weren't for him. At five, he began reading and math lessons in an isolated prayer room, studying at the hands of the half-crazed, roving-eyed priest Cyril. Cyril was the only man Akul trusted to keep quiet about Larin's outbursts, even if Larin knew that trust was bought by silver with every handshake. At six, Akul found him a job cleaning offerings to Emja in an isolated temple storeroom, where his outbursts could be swallowed by thick walls and shelves of knickknacks.

By the time he'd turned seven, he'd grown so bored polishing cherrywood boxes and brass bowls, he thought he'd run screaming from the Wormpile until some Imperial Guardsman smashed the butt of a halberd into his skull. Instead, one day, he decided to steal upstairs to the temple library, where ship-sized Priest Tewin watched the door from his chair while eating enormous sandwiches and leafing through thick tomes.

"The books are for the priesthood, not seven-year-old boys," Tewin said between chews, raising a massive arm to block Larin's entrance to the library. He swallowed and stared from beneath sweaty brows. "What do you want up here anyway? You should be playing with other boys, not reading dead history."

"Not much to do around here, and I can't leave these four blocks," Larin pouted.

Tewin tapped one fleshy cheek. "I suppose Akul does have you boxed into this little patch of cobblestone. Do Oarl's cretins really cause you so much mischief when you step into the rest of the Wormpile?"

Larin shrugged, looking at his torn shoes. His uncle's solitary war against Oarl's gang had mostly left him unaffected, especially since he spent most of his time inside Akul's Oarl-free zone. But as Akul's boy, his status outside those four blocks was always touchy. Anyway, he wasn't about to say anything that made him seem less sympathetic.

"I just want to learn what you know."

Tewin's gaze softened. "Well. Still, I don't think I'm supposed to let you in here." He shifted his enormous girth, provoking a terrible cracking noise from his chair. "Maybe come back when you're a little older."

"I brought you this," Larin said, fishing the wrapped honey cookie from his pocket.

Tewin glanced at the stairway entrance, then squinted at Larin. He took the cookie, removed the paper wrap, put the entire disc in his mouth, and looked down at his tome. "Fine," he squelched, "but stay away from the Lyrashi scripts. Carver magic and ignorant boys do not mix."

The library quickly became Larin's favorite spot in the temple. The morning lessons with Priest Cyril would begin in a state of sanity, but they would devolve by noon into a conversation between the priest and the alabaster statue in his lap. Larin tiptoed out during these times, listening to Cyril's excited tones fade into the solid oak walls. From there he padded to the storeroom, where he polished just enough of Emja's offerings to keep Akul from grounding him. After that it was straight to the library, to immerse himself in dreams of faraway lands, divine battles, and mysterious legends of the deep.

Larin developed a ritual whenever he stepped through the library's jade doorway. First, he'd issue a lighting spell on the vast crystal chandelier, though it always failed miserably outside the week of Apex. Then, beneath the unlit chandelier, he'd inhale the scent of cedar, eye the brilliant tapestry reliefs of the City of Aldive, gaze out the window overlooking the Wormpile's grimy flat rooftops, and wait for Tewin's snores.

When the rumbles vibrated the cedar walls, Larin padded quietly to the section dealing with the ancient creatures known as Carvers, whose Lyrashi language was the foundation of the world's magic. He read about those godlike beings, now long removed from the earth, and the mysterious glyphs that had given humanity keys to their power. He memorized long, violet-sash spells he had no hope of ever casting, marveling at the shape of the words on his tongue.

When Tewin's snores were replaced by chewing, Larin kept to the religious tomes on the theory that no self-respecting priest would scold him for reading scripture. Here, he learned about the three monstrous forces that still ruled the world—New Gods, Old Gods, and Demons—and the perpetual enmity between them. Under those vaulted ceilings, he read about the religions of all three, though the Demons were only worshipped by one strange cannibal tribe called the Sudmen, in the viney jungles of the Southeast.

And it was while reading about the Sudmen that he received his first clue as to who he was.

In one passage, he came across the term *Kineshe*, which sounded very much like the beginning of his Phrase. When he encountered the word *Varushen* a minute later, he felt the familiar sensation of spiders crawling up his spine. Burning liquid pulsed through his veins, and a terrible heat throbbed in his head. He ground his teeth and gripped the table, but the fury was unstoppable.

Larin shot to his feet, his chair scraping the floor.

"*Kinech!*"

Tewin's chewing stopped.

"*Aklad! Vahrusen!*"

He remained frozen as the outburst faded away, yearning to shrink into a tiny ball. Numbly, he gazed out the library's enormous window to where the flat rooftops of the Wormpile blended into the bone white squares of the Port District in the distance. All of it shaded blue by the moon Spellgiver, now close enough to resolve its oceans and clouds.

A slow dripping noise caused Larin to turn. There, Tewin stood gaping, a half-eaten chicken leg clubbed in one fist as it dropped grease onto the floor. Absently, Larin realized he'd never seen Tewin stand.

Tewin mumbled something, and the chandelier lit.

"How do you do that?" Larin asked, grasping for any subject other than the obvious.

Tewin blinked. He looked out the window to where Spellgiver hung large in the heavens, then back at Larin. "Well, most people can muster a lighting spell four weeks after Apex. Can't you?"

Larin shook his head, now even more miserable.

Tewin wiped sweaty cheeks. "Well now, no matter. There are many who haven't much magical power. You know, most of us don't get much use out of Lyrashi, except to boil a pot of water around Apex or light a candle a few months out of the year. Hardly something to worry about."

Larin nodded, looking down.

"So, erm. What just happened there?"

"I sneeze really hard," Larin mumbled.

Tewin's mouth opened and then snapped shut, jiggling multiple chins. "Larin, I hope whatever demon you expelled with that sneeze flies far from here."

Neither Larin nor Tewin knew how close the priest had come to the truth.

From that day forward, Larin vowed to do his reading beyond earshot of any priest. The next day, he slipped a library book into his bag, tiptoed past Tewin's giant sleeping form, exited the temple, and then pushed through the chaos of shouting cart vendors and bargain hunters to reach the boundary of Akul's four-block zone. Breathing deeply, he lowered his head and stepped into wider Wormpile, where the alley corners were lined with trash and one could slink beneath smoke-charred brick overhangs for minutes without bumping into a soul. This was Oarl's turf, a place as different from Akul's four-block zone as porridge and chimney soot. He snuck through abandoned courtyards and empty alleys until he reached Madam Shembri's brothel at the boundary of the Port District.

To Larin, the Port District existed in a completely different plane than the Wormpile's dog pile of dirty alleyways. The port's square, brilliant white buildings sloped sharply down to the sea, traversed by winding streets impossible to descend without breaking into a run. The entire district rested on stone pillars, raising it above the high season tides, and the stench of seafood pervaded every corner. Shouts drifted from the docks as port workers hauled great bags of crab and shrimp from the ships.

Larin soon found a sheltered alcove high above the bustle, with views of the district and the endless sea. Keeping his book closed, he breathed deeply of the salt air as he gaped at the rich vista below.

It was four weeks after Apex, that time of year when the ocean's low tides sweep beyond the houses, leaving hundreds of fish in the nets strung between stone columns. Everywhere, men flipped those nets with winches, spilling piles of slippery fish onto the cobblestones to be scooped into hemp sacks. Nearby, children picked away seaweed accumulated from the district's time under the sea, while idlers played the strategy game Thirazi on stone benches. In the plaza behind Larin, workers pounded nails into wooden planks, building the five-hundred-stall fish market on land submerged by the tides only last week. All of this under the moon's turquoise shadow, for this close to Apex, Spellgiver hung in the heavens like a vast blue god.

Throughout this kaleidoscope of motion swaggered Sajuk, an enforcer for Oarl's gang who was perpetually trailed by two sycophants. Larin always thought "enforcer" too strong a word for eighteen-year-old Sajuk, but backed by Oarl's slackjaws, he held the power to extort silver from any fish merchant selling into the Wormpile. This portside robbery was then turned into a visible taunt, as he stuck his coin pouch partway from his pocket and strutted about the Port District like a King of Thieves. Everyone knew Sajuk barely touched the silver before his master took it away.

Larin learned to ignore Sajuk's terrible trio on his regular visits to the Port District, casting his eyes down when they glanced at him. This gesture of submission was really all Sajuk needed from anyone, and with that, Larin began focusing on his books. He read more about Emja and the rest of the New Gods. He read about Demons and their Lord Haraf, and the long war with the Old Gods—the *Eldegod*—that had banished the Demons to the Gray Lands.

But to Larin, more important than any book was freedom from the Wormpile. He loved the stern bustle of the Port District, its sense of urgency, the hint of wild adventure implied by the docked ships. After the temple's close quarters, the fresh sea air was a powerful drug, untainted by inebriated priests or musty prayer chambers.

Until his outbursts brought it all down one day.

He'd been avoiding reading about Sudmen since his explosion in front of Tewin, but on this particular day, a book on those remote peoples intrigued him enough to try again. He pulled it from the library's shelves, blew dust off the top, and scanned for any hint of the Phrase.

An hour later, he was reading chapter two as he leaned against a pillar high above the docks, and saw he'd missed something—that word "Kineshe" again. The heat rose behind his forehead, and boiling liquid pulsed through his veins. After a desperate momentary internal battle, he dropped his book and raced into a rancid alley behind the cannery. There he pumped his fist, stomped his foot, and passed through every stage of his curse, shouting the Phrase to the heavens.

Larin bit his lip as the outburst faded, trying to keep from crying. Losing control this way was terrifying, like being chained to a jailer who could steal his mind at will. It felt as if some enormous spirit played him on puppet strings, moving his arms and expelling meaningless bellows from his lungs. He watched a rat burrow through a pile of garbage, resolving never to read another word about Sudmen. After several minutes, he wiped his eyes and stepped out of the alley.

And froze at the sight ahead.

Shadowed by a pillared house, Sajuk held Larin's book open, deliberately mangling the Sudmen's language as he recited the text to his two grinning followers. He scratched his head and turned the book upside down. "Look, it makes as much sense in this direction."

"Hey, give that back!" Larin yelled, running at Sajuk.

Sajuk's eyes widened, and he made a sarcastic "oh" with his mouth as he threw the book to a cohort. "But Ajay wants to read it, too. Come now, don't be stingy."

Larin began running toward Ajay. "That's not my book, it's the temple's! Give it back!"

"Yet it flies so well." Ajay laughed, throwing the book back to Sajuk. Larin heard the terrible sound of a page ripping, the same sound his heart would make if the temple ever banished him from the library. He whirled around and ran to Sajuk, who held the book high above his head. At eight years old, Larin had as much hope of reaching it as he did of standing on Spellgiver.

"Give it back!" Larin said, hating the pleading whine in his voice.

"And what if I don't, you little puss boil? What exactly are you going to do?"

If Larin had thought about it for an instant, he'd have lost his nerve. But everything happened too quickly for that. He yanked the coin pouch from Sajuk's pocket, darted to Ajay's left, then raced down the hill to the docks, weaving around busy workers and jumping over thick chains as Sajuk and his crew bellowed behind him.

"You're going to die, you little insect!" Sajuk screamed, as they jumped over nets and pushed through crowds of workers. Nobody wanted to be seen resisting Oarl's gang, but no one really wanted to help, either. Burly dockworkers moved slowly out of Sajuk's way, giving Larin precious seconds. He flew over the cobblestones, swinging around Port District pillars with one arm, jumping over piles of fish, and racing up another hill as a blur of gaping people passed through his vision.

Finding himself out in the open, he darted into an alley, then realized it was a dead end. He scrambled out again, scraping grit off the decaying brick wall into Ajay's eyes as the boy's fingers grasped Larin's shirt. Larin twisted away, hearing Ajay shout something unintelligible as he jumped over a giant crate of shrimp and swerved around a stand selling crab. From behind came a loud thud and crash as Sajuk collided with the vendor. Larin burst from the market and, after a panicked second, raced to the edge of the sewage canal parallel to the wooden fish market stalls, only two hundred feet from where he'd started. He skidded to a stop and gasped desperately, staring at the brown ooze flowing from Aldive's richer districts out to the sea.

Hand shaking, he held the coin pouch over the canal as Sajuk's trio raced up the hill, their sandals slapping the cobblestones. They halted twenty feet away in a symphony of gasps, Sajuk's eyes wide at his pouch's precarious position.

"You," he wheezed. "You have exactly ten seconds to give that back." His few chin hairs were dripping with sweat as he bent over, sucking air.

"Book. First," Larin said, gasping.

"You have made"—Sajuk gulped—"a giant mistake." He straightened. "You little shit, that's Oarl's money. Think what he'll do to you if you lose it."

Larin stepped back, eyeing the gathering crowd. He turned back to Sajuk. "Think what he'll do to you, if *you* lose his money."

Sajuk's face paled. He opened his mouth to reply, but a sudden lull in the Port District's buzz caused them both to swing around. There, bobbing above the newly installed fish market booths like a floating blowfish was Akul's bald dome. It floated purposely over the stalls, causing the stall owners to stop their conversations and watch nervously.

Larin gaped. How had his uncle known he was here? Had one of Akul's contacts spotted him?

Akul burst from the fish market like some scowling mountain troll, a shiny-domed creature beset by scars and pointed instruments that jutted at every angle from a thick leather belt. He stopped in the plaza's center, the hilt of his back-strapped long-sword shading a neighboring stall. Shielding his eyes with one hand, he spied Larin and began striding purposely uphill toward him.

Larin was still too young to fully grasp who his uncle was, and he didn't understand why all motion stopped as Akul stomped up the hill. He knew about his uncle's war with Oarl, of course, knew that Akul single-handedly kept four Wormpile blocks free from Oarl's entire gang. Yet until that moment, he'd never realized just how intensely everyone followed this local battle. He watched several fish haulers lower their bags to stare at Akul, wary respect on their faces.

Then Akul's giant shadow darkened Larin's view, forcing him to look up.

Akul's jaw unclenched, clenched, and then unclenched again, as if manually trying to hammer his face into a more pleasant expression. His endless forehead became bunched with wrinkles, the way it did whenever he tried to soften his demeanor.

"Sprite," he said finally. "Time to return to the temple."

Larin's heart sank. "Well, maybe today, but—"

"No, permanently. You need to do something a little less public."

Larin's chin quivered; he knew exactly what wasn't being said. His forsaken outbursts again. Never mind that today was his first one in three weeks at the Port District. Never mind that he'd go crazy living in Akul's four-block zone the rest of his life. For the first time, Larin felt his curse settle into his bones, wrap his chest like a thorn tunic. He started pouting, though he knew it would get him nowhere.

"I can't leave yet," he said petulantly. At this, his gaze flicked toward Sajuk, who watched the exchange with wide eyes.

Akul twisted to consider Sajuk. His hard stare traveled from Sajuk's pale face, down his trembling arm, and to the book in his hands. Then he glanced at Larin's coin pouch, dangling over the canal. His mouth twitched, the closest thing to a smile Larin ever saw on his uncle.

"The book," Akul said to Sajuk, his hand outstretched.

Sajuk looked like he needed new breeches. His eyes flicked up and down the bristling mobile armory that was Akul. Saying nothing, he gave him the book.

Akul nodded to Larin, and with enormous relief, Larin traded the pouch for his book. Akul turned to Sajuk, dangling the pouch at eye level.

"This is Oarl's money, is it?"

Sajuk folded his arms. "That's right. Oarl will be very unhappy if any part of it goes missing."

"Good."

With that, Akul opened the sack, scooped up the pile of coins and threw them to the watching crowds, amid Sajuk's horrified yell. A mad scramble ensued as port workers dove for the silver in a frenzy, and gasps of delight sounded even from those unable to reach the bouncing coins. It wasn't often Oarl's crew got stiffed.

"Come on, Larin," Akul growled. He whirled around and stomped back down toward the fish market, completely unconcerned by Oarl's three armed henchmen at his back. Larin raced to catch up with his uncle, his stomach twisting into triple knots. The war between Akul and Oarl had just gotten more personal, and now he was a field mouse between two armies.

As they reached the corner, Larin twisted to see Sajuk's desolate face. Sajuk's eyes held no animosity, no desire for revenge—only anguish. In that moment, neither could Larin muster any satisfaction at a bully's comeuppance. Instead, he was filled with an odd kind of sorrow and a peculiar sense of doom.

He never saw Sajuk again.

"Would we have still succumbed to the Darkness had Emja's cloisters adhered to their original sacred mission? No one knows. But into the void of apathy, the rush of hatred easily finds purchase."

Preface opening, "Complete History of Tanbar, Maldovin Dynasty," 3rd edition

II

As Larin got older and better able to control his outbursts, he began sneaking out of the temple storeroom during work hours. By eleven years old, he regularly ventured out of Akul's four-block safe zone into the wider Wormpile, where Oarl's gang owned the streets. There, he watched other boys play bruiseball from the sidelines, never joining for fear the game's violence would trigger an outburst. He'd learned the hard way that his misery clawed out of its cage whenever he let anger overwhelm him.

On one particularly sticky-hot day in a courtyard enclosed by terraced gray buildings, he found himself watching a bruiseball game descend into a shouting match between Uli and Loika, the latter a disheveled, red-haired urchin endlessly harassed for being the only Nydyn boy in the Wormpile. Everyone grumbled about the Nydyn nobility, but that could be because everyone Larin knew was Tanbari scum, like him. They all said that after trying for centuries to emulate Tanbari culture, the Nydyns had finally resorted to murdering Tanbari kings and crushing the people who'd founded the empire they craved. Larin didn't care about any of that, but he did know Loika was out of luck. With the flame-headed Nydyns running the Tanbar Empire, red hair was as common in the Wormpile as gold coins in the sewers.

"It hit you square, you Nydyn reject!" Uli was shouting.

Loika's jaw trembled. "The ball only glanced me, and you know it."

"Your scab-red hair might make me sick to my stomach, but my eyes still work. I saw it hit your back."

"You know it was a glancing blow," Loika repeated.

"Well, since your father is the only Nydyn stupid enough to have to live in the Wormpile, you probably wouldn't know the difference between glancing and a full strike," Uli said, provoking much laughter.

Larin's anger peaked; everyone could see Loika hadn't been hit square. The group fell into a hush as the rock-headed Uli stared contemptuously at Loika, his out-thrust chest daring Loika to throw a punch. From a second-floor balcony, a rotund man leaned over the railing to watch the altercation, dropping pistachio shells to the cobblestones. Warm breezes rattled a defaced Imperial edict and brought the faint whiff of garbage, as the boys stared at each other without blinking. Finally, Loika mumbled something and turned away.

Larin bit back panic as his anger walked the precipice of outburst. His forehead tingled, hot liquid coursing through his neck and arms. Without a word, he backed away.

Uli turned to Larin, scowling. "Hey, where are you going?"

"I have to get home."

"Nah, stay a minute," said Candro, a black-haired, spear-thin boy with torn shoes and an almost permanent smirk. He grabbed the ball. "Why don't you play the next game? I never see you join in." But Candro wasn't smirking now; he seemed genuinely curious. Of all of them, only he hadn't laughed at Uli's taunts.

Larin quelled his growing panic. He'd just opened his mouth to reply when he was saved by the king himself. From the next alleyway, shouts echoed off the stone walls, followed by the clang of steel and pounding of hooves. Everyone stopped and twisted to listen, as screams tore through the stiflingly hot day. After a frozen moment, Uli whirled back around.

"Purple cocks! Run!" With that, he sprinted in the opposite direction, faster than Larin had ever seen him go. The rest of them walked away quickly, darting glances behind. Only Uli was old enough for the purple cocks—so named for the rounded purple helmets of the Imperial Impressors—to draft into the army. Through a narrow alley into the next courtyard, Larin saw one running man fall to the ground, a looped rope entangling his legs. As Larin rounded the corner out of view, he caught sight of a purple-helmeted soldier pulling his horse alongside the tethered man.

The screams faded into the distance as he turned another corner, and with that, Imperial press gangs were almost immediately forgotten. He had a much more personal problem. More than ever before, he wondered what he was going to do about his cursed outbursts. Today's close call could have ended any hope of a social life.

The incident was a lead weight on his spirit as he attended the temple's Ritual of Answers later that day, surrounded by fifty bored Wormpile residents and enormous tapestries of Emja astride his chariot. He could almost hear the metronome in the adults' heads as they droned along with Priest Paku, for an hour of worship here bought a night's free ale in the temple alehouse. It was a promise that drew Wormpile residents to Emja's prayer rooms like ants to spilled sugar. Akul stood next to him in a stained purple tunic, his wide jaw clenching and unclenching in some internal debate as he stared at the God Emja's statue.

Larin scowled at Akul's faraway look. He knew his uncle was trying but failing miserably to be a good father, and that he only brought Larin here so that they could claim togetherness without actually having to speak. Larin was used to days passing with only grousy, one-word jabs from Akul, until one morning, after his system had cleared of all the khald drug he'd ingested, he perked up and decided that today was the day they'd attend prayers like a normal family. Now, after that brief flowering of humanity, Akul was back to his usual sour existence.

Today, Larin didn't care. The incident at the bruiseball game bothered him; it was only a matter of time before this curse of his ruined his life.

"Emja protectsh us from the Eldegods," came Priest Paku's drunken slur.

"His shield gives us power," Larin intoned with the crowd, shaking his head. *Someone* in this decadent temple must have the answers. He just couldn't continue like this.

"Emja keepsh the Demonsh below," said Priest Paku.

"He confines them forever," Larin mumbled with everyone else. He knew Akul would flay him alive for talking to a priest, but he just couldn't keep it bottled any longer.

"Hish protection is truth. Hish worship keeps us happy."

"Let him guide us," the crowd responded.

Larin bit his lip. If Emja truly wanted him to be happy and truthful, then keeping his curse hidden was ridiculous. One of his priests must surely see that.

The service ended, and Larin watched the crowd shove each other through the door, each racing to secure a premium spot at the temple alehouse bar. He glanced at Akul, but as usual, his uncle's massive cheekbones were clenched in thought as he followed the crowds, his eyes ringed black from years of dabbing khald on his tongue.

Larin exited the prayer room and walked through the central ranunculus gardens to the temple's east wing. He strode past jade-covered meditation chambers and climbed the winding stairs to the Tower of Devotion, where his priestly friend Ulysse sometimes ran afternoon prayers. Though "friend" was a loose term when it came to Emja's clergy. Temple priests were usually engaged in drinking, chasing women, or overeating, and Larin's interactions typically focused on assisting those efforts. Still, Ulysse had a nice smile and a warm handshake, and gleamed sincerity when he asked how Larin was doing.

He found Ulysse sweeping the hallway just outside the tower's top prayer room, a suspiciously unlikely task for the man directly beneath High Priest Tierre. Larin stopped and rehearsed his speech, but Ulysse looked up first, hurrying to Larin with his broom in the air.

"Ulysse—" Larin started.

"Listen, my little mosquito," Ulysse said, pointing at the prayer room. "In there is one of the clock master's daughters, making a rare visit to the Wormpile. You should buzz in after the Song of Moon and tell her brother Ulysse needs to see her, eh?"

Larin paused, then launched into his speech. "Ulysse, I say these words sometimes—"

"I know, I know." Ulysse waved a hand dismissively. "But she's never been here, she won't know about that. Have you seen his wife and his other daughter? Well, lengthen the other daughter's legs, imagine bluer eyes than the wife's, and that's the beauty who's reciting the Call of Answers as we speak."

"Ulysse, I have this problem—"

"Hurry, brother, the door is opening!" Ulysse hissed, and then whirled around with his broom.

Larin sighed, watching Ulysse sweep the floor furiously. With that, it was crystal clear he'd never discuss his problem with any temple priest. He turned to enter the prayer room but was shoved backward by hordes of people barging through the oak door. Anyway, he soon watched, bemused, as Ulysse's broom "accidentally" touched the leather slippers of a tall black-haired woman as she shuffled behind the crowds. This led to apologies and laughter and a loud conversation that grew fainter as the last worshippers stomped down the spiral staircase.

As the voices faded into silence, Larin felt a hollowness in his stomach unlike anything he'd ever experienced. For the first time, he wondered if there was any hope for him. He gazed out the tower window, feeling the Phrase's curse sink into his bones.

Below the temple walls, the Wormpile spread out in a dingy maze of flat rooftops and balconies, obscured by grimy smoke from a hundred chimneys. The surrounding four blocks were as dense as tightly crumpled parchment, with street signs packed into every square inch and cobbled streets bustling with cart vendors. Outside those blocks, the Wormpile's shops became sparser, wedged between squat multistory residences that turned into the stately buildings of the Flerrindor District across the river. To the east, the Mount of the Empire rose high above the city of Aldive, with the Imperial Compound's spires glinting gold from the sun's rays.

Larin turned away from the window, trying to keep depression from swallowing him. He'd always known he couldn't rely on the temple priests for any subject that really mattered. Today was just the final spoke in that wagon wheel.

Yet one of Emja's servants might still help—a warrior priestess named Trana he'd known since tykehood, a woman whose laugh was so ground-shaking, Larin used to think she was part elemental. She was usually traveling, but he thought he'd seen her riding her horse into the temple stables earlier today. If so, there was only one place she'd be.

Later that evening, Larin stomped through the dinner prayer room and climbed down steps smelling like stale alcohol toward the single place Akul had expressly forbidden him.

He stood at the temple alehouse doorway, watching the mayhem inside. Tonight, it seemed the entire Wormpile had descended on the alehouse at once. Dust clouds drifted about as moving chairs, flying mugs, and falling men kicked up the dirt floor. Drunken singing warred with loud yells as priests and Wormpile residents shouted lies at each other, and Madam Shembri's girls laughed easily with the men. Next to the sword rack, Emja's statue stood lonely and dwarfed by the warder gargoyle, as if the god were an afterthought in this place.

Larin squinted through the dust, focusing on Trana's stocky figure at the bar. He weaved around discarded plates, overturned chairs, and prone men, then climbed atop a nearby stool.

"Ho, Trana."

Trana paused in mid-drink, her eyes wide. She lowered her mug and cracked into a broad, gap-toothed grin. "Well, now that's a sight. Is Akul finally going to make a man out of you?"

Larin marveled at Trana's well-inebriated face, topped by a forehead red enough to burst. She was a battering ram of a woman, with a shock of wavy brown hair and a thick frame that refused to be ignored. No dainty thing was Trana, but she possessed a light of sweetness that years of battle had never extinguished.

Not sure whether Trana's question referred to alcohol or Madam Shembri's girls, who floated about the alehouse like lovely wraiths, Larin decided the first assumption was safer.

"I don't want any ale."

"Well, then I guess you'll never make it to the priesthood," Trana said, then issued a clap of thunder-laughter that bounced off every alehouse wall. She squinted at him from behind reddened cheeks. "But since you're learning to sit at the bar, let's swap war stories."

Larin smiled. "I don't know any war stories."

"Well, I do, so I'll start. Way back when I was in the Haques mercenaries—"

"Trana, I want to talk to you about something."

She stopped and wiped her mouth with her sleeve. "Lad, if you preface every sentence with 'Now I'm going to say something,' you won't get far. Speak."

"Well, uh. . ." He looked into her wrinkled, curious eyes, and his tongue froze in his mouth. She watched him for several seconds until Priest Roald, who was manning the bar in Akul's absence, slammed a bowl of stew in front of her. She mumbled a few words over her bowl, then turned back to him calmly.

Larin nodded to her bowl. "A spell to keep the parasites out. I can't even do that."

"Pretty useless, young'un. I got no idea if it even works."

"If I tried to cast it, it *definitely* wouldn't work. I can't make Lyrashi words dance until Spellgiver is practically right on top of me."

Trana ran calloused fingers through brown wavy hair. "Most people got their little bit of power—some more, some less. Training can take you up a notch, but unless you got enough to get into the one of the four academies, it's pretty pointless. Anyway, if I die of a parasite after all these stupid calamities I force myself into, the world would be a funny place." Her eye twitched. "Is that *really* what you wanted to talk to me about?"

In the background, a steady singing began, and Larin watched Trana try but fail to maintain her serious expression. Soon, the "Hero's Lament" began a rising crescendo throughout the alehouse to the steady pounding of ceramic mugs on wooden tables:

"Jathan gouged the earth in two,
A chasm mighty, deep and true.
Drained of power, he stopped to swoon,
Fell to the earth like a shriveled prune.
Commander Lukas won every attack.
Lizards and Seridor, he beat them back,
Tanbar's savior, time and again,
Till magic speared him like a dinner hen.
Others may die or become unhale
To save the realm and spark new tale,
But I will sit and lift my glass
For heroes be glad, but I'll have more ale!"

The last sentence was shouted to the rafters as everyone lifted their mugs. The song stopped as they all took a drink, then began the next chorus. Trana guzzled her ale, then pounded her mug on the bar as she began bellowing with the rest of the alehouse.

"King Tunos fought to save us all,
But a poisoned arrow made him fall . . ."

"Never mind," Larin mumbled, getting up.

Trana stopped singing and darted a hand to his shoulder. "Lad, there's no rush. Many men sit here for hours without a word. You'll speak yours when you're ready."

Larin looked up gratefully. Here in the temple, Trana stood out like fresh air in the underground lavatories. To Larin, she was a grounded anchor in a sea of frivolity.

He climbed back onto his stool. "Trana, why are you so different from the other priests?"

Her eyes crinkled. "Well, if Akul hasn't explained the difference between men and women, then it's not my place."

"No, that's not—"

"I know what you meant, lad," Trana said, as the singing died away. She turned back to her stew, mug in one hand and fork in the other. "There are many ways to worship Emja. Our beloved clergy revere the Five Pleasures, but some of us believe Emja's service carries responsibilities beyond the flesh."

"But you're a priest, too."

"Aye, young'un, but there're several orders of the priesthood. I'm from the Atlaran School; we're trained to fight, to defend the believers. These men"—she nodded toward Priest Yuri, whose latest drinking mishap had spilled beer all over his robe—"are more concerned with earthly pleasures. They're of the Ealanian order. At one time, this temple's priests cared more about serving the people than their own pleasures, but those days are long gone." She speared a piece of meat in her stew and popped it in her mouth.

"Is that why you travel? To defend the believers?"

"Aye," she said, chewing. "They need defending these days. My order sends me to the empire's southern reaches to protect the flock wherever Old Gods encroach."

"Old Gods? Are they older than Emja?"

Trana peered sideways at him from above her bowl. Then she shoveled another helping into her mouth, holding up one finger for him to wait.

Larin sighed, focusing on Akul's etched mugs on a shelf high above the spouts. Mugs with words like *Hefbranau*, *Ordaenth*, and other tongue-twisting names from the Northern Mountains. He'd heard some of the priests placing bets on what the names meant, though he doubted any would ever collect. Another meaningless clue to Akul's past.

"Seems your uncle's gotten lazy with your education," Trana said finally, swallowing her food. She picked her fork out of the stew, grabbed another nearby fork, and leaned them diagonally against each other so that their prongs intertwined. Then she put a knife along the bottom, touching the ends of the two leaning forks.

"Know what we have here?"

"A mess that someone's going to have to clean?" Larin ventured, pointing to where her stew fork dripped gravy onto the oak.

Her eyes flicked to the brown pool. "Lad, this bar's absorbed enough sauces to feed an army of troubadours for a year. No, this is a triangle. But not just any old three-pointer—this is the triangle of enmity that rules the world!" Her eyebrows arched inward in a falsely sinister expression, and Larin smiled.

"You see, Emja and the other Human Gods sit at the top corner," she continued. "Seven thousand years ago, glorious fire vomited forth humanity, our gods, and the other four-legged creatures—horses, dogs, and so on. Then here, on the bottom left corner are the cursed Old Gods, who've been around forever. They're the rulers of the six-legged indigen creatures—grombits, tagalanths, thrukk, and the lot."

Larin's eyes went wide. In truth, he'd read a little about the Eldegod, but never knew they were kings of the indigen creatures. One didn't see too many indigen creatures in the city, and Larin was fascinated to learn they had their own gods.

"And at the bottom right corner of the triangle are the thrice-cursed Demons, who would stomp us all into flatbread if they escaped their gray hell." Trana knocked a fork over, and the triangle collapsed. "And let me tell you, young'un, all three corners of that triangle hate each other fiercer than a mama bird attacking a cat. That balance of hatred keeps the other two from wiping us out."

Larin watched her face. "Demons. And the only people who worship them are the Sudmen, right?"

Trana leaned back, surprised. "True enough. How do you know that?"

Priest Yuri's forehead chose that moment to slam against the bar, making Larin jump. He returned to reality.

"Trana, my problem. I—I have these outbursts . . ." He waited for her to interject or change the subject, but she just watched him, resting one hand on the bar. He gulped and continued. "Sometimes I shout these words for no reason. The first one is *Kinech*. Then the second word is *Aklad*. I can't say the whole thing because—"

Trana seized his shoulder in a crushing grip, her beet-red forehead now crisscrossed by throbbing veins. Her eyes blazed, and Larin suddenly thought she looked more sober than ever. She jumped to the ground, holding out a hand for him. It trembled slightly. "Larin, come with me."

He climbed off his stool and followed her through the alehouse doorway, but stopped at the foot of the stairs. "Where are we going?"

Trana grimaced. "Lad, I know this was supposed to be between us, and I know you don't want Akul to know you told me. But it's very, very important we talk, just the three of us. Will you trust me?"

Larin's stomach sank as he imagined Akul's coming tirade. He nodded reluctantly, and with that, they climbed the alehouse stairway, walked through a temple courtyard, and stepped into the Wormpile.

III

A thousand years ago, some hopeless romantic had beheld a dragon in the contours of the Tanbar Empire, and the term "Dragon Empire" had stuck. This in turn had birthed all kinds of silly analogies: Tanbar's capital Aldive was said to be the beast's heart, its four main roads regulating the empire's flow of commerce. Aldive's four magical academies were the chambers, pumping power across the land. The Great Chasm at the empire's vertex was the dragon's mouth, yawning wide to crush the Lidathi tribes to the north. All this despite the fact that every drawing depicted dragons as six-legged beasts, which meant they were indigen. And everyone knew indigen creatures had no hearts at all.

By that comparison, Larin thought, the Wormpile District was a cancerous lesion on the heart: dead to the body's commands, spreading poisons throughout otherwise healthy tissue. In that neighborhood of narrow alleys, royal edicts were used only for fish-wrap, and any Imperial presence was limited to a few crude paintings of Maldovin IV, hung for archery practice. By the same silly analogy, Akul's four-block zone was a tiny patch of healthy tissue within the Wormpile's decay. As they approached the upstairs apartment Larin and Akul shared, Larin and Trana passed narrow shops and eateries bunched so close together, many had eliminated the interior walls to save space. In this tiny slice of the neighborhood, shopkeepers paid Oarl no protection money.

Everyone wanted to be here.

As they turned the corner onto Larin's crowded street, Larin noticed a skinny black-haired boy with toes sticking out of his shoes, in a tunic that appeared patched together from curtains. He stood across the street from

Larin's upstairs window, holding a ball and looking lost between a rug rack on one side and fruit trays on the other. Trana began crossing the street to the glassblower shop on the bottom floor beneath Akul's apartment, but she stopped as she saw Larin heading in the opposite direction.

"Hey, Candro," Larin said as he approached, though his voice was drowned out by rug vendor's shouts.

"What?" Candro yelled.

"How's it going?" Larin yelled.

Candro nodded. "I thought—" He stopped as the fruit vendor screamed into the street crowds, something about apples fresher than a baby's first words. "I thought maybe you wanted to play a game of bruiseball just us," he continued quickly. "You know, because Uli is a granite head. Sometimes it's better to leave him out of it. Anyway, the purple cocks probably got him."

Larin felt a small warmth that was his only really good feeling on this miserable day. He was about to accept eagerly, but he remembered how the other boys talked to each other and bit back his enthusiasm.

"Yeah, without Uli there, no one will see how completely I destroy you at bruiseball."

Candro stared intently, then broke into a grin. "If you're as bad at bruiseball as you are at bluffing, you'll be easier to beat than my Nana. And she's dead."

"Larin, can this wait?" Trana interrupted, just before a piercing yell from the rug vendor caused them all to wince.

"Och, will you shut up!" Trana said, whirling around. The rug vendor stared at the scowling, red-faced woman, glanced down at the blade hanging from her belt, and shrank back.

She turned back around. "Larin. You and I and Akul need to talk, and now's not the time for chest-thumping." Her face softened, and she tousled his hair. "Never understood what you lads saw in that game, but some things are meant to stay mysteries."

Candro paled at the mention of Akul. He looked up nervously at the Imperial green dragon tapestry draped from their window, as if realizing for the first time that he was in the warrior's direct line of sight. It was a common reaction from people who didn't know Akul personally, and even from a few who did.

Trana began crossing the street, and Larin nodded quickly at Candro. "Yeah, I'd like that. I know a mostly empty courtyard a few blocks from here where we can throw a ball around."

Candro smiled. "Right."

Larin raced to catch up with Trana, who was already entering the glassblower shop. He ran through the door, climbed four flights of narrow stairway past Trana, and opened the front door.

"Akul—Trana's here."

There were several thumps from Akul's room, then the door flew open to reveal Akul, bald head shiny with sweat and eyes ringed with black. The scar between his left ear and nose was inflamed, and his wide chin was clenched in misery. All the signs of a post-khald binge evening.

"What the . . . Trana?" Akul said stupidly.

"Hello, sunshine. A forest glade filled with butterflies and poppies, that's what I see when I look into your face." Trana grinned at Larin, but he shook his head.

"Oh—" she said, then nodded. Akul's khald problem was well-known in these parts, but not well-mentioned.

Akul sprawled into a chair and cradled his head, his royal dragon earring glinting in the window's light. "What do you want?"

"Akul, I'll be blunt. This secret of Larin's—he must never reveal it to any other Emjaian priest. The consequences would be dire."

Akul lifted a pale face from his hands. "And how do *you* know his secret?" He turned to Larin with a hard expression. "You *told* her?"

Trana raised a hand to still Akul's growing temper. "That's not the point—"

"Why in Emja's name would you discuss your outbursts with a priest?" Akul yelled at Larin. "I warned you this would trigger some stupid superstition! Have you no sense?"

"Akul," Trana said flatly. "Now I know why I never see this young'un. He's relegated to the storeroom, as if he were some servant. I'm guessing you've told him not to be seen anywhere in the temple, and he can't say why. How long did you think *that* was going to continue?"

The evening after overdoing khald, it was safe to bet Akul would either launch into an angry tirade or an orgy of self-loathing. Larin had just checked off angry tirade when Akul's face twisted with sorrow.

"Oh, Trana, I know." He closed his eyes, wrinkles of guilt lapping against an endless forehead. "His condition is unheard of. I've consulted physicians and mages, but no one has any idea."

"You have?" Larin asked incredulously.

"Of course, Sprite. Last year I talked to an Influence mage, but he said it's lasted too long to be based on Influence magic." Akul narrowed his eyes at Trana. "But you seem to know."

Trana looked away, her chin trembling. "Yes, and sure as the red welt on my side, this is no superstition. Akul, by not acting on this, I'm violating every oath I've sworn. If I speak it aloud, I will be beholden to Emja to take this sweet boy to the nearest temple and place him in the hands of its High Priest. None of us want that."

Larin clenched his fists; of all the outcomes, this was the last one he'd expected. Trana knew exactly what the Phrase meant, but she couldn't tell him.

He gazed toward the cracked window, trying to keep despair from eating his insides. Evening sounds drifted from the streets below: The six-legged clopping of tagalanth-pulled carts as they returned from Westmarket, men shouting at their animals and each other, grinding metal as the ground-floor shopkeepers locked their stores for the night. From somewhere, the hollow smacking of two boys practicing with wooden swords.

He willed his eyes to remain dry. He didn't much ponder his dead parents anymore, but times like these revived a familiar desperation, an aching desire for someone to talk to other than his morose, drug-addled uncle. A man who was probably wanted by the Imperials, and who wouldn't provide a sliver of information about his prior life.

After a heavy silence, Trana sighed. "Akul, listen to me. If High Priest Tierre finds out, Larin will be banished. Actually, Tierre's oath requires much more than that."

Akul shot to his feet, dark khald eye-rings turning him into a huge, angry raccoon. "The puddings who run our temple care only for their own pleasures," he snapped. "I keep these four blocks safe from Oarl's rats, and I tell the shopkeepers to donate to the temple one-fourth of the money they'd pay Oarl. Then I man the alehouse, stop the fights, and they still pay me the same as the head groundskeeper. They wouldn't give all that up to banish my boy."

Trana sighed. "You're wrong about that." She walked to the window and gazed outward, running a hand through her wavy brown hair. "You know, you might be able to stop these outbursts."

"How?" Larin and Akul blurted together.

"As you said, Influence magic is useless here, but Enchantment might work. You need a powerful charm, magicked by at least a green-sash." Her eyes crinkled at the corners. "I once knew a man who shouted whatever was in front of him at that moment. One day I saw him with a scar on his face—apparently, he'd shouted 'brown lizard' to a Lidathi warrior . . ." Her guffaw shook their small apartment, and Akul wrapped huge hands about his head in khald misery.

"Anyway," she said, wiping her eyes, "he paid an enchanter to craft a charm to stop his outbursts. I'm guessing it didn't cost more than eighty crowns."

They both stared.

"Ehh . . ." Akul gurgled.

Larin bit his lip. If the curse had been a thorn tunic before, it had now become heavy chains, chains whose lock had no key. He shook his head, spun around, and walked into his room.

At eighty gold, he'd be shouting the Phrase well into old age.

"In fire and magic, sent away
To a land of mists, where all is gray,
Demons live where no one sees
Eating tykes who don't say please."

Children's nursery rhyme admonition,
Origin unknown

IV

L arin's life changed before he could ever have that bruiseball game with Candro. Trana's visit convinced Akul to find Larin a job outside the storeroom, and in a triumph of optimism over common sense, Larin was assigned vegetable-buying duty, traveling daily to the sea of market stalls in Westmarket to buy the temple kitchen's fresh produce. It was a job that took him outside Akul's four-block zone, a fact they'd dusted under the rug by convincing themselves Larin was mature enough to hide his outbursts. Deep down, Larin had always known it was wishful thinking.

It happened one day, as he returned from Westmarket with a full cart. He'd stopped to watch a particularly violent bruiseball game play out beneath Enatt's suspicious eye, though today's extra aggression had nothing to do with Enatt's status as Oarl's informant. It did, however, have a lot to do with Lenorre, Ferena, Trulette, and Onie, who stood halfway down the street, whispering and laughing as they stole glances at the players. Larin had seen that whenever the girls were watching, the ball was hurled with extra strength and curses were bellowed with extra enthusiasm. To Larin, none of it mattered. Only one of them drew his attention like a clap of thunder: Onie, a waifish, dimple-cheeked beauty with blonde bangs and a thoughtful expression that seemed to notice deeper things than what anyone else was wearing. And he doubted she cared how big a bruise the boys could inflict on each other.

With the extra violence of that game, it wasn't long before the inevitable happened. The ball slammed into his cart, spewing tomatoes, onions, and potatoes in every direction. He stared, horrified as the cart tipped over, and soon knew another type of horror as heat rose behind his forehead. This time, his outburst would be unstoppable.

Scalding liquid flowed through his veins, throbbing heat threatened to burst his forehead. Dark spirits moved inside him, lifting his arms and stiffening his spine. He arched his back, pumped a fist over his head, stomped his foot hard on the cobblestones, and shouted his Phrase to the sky, while everyone stood in stunned silence.

The outburst faded away, leaving his stomach a cold lump. Tomatoes lay strewn about the cobblestones, the game had stopped, and everyone was staring at him like some indigen creature just slithered from the Shernock Swamps. He chanced a brief, shameful glance at the girls to see them staring with open-mouthed shock and hilarity. Only Onie's face held no mirth, but the pity in her eyes was somehow worse than laughter.

Unsure what else to do, he stooped and began picking tomatoes off the ground. The utter silence was filled only by the sounds of a wagon clattering through a neighboring alley and the low hiss of tagalanth scat. Musty scents of drying clothes drifted from a nearby clothesline.

"The Wormpile has a new village idiot," Enatt wheezed finally, his mouth stretched into a wide, bucktoothed grin. His single good eye narrowed as it stared at Larin in cruel amusement, and he seemed oblivious to the trail of mucus hanging above his upper lip.

Larin stood, giving Oarl's lackey a hard stare. "Enatt, if that snot dangles any lower, you'll be able to play the harp."

Candro snorted, and Enatt shot him a withering look. He turned back to Larin. "Your old man can't protect you forever. I'd watch my mouth if I were you."

Larin picked up a tomato and threw it in the cart. "I don't need protection from you, Enatt. I only need protection if your puppet master sends his whole army."

Enatt spat. Then his wheezing became higher pitched, like a bat in a wind storm, and shortly, Lyrashi words tunneled through labored breathing.

It was three weeks before Apex, that high-magic time when the moon Spellgiver was already giant enough for its blue light to impart the Wormpile's drab stones a dimension of color. That time of the year when everyone thought they were a wizard, even unlit candles such as Enatt.

Larin clenched his fists, recognizing the words. It was a pain-in-the-neck spell, quite literally—the type of spell small boys threw around before they learned better. He clapped his hands over his ears and yelled the word of negation, the only magic he could wield that worked every time. Sure enough, he soon felt the minor cooling that always accompanied power's dissipation. Angry and humiliated, he shouted his own spell, a simple Lyrashi dweomer intended to stick Enatt's fingers together for the next hour. Yet he knew from Enatt's puzzled look that his Lyrashi was almost unintelligible and the spell wouldn't work.

That was his other problem.

"No, Wiz, that's not how you do it," Candro groaned, his gaunt face twisted with discomfort. It was as if Larin's mangling of Lyrashi words had pained him personally.

"Wiz! That's great!" Uli guffawed, and they all began laughing uproariously.

Larin closed his eyes, knowing the humiliation would never end. He chanced a miserable look ahead and saw that Candro wasn't laughing with them. Instead, his face held curiosity and apology; he hadn't meant his comment to provoke the response it did. Larin nodded in silent understanding and grabbed the cart handle.

"Hey, *Wiz*," Enatt said gleefully when the laughter had died down. "I'm telling Oarl everything."

All conversation stopped abruptly then. Larin scanned every face in that courtyard, watching his social implosion take form. Somewhere, a shutter banged against a high window and, further away, they heard the muffled sounds of someone beating a rug. He closed his eyes a moment, trying to forget that the thing he'd always feared most had finally happened. Finally, he walked away with his cart, feeling like a hollow shell.

He'd gone only twenty steps before stomping drowned the clatter of his wagon's wheels, and he turned to see Candro racing toward him.

"Quite a show," Candro said, as he caught up. "Maybe once Enatt blows the snot out of his brain, he'll forget it happened."

Larin stopped, blinked at Candro, and then glanced down the alleyway. Uli, the girls, three other boys, and a scowling Enatt were all still watching them from the courtyard.

"Candro, do you *really* want to be seen with me? After this, I'll be lower than a kitchen cockroach, ready for Oarl to smash under his boot. Scurry alongside, and you'll be next."

Candro waved a hand dismissively. "I run too fast for any of Oarl's garbage flies to keep up. Anyway, they're too busy buggering tagalanths and bullying old ladies to care about me." His face brightened. "So I like what you did there, insulting one of Oarl's own. We don't see enough of that around here."

Larin smiled, turned around, and began walking again. "And I like how you can call me stupid and still pretend it's a compliment."

Candro laughed. "Stupidity, bravery, two crusts from the same loaf. Speaking of that, how would you like to help me steal the turquoise ring off fat Watchman Heddis's finger? He's supposed to be guarding the west-end spice store at night, but he's usually sleeping like a baby by ten. That ring will feed us both for a month."

Larin had always wondered how the Wormpile's orphans made enough to eat. He shook his head. "Candro, does it look like I need more enemies right now? Though I guess after Oarl's crew pounds me into jelly, having Watchman Heddis slit my throat would be a relief."

"Emja, you are a morbid one, aren't you? Do you like dwelling on all the different ways you can die?"

"It helps not to have high expectations."

Candro shrugged. "I guarantee we can do it without Heddis ever being the wiser. You just don't know how good I am. Did I ever tell you about the time I stole the daggers from a squad of Imperial Guardsmen while they stood around picking their noses?"

"What? None of them looked down?"

"Nah, they were blathering about how many people they'd arrested last week. I took them right out of their sheathes as they stood there, one by one . . ."

Larin seriously doubted that one, but he found Candro's excited jabber pulling him away from his dark misery, and he was grateful. Somehow this gaunt, thieving urchin was the only neighborhood street rat who didn't care what Oarl's crew thought of him.

They continued to talk until they reached Deepwell Plaza, with its ancient brick well, crowds of people, and old walls plastered with paintings of the Council of Twelve. This close to Apex, advertisement for the annual magic contest was in full swing, and the faces of the High Council were everywhere. Larin breathed a little easier as they stepped past the clock tower and into the plaza. It was still two blocks outside Akul's safe zone, but Oarl's gang stayed away anyway, for their one-time tax on water withdrawals had resulted in a full-scale Wormpile riot.

Candro stopped, nodding northward. "Well, this is where I make my exit; the Netrina is that way." He brushed black bangs from his eyes. "You know, this might all blow over in the end."

Larin looked north, knowing that the abandoned building where the Wormpile's orphans made their beds was worse than anything he had to deal with. "Yeah, I'll tell myself that. Well anyway, thanks."

"For what?"

"For sticking with me, even after I—uh, you know."

Candro squinted. "You're not going to get all soupy on me, are you?"

"Go eat pigeon scat."

Candro's face flashed a grin that disappeared almost instantly. "One day, you'll have to tell me what it was we just witnessed. I've never seen anything like it."

"I promise I will, if I ever figure it out myself."

Candro nodded and slipped out of the plaza, toes sticking prominently through his decrepit shoes. Larin watched him go, breathing deeply. With Candro's animated chatter gone, he had to face his life again, a life that had just gone from bad to horrible. Head hung low, he pulled his cart back into his four-block prison.

Word of Larin's condition raced through the Wormpile. It wasn't long before Oarl's crew surrounded him whenever he left Akul's safe zone, dancing madly to trigger the hilarious seizures. Eventually, they found that a good gut punch while he was held helpless did the trick. Yet they also found that they'd better hold his arms until they'd walked away because, if not, he was liable to strike back. Larin dented more than a few cheeks and, in one case, broke a nose before this lesson really sank in.

No one—*no* one—struck back at Oarl. Soon, Larin became a target worth attacking for far more than the hilarity of his seizures. While the threat of Akul's steel prevented Oarl from using anything but his fists, there were other ways to hurt. Before long, Oarl began bullying anyone daring to associate with Larin, a fact that kept everyone else away as surely as if he had the pox. Everyone except Candro, who for some reason seemed completely unimpressed by Oarl's threats. Larin never figured out how Candro escaped Oarl's punishments, but he assumed his boast was true— Candro could outrun just about anybody.

The first time Oarl's gang used steel against him was a defining moment in the war for the Wormpile. A man named Lafrikas, one of Oarl's lieutenants, threw a dagger at Larin as he ran away, gashing his calf. Then he threw another one that missed.

Later that night, Akul donned his gear, stomped to Lafrikas's upstairs flat, and pulled him out of bed where he'd been sleeping with one of Madam Shembri's girls. Two of Lafrikas's henchmen came to their commander's rescue as Akul dragged a screaming Lafrikas through the grimy alleyways, both of whom Akul flattened without even drawing his sword. A few more blows silenced Lafrikas, and Akul dragged his limp body to Clocktower Plaza. There, he beat Lafrikas into jelly, broke both his arms, and draped him over the walkway parapets.

Lafrikas was unlikely to hold a sword for the rest of his life. Despite everything, Larin felt no joy at this; it was a fate he couldn't wish on anyone. Yet his uncle was a different breed—one accustomed to fighting threats with every means at his disposal. There was no denying its effectiveness, for the rest of Oarl's gang got the message very clearly: using steel was a line that could not be crossed.

None of them ever tried it again.

Still, Akul's protection only went so far. He couldn't stop every beating, only the dangerous ones, and while Larin mostly tried to hide his bruises, he doubted Akul was fooled. When Akul did see them, he always asked three questions: "Did they use steel?" "Did it happen in these four blocks?" and "Did they break anything?"

If the answer was no to all three, then he let it be.

After four weeks of overturned vegetable carts, Larin's new job ended for good. He was reassigned to polishing Emja's gifts in the temple storeroom, and his burgeoning loneliness now became black despair. The walls of his storeroom prison became indistinguishable from Oarl's wall of isolation, barricades from which there was no escape.

The only break in the loneliness came from Candro's occasional visits. On Baker's day, Candro often showed up with a ball in hand, dragging Larin out of his apartment and his depression for a game of bruiseball. They played in the temple's ranunculus gardens, the only open space in Akul's four-block zone—at least on Baker's day, the one day of the week that the alehouse was closed. It was a game not known for its gentleness, and while they flattened more than a few flowers, most were replanted by the priests the next morning, before they'd started the afternoon libations.

"Only for Akul's boy," declared Sandre, whose love for gardening despite near blindness turned his words into an obvious lie.

Candro's occasional visits weren't enough to banish Larin's utter isolation. Late in his fifteenth year, Larin reached his low. After breaking two wine glasses in two separate outbursts, he walked home and went to bed. He'd refused to get up the next day, despite Akul's threats and enticements. On the second day, Akul walked into his room and sat at the corner of the bed, fat rolls behind his bald dome sweaty from the evening's heat.

"I was waiting for your fifteenth birthday, but I think we can cure you." He sat forward, giant arms on his knees. "Anyway, it's better now, only six weeks before Apex."

Shocked, Larin sat up. "You have eighty gold? That would feed us for two years!"

Akul looked pained. "Fifty. But it'll be enough."

Larin shot forward, wrapping Akul in a hug that caused his uncle no end of discomfort. After a frozen moment, Akul awkwardly extricated himself. "Well, all those broken plates aren't cheap," he said gruffly. Patting Larin's back, he got up and walked out.

Locating a green-sash enchanter was no easy feat. In the city of Aldive, they were midlevel nobility, the kind of person who lived in one of the beautiful stone houses lining the Kanic, or who attended performances in the Grand Playhouse overlooking the Tanbar River. Finding one willing to stomp through the city's worst neighborhood just to cure a street urchin of loud yelling should've been impossible, despite Akul's promises to escort them through Oarl's turf.

Yet Akul had his resources. They were resources from another place and another time, a time upon which Larin's questions never shed the smallest light. Somehow, against all odds, one of those old contacts had found just what was needed. As often happened, Larin wondered exactly who Akul had been before he'd come to the Wormpile.

The enchanter was actually an enchantress, and she marched through the Wormpile with no escort needed. Apparently, her myriad charms were more than sufficient to dispatch any dim-witted street rat who dared cast her a second glance.

She strode through Akul's open door and looked straight at Larin. "This is the one, is it?"

Larin stared. She was commanding in the same way the ocean was damp. Beautiful was too narrow a word; her face radiated power, both magical and charismatic. Wavy red hair cascaded around a striking face marked by the sharp blue eyes and high cheekbones of the Nydyn peoples. Her slender frame was draped with a dozen silver circular charms that glinted at him from prominent breasts, a place upon which Larin knew very well not to concentrate. She was a completely different creature than the coquettish Wormpile girls he'd once talked to—this was a woman of confidence, one whose intelligence radiated like a beacon.

Larin was mesmerized.

The enchantress's sharp face twisted in annoyance, and she turned to Akul.

"Does he speak?"

"Did you make all those charms?" Larin blurted.

Her mouth twitched. "Of course." She walked to Larin and put her open palm on his forehead, which triggered a small spark. "These outbursts. Always the same three words?"

"Yes."

"Repeat them."

Larin's face fell. For some unexplainable reason, he was embarrassed to have this woman witness his seizures. *"Kinech Aklad Vahrusen,"* he said, steeling himself. The heat began in his forehead and traveled into his arms. A moment later he repeated the Phrase, this time with much more power.

Akul stepped forward. "See the hands? He always drops what he's holding."

She stared at Larin thoughtfully, her eyes blue as the ocean. "Those words, that language. It's familiar, but I can't place it."

"The Sudmen?"

She cocked her head, as if studying a strange insect she'd found in her garden. "Interesting you say that. But no. The language of the Sudmen is full of glottal stops and, anyway, they do not know the sound of 'V.'"

"Look, can you cure him?" Akul asked, annoyed.

The enchantress whirled around, seeming to truly focus on Akul for the first time. "No one can cure him." Her withering look would have intimidated any normal man, but Akul's jaw remained set in a hard expression.

Larin's stomach clenched, and he leaned against the wall for support.

She turned back to him with a softer face, as if only now realizing he was human. "But yes, I can make a charm that will arrest the outbursts. I'll need a patch of skin, and it will take six weeks—this charm must wait for Apex Day." With that, she extracted a small knife and shaved a sliver of skin from Larin's arm.

For the first time in Larin's life, a tiny glimmer of hope peeked through the blackness. "Thank you," he whispered.

The mage's smile transformed her already fine features into a brilliant gem. "I think I like this one." Her emphasis on the word "this" provoked a tight scowl from Akul.

"What do your charms do?" Larin asked, not wanting her to leave.

"I have charms to ward against every misfortune. For example, this one here"—with much clinking, she uncovered a gold disk hidden beneath several others around her neck—"will deflect a sword. So if some lowbrow, such as this man behind me, attempts a strike, the blade will slide past as if I were sheathed in armor."

Akul nodded, as if he'd not just been insulted. "But our fine wizardress neglects to mention that any charm holds only so many Lyrani threads. Once those threads are spent, the charm can't be reused for several seconds." He fixed her with a pointed look. "So, the next blow sometimes finds the charm-wearer defenseless."

She scowled, and her eyes traveled up and down Akul's imposing presence. Then she turned back to Larin, as if speaking through an interpreter. "Just so. But it's also true that green-sashes can weave many threads into a small area, enough to absorb three to four blows."

"Which only requires speed," Akul cut in smoothly. "It's said some swordsmen can strike fast enough to defeat any charm."

Larin wondered if Akul could still claim that ability after sixteen years of khald stupor, but he said nothing.

Now the enchantress turned to face Akul directly. "Oh, indeed?"

"Madam, I've fought green-, blue-, and violet-sashes, and I still stand. They were of Seridor, but I don't believe magic works so differently between the two lands."

A flash of interest crossed her face, turning to curiosity as she focused on Akul's royal dragon earring. "Do I know you, sir? You look familiar."

With that, Larin felt the sudden pangs of an impossible jealousy. "How do Lyrani threads work?" he asked quickly.

The wizardress tore her eyes from Akul to look back at Larin. "Lyrani threads are strands of energy which have been laced through the world's very existence by the ancient Carver race. The Carvers crafted the Lyrashi language to manipulate those threads, and with correct pronunciation, most people can control them a little. As an enchanter, I bind those threads to physical objects, but there aren't many who can control Lyrani threads unless Spellgiver is close. The few who can control them all year become wizards and wizardresses, yellow-sash and above." She turned back to Akul. "And somehow this shiny-vertexed lout has fought several of those. How is that?"

Akul said nothing, and after a long moment, she cast a distasteful look around the small room. Narrowed eyes traveled past the frayed rope leading to the roof trapdoor, swept over the hearth with its pile of dirty pots, glided past the congealed stew on the oak table, and settled finally on their pitted door, pockmarked by years of dagger-throwing practice.

Mouth pursed, she glanced at Akul. "Well, I think we're done here. Would you care to escort me out of this rubbish bin you call a neighborhood?"

"You didn't need an escort earlier," Larin blurted.

Akul beamed, offering his arm. "I'd be glad to. The Wormpile does get a bit rougher around dusk."

The enchantress took Akul's arm, and her half-smile in Larin's direction told him that she'd read him like a book. Larin felt his face color as the door slammed shut.

The charm arrived seven weeks later through a courier, and while Larin felt slight disappointment it hadn't been delivered by his enchantress, he was too excited to dwell for more than a second. It was mounted on a belt he could wear under his clothes, and it came with a note:

I put in something extra. Enjoy. —L

Larin stared at the note, wondering why he'd never learned her name, but he couldn't wait. He immediately fastened the belt and muttered the Phrase.

The heat gathered behind his forehead, and for a heart-wrenching moment, he thought the charm would be useless. But after a few seconds the fire dissipated and the outburst faded away, like a rain puddle on a sunny day.

Larin gazed through the window, reveling in the dance of sunlight on the balcony railings. He was cured.

With the outbursts gone, he felt he'd gained a new beginning. He could wander the temple hallways without fear, and he even managed to land a new job cleaning tables in the temple alehouse. Still, while his life did change, the loneliness never really left. Oarl still hated him, Candro was still his only friend, and threat of physical harm kept him within the same four blocks of the city day after day. While the promise of Akul's swift blade prevented Oarl from using steel, he was almost guaranteed a beating if he ventured outside Akul's zone. As was anyone who dared talk to him.

Still, over time he imagined his outbursts had been only a long nightmare, their mystery unimportant. So when the solution finally appeared, it was long after he'd stopped looking for it.

He was in the temple library, perusing a tome on warship construction, when Trana strode by with a pile of books.

Larin looked up, surprised. "Ho, Trana. What brings you here?"

"Ho, young'un," she said, balancing a stack of books with her chin. "Studying the Chandor language for a trip to the disputed region." A book fell as she passed, and Larin bent to retrieve it.

"Don't you want this?" he shouted, as Trana pounded down the wooden stairway.

"You keep it. I've got too many," she called over her shoulder.

Larin had just shoved it to the side when his breath caught at the title: *Sudmen: Tribal Worship in the Southeastern Foothills.*

Nothing to do with Chandor. Trana was giving him the most direct help she could.

He flung the book open, but his initial enthusiasm waned quickly. The reading was slow going, and dry facts filled his mind: the Sudmen were unrelated to any surrounding human tribe; they'd worshipped Demons for as long as records had been kept; their numbers were less than fourteen thousand; and so on. From the few language snippets, Larin concluded that the enchantress was right: the Phrase couldn't be related to those backward, remote peoples.

After an hour, he came to a more interesting section, one discussing Demons. These creatures fascinated him, for in all the legends, Demons were described only as the gods' dark enemy. He reread the one story everyone knew: after a long war, the Demons were banished to the Gray Lands by the Eldegod, where the Demons' force was muted. Today, a shadow of that immense power entered this world only when they were summoned from the fog by the highest-rank wizards. With that ancient fury buried deep in the gray mists, Haraf—Lord of Demons—had vowed to wreak vengeance on the world that had condemned him.

It was several pages later that the first chill wormed down his spine. He encountered that word again: *Kineshe,* meaning "Master" or "Lord." Blood freezing in his veins, Larin hesitated, dreading what would come next. Finally, he lifted the next brittle sheet, and there, in letters that seemed to waver in and out of his vision, was the Phrase. He shot forward in his chair, gripping the book with white knuckles as he read those impossible words over and over again.

Uttered by Haraf, Lord of Demons, the Phrase was not in the language of the Sudmen at all—it was in the language of the Demons they worshipped.

Kineshe Aklad Vahrusen: "The Lord Escapes His Prison."

> "If I had a copper ducat for every loyal citizen in the Wormpile, I'd have two copper ducats."
>
> Maldovin III, responding to an ambush and theft of weapons from the last Imperial garrison ever stationed in the Wormpile.

V

"Someone is watching us."

Larin turned away from the window as Akul spilled another vial of khald onto the pitted oak table. Akul raked gnarled fingers through the red powder, dabbed them on his tongue, and then looked at Larin with pupils as wide as plates.

"Well then, good," he said cheerfully. "Let no one say they couldn't watch!"

Larin scowled, turning back to the window. The street below was thick with the usual traffic of late morning. A cheese vendor had established himself too far from the stone walls, partially blocking a tagalanth-led caravan heading to Westmarket. Cursing echoed across the narrow street, laced with Lyrashi phrases, which might have been effective later in the high season. The air was still and hot, and sounds of clanging metal from a nearby blacksmithy made Larin wonder how anyone could operate a forge today.

And the man with the inward knee was gone. Larin had seen him twice now, limping under the awnings across the street, looking up at their window. At first, Larin'd paid no attention. Akul had long ago draped Maldovin IV's green dragon standard from their balcony railing, and the sight of an Imperial symbol in the Wormpile's heart had provoked odd looks over the years. The second time, Larin had caught his eye. A portly, limping man with the features of the Yulish peoples: sunken eyes in a yellowish face, hair twisted into a single braid. He'd been looking up directly into their window.

Larin turned back around. "Akul, I'm serious. Do you owe money to any Yuls?"

Akul considered the table, where he'd created an intricate hash pattern from khald powder. His faded tunic was stained, wet with sweat dripping off that massive chin. Ashes from their untended hearth clung to his shirt, where he'd been trying to boil a pot of water minutes before.

"Money, money . . . why all this talk of money? Do you need some?"

Larin exhaled loudly. "Akul, listen! If you don't owe a Yul some money, then that man out there is an Imperial spy. Probably measuring whether the street's wide enough for a phalanx of city guards!"

Akul craned his neck, pretending to look out the window, then burst into laughter. However, his breath scattered the khald on the table, and he stood frantically, sweeping the wayward powder back into a pile.

Larin averted his gaze. Akul's shame had completely deserted him lately, as well as his natural suspicion. Over the years, Akul's highest fear had become Larin's own—one day, Imperial soldiers would march through the Wormpile and drag Akul back to the palace to answer for whatever crime he'd committed. A single mantra had been repeatedly pounded into Larin's head: keep a watchful eye on traffic outside. The king's men could find them at any time, but anyone lingering on their street was casing it for a raid. It was nearly impossible to watch for, since as part of Akul's four-block zone, the street outside was always packed with vendors and buyers. Yet this man had definitely been focused on their window, and now Akul was too far gone to care.

He tried again. "Akul. Someone. Is. Watching. Us. Do something!"

Akul waved his hand, not looking away from the table. "Let them in. There's enough for everyone."

Familiar desperation descended on Larin like a chill rain. The only force stopping Oarl from owning the entire Wormpile was sitting before him, lost in a hell of his own making. If Oarl's crew knew when to strike, they might just bring him down.

He closed his eyes, imagining a different life. One where his parents hadn't died three months after he was born, one where his only other family member didn't regularly leave the world. Without another word, he walked out and slammed the door, stomping down the stairway in frustration.

He exited to the street, squinting in the bright sun, trying to ignore the hollow feeling in his stomach. The smell of unwashed tagalanth mixed with the pungent aroma of exotic cheeses as he threaded through the stopped caravans, searching for the Yul. The cheese vendor and his son were face-to-face with three cart drivers, and Larin wondered who'd be the first to draw a knife. Stopping next to an immobilized caravan, he scoured every bottom-level shop doorway for signs of their mysterious Yulish spy.

Without warning, a giant stubbled head thrust into Larin's face, accompanied by a cloud of bored affection and the urge to scratch his chin. Smiling, Larin raked his fingernails across the tagalanth's scaly chin as he stared into the creature's four black orbs, arranged in a semicircle around its triangular head. They appeared to be shiny black balls, but close up one could see the patchwork of small ovals that were the beast's true "eyes." More strangely, the ball's outer covering was said to vibrate with noise, allowing tagalanths and other indigen creatures to hear sounds through those same orbs. The tagalanth's oddly pointed head was mounted on a scaly neck that protruded from a six-legged body, covered by fur strands thick as ropes.

He removed his hand for an instant, feeling a renewed urgency to scratch his chin. Grinning, he resumed his duties, always amazed by the ability of indigen creatures to project their emotions. Yet for all their bizarreness, tagalanths were placid in their six-legged gait, and Larin preferred them to the horses some cart vendors used.

He reached behind the bumps atop its head and felt the long, crusted groove of a whip mark. The tagalanth shook its head uncomfortably, and Larin caught a fleeting image, filtered through the beast's eyes: a memory of dumb, helpless pain, dueling affection and confusion as the food-giver struck it again and again.

He peered again sadly into the four gentle orbs. "Who did this to you, sweet girl?"

"Ho, Larin," came a voice from behind, and he turned to see Nitalen the leather-tanner descend from his cart, his ruddy face straining. Nitalen was short and cylindrical, like a plump lamppost, and today he wore a brown doublet and felt hat, a combination that looked miserable in the heat. It took a moment for Larin to realize Nitalen actually wanted to speak, since like everyone else, he ignored Larin outside Akul's four-block zone.

The smell of lime and urine assaulted Larin as Nitalen approached, and Larin wrinkled his nose. "This fiasco is preventing me from delivering a message," the pudgy man said, seemingly unaware of Larin's discomfort. He held out a scroll. "How about two coppers to get this to the house of Morphat: one now and one after delivery?"

Larin blanched. *Morphat.* "You mean that cult on the south end of the Port District?"

"Hardly a cult." Nitalen chuckled. "Half the world worships in such temples."

Larin's eyes widened. He'd known since he was a tyke at his first dinner prayers that the Eldegod temples were the fountainhead of evil, and Morphat was their chief. The six-legged Old Gods were ancient like the Carvers, that mysterious race which had once ruled the world. But unlike the Carvers, the Eldegod were a malevolent force, demanding blood and pain.

Or so he'd been taught all his life.

Larin shook his head. "Nitalen, you've been breathing your leather fumes too long. You can't be actually worshipping that six-legged monster."

Nitalen's eyes flashed. "And what have your priests done for their flock lately? Made a stronger batch of ale? Slept with their worshippers' wives?"

Larin flinched under the pudgy tanner's intensity, trying to remember if Ulysse had ever slept with Nitalen's wife. "Well, the priests like their pleasures," he admitted. "But that doesn't change—"

"Forget the lifetime of lies they've fed you," Nitalen spat. "Emja's priests have done nothing—*nothing*—for us. They let Oarl run the Wormpile, let the crown raid us for fodder in Maldovin's endless wars. None of it matters, as long as we pray every evening."

"But Morphat? The god of the Lidath and Seridor demands blood sacrifice . . ."

Nitalen's anger melted into benevolent smugness. "Emja's drunkards have lied about him so long, I can't fault your ignorance. The Lidath may sacrifice, but the lizards have their own ways that have nothing to do with worship. As for Seridor, they only execute criminals and traitors. That's no different than what we do here in Tanbar."

"Don't they do it publicly?"

"Have you ever been to the Uranim District? There you can watch criminals hang every month."

Larin breathed deeply, at a loss for words. Nitalen's perspective was strangely compelling, radically different than the one he'd heard all his life.

"Still I don't see how Morphat—"

"That's where you'll be enlightened," Nitalen interrupted, his voice shaking with fury. "Unlike Emja, Morphat provides true sustenance instead of ale bribes. He heals the sick, gives food to the poor, but mostly he teaches us to fight back!" A shiny dangle of spittle appeared at Nitalen's mouth as he waved his hands wildly.

"Does he teach us to wipe our drool?" Larin mumbled.

"Eh?"

"He teaches us to fight against who?" Larin said, a little louder.

"Against those who would oppress us! He'll destroy Oarl. The crown will take longer, but they'll also go down. Maldovin, the coward, sends his army to steal from the people without giving us protection, roads, or services of any kind! I'm joining the Morphasti myself, the temple's army. If I pass the warrior's test, they'll let me wear the red and black tunic . . ." His voice trailed off as he realized he was losing his audience. "So, you'll take the message?"

Larin shot one last hopeless glance down the street, but the Yul was gone for good, and two coppers would help buy the book of seafaring legends he'd seen at the south-end market. He nodded.

Smiling, Nitalen handed him the scroll and a copper coin. "Deliver to Kamithan, third-rank priest of Morphat. He'll give you the other copper."

Larin winced. Walking under the marble archway was bad enough, but speaking to the cleric of a six-legged god was ultimate blasphemy. "I didn't plan to talk to a priest."

"You'll like him, and he can explain more."

With dread, Larin watched Nitalen return to his cart. Now he was stuck. Swallowing, he put the scroll in his pocket and the copper in his shoe, then turned away.

He pushed his way through the throngs and out of Akul's four-block zone, slipping into deserted alleyways as he mulled the conversation with Nitalen. At fifteen, he'd long figured out that Emja's servants were as useless as horns on a pillow. Were there priests who actually helped their flock, provided order amid the Wormpile's chaos? It was hard to shake an icy chill whenever he heard Morphat's name, but he had to admit, that was likely due to years reciting the Ritual of Answers.

From Akul's lips, Morphat's name always evoked a shudder and grim face, but that had nothing to do with temple teachings. That one was personal. The only thing Larin knew about Akul's past life was that he'd spent part of it in the Imperial khula knight brigades on the frontier with Seridor, the land to the south. Having fought Seridor for so long, Akul hated everything about that land, especially its gods.

As he walked, he resolved to peruse the temple's library for books on the Eldegod origins. The temple owned many volumes of the Tiyani Codex, though he was allowed to see only a few. Yet there were several commentaries he could read, even if they didn't have all the original Lyrashi passages. Plus, other sources existed beyond the temple. He mulled it over, wondering if he should apply the two coppers to a true history of the Age of Gods. He tallied his money, and as often happened, his mind turned to reading.

He was so lost in his mental catalog that his usual caution escaped him, and he stepped around a corner directly into Utra's expansive belly. He spun around in panic, but Utra's three henchmen moved to block his path. After only two steps, the tall one grabbed him from behind. Whoops of joy rang out as Larin was immobilized, and he twisted so violently that two of them had to hold him back

"Beautiful," Utra said, his fat face beaming. "It's been months since Larin's done the dance." He motioned to the other three. "Bring him out to the plaza so everyone can watch the show. No need to be selfish about this." With that, Oarl's senior lieutenant spun around and marched toward Westmarket, his thugs dragging Larin kicking and cursing behind.

They burst into the plaza, and a blur of faces wavered in Larin's vision as he struggled in their grip. At fifteen, he was no match for their adult strength. They set him down in the center, one of them still pinning his arms. Larin saw that activity among the outdoor market stalls had halted, as people stopped shopping to watch. Some grinned, others wore grim expressions, but he knew none would brave Oarl's wrath to help him.

Utra's smile dug into his fat cheeks. "Too bad Oarl's not here," he said loudly, playing to the market crowds. "He's missed the puppet show."

"Well, I guess after Oarl sticks it to you in the morning, he refuses to be seen with you the rest of the day," Larin said.

Muffled laughter rose from the crowds, and one of Utra's henchmen, a square-headed hyena-faced man whose name Larin forgot, shot warning looks at the wooden stalls. Utra's mouth became grim, his eyes narrowing behind sweaty cheeks. But his light expression quickly returned.

"Ah, Larin, you never learn, do you? That's what makes this so much fun." With that, he stepped forward and shot his fist into Larin's stomach.

Larin doubled over, expecting aching fire but feeling only a hard slap. He sagged in the grip of the tall one, pretending dire pain. What was this? Why was Utra pulling his punches? Yet one look at Utra's savage expression told him the blow had been as strong as ever.

Then, the familiar heat blossomed behind his forehead. He straightened, and his four tormentors exchanged wide grins, recognizing the beginning of an outburst. They released his arms and stepped to Larin's front, knowing Larin would be helpless to run, defend himself, or do anything.

Except that this time, the charm would stop the outburst dead.

As the outburst faded away, Larin continued going through the motions, furiously considering how he could use this one-time chance to stick a finger in Utra's eye. He pretended the heat spread down his arms, then into his hands, as it used to do.

In synchronicity, his four tormentors bent their legs in imitation of Larin's mid-outburst stance, watching each other through open-mouth grins of pleasure. As Larin pretended the heat reached his fists, they all, in one motion, clenched their fists and shut their eyes in perfect copy. There was scattered laughter among the marketplace crowds.

As Larin shouted the first word, they shouted it with him, bent down with hands flared, eyes shut as though preparing for overwhelming rapture. When he shouted the second word, they straightened up, turning chins upward with Larin. With the final "*Vahrusen!*" they flung their arms in the air, shaking and dancing. Utra's fat face was raised in closed-eye abandon as he shouted to the sun.

So it was that Larin's fist slammed Utra's teeth through his tongue so hard, Utra staggered back several steps and fell, mouth spurting blood.

Cries of surprise, laughter, and a few shouts of pleasure erupted from the crowd. Larin watched Utra roll to his side in a daze, reveling in the feel of crunched teeth on his fist, knowing he would pay well for that pleasure.

The others came at him in fury then. He managed one glancing blow on hyena-man's chin before a rain of fists beat him down, and his vision became a blur of knuckles. Yet within a second, wonder engulfed him: the blows were muffled, as if he'd donned leather armor. Larin curled into a tight ball, thinking furiously.

I put in something extra.

The charm wasn't completely effective, and blows further from his waist seemed more painful, but the impact was a fraction of what it would have otherwise been. He gave silent thanks to his enchantress. *If I can ever repay you, I will.*

Utra finally picked himself up. The others stopped their beating, keeping Larin pinned as Oarl's lieutenant lurched forward with drawn dagger. He stood above Larin with an incomprehensible expression, turning his weapon in small circles as a stream of mouth blood splattered on Larin's forehead. He let the dagger drop to the cobblestones, its clang loud in the hushed silence of Westmarket Plaza.

"We don't have to use steel. We can just break every bone in your body."

"*Utan*, let it be," said the tall one, softly. "We don't need the old man's wrath."

Larin smiled grimly. At fourteen, his nose had been broken by weasel-faced Terris, Oarl's short, stocky and mean right-hand man. A day later, Akul had descended from their apartment like a vengeful god. He'd swept through six of Oarl's twenty, knocking them unconscious using only the flat of his sword, all without himself receiving a single cut. Terris had fled like a rabbit from a forest fire, and the story had reached legendary status in the Wormpile. Best of all, after a flat-bladed forehead slap that'd marked Utra for months, Oarl's lieutenant would never shake the nickname "Flatface" that had stuck to him like honey.

Larin turned painfully to hurl the dreaded nickname into Utra's face. But his body was on fire, and after a shaky moment, he lowered his head back to the cobblestones. For once, firing back at Oarl's jackals seemed less important than being able to walk tomorrow.

Utra curled his lip. "You better stay down, you rot worm. And don't think we won't catch Akul sometime when he least expects it." He kicked Larin in the ribs, retrieved his dagger, and motioned to the others. They walked away, hyena-man giving Larin one final kick as he rubbed his chin.

Larin lay on his back, eyes closed, almost wishing Utra had used his dagger. Throbbing pain warred with deep humiliation, humiliation at the public beating, at having a hundred people witness his outburst. He rolled to his side, watching the crowd turn away. By the time he sat up, Westmarket was back in full swing, with only two spectators left: Onie, the girl he'd once pined for along with just about every other neighborhood boy, and a chubby, curly-haired man on the plaza's far side.

Larin rose slowly, trying not to cry out. His rib and stomach bruises seemed to be healing already, though those on his arms hurt quite a bit. The charm's powers diminished rapidly when it came to his face; he'd have a black eye tomorrow.

Head spinning, he debated returning home. He had no desire to see Morphat's temple, but with the copper, failing to keep his word would only earn another enemy—and that was the last thing he needed.

In black despair, Larin limped across the plaza toward the west end, expecting his two remaining watchers to turn away. But Onie stayed put, her drab homespun dress eclipsed by radiant blonde hair that cascaded over perfectly dimpled cheeks. Larin stared, caught himself, and then bit his lip. After seeing his outburst a second time, she must think he was a pure imbecile.

To his surprise, she didn't turn away. He remembered that sprinkle of freckles around her nose, the way her bangs shrouded her eyes. He opened his mouth to say something, anything. Then he noticed Enatt watching from the market crowds, and he knew he couldn't put her in danger. Gritting his teeth, he turned away.

Onie's face fell as he passed by.

"That was pretty stupid, you know," she shouted to his back.

Larin stopped and turned around, wincing from pain.

"Which part? The part where Utra slugged me while I couldn't move? Or where they all took turns playing bruiseball with their fists?"

She stared. "The part where you gave Utra a bloody lip. And where you insulted him in front of his crew."

Larin nodded, feeling his bruised right eye. "I know." He cast his gaze downward, not wanting the conversation to end but not feeling particularly witty at the moment. His ears had started to ring, and the high-pitched tone was drowning out other noises.

"But it was brave, too," she said softly. "I've never seen anyone insult Oarl's trolls, let alone hit one."

Larin smiled weakly. "I'd be long buried without Akul's protection."

She brushed her bangs away from her face. "Still, no one else utters a word out of place to them. You could make less trouble for yourself if you kept your mouth shut. Why do you do it?"

Larin stood silently, the light breeze cooling his neck. Why did he do it? Poking a finger in Oarl's eye had become so ingrained, he had to dig deeply to remember how it started.

"Because they shouldn't get away with it," he said. "They extort, they murder. What right do they have to force monthly silver out of all the shopkeepers when the only protection they need is from Oarl?"

"None at all." Her eyes gleamed. "But it's still dumb, even if it is brave."

"You know, talking to me in public isn't so smart either." He nodded toward Enatt, who watched them from the market, buckteeth in full view as he breathed heavily. "That one with the tusks, he'll tell Oarl everything."

Her smile dropped. "Are you telling me to go away?"

Larin winced; that was the last thing he wanted. "No, no, but—"

"Well, if you're brave enough to hit Oarl's creatures, then I can be brave enough to talk to you in public."

They locked gazes then and, entranced, Larin imagined diving into her blue eyes. Emotions swirled through him, a mix of fascination, hope, and a desperate desire for a friend other than Candro. He struggled to speak, not wanting this to end. Yet he knew that if it went on much longer, she'd feel Oarl's wrath.

"Come by the temple sometime," he said finally. "I'll get you into the alehouse without going through the prayer rooms, and Akul will give you a free ale." He regretted the words immediately.

Onie wore a merry smile. "Silly. Why would I want a free ale?"

"I mean—none of Oarl's flat-faces come near the temple."

"Everyone knows that."

"Look, some other time I might be better at playing these games. I just mean, come by the temple, and we can talk without worrying about Oarl. I'm there every evening."

Onie was immediately apologetic. "I—I will come by. And maybe I can try an ale . . ."

Larin smiled, but it dropped as he saw Enatt disappear into the crowds. "I have to go. You'd better make yourself scarce, too."

He turned away, Onie's final sweet smile burned into his memory. His first ray of sunshine in a very long time. He became so lost in wonder that he forgot about his other observer, sitting on the bench, until the man spoke out.

"Haraf's servant. Heh, that's funny."

Larin froze. "What?"

The man's round face was red from mirth. Greasy curly hair framed a sweaty forehead as he considered Larin with an amused expression. He wore a simple green robe, which bunched around his midsection in rolls of fat as he leaned forward on the bench.

"Oh, the dance, the words. *Kinech Aklad Vahrusen*. I've seen likelier demonic servants."

All other thoughts evaporated into the warm afternoon air as ice crept up Larin's spine. "What do you know about it?" he hissed. "What prison is Haraf escaping from?"

The man's rosy cheeks puffed out, as if verging on laughter. "Well, as you'd expect, it's the prison preventing him from wreaking vengeance on the world." He turned to his right, and his eyes widened. "Ah, the children.

They do enjoy themselves."

Larin followed his gaze to Jinett and Lophan playing in the plaza, their five-year-old screams of delight piercing the dull roar of the marketplace crowds.

He leaned forward. "Why are you calling me Haraf's servant? For Emja's sake, do you know why I shout these cursed words?"

"Emja has nothing to do with it," the man said, keeping his gaze on the children. He pulled out a sweetmeat wrapped in paper. "They're so lovely at that age, aren't they?"

Larin blanched. "You mean cute?"

He glanced at Larin, pushing curly locks from his eyes. "Sure." He turned back to Lophan. "Would you like a treat?"

Larin stepped back in horror, then turned to Lophan. "Don't!"

Lophan's face scrunched tight. "I don't have to listen to you." He began to walk forward to accept the treat.

Larin shut his eyes. Even the Wormpile's children had been taught to ignore him. He did the only thing he could think of: he drew his dagger and walked menacingly to Lophan. "I'll cut your throat if you take another step."

Lophan stared with wide eyes and then, crying, ran back to his family at the market. Larin stared after him with a sinking feeling. Another enemy.

"Och, I don't hurt them, I just want to hold them a while," the man said wistfully. "Was that really necessary?"

"Yes!" Larin sat as far away as possible, staring at the man with disgust. "What do you know of Haraf? And what does it mean to be a Demon's servant?"

"Well, it's a little like being King Galin III," the man said, fist in his mouth to contain laughter. "Maybe just like it." He erupted into loud guffaws and, for the first time, Larin realized this man was mad. Yet something real lurked beneath the mania, and Larin was fascinated.

At Larin's hard look, the man stifled his guffaws, his face tomato-red. "Well, surely you've heard of King Galin's disease," he said, wiping a patch of spittle.

"Of course." Every boy learned about King Galin's many personae, each knowing nothing about the other. For ten years the empire had been ruled by four different kings in one body, often suffering repeal of a royal decree issued two days earlier. After the Imperial Guard had ceased enforcing laws from sheer confusion, the king had been declared mad, and replaced by his son. "So what?"

"Well, let me tell you," the man said conspiratorially. "It's not all it's cracked up to be."

Larin closed his eyes. "What in the name of all the Demons are you talking about? For Emja's sake, can you carry a conversation for more than one minute?"

The man pursed his lips and rolled his eyes, dissecting Larin's words. "Emja, Demons. Those two don't fit." Then, a flash of lucidity crossed his sweaty face. "Forget Emja. The only players here are the Old Gods, and those you call "Demons." Only their war matters; only their conflict will destroy everything. And, my dancing, shouting Harflet, whichever side wins, it will not be good for humanity."

Larin was fascinated. "What about the Human Gods?"

The man waved a fat hand full of stubby, jeweled fingers. "Emja: decadent. Rakva: lazy. An-Dhura: Self-absorbed. The Human Gods will watch from the sidelines, but when it's over, they'll be the victor's plaything."

"So what am I supposed to do?"

"Eh, you might want to leave," the man said, pointing to where two members of Oarl's gang exited the Westmarket crowds. He turned away, a broad smile lighting his face. "Oh, there he is again!" He clapped his hands as Lophan peeked around a stall, staring at the bench but coming no closer.

Larin got up, eyeing the approaching men warily. "I'd advise you to go, too, or you may get a beating."

The man continued staring at Lophan. "Oh, yes, I'm sure they're very frightening."

Larin sighed, considering trying to scare Lophan away again, but Oarl's wolves were too close. "Fine, it's your skin." He walked away, and the man turned his attention away from Lophan.

"That's not the way home, is it?"

How did he know that?

"I'm delivering a message to the house of Morphat," Larin said.

"Morphat? Straight into the enemy's lair. Well, no one said Haraf's servants were timid."

Larin spun around, scowling. "Morphat's not my enemy. And I'm no one's servant!"

"Mmm . . . just don't sing your Phrase in a Eldegod temple, or you'll end your day in a relaxing bath of bubbling oil."

Larin stared, wanting to say more. He glanced toward the market, where Oarl's goons were striding toward him purposefully. It was getting too unhealthy around here. Without another word, he turned away and disappeared into the alley.

Their [untranslated] imprisoned them, [untranslated] freedom weaned them from pain. Pride gave spirit away, yet what was done had never been. When spirit and [untranslated] no longer join, only pain can return to what once was.

"This Lyrashi script from the Carvers is one of the most mysterious known snippets of their language. Early commentators point out that the Lyrashi usage of 'they' differs from human connotations, implying a nether state between 'us' and fully 'other.' Based on this, some claim this passage depicts an early split between factions of the Carvers. A small few [See reference 19] boldly posit that this carving depicts the creation of the Old Gods themselves. However, no relationship between the Eldegod and the Carvers has been widely accepted."

Tiyani Codex: Volume 24, Chapter 8—"Theories on the Rise of the Old Gods."

VI

Larin limped through the Wormpile's west end, his mind churning. The twisted lunatic on the bench had answers he wanted, but when would he ever see him again? Now his book-buying priorities shifted. He must have more information on Demons, and the beginnings of their war with the Old Gods. The legends weren't enough; someone must have the real story in all its details.

He passed Madam Shembri's brothel, entering the Port District. From there he turned left, traveling south for several blocks along narrow and hilly streets that occasionally opened into courtyards enclosed by terraced buildings with pointed rooftops. The Port District's south end rested on cliffs high above the Apex tides, and it was free of the pillars seen elsewhere in the district. He walked alongside ivy-covered stone walls, then turned right onto a cobbled street that sloped sharply down and dead-ended just before the cliffs, giving way to the vast blue expanse of the Kanic Ocean. At the street's end was the marble four-spired temple of Morphat, encircled by a line of people waiting to pass through the arched gate. The arch was mounted by a giant statue of Morphat, the god's concave head ringed by eight black orbs that surveyed the city with an unreadable expression. It stood on six scaly legs, each ending in an eight-pronged claw.

Whatever deep reservoir of Larin's soul birthed the Phrase evoked an immediate, nauseous reaction at the sight of the six-legged god. He stopped, averting his eyes and trying to let his stomach settle. Breathing deeply, he pulled the scroll from his pocket and forced himself to continue.

As he approached, he saw tables of food surrounded by acolytes in red and black, and he realized that temple workers were distributing food to the poor. Armed men in red and black tunics paced the lines, keeping order and watching for cheats. Larin guessed these were the Morphasti, Morphat's temple guards. The line stretched around the temple, and the acolytes seemed harried as they raced around with ladles and plates.

Larin received dirty looks as he approached the archway. One man balled his fist. "Hey! Stand in line!"

Larin hesitated, wincing as the bruise on his chest flared. "I'm just delivering a message . . ." Yet shouts of anger and two Morphasti heading his way turned him around. Dismayed, he limped away. Surely he wouldn't have to stand in this line just to earn an Emja-forsaken copper.

"A message? Why, do come inside."

Larin turned to see a baby-faced blond man in a red and black robe beaming at him. Three golden sunburst pins lined his sleeve, now pulled back around an outstretched hand.

After a moment's hesitation, Larin walked forward. "I'm—I'm supposed to deliver this to Kamithan . . . and I'm due a copper . . ."

"Of course," the man said, taking the scroll. His smile immediately put Larin at ease. "I'm Kamithan, and let's see what I have for you today . . ." He pulled two coppers from a fold in his robe. "Here we are. This is for the extra determination, as it looks like your trip was eventful." He pointed to Larin's bruised eye.

Despite all expectations, Larin liked the man instantly.

"Why don't you come inside, and we'll see if we can heal that eye?" The priest's face was soft and rosy-cheeked, the image of a man at peace. Larin nodded and followed him into the temple, ignoring a twinge of fear.

Inside, the Marble Temple was bright and clean. Red-black cloths draped the walls, which were adorned with glass-encased metal rods, each sporting a beautifully carved wooden handle. The floor was polished tile, smelling of lye and incense. At one wall, an unassuming altar depicted the god upright on two legs, four upper legs in the air. A glass bowl sat before Morphat, filled with copper, silver, and pieces of silk. At various points in the room, priests and acolytes conversed with the townsfolk in hushed tones.

Larin and the priest walked to a back room filled with bread and medicines, and Kamithan pulled a vial of liquid from a shelf. "Let's try a simple healing spell," he said, dabbing the liquid onto Larin's eye. "It would be better were we further into the high season, but I think we can reduce the bruising."

"Thank you." Larin peered around the room without moving his head. "You're feeding a lot of people out there."

"We do what we can. The people have been neglected so long, it's hard to know where to start." Kamithan mumbled a few Lyrashi words, then stepped back. "That should do it. I hope whoever did this thinks twice next time."

Larin shrugged. "Utra? He'll do it again. Though I definitely gave him something to think about."

The priest nodded. "You know, here we teach our flock to regain their lives. We're looking for those willing to break chains of powerlessness."

Larin noticed how Kamithan's rosy cheeks dimpled as he talked. If someone were to create the exact opposite of what he thought an Eldegod priest should look like, Kamithan would have been very close. He suddenly wanted to understand more about this much-maligned religion and could almost ignore the tiny voice screaming from the pit of his stomach.

"And how do you help the powerless?"

"We teach them warrior skills. We teach that even if their king casts them down, they are not low. Only the gods can designate such status, and their criteria are different from mankind's." The priest pointed to the temple's main room, his red-black striped sleeve draping to his waist. "In there, a man named Hulyis is learning to resist his oppressor. He was beaten by a group of men, but now he learns to assemble his own group, to fight back. We can teach you the same thing."

Larin's eyes widened. He knew Hulyis. Hulyis had been caught robbing several businesses, and in the lawless Wormpile, the shop owners had taken matters into their own hands. Larin wondered what warrior training would do for the conniving drunkard. Still, he was intrigued.

The priest smiled as Larin's face played out his thoughts. "I see you already have the warrior spirit. I will show you how we can strengthen it." He stepped to Larin's side. "I want you to imagine the face of your oppressor. Think about it in detail."

Larin turned to stare at Kamithan.

"Just picture it for a moment. Think hard."

Larin turned back around, picturing Oarl's chiseled face pulled back into his typical sneer. Within seconds, Oarl's form materialized before him, and Larin jumped.

"What in—" Larin started, stepping back. The image faded away.

Kamithan chuckled, a merry sound that made Larin smile.

"That's the typical first reaction," Kamithan said, eyes crinkled. "I have some skills with Influence magic. Outside the low season, I can usually manage an illusion or two. Only the Influence type of course, not the light-bending shadow magic of a true mage. But it should be enough for our needs." He placed a friendly hand on Larin's shoulder and stepped backward. "Let's try it again. This time keep the image in mind, and when it materializes, strike with all your strength."

Larin imagined Oarl's face again, marveling as Oarl came to life in full detail. The homunculus sauntered forward, and Larin struck its chin hard, wincing at the sharp pain in his shoulder. He was surprised to feel the crack of bone as the illusion reeled backward and fell. It lay on the ground briefly, before fading away.

"Excellent!" said Kamithan.

"I felt that!" Larin exclaimed, looking at his fist in amazement.

Kamithan nodded. "With the Influence illusions, all the senses can be engaged." He fished in his robe, pulling out a rune-covered golden pommel dagger. "You've passed the first warrior's test, but now comes the difficult part. In battle, mercy may be applied to soldiers, but if one grants the oppressor a single opening, he'll defeat you with it. So the most difficult part of warrior training is hardening your heart." Kamithan handed Larin the dagger, and Larin suppressed nausea as he clasped the glyph-carved pommel.

"Imagine your oppressor again," Kamithan said. "This time he's trying to trick you into releasing him."

Larin's face drained of blood as Oarl's form materialized before him. This time Oarl was manacled to a wooden frame, crying.

"*Please don't,*" the illusion gasped, and Larin stepped back in horror.

"You must be strong," Kamithan said. "Don't let his tears fool you. If you unlock his manacles, he'll kill you. It's you or him."

Larin stared at Oarl's image, blubbering in terror, and clenched his jaw. Years of beatings steeled his nerve, bringing his dagger hand up. How good it would feel to plunge that icy metal into Oarl's chest. But the tiny screams that had been fighting for his attention since the beginning had now become a full-throated roar. His hand trembled, the dagger wavering in the air as he stared at Oarl's tear-streaked face. Finally, he stumbled backward, dropping the dagger.

"I—I can't," he said, shamed by the priest's disappointed look. He searched for some way to right the situation, to make Kamithan like him again. "I have the same problem in sword practice. Akul always tells me I won't master the sword until I learn to kill . . ." Yet he knew Kamithan's request was far different than killing an enemy in combat. His shame deepened as he imagined Akul staring aghast at his comparison.

Kamithan nodded understandingly, bending to retrieve the dagger.

"Well, one cannot become a warrior overnight. It will take practice. But we can help, and if Akul wants to visit us, he'll be most welcome."

Kamithan's strange inflection at Akul's name caused Larin to look up sharply. With sudden revelation, he realized the priest hadn't broken the message's seal.

"There never really was a message, was there?" Larin said. "This isn't about convincing me—this is about convincing Akul."

Kamithan's face registered surprise and a sly smile all in two seconds. Finally, he nodded, looking at Larin with respect.

"Well, I must say, we like our warriors smart, and you are that." He smiled and clasped Larin's shoulder. "Whenever we establish a new temple, we identify the powerful forces in the area and bring them to Morphat. Since we've built this temple, we've heard much about Akul. We know that for ten years he's single-handedly withstood a small army. We respect such strength, and we know he'd make an excellent warrior for Morphat."

Larin choked back laughter. Akul would rather run full force into a brick wall than shake hands with an Eldegod priest.

Kamithan misinterpreted Larin's smile and beamed back, dimples widening. "Yes, we can strengthen even Akul and eliminate his enemies. We are powerful, and becoming more so." He put his hand on Larin's back, escorting him out. As they reached the door, Larin turned around, realizing his eye was doing much better.

"Thanks for the salve and the healing spell."

"Of course," said Kamithan. "Come back next week if you'd like to continue your training. And remember to bring Akul for a visit."

Larin nodded and walked out. As he exited the Marble Temple, the knot at the pit of his stomach loosened in a sweet flow of relief, and he breathed deeply. Ascending the sloped street, he replayed the past thirty minutes in his mind. The whole experience was a dream; his usual cynicism had deserted him, leaving vague impressions of smooth arguments that yet concealed a hidden flaw. Yet he could not for his life identify what was wrong. It was as if entering Morphat's temple had turned him into a naive child.

I have some skills with Influence magic.

"Out of the dragon's lair alive, eh?"

Larin whirled around to see the chubby, curly-haired man limping toward him, looking like he held a bruiseball under that loose robe. For the first time, he noticed the man had difficulty walking.

"Are you following me?"

"Eh, just curious to see if you'd leave Morphat's hive in a robe of red and black, or in a plume of smoke." He snorted, then burst into laughter, then snorted again.

Larin thought furiously. He wanted to ask this strange man so many questions—were the legends of the Demon Lord's imprisonment true? Why had Haraf chosen him? Yet with limited time, he had to ask the question that'd plagued him since childhood.

"Who am I?"

"Good question," the man said smoothly, as if Larin had just asked his favorite food. "Let's just say you're here to do Haraf's bidding."

"And that would be?"

"Dense boy, consider the Phrase you utter." He said this in a distracted tone, and Larin saw with disgust that the man's gaze had settled near Morphat's temple, where some children stood in line with their parents.

"I'm supposed to release the Lord of Demons from prison? Are you crazy? Never mind, I see that you are." Larin walked to stand directly in front of the man, blocking his view of the lines. "Why in Emja's name would I release a being that all the legends say will enslave humanity and destroy the world?"

A pained expression crossed that chubby face. "Och, I've told you, Emja and Haraf don't go together." Madness returned to the man's eyes, and he began to hum, moving his hands in a small dance.

"When Haraf ascends, all must bow
Then get away, I don't care how;
For if He's here when you arise,
He'll flay you bare and gouge your eyes."

Larin shook his head. "You're insane. I'd rather work for Morphat." With that he stalked away, feeling the man's eyes bore into his back.

"What kind of warrior training teaches one to kill a helpless enemy?" the man called.

Larin halted in his tracks but did not turn around.

"And they'll help the powerless, I suppose. What an odd philosophy, to teach that the powerless are always right, no matter their battle."

Larin thought about Hulyis, and how the temple priests were teaching him to exact revenge on the Wormpile's honest shop owners after he'd stolen from them for years. Yet his anger and frustration wouldn't let him acknowledge the point.

He spun around. "Why should I listen to a twist like you?"

The man shrugged. "Don't spear the message because you don't like the messenger."

"I think that's backward—"

"I have a riddle for you," said the man, his eyes gleaming. "What happens to a wizard with King Galin's disease?"

Larin froze, hesitating between deep fascination and the desire to escape this lunatic. "I don't know."

"His personae become real people." The man chortled, then began limping away.

"That's not funny," Larin shouted, as the man hobbled up the street. He glanced at Morphat's temple, seeing it in a new light. The lunatic's earlier comments had hit home, and he now knew why Kamithan's arguments bothered him. He had a sudden desire to understand more about this being he was supposed to serve.

"And what do Haraf's servants believe?" he called loudly after the man, now climbing the sloped street. Several people in the lines below looked up curiously.

The man turned around, and Larin saw approval on his face, as if he'd finally asked the right question. "They believe in justice. They believe some wrongs are so grievous, not fixing them will bring time itself to an end." With that, he turned again and crested the hill.

Larin gazed at the sea for a long moment, chewing on the events of this strange day. He stole a nervous glance at the temple, then walked quickly up the street.

He was crossing into the Wormpile when a familiar jet-black-haired figure turned a corner, limping toward him. Candro's face was a dark cloud, the ring around his eye darker still. Larin stopped, watching his friend approach, head low, until he was a few feet away. Candro raised a beaten face, his one good eye widening as it contemplated Larin.

"Emja, I thought I was bad! You look like a thrukk stomped on your head and dragged you around the city. Actually, it's a better look for you."

Larin smiled weakly, nodding at Candro's eye. "Oarl?"

Candro shook his head, his thin face haggard. "The usual three. They think they own the Netrina."

Larin was silent. Whatever his woes, at least he had Akul. Candro had no family save the denizens of Netrina, the abandoned building where Wormpile orphans spent their nights. A place where older, more powerful boys got food and shelter at the expense of the rest. Which was to say Candro really had nothing at all.

Candro blinked his good eye, black hair in disarray. "And who do you have to thank? Oarl?"

"Utra. Might as well be Oarl." Larin drifted away to happier thoughts. "Onie was there too—she actually said she'd visit me in the temple sometime. I don't know why watching me get beaten made her *want* to talk to me, but I won't complain."

They stood in silence for a moment. Candro looked toward the river. "You know what I feel like doing right now? Hitting the king. I want to hit the king hard. You in?"

Larin nodded, and they turned northward, walking over the Hodjat Bridge and into the Flerrindor District. They passed the beautiful stone walls of the fine houses in that district and the stately trees lining its boulevards. Dirty Wormpile street urchins were as out of place here as rats in a pudding, and they kept to the shadows, pointedly ignoring wrinkled noses from passers-by. When they saw an Imperial Guardsman, they scurried down a narrow footpath to the river, down the high banks and below the monstrous stone walls of the mansions above.

They walked in silence along the roaring river until they found their usual spots beneath the Flerrindor Bridge, sitting far apart on either side of the stone arch. Together but alone.

Someone once had the brilliant idea to suspend the likeness of Maldovin IV over the river from the bottom of the bridge, though no one above could see it. That banner was now ripped and shredded in a dozen places where their stones had found their marks over the years. The king's red Nydyn hair appeared shaved in one spot directly above his forehead, a fortunate strike they had laughed about for days.

A stone flew from Candro's position directly into the king's ear. "Ha, now he's deaf!" Candro called out. "Even less likely to listen to our complaints . . ."

Larin sat back, letting the river's roar flow through him. He thought again about Akul's morning khald flight. If Oarl's crew knew when to strike, it might be all over for them, and Larin knew such episodes would only become more common. He looked to the future, seeing life as he knew it coming to a close. He wouldn't have Akul's protection forever, and when the sorry day arrived, he'd better have found a good hiding place for both of them.

He stabbed a sharp rock into the dirt, wondering why, if he was to serve the Lord of Demons, he had no magical power. Did Haraf expect him to open the Gray Lands by strumming a lute?

As Larin's rock hit the dirt, the lunatic's words sprang unbidden into his mind: *What happens when a wizard gets King Galin's disease?*

His personae become real people.

He looked into the river, a creeping suspicion dawning. Then his eyes widened, as the day's events hit him with full force. The Yul outside their window, he'd had a twisted knee. Larin tried to picture the lunatic's limp as he walked away from Morphat's temple, and with icy water in his veins, he knew one thing for sure: the Yul and the chubby curly-haired man were one and the same. Two personae of the same man—a wizard with King Galin's disease.

Which meant one thing: the Yul had not been looking for Akul. He'd been waiting for Larin.

VII

The snowfall would not stop. It fell in a solid white haze, obscuring everything—the tents, the forest, the thrukk, and any other sign of the massive army that spread across the forest floor, huddling between the great pines to wait out the winter. The wind had died somewhat, but still the snow fell, as it had fallen almost every day in the past week, a nonstop punishment from the skies. It would be months before the first shrubs poked through the layer of white, and weeks beyond that before the snows would melt to reveal the ferns and the pine needle floor. A brief burst of life that would last two months here in the North, before it all began again.

The glare reduced visibility to just a few feet, and Kemharak finally stopped, adjusting his frontal pods to shift emphasis from vision to hearing. Immediately, the small surrounding noises came into focus—light wind rustling through pine, distant crackling of high branches as they gave way under the weight of snow, the occasional snort of the tethered thrukk invisible behind a curtain of white. The low whistling of his troops inside their denarin-skin tents also became audible, and he concentrated on Manek's soft voice. Pulling his heavy coat tight, he began walking the short distance to the war tent, his lower booted claws rising high to plow through the deep snow.

It was cold, brutally cold in the Northlands, and would be so for another two months. A thousand miles to the south, across the Great Chasm, the stolen lands would be basking in the warm sun of late spring, enjoying blue skies or, at most, a light rain. Kemharak considered the white glare around him with his diminished vision and tried to banish the image of a sunny land filled with rolling green hills.

He could not. He forced himself to stop, taking a deep breath and concentrating on the sharp, freezing air rushing through his neck flaps. Sheathing his pods in misery, he used his upper right claw to unwrap the thrukk-wool scarf, forcing himself to feel the new snow drifting onto his scales. He stood for a moment, ridged head exposed to the bitter cold, clenching all four claws and glad none of his subcommanders could see him through the white glare. Yet moments like this were necessary—they hardened his resolve and reminded him why he had come this far.

For he hadn't assembled this army to glorify his people's cruel, capricious Creators. Nor had he conquered every one of his people's tribes from the Great Chasm to the Great Ice just so that his name might be whistled around the birthing dens for eternity, though that would certainly be so. Nor had he sought glory for the Created Ones, his people, the ones the humans so demeaningly called "Lidath" or "lizard-like" in their ancient language, as if his people resembled any of the four-legged invaders. No, this army had been assembled for one reason, and one reason only: to recover what was rightfully theirs. To steal back what had been stolen.

Thrusting out his torso, he removed his coat and upper coverings, keeping his pods still and his feeding orifice closed as he forced himself to feel every snowflake on his newly exposed scales. He spread out all four arms, letting the snow accumulate on them as if they were branches from the giant pines above.

He'd forgone the rite of dominion time and again. When defeated chieftains bared their necks to him, he'd turned his back, refusing to put them to the sword, refusing to honor a tradition dredged from the Creator's insanity. All had been given a choice: "Stay, learn how I have defeated you and every other tribe, and help us win back the stolen lands. Or leave my sight." Some had stayed, some had gone, and some had tried to kill him, thinking him weak. These had been quickly dispatched.

Of those who stayed, none had believed the stolen lands recoverable. For too long the vast empire south of the Great Chasm had been known as the "human lands," the result of a war long ago fought and lost. Among a people who'd accepted their vanquishment, the battles with the humans were joined only to allow relief from the gods-stoked bloodlust. Tanbar itself could never be defeated.

Yet Kemharak needed commanders who shared his vision. Against stiff faces and extended claws, he'd badgered them to see what he had seen. He forced them to touch the storytellers, the diseased caste, to experience memories formed so long ago and now passed down through direct mind contact from one generation to the next.

Together they had witnessed the day, five thousand years ago, when the four-legged alien creatures had first crossed the mountains. The humans had arrived in a swarm, together with their four-legged brethren: the horses, goats, elephants, dogs, cats, and other creatures never before seen in the world. They swarmed the lower valleys, displacing the natural creatures of the world, the six-legged ones. Displacing his people. Even the forest had been different then, full of the blue-green vines that moaned in higher pitch with the wax and wane of the moon. It had taken only a thousand years before the last of the *Maranth* vines was gone, replaced with these cold dead pines that offered no song to mark the seasons.

How had these weak, two-armed creatures defeated the mighty Created

Ones, a people who could wield pole-arms heavier than their largest warrior? It was a question he'd struggled all his life to understand. Clearly human ability to use the remnants of the creator's energy—what they called "magic"—was a clear advantage when the moon was near.

Yet human magic was not the true core of their power.

Feeling he'd endured enough motivation for one day, Kemharak re-donned his coverings and wrapped the scarf around his head. Maximizing hearing in his two frontal pods, he focused on the noises around him, trying to separate Manek's voice from the sounds of wind and falling branches. After a moment, he turned and began his forward trek again.

Within minutes, the brown of denarin skin stood against the white onslaught, wavering in and out of his vision like a mirage. He slowed his pace, stopping finally just outside the war tent, his heavy boots sinking into the new snow. For a moment, Kemharak stood, listening to the soft whistle of his subcommanders as they discussed strategy. The higher-pitched whistling of wind through the great pine branches created an eerie counterpoint to the conversation, as if they debated nature herself. From somewhere in the white haze came the creaking of hanging wooden arms, as the wagon-mounted sling swayed in the wind. Feeling a sudden longing for warmth, he burst through the tent flaps.

They stood as he entered, all except the chained human on the far side. Kemharak's throat bulged as the air entered his neck flaps, a breath of sweet warm air from the glowing rocks in the tent's center. He closed his pod sheaths in pleasure but realized the tent had fallen silent as his six subcommanders stood around the war table, their front pods brown with deference. He lowered his upper right claw in the sign for "sit," and after a moment they sat, continuing their conversation.

He turned to consider the chained human, who watched him with an expression Kemharak had come to understand was fear. It was right to be fearful. Yet he'd resisted the Creator's commands to subject it to the excruciating torture-killing mandated by ritual, for although the gods required pain, Kemharak was not yet done with this human. When he was, he would defy the Guardians of the Creator by giving it a quick, merciful death.

Kemharak walked to the human and sat before it. He felt his commanders' hard stares of disapproval but paid no attention. Crossing his two upper arms, his lower right claw dug a flat of salted thrukk meat from his pouch and held it out to the human.

"Take," he whistled slowly, shaping his notes around the strange human language.

Never removing its eyes from the Lidath commander, the human leaned forward slowly, taking the hard meat from Kemharak's outstretched claw. Kemharak marveled at this—the human starved, yet its actions were slow and deliberate. With certain death nigh, what did it care about dignity? So much yet to learn about these creatures.

"When will you kill me?" the human asked, keeping its vision pods focused on Kemharak.

"I do not know," Kemharak said. "Soon."

The human leaned back, putting the hard tack in his mouth and watching Kemharak as it chewed. Its actions were measured and relaxed, though Kemharak knew this was a lie.

Kemharak in turn watched the human with fascination, its weak teeth barely able to tear the hard meat. The strange elastic substance covering their bodies had never bothered him, nor their rows of flat bottomed teeth. It was the facial differences which disturbed him most. Both humans and the Created ones had heads, necks, and faces, and both faces held sensor pods on the top and feeding orifices on the bottom. Yet the human sensor pods were three colors and used only for vision, with separate pods for hearing on the sides and a strange protuberance in the middle for sensing things Kemharak could only guess at. Whereas, Kemharak's four bulbous pods were evenly spaced around his head, each functioning independently for vision or hearing. In addition, the human's vision pods never revealed its intent through color, as did his people's. It was as if the human creator had been drunk on the fermented fruits of the forest or was new to the act of creation. In every physical way his people were better designed.

Yet somehow, against all logic, these weak creatures had bested his people time after time. Though he felt close to cracking their ultimate secrets, much remained unclear to him.

"You will tell me your thoughts," Kemharak commanded, leaning forward.

The human's feeding orifice turned upward at its corners, and Kemharak studied it with interest. He rarely saw this expression, but it usually occurred when he commanded this type of response.

"I'm thinking there is no way to escape," said the human. "You've well-confined my power." It pointed with its small, ineffective claw at the runes covering its chains. A necessary precaution, as this one was rumored to be a powerful wizard among its people.

"Yes," Kemharak whistled. They were both silent a moment, while Kemharak waited for the human to say more. When it did not, Kemharak spoke. "What do you feel now?"

The upward curve in the human's feeding orifice became more pronounced, and a small sound escaped. The sound was new to Kemharak.

"Why do you make this sound?"

"It's called laughter," the human said. "We feel humor when something is like something it is not." It apparently had learned to read the amber color of confusion in Kemharak's pods, and it exhaled. "The High

Commander of the greatest Lidath army in history asks me how I feel today. This is something my wife would ask, so I feel humor, which brings laughter." The human's vision pods darted in several directions.

Kemharak leaned back, considering this. He sensed humor was a good thing and, with sudden insight, realized it was a key to human bonding. He sheathed his vision pods, feeling he'd discovered an important truth.

For the human secret, the core of their power, was their ability to bond. An intangible, seemingly inconsequential thing, yet powerful beyond the gods themselves. It was not that his people could not feel respect or loyalty to tribe. Yet human bonding was something far different, a capacity that allowed them to move with unity on the battlefield, to persevere against certain defeat in order to save other members of their tribe. Kemharak had seen it too many times. Bands of humans cut off from their main unit, fighting not for glory or empire, but for one thing only: to save their brethren. Whereas his people fought as warriors do, alone and with valor. For the Creator filled them with anger.

His incorporation of the human secret was but a poor imitation, yet it had brought every tribe of the Created Ones under a single chieftain for the first time in history. He'd formed his soldiers into small units, keeping them isolated from each other. He'd forced his soldiers to share their thoughts every night, without fail. He'd ordered that they remain together at all costs—if their lines were overrun, they were to make every attempt to save all members of the unit.

Had it worked? It had certainly allowed his own tribe to extend its dominion to every part of the Northlands, planting Kemharak's banner on every northern mountain from the Great Chasm to the Great Ice. He couldn't say whether he'd created true bonding or whether they had followed his orders only. Yet, though the gods had initially created them to work the metals of the land and not to form great societies like the humans, he knew the capacity for bonding was buried deep within his people.

"And what do you feel today?" the human countered, breaking Kemharak's thoughts.

Kemharak heard his commanders rise, and he shot his lower right claw outward to decree silence. They could not understand the human's question, but they knew it had spoken out of turn. It was a mistake that could normally cause a prisoner's immediate death.

"I have given it permission to speak as it wishes," Kemharak whistled, and after a moment, he heard them sit again. He opened his rear pods, watching as the red glare of anger in his commanders' pods became superimposed on the human's fearful face. He struggled to contain his disappointment, wanting nothing to reduce his chances of hearing honest truth from this creature.

"I have told them you may speak as you wish," Kemharak said to the human. He closed his rear pods, and the ghostly images of his commanders disappeared. "Repeat your question."

The human's vision pods shifted wildly, in what Kemharak assumed was lingering fear. "Will my death be quick?" it asked in a low voice.

Kemharak swallowed his anger. This one did not always do as it was commanded. "I will make it quick," Kemharak said. "Now, repeat your question." He tried to force a commanding tone, a difficult endeavor given his halting attempts to shape his whistles around the strange human language.

The human stared at Kemharak a moment. "What do you feel today?" Its voice had a different tonality than Kemharak had heard the first time, almost mechanical, and the corners of its feeding orifice were no longer twisted upward. In fact, they now had a downward tilt, and Kemharak wondered if this was the opposite of humor. Was such a thing possible?

Kemharak searched inside himself, sensing this interchange was particularly critical to his understanding of human emotion. He struggled to evoke a feeling but had difficulty.

"I feel nothing. Do humans always feel?"

The human shifted positions, as if thinking. "Perhaps not always," it said. "But usually we have some internal mood, if we look hard enough."

Kemharak sheathed his vision pods. He hadn't understood every word, but the basic meaning was clear. He needed to search inside himself. He sat in silence for several moments, filtering out the low whistle of his commanders and the heavy breathing of the human as it waited for him, searching inward for some—mood—as the human had called it. Probing beneath his thoughts, he searched for an underlying feeling, finally touching something in his mind. He unsheathed his vision pods.

"I feel anger. The gods give us—" He did not know the word for dream, so he searched his human vocabulary for the right expression. "The gods speak to us as we rest," he said finally. "They bring us war, command us to bring pain to others. They make us angry, so we can do these things."

The human leaned forward, seeming interested by this. "Is that all you feel? Do Lidath—Created Ones—feel only anger?"

Kemharak was silent, searching deep within himself. He found the evocation of emotion became easier with practice, a fact that gave him hope for his people. There was something there, just below the surface. What was it? The clear precise actions that governed his life had some undercurrent; it hung in the background, like difalli vines draping from the canopy in the summer.

"I feel doubt," he said. "We have been defeated for so long, I wonder that we will recover the stolen lands." A cascade of emotions flowed in response to his own words, as if he'd opened a gate and he wanted nothing more to do with this conversation. He'd gone too far; furthermore, he couldn't believe he really felt thus. Doubt had never risen long to the surface; it was not an emotion to which he gave much thought. Surely his outburst was false.

The fur above the human's vision pods lifted, and Kemharak mentally catalogued this as an indicator of surprise. Fortunately for its own health, the human had the good sense to stay silent. Kemharak leaned back, wondering if he should end the conversation. Yet despite his discomfort, the discussion had been fruitful today.

Howling wind and a burst of snow saved him from that decision, as one of his guards opened the tent flaps and stepped inside. "Revered one, the emissary is here." His lowered whistle at the word "emissary" changed the connotation from neutrality to disdain, a disrespected enemy.

Kemharak twisted around and stood up, the chained human now forgotten. He wondered whether he should make the human emissary wait outside longer, but dismissed the idea as a petty torture influenced by his dreams. It was therefore unnecessary and inefficient.

"Send it in."

The guard whistled a command and, in a moment, the human entered the tent, followed by another guard. The human carried a case made of some kind of animal skin and was bundled in many layers of clothing. Shivering, it moved toward the glowing rocks and began removing its head covering. A guard smacked it with a bunched claw, and the human turned in surprise.

"He is telling you to make respect," Kemharak said to it in the human language.

The human became agitated and turned to face Kemharak. "I am sorry, Great One." It bowed profusely. It removed the shawl wrapped many times around its head, then bowed again. Kemharak waited while his six high commanders left their table to stand next to him, keeping a wary gaze on the human.

"Great One—as you know, my master has sent me to you with information," the human finally said, shaking noticeably from the cold. "I have brought the location of the wizard camp, a place the empire's magic corps will wait until the start of the campaign next winter."

With a loud, guttural sound, the human in chains ejected what looked like water from its feeding orifice, and both Kemharak and the emissary turned in surprise. Kemharak assumed this was a gesture of contempt, and he did not disagree. With interest, he turned back around to watch the other human's reaction.

The human emissary's vision pods became half-sheathed, and its voice took on a low tone. "I know that one. Give him to me; I will serve our common gods by providing him a long painful death." Its feeding orifice turned upward at the corners, but Kemharak didn't think this was humor.

An interesting variation.

"You will not," Kemharak said. The human waited, perhaps surprised, for Kemharak to say more. When he did not, it began fishing into its case, its movements agitated. It pulled out a parchment map, a highly detailed design that showed with great precision the valleys and gullies surrounding the Avensai Passes.

"The highest-rank wizards, the Council of Twelve, remain in the capital," it said. "However, aside from the Council, Tanbar's next most powerful mages have begun the northward journey with the army, and will be at this location"—it pointed to a valley several miles north of the passes—"within two months. After that point, an attack on this camp can destroy the empire's magical might in a single stroke."

Kemharak considered this, neck flaps expanding as he breathed in and held. This was the information he hoped for, but his suspicions were high. "Why would the humans move most of their magical power to one place? It is"—he searched for the word—"unwise. They have never done this before."

The corners of the human's feeding orifice turned upward, and Kemharak wondered if it were feeling humor and, if so, whether it was a bad or good thing. "My master is very high in the empire," it said. "He has great power and will arrange it to be so."

"And what of the Council of Twelve?"

"They will be taken care of," said the human. "They will never make it to the camp."

Kemharak's claws shot out of their sheaths, and he lunged at the human, stopping just inches from ripping its face to ribbons. "Do you think us fools? We will mount an attack on this valley only to have a fire poured upon us by Tanbar's most powerful wizards from the forest above. Have you come here to die?"

The human's face went completely white, an expression of fear Kemharak knew well, having witnessed it on countless human soldiers moments before he killed them.

"N-no, Great One! He will remove the Council of Twelve, I swear. You still have scouts in the capital, do you not? Keep them there until the Apex festivities. They will see the end of the council for themselves!" The human began shaking, though the tent was warm.

Kemharak stepped back a small fraction, enough to let the human breathe. "And how do I know your master will do as you say? Be careful what you say—if I think you are lying, your death will be painful." He almost wished it were so. Every night, the gods assailed him with dreams of the rituals, wishing him to force a long, painful death on the chained human. The Creator's will was revealed in other ways as well, for every few days, the Guardians of the Creator demanded anew that he give the human to them for use in their horrors. He'd much rather apply the rituals to the human before him and gain a reprieve for the other. Yet, if this creature wasn't lying, the opportunity to defeat all human magical power in a single onslaught could not be ignored.

The human became more agitated. "You can see for yourself," it said in a high voice. "The wizards will occupy this valley for many months before Nadir." It stopped and looked at Manek, who, unable to understand the conversation, was holding out his upper right claw. The human placed the map in Manek's outstretched claw, then looked at Kemharak, the fleshy covering under its feeding orifice trembling. "Send scouts to report before you move—if the wizards are not there, you've lost nothing. If they are, you've gained everything."

Despite his contempt for this human, Kemharak saw wisdom in this. "It may be so." He was silent a moment, while Manek looked at the map. "Why does your master do this?"

"We share the same gods. Surely we can fulfill their will together?"

This did not ring true to Kemharak. Though he was sure the gods did indeed wish to extend their dominion over Tanbar, the massive human empire south of the Great Chasm, he knew this human was hiding something. The human cults that worshipped his gods were riddled by infighting and betrayal, and rarely did they do anything purely to please the gods. Their infighting was similar to that of his people before he'd united them, a direct consequence of serving insanity.

Not for the first time, he wondered that any humans worshipped the Creator, the one humans called Morphat. In his study of human motivations, he'd found no reason why some humans would follow such cruel and malicious gods. His own people had no choice, for the beings called "Old Gods" by the humans were the Creators, and they had a hold on his people that was almost physical. While there had once been different Creators—rational beings who'd designed his race for work, not pain—they'd not walked the earth for ten millennia.

Kemharak faced the human. "We will consider your plan," he said, then turned his back, the audience clearly over. To his guard he whistled, "Remove this one before I disembowel it."

The guards escorted the human out of the tent with great haste, not giving it a chance to don its protections from the bitter cold.

Kemharak looked at his commanders, who watched him with gray pods.

"Come next winter, we shall be ready," Kemharak said. "Let the humans come."

Let them come.

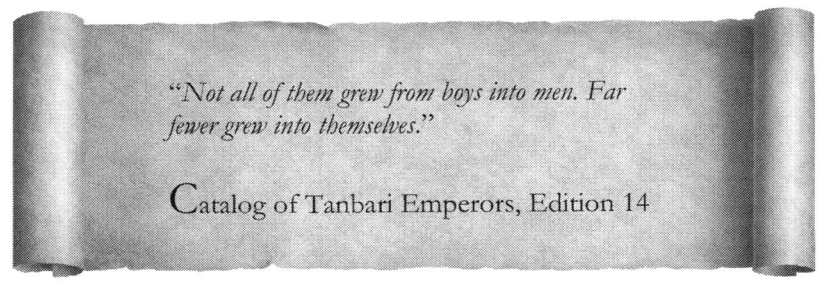

"Not all of them grew from boys into men. Far fewer grew into themselves."

Catalog of Tanbari Emperors, Edition 14

VIII

Emperor Xartusius Maldovin IV, ruler of Tanbar, Lord of the Outer Reaches, High Sovereign of the Haques valley, Master of the civilized world from the Great Chasm to the Southern Marshes, was amused. The fool balanced a fish on his nose—on his *nose* of all things, and Maldovin could no more contain his giggle than he could sprout into a mushroom.

The King wiped spittle from the corner of his mouth. "Look, Talin—is that not the most ridiculous thing you've ever seen?"

General Talin lowered the map, his rows of medals glinting under the colored light of the arched Great Hall windows. He tried to force his wan smile into something brighter.

"Your Majesty, most amusing."

Maldovin snorted and pinched more khald from the gold plate at his side. The fool, sensing his hold on his royal audience had slipped, promptly began waltzing with the fish as if it were his greatest love. Maldovin smiled, then frowned, all within an instant. His head felt submerged by water, the Great Hall's kaleidoscope of motion seen through swaying vision. He motioned the fool to move on, suddenly sure that his khald-quickened heartbeat matched the steady pounding of drums from the minstrels below.

"Your Majesty, if we can but consider the map again," Talin started. His voice trailed off as he saw Maldovin's eyes drawn to the spinning gowns of the dancing courtiers, twirling through the Great Hall in a festival of colors. The chattering classes of the Imperial District, always eager to attend royal parties, had been delighted at the royal decree for ten days of revelry to mark the beginning of the High Season. Maldovin watched the be-quaffed lords and ladies gaily swirl around each other, wondering why he hadn't decreed a color theme this year. With khald's sweet flow through his veins, such wonderful ideas popped into his mind.

"Talin, do you see those streamers trailing from the hats?" He pointed to the conical hats of the ladies, festooned with lace and colored ribbons that trailed behind them as they danced. "What if I decreed that, tomorrow, each lady must affix a straw from mouth to the hat's peak so that our lovelies could blow the streamers behind them as they waltzed? Would that not be beautiful?"

"Yes, Majesty," Talin said flatly. Something in his tone caused Maldovin to look directly into those hard eyes. Warrior's eyes.

Scowling, Maldovin glanced toward Queen Relena and Panjus, his advisor. Relena was beautiful as always, her black hair braided and looped atop her head, held together by a silver headband engraved with the royal charging green dragon. Her gown was purple and red, beautiful colors for a beautiful woman, and gaily suited to these happy dances. So why were her eyes so desolate?

She watched him with an intensity that seemed to match Talin's. Maldovin turned to Panjus for support, but the Royal Advisor was sitting in a chair with his head down, not looking at him.

What was wrong with them?

He gazed back at the Great Hall, fascinated by the way the light from the massive arched windows glinted off the shields lining the oak walls, illuminating the glyphs that flowed down the rafters. Though those glyphs had the important task of banishing all magic from the Imperial Compound, now they were a flowing river, spinning in his vision. In the dappled light of the great windows, which overlooked Aldive all the way to the sea, the courtiers danced like butterflies on a sunny day, stained glass casting their gowns in hues and shadows.

"Your Majesty," Talin said, interrupting his fantasy, "events in the North truly demand our attention."

Maldovin rubbed his eyes. "What, exactly, is your worry, Talin?"

Talin's jaw tensed. "Majesty, as I said earlier, we have intelligence that our enemies to the north have united under their old leader Kemharak, who assembles the greatest Lidathi army in history."

Maldovin felt the room shift, as the khald kicked up a notch. He waved a hand in dismissal. "Commander Lukas knocked that wily Lizard down for good."

"Your Majesty, that was nineteen years ago."

Trumpets sounded, as a silver inlaid float wheeled through the massive double doors of the Great Hall. Maldovin clapped eagerly as Lady Annali pirouetted on the wheeled platform, her black-clad suitors dancing around the cart as it entered the room.

Maldovin laughed. "Is that not wonderful, Talin?"

Talin bent to return the map to its satchel, his long red hair draping over his knees. "Yes, Majesty. Perhaps another time would be best for this discussion."

Maldovin slammed his hand down on the throne's bejeweled arm. "You are too dour, Talin—lighten up, man, I command you." He gestured toward High Wizard Emderian, who was talking with a nervous baroness as he waved his brilliant white gloves in oddly hypnotic patterns. Those gloves were the only features that made that drab man noticeable. "There, you see, even our power whirlwind is enjoying the festivities, and he is not known for social pleasantries."

Talin's hard eyes and granite-carved cheeks were as distant from the Great Hall's merriment as they were from Spellgiver. Yet his words conveyed nothing of his expression. "Majesty, I fear I'm too tired for celebrations. Perhaps another—"

"And even—even *Pig Intestines* seems to enjoy himself," Maldovin spat, unable to utter Hekrian's name. He pointed to Duke Selton's servant, the bearded man with a half-empty mead glass sitting next to Maldovin's simpleton brother.

Talin squinted as he considered Hekrian, and Maldovin knew that at least on this, they agreed. Hekrian's presence in the royal court was but the latest miserable indignity forced upon him by the thrice-cursed Treaty of Gifain. A treaty whose larval birth was spawned by a civil war over the impossible provincial taxes levied by Maldovin's infamous grandfather, Maldovin II. That treaty, negotiated by Duke Selton's grandfather, had emasculated the entire Maldovin line, forcing Tanbari emperors to beg their own subjects for levies and accept provincial stooges in their court. Stooges like this Hekrian, loyal to the Province of Aimes, but officially an "advisor" to Maldovin's simple-minded brother, Yalinus. As if Yalinus needed any advice beyond when to put away his toys and when to eat.

Talin stood, and Maldovin blinked up at him, the bright chandeliers burning his khald-addled vision.

"By your leave Majesty?"

Maldovin turned back to his dancing courtiers, finding his khald mood melting into dirt and worms. He waved a hand in resignation. "Go, Talin."

Talin departed, and Maldovin gazed back at the spinning gowns, willing himself to return to his sweet daylight dreams, to bask in spring's hazy colors. He felt himself gliding toward his sea of calm but for a thin string pulling him to shore. A gnawing tug that kept him anchored to land, unable to reach sweet paradise.

Shame.

He stood shakily, grasping the arm of the throne, watching Talin weave through the crowds toward the door.

"Talin!"

The music stopped, and from his peripheral vision, Maldovin noticed

Relena and Panjus jerk their heads in his direction. He swept his gaze over the assembled lords and ladies, all frozen in place as if by strong magic that could never actually work in this place.

"All of you, leave us now. I would converse with my council in peace. You may return when I'm done."

The Great Hall buzzed with murmurs and the rustle of fabrics as ladies lowered their masks and men mingled with them on their way to the doors. Maldovin looked around the Great Hall, seeing only Hekrian and Emderian standing fast.

Maldovin scowled at Hekrian. "You. Especially you. Out."

Hekrian's mouth was tight behind his tightly cropped beard. "As royal advisor, my place here is ordained by articles two and seven of—"

"You are not *my* advisor, and the Treaty of Gifain mandates no provincial attendance at close councils," Maldovin snapped. His eyes darted toward the door halberdiers. "Is there anything else?"

Without a word, Hekrian stood. He offered his arm to Yalinus, who blinked at him stupidly and put down his coloring book. Maldovin watched them descend the steps of the royal platform as Relena glided close.

"And him," she whispered, nodding to Emderian. The High Wizard stood with his hands clasped in front of him at the far end of the Great Hall, the very picture of meekness.

Maldovin had never understood his wife's distaste for the empire's glove-wearing, mild-mannered High Wizard. Yes, Emderian worshipped Morphat, but despite the man's ugly gods, he was always the perfect gentleman, slow to anger, eager to placate. As the strongest wizard in a hundred generations, he was Maldovin's ultimate weapon against Seridor.

Maldovin rubbed his forehead, trying to see clearly through his khald haze. Still, his wife and Panjus served as his most trusted advisors. When her request was made in private, as it was now, he almost always conceded. He looked across the hall to Emderian.

"High Wizard, please excuse us. You may return to the festivities when we are done."

"As you wish, Majesty," Emderian said. He bowed and left by the great arched doors, to Maldovin's secret relief. Maldovin often found himself immensely grateful for the layers of runes carved into the rafters over the centuries. Runes that turned the most powerful wizards into ordinary men while they stood behind the Imperial Compound walls.

The guards pulled the great doors shut, and then it was just the four of them. Talin approached the platform and mounted the steps, his long hair feathering against the rows of medals on his uniform. He reached the top, relief and a modicum of respect returned to his eyes.

"Thank you, Majesty."

Maldovin looked away, wondering why he so desperately clung to that tiny sign of esteem. What emperor cared about such trivialities? Yet he remembered a time when he'd been king in action as well as in law, a time when he and Commander Lukas had brought Tanbar's might to the edges of the inner kingdoms, extending the empire's borders far beyond anything in history. For those distant memories, for the man he'd once been, still he cherished Talin's respect.

Then there was Relena—how long had he ignored the desperation in her eyes, as he slid down the path of khald madness? How many times had she tried to organize this meeting, finally arranging it during one of his endless parties simply because he'd left her no option?

He flopped into the throne, rubbing his temples as if he could clear the khald from his mind. "Tell me, Talin. What danger do you see for the empire?"

Panjus, Relena, and Talin took turns describing the latest intelligence, the pincer that would envelop the empire in two years. Talin unrolled vellum maps showing troop movements along the southern border, where Seridor quietly prepared for the most massive invasion in centuries. He described the latest information from the north, where the ever-resilient Lidathi commander Kemharak had returned from the grave after being crushed by Lukas, unifying a hundred fractious Lidathi tribes under his banner.

"So," Maldovin said finally, "within two years, we'll be flattened by Morphat's forces from south and north, no matter what we do? I propose mobilizing our yeomen. I describe plans to draft over thirty thousand from the cities within the empire. Each time, Talin's answer is that it is not enough. Are we all doomed then?"

Relena, Panjus, and Talin darted glances at each other, and Maldovin knew it was bad news.

"Out with it!" he yelled.

Relena was the only one who could say anything to him without consequences. She stepped forward, her purple and red gown draping along the hard wood of the royal platform. Maldovin thought her so beautiful, with her black hair braided and styled, her desert brown skin smooth in the light of the arched windows. He found his khald stupor pulling him into her radiance, and forced himself to pay attention.

"My love, the standard 10 percent provincial levies won't be enough," she said. "We'll need each province to contribute 50 percent of their troops."

Maldovin bolted forward in the throne. "Impossible! That would mean a Council of Lords!"

Panjus grimaced, and Talin looked away. Only Relena met his eyes. "Yes."

Maldovin's spirit turned to ash. Gifain's highest indignity—in times of emergency for the empire, the king had to *ask* his dukes for levies. The last thing he needed was the vitriolic rancor that would accompany his lords' presence in the royal court. He'd held but a single royal council in his thirty-seven-year reign, and the spite and anger of it had bubbled through his dreams for years. Surely there was another way.

Talin stepped forward hesitantly. "If it helps, Your Majesty, the actual council won't occur before another year. It will take months for word to reach the empire's corners, months beyond that for the lords to prepare, and many beyond for them to travel. This is why we bring this to you now. Kemharak and Seridor will not be ready for war for two years. If we act now, we can fortify our borders in time."

Talin stopped, his face paling at the expression of pure rage on Maldovin's face. Maldovin's neck burned, his fists clenched in anticipation of the verbal battles that this farce would surely produce. His anger had nothing to do with Talin, but it was raw enough that it boiled to the surface, his khald-thickened blood only inflaming him further. In younger days, he might have lashed out at all around him. Now, he forced himself to swallow his spit.

He unclenched his fists, rubbed his forehead, and leaned back in the throne.

"If we must."

The three of them exchanged looks, and Talin's face melted into relief.

"I will take care of it," Relena said.

Talin bowed. "It shall be done, Majesty. Shall I tell the courtiers to return on my way out?"

Maldovin tried to muster the soaring exuberance of an hour ago, but he knew it had curdled beyond all recognition. Now all he felt was khald's ending tremors, and the darkness of spirit that traveled with them.

"No. Leave us."

He watched them go in a melancholy haze, their footsteps loud on the polished oak of the Great Hall floors. The enormous doors closed, and Maldovin sat back in the throne, gazing sourly at the rows of shields lining the walls. Each bore a coat of arms from a previous Tanbari emperor, their colorful heraldry clashing with the pit of blackness in which he now found himself. He focused on the shield of Maldovin II.

What curse you have brought upon your line, Grandfather?

He remained motionless until the setting sun bathed the Great Hall in shadows.

IX

Larin saw her again next to the roleike stand, where a loud vendor hawked those strange indigen plants to a crowd of onlookers. Onie was dressed simply, a rough-spun gray kirtle tied with rope and torn flat shoes long past their due. She wavered in and out of his vision as people swarmed the vendor, but her bright blonde hair was unmistakable through the crowds.

He sidled next to her, but she turned to him first, eyes shrouded by yellow bangs.

"It's about time."

Larin folded his arms. "Nice try. I've been wandering the market all morning. I saw you walk in."

She grinned, then turned her attention to the vendor. "Watch this— these are the biggest roleikes I've ever seen."

Larin watched, somewhat impressed, as the vendor held the bluish plant by its stem, the two mottled leaves wavering in the breeze. They were indeed large roleikes; the flapper leaves could have spanned his whole arm. With a completely unnecessary cry, the vendor released the indigen plant into the wind, and the crowd turned to follow the ragged blue leaves as they flapped like a bird through a gap in the Port District pillars, pink veins glinting in the morning sun. Crying again, the vendor extracted a sack of crushed Jouane root, spreading it over the cobblestones. The roleike circled the upturned heads for another minute before finally spiraling inward to settle on the Jouane powder. It immediately shot tendrils along the ground, trying to burrow into the Port District's dirty cobblestones. The crowd clapped politely, and some children pulled their mothers toward the vendor, for roleikes were much coveted as toys.

Onie grabbed his arm, her attention already elsewhere. "Follow me. I know a place where they sell the best spiced octopus." She disappeared into the fish market chaos, and Larin struggled to keep sight of her blonde hair as it weaved through the crowd. He tried to understand how, in all the Demons' names, he'd ever thought Onie was demure.

The fish market was vast, an endless expanse of makeshift stalls bursting with seafood. Like the ocean on Apex day, it flowed around the thick stone columns that supported the Port District's houses. Cast in darkness from the houses above, the fish market kept its rows of fish cool as shoppers from across Aldive picked over the city's freshest seafood. All the stalls sported the grooves of easily disassembled planks, for this market would be dismantled two months before Apex to make way for the ocean's rush.

He caught her in front of a stand selling ground meat in bowls of bread.

"I don't know what spice they put in this ground octopus, but it's the best I've ever had," she said, without glancing behind her.

Larin blanched. "How did you know I was even here? You flew off so fast, I almost lost you!"

She turned around, smiling. "You stomp around like an injured thrukk. I can hear you a hundred feet away, even in this crowd."

Larin wrinkled his nose, and they eventually jostled their way to the vendor. At the last minute, he shoved his way in front of Onie to pay for both their food. It was his last copper, and he wouldn't get more for another week when Akul doled out his pay from the temple coffers. Yet Onie's grateful smile lit her entire face, and just then he'd have paid a gold crown if he'd had one.

Larin had just grabbed their bread bowls when he was pushed from behind, and he barely escaped dropping his food.

"I'll take all the rest of your spiced meat," came a gruff voice. They turned to see that the crowd behind them had been shoved aside, where three burly men sporting red-black armbands had commandeered the area in front of the stall.

Morphasti.

Larin pulled Onie back warily, and they watched as the overjoyed vendor began shoveling every bit of meat into giant wooden bowls. The crowd grumbled behind them, and finally a Njord warrior spoke up.

"What about the rest of us? Who in Dalik's name are you to take everything?"

All three Morphasti turned around, and the Njord's eyes darted between them.

"And who are you to complain about finding another vendor when the hungry have nothing?" barked the lead Morphasti, a stocky man with a permanent anger crease between his eyes. "You invoke Dalik's name, but none of your Human Gods feed the starving. Your Nydyn king and all his useless gods care nothing about the people."

The Njord put a hand on his pommel but stepped back, eyeing all three men nervously. Seeing no further challenge, the Morphasti turned back around and produced two gold coins. Larin studied the men, ignoring Onie's anxious tugs. He had a hard time believing any of them cared about feeding the poor. Yet he'd seen the line around Morphat's temple; he'd watched the acolytes doling food to any who asked. He shook his head, trying to understand just who Morphat was. The god's followers were doing good things, but the curly-haired man's words would not leave his head: *"What kind of warrior training teaches one to kill a helpless enemy?"*

Onie's tugs became more insistent, and Larin finally turned away. They walked through the crowds toward the center plaza, out from under the houses and into the full, glorious sun. Onie's pace had lost its excited frenzy, and he kept up easily until they reached a stone bench at the plaza's south end. They sat, and Larin almost yelped from the sharp edges of dozens of dead sea creatures crusted to the bench. Proof positive that this plaza sat underwater for half the day, two months out of the year. He found the most comfortable spot, and within moments they were scooping meat with crusts of bread, watching the crowds swarm through the markets.

"My father says all this feeding the poor talk is a trick," Onie said between chews. "He says they're just trying to drive up prices."

Larin chewed a flavorful mix of spiced octopus and bread, watching a small-time magician spin swirling lights in the air. "Well, whatever the reason, they really are feeding the poor. When I entered the Marble Temple last month, I saw a line of people circling the block."

Onie stopped eating and stared at him through ice-blue eyes.

"You *entered* Morphat's temple?"

Larin winced. He'd gotten so used to the miracle of Onie's attentions, he'd forgotten she didn't really know him yet.

"I—I—Nitalen the tanner gave me a message for a priest. I delivered it for two coppers. It was where I was going when I saw you in Westmarket that day."

"But why in Emja's name would you *enter?*"

Larin tried to ignore her cold tone. "The priest invited me in. And he healed my eye. But—that was it, and I'm definitely never going back." He disliked the pleading note in his own voice and turned back to his food. "Anyway, the only reason they cared about me was to get to Akul. They have some fantasy that Akul's going to join that pack of hyenas."

Onie's eyes softened. "I'm sure Morphat would love that. Any man who can single-handedly defeat Oarl's gang could probably outfight a platoon of Morphasti. With Akul, they'd be unstoppable in this part of the city."

"You'll never have to worry about that," Larin said. "Maldovin IV will grant me a duchy before Akul ever joins Morphat. Take your father's dislike of the Eldegod, multiply it by a thousand, and you'll have a tiny idea of how much Akul hates all the six-legged gods."

Onie nodded, and they ate in easy silence for a few minutes. Larin finished first and sat back, sure without knowing how that Onie was as comfortable as he was. He shook his head, trying to understand how he'd come to be eating spiced octopus next to the prettiest girl in the Wormpile. Outside Akul's four-block zone, no one favored him with a simple "good morning"—yet here was the girl everyone wanted, treating him like he wasn't the neighborhood's biggest outcast. Granted, they were here in the Port District, where Oarl was unlikely to see, and granted, this was just friendship. Everyone knew Onie's romantic attentions were focused on Thanakil, a strapping boy two years older and one of the few who'd escape the Wormpile's misery, having received a post in the Imperial army officer's academy. Yet despite everything, Larin was grateful. He just wanted to satisfy himself the whole thing wasn't some giant mistake.

Onie finished her food and reached into her bag, pulling out a wood carving. She handed it to Larin.

"I made this for you."

Larin took the carving reverently, staring at the beautiful mix of woods. It was a strange, impossible creature, yet Onie had carved it as if it'd paraded across her front doorstep this morning. An animal combining two worlds—one with a horse's head and tail, but a tagalanth's body, complete with ropy fur that drooped almost to the creature's horselike hooves. A six-legged mix of the indigen and non-indigen, charging on hind legs, the way a horse would.

"It's beautiful," Larin said, truthfully.

Onie concentrated on her bag, from which she pulled a knife and a block of wood. "I've always wondered why all living things are split into two such different categories. Indigen. Non-indigen. I like to see them come together in the wood." She mumbled this without looking at him, as if afraid to see a different opinion on his face.

Larin studied the carving. Every detail was intricately crafted, down to the horse's hooves sprouting from the tagalanth's scaly, very unhorselike leg.

"You are very good at this."

"Thank you," she said, then began murmuring familiar Lyrashi words.

"I know that one," he said. "A spell of pliability, to make the wood softer and more easily carved."

Onie finished, then turned to him with raised eyebrows. "Do you carve? That's a pretty obscure spell only those who work with wood normally use."

Larin shook his head. "I spend a lot of time studying history and magic. I can get my hands on some pretty advanced books in the temple library, even parts of the Tiyani codex. I like to learn spells of all types, even violet-sash spells I'll never be able to use. And I remember everything I read . . ." The words came out in a rush, and he stopped suddenly, embarrassed. Candro gave him endless grief for his constant reading, but somehow he felt comfortable talking about it with Onie.

"Hmm," she said, amused. She turned her focus back to the wood.

Larin watched her through the corner of his eye. She sat with her knees bent and feet flat on the bench as she carved, the lower part of her peasant's kirtle pushed aside to reveal thin, perfectly formed legs. Wisps of blonde hair trailed over dimpled cheeks, her fine features intent as she worked the wood. A girl from the very bottom of Aldive's class structure, but one whose beauty shone through her rough-spun clothing like a butterfly on a chamber pot. For the thousandth time, he wondered that she spoke to him.

"It's rare for a girl to whittle wood," he said. "I feel like I should be giving this to you."

She shot him a strange look. "How would you know what most girls like or don't like?"

Larin sniffed. "Well, I know a lot about girls. I talk to Trana every couple months in the alehouse, whenever she's back from one of her trips. And sometimes I speak to Madam Shembri's grombit when it flies up to my window. Though it doesn't talk back, and I think it's one of three sexes like all the other indigen creatures, so I'm not sure it's actually female."

Onie laughed, a throaty sound that seemed out of place from this slip of a girl. "Actually, you're right. Maybe I am unusual. Maybe that's why I like you."

Larin smiled, but then the words gushed out. "Onie, why do you like me? I can't leave Akul's four blocks without getting a fisticuff lunch. No one except Candro and a few Emjaian priests acknowledge my existence, and I've got these horrible—" He stopped, unwilling to mention his outbursts, though she'd seen them twice now. "And I'm not really good with a sword, or anything else. And you, well. You can have anyone you want."

She stopped whittling, putting the knife and wood down on the bench. She straightened her legs and smoothed her dress, looking out at the crowds. Larin mentally cursed himself, wondering if he'd just reminded her that he was untouchable.

"Maybe because I'm as different as you are," she said finally. "I can't stand that Oarl gets away with beating who he wants, taking what he wants. I watch him ruin good, honest men, simply because they can't pay him, and no one dares speak a word out of place." She pushed a strand of blonde hair behind her ear. "Then there's you—and your uncle. You two are the only ones willing to shove a thumb in Oarl's eye, to let him know he can't have everything."

Larin leaned forward. "So that's it then?"

"No. I happen to know the only reason old man Higlen is still in business is because you gave him a few coppers a week so he could make Oarl's payments after Utra trashed his store."

"Well, actually Akul ended up helping too . . ."

"The point is no one else does things like that."

Larin smiled weakly. "So I guess it's not my stunning looks or brilliant charm . . ."

"Well, maybe some of that, too." Onie said. "Plus, I like them desperate. This way, I can treat you however I want and you'll still like me."

Larin grinned and reached out to mess up her hair, while Onie laughed, trying to block his hand. Their arms intertwined, and for a brief moment, he fell forward, finding his nose a few inches from hers. Mortified that he'd ruin everything, he pulled back quickly. The last thing he wanted was to end this friendship over a misunderstanding.

Yet Onie's look was mischievous as they disentangled, and she held up three fingers. "Three times we've seen each other now, and still you haven't tried to kiss me. I'm not sure what to think."

Electrified, Larin almost dropped the carving. Could she really want that? From *him*? "I didn't know if—" he started. Without any further hesitation, he bent down to kiss her, wanting nothing more in his entire life. She pushed him back gently, eyes merry.

"Well, not now, thickheaded boy. It can't be after I just asked you."

Larin stared, equal parts disappointed and confused, his first glimpse of just how complicated girls could be. In this, he suspected Onie wasn't so unusual.

"Justice! And love!" The booming voice interrupted Larin's thoughts, and they both twisted around on the bench. In the center of the plaza, two men in Morphat's red and black priestly robes stood like lone warriors, addressing the mildly curious crowds. One was a dark giant with hair in long braids carrying a leather-bound book, while the other was a fair-haired, baby-faced man Larin recognized.

"This Morphat brings to his worshippers!" yelled the dark-haired man. He thrust his hands in the air, and Larin noticed five sunburst pins lining his draping red sleeve. "Where other gods tell you to find your own way, Morphat lights your path. Where the Human Gods bribe their followers with spirits, Morphat provides true nourishment! Where our king steals the poor to fight his wars, Morphat stiffens their spines and teaches them discipline!"

A lone Imperial Guardsman stepped forward but halted immediately, his eyes darting between the Morphasti dotting the crowds.

Onie's mouth set into a hard expression. "That one yelling, that's

Goullard—Morphat's High Priest in the Port District. My father says he's responsible for building the Port District temple, and buying up all the food." Her eyes narrowed. "Whatever pretty words he spouts, he has a cruel face."

Larin nodded. "That one next to him is Kamithan. I recognize him from—" He stopped at Onie's sharp look. "I—I've heard he's second in command," he finished lamely.

"My neighbors, I bid you to discard your assumptions and see Morphat anew," Goullard shouted, spreading out his hands. "The priests of the Human Gods spout lies, but you are not sheep, my good people. You must decide for yourselves, based on your own eyes and ears. Come to the Marble Temple and watch us teach the powerless to control their lives. Come see how we provide food to those the king has forgotten!"

"Except to Hemeks," called a voice from within the gathering crowds. "Tell me, why does your temple provide smaller portions to those with Hemek blood?" The man stepped forward, and Larin saw that he had the tan, leathery skin of the Hemek peoples. The Hemeks were originally desert dwellers, a tribe whose trader ancestors had come to Aldive in such numbers that Hemekish had become one of Aldive's three unofficial languages.

Goullard's eyebrows lifted in what looked like genuine concern. "My good sir, it cannot be so! Morphat provides sustenance to all who ask, regardless of origin. Surely you came to us on a bad day—we feed hundreds, and maybe you were shortchanged." He turned to a Morphasti in the crowd. "Elios, please talk to this man and address his concerns. We must ensure all the poor are fed!"

The Morphasti approached the Hemek trader, who suddenly seemed nervous. They disappeared into the crowd, and to Larin, it seemed as though the Hemek was being dragged away.

Goullard turned back to the crowds. "Who amongst you has not felt the lash of destiny's whip? Who here denies that the Human Gods have deserted their followers? The temples of Emja purloin their offerings from the backs of the poor, while providing not a single service. My people, you've endured this for so long, it has come to seem normal." There were low murmurs of assent, and Goullard swept his growing audience with his gaze. Then he opened his book and began reading. "'And in the days of creation, the Eldegod protected humankind from the dangers of the indigen. They bathed mankind's heart with love and taught him to exist within nature. They shared their Lyrashi, that humanity might use the raw forces at their fingertips. Despite this benevolence, humanity turned away from the Eldegod . . .'"

"I've heard enough," Onie said flatly. Larin nodded, and they got up and walked back toward the fish market. They were silent as they meandered through the crowds, but as they reached the edge, Larin put a hand on Onie's arm.

"You have to go back to the Wormpile alone."

Onie whirled around. "I don't care what Oarl thinks. Let him see us— you spit in his face all the time, why should you care about his opinion now?"

Larin shook his head. "Onie, it's different when I'm the only one paying the price. The reason I'm still alive is because Oarl knows Akul will skewer him if he touches me with steel. Otherwise, they'd have probably diced me into small bits by now, maybe slit my throat into ribbons—"

She punched him in the chest. "Stop it."

"The point is people who talk to me don't have the same protection."

Onie closed her eyes. "Larin, I know all this."

"But you don't know how bad it can get. Oarl will beat you hard, Onie; it doesn't matter that you're a girl. Eventually, he'll go after your family."

At this, Onie's face lost its irritation. She watched him intently.

Larin looked into those blue eyes. "Come by the temple alehouse later in the week; Oarl will never set foot there. But don't take stupid chances for no reason."

She nodded slowly. "All right. But I will come see you in the alehouse. You're not getting rid of me that easily."

Larin shook his head stupidly, unable to keep the grin off his face. That Onie could even hint he didn't want to see her was ludicrous. He said only, "I really hope you do."

He watched her disappear into the crowds, swimming with heady thoughts. *Three times, and you haven't tried to kiss me.* He could barely believe she wanted that, would have never thought it possible. He began wandering the fish market, absently noting several more stands where Morphasti were buying all the available food. Still, he didn't dwell on it. His head was filled with images of Onie's lips, inches from his.

He was so lost in his own world that he was unprepared for the wave of fear and confusion that washed over him like a summer flood. Startled, he looked up to see a tagalanth's stubbled head a few inches from his face, its four orbs shifting right and left with terror. The sharp crack of a whip could be heard on the tagalanth's back, and a wave of the beast's pain washed over him before he could move away. He stumbled backward with the rest of the crowd, making way for the giant cart plowing its way between the Port District pillars. Atop the cart, three Morphasti sat with several large open sacks, one of them counting a stack of coins.

"Turn right just past the high tide mark," the lead man was saying. "We'll follow the street of knives directly to the Westmarket plaza."

Larin stared after the cart as it clattered away. Westmarket—the Wormpile's biggest exchange. Nowhere near as big as the Port District's fish market, but the place the Wormpile bought its food. Those open sacks, and all those coins. Larin narrowed his eyes, knowing exactly what they were about.

The Morphasti were going to start buying all the food in the Wormpile.

A chill chased away his pleasant mood. Whatever Morphat was up to, Larin doubted it would be good for anyone except the Marble Temple. All thoughts of Onie banished, he watched the cart disappear into the fish market crowds.

> "The Darkness sprouted from the fetid decay of a hedonism practiced by those sworn to its opposite. From there, it strengthened like a black rose growing from a rotten corpse."
>
> Jen Lothan's "The Forces Gathered."

X

One Year Later

It wasn't until 4115 CH that enough obelisks had been found in Shernock to give birth to the disciplines of lightbending and transmutation. This is one of the central mysteries surrounding the race that once ruled our world: Why would the Carvers arrange their cryptics such that the weaker magical disciplines were more easily discovered, while words relating to time, light manipulation, and other powerful disciplines are buried deeper within the swamps? Could these strange creatures truly have imagined our existence? Yet nothing surpasses the central mystery of them all: why do Lyrani threads exist, and how did the Carvers use them?

Larin looked up and twisted around at the bar, suddenly paranoid that Akul was scowling over his shoulder. Reading a book here was dicey, given that he was supposed to be *working* at the temple alehouse now.

He squinted into the alehouse through the greasy fireplace smoke, noticing the usual drunkards in attendance. More rushed in every minute, brushing snow from their hair as they raced past the devotion rooms, taking advantage of Sandre's blindness to avoid dinnertime prayers. Madam Shembri's girls floated through the chaos like purposeful butterflies, placing their hands lightly on men's backs and talking softly into their ears. Naela, the temple's stunning serving girl, received more attention than Madam Shembri's girls, but as these things often go, she wasn't for sale.

Larin studied the dusty room, feeling something was off. After a moment, he had it: many of the patrons were men who'd disappeared ages ago, Wormpile misfits who'd stopped showing their faces in the neighborhood. He was surprised to see Ropalek, a brooding, long-haired giant who'd failed every apprenticeship he'd tried, sitting alone without a single empty mug. There was Kelenas, an ex-soldier known for crazy angry tirades, rolling beads between his fingers, and watching Madam Shembri's girls from furrowed brows. Plus several others whose names he'd once known, but whom he hadn't seen in years. At one table sat a completely unfamiliar pockmark-faced man in a brown robe, hollow cheeks etched in shadows beneath his hood.

Larin scowled; it was unusual to see so many new faces here. He stared at the brown-robed man, then tore his gaze away to unenthusiastically scan for dirty tables. Seeing only two, he turned back around.

The fact that people drank, yelled, and sang while he read quietly at the bar barely bothered him anymore. He was a ghost here anyway, for few acknowledged his existence besides a few regulars. Although Emja's temple was free of Oarl's mouth-breathers, most wouldn't chance Oarl's wrath by talking to Larin where others could see. The loneliness of his storeroom job had been miniscule compared to fifty people pretending he wasn't there.

Yet in the year since he'd met Onie at the fish market, he'd managed to shrink that loneliness into a tiny ball. Onie's first alehouse visit had come on his sixteenth birthday, a day of blustery winds and smells of hot tomato soup wafting from the kitchen. Soon she was visiting twice a week, sitting at the bar sipping melon juice while he drank ale in a secret bid to impress her. They talked of simple things, sometimes joined by Ruldir the armorer, a burly, religious man who felt the need to comment without regard for such trivialities as private conversation.

Larin remembered well the first time they'd walked to the storeroom together, searching for privacy as Ruldir grinned slyly and Akul pointedly ignored them. Nervous as a first time stage bard, Larin had talked incessantly, not sure what to do once the silence started.

"And see, here's where the temple priests bring all of Emja's offerings," he said, waving at bauble-filled shelves. "Figurines there, rare stones there, and brass bowls and cutlery over there. Then my job was to polish them and make them presentable—"

"This is a place of loneliness, I feel it," Onie interrupted. She stared at a shiny brass serving spoon, not looking at him. Larin felt her closeness, breathed the smells of her skin cream. A magnetic pull that for some reason he found himself resisting as hard as he could.

"Not really," he muttered. "See, I also stored my books in here, and I spent a lot of time reading about—"

She yanked his tunic, pulling him close to her. He stared at the freckles around her nose, feeling his entire head go numb. Wisps of wavy blonde hair dangled over dimpled cheeks; she was so, so beautiful. He felt paralyzed, able only to blink.

"Larin, this place was your hell, I know. But we're done with that." With that, she pulled his mouth to hers, and everything changed.

Since then, they hadn't bothered to spend much time in the alehouse. When Onie arrived, they headed straight for the storeroom, too eager to be in each other's arms to wait even a minute. Soon, that room turned from Larin's private prison into something much sweeter, something he'd never imagined. And in the last few months, something more—talk of running away together, escaping the viper pit that was the Wormpile.

Larin sighed, glancing wistfully toward the alehouse door. Unfortunately, today wasn't Onie's usual day to visit. He returned his attentions to *On the Foundations and History of Magic, Volume II*, a tome he'd found in an unused cubbyhole within the temple library. Not scholarly enough to be noticed by the priests, to Larin it was still a lot easier reading than the Tiyani Codex.

For one thing, we know Lyrashi was the language of the Carvers, and the Lyrani threads respond to Lyrashi words. Yet Lyrashi is also our language of magic. So, were the Carvers unable to even say hello without invoking powerful dweomers? Did every conversation, every discussion pluck the chords of the earth, causing great forces to flow? Scholars have debated this point since the first obelisks were found. It is now commonly believed that the Carvers were able to use pitch to create power words from normal speech. Indeed, it is long-accepted magical theory that finishing the most powerful violet-sash spells with an upward lilt increases their—

"Ho, young'un," came a booming voice from his left. "Emja's flowing mustache, but you've grown!"

Larin looked up, wincing as Trana pounded his shoulder with the force of a blacksmith's hammer. Trana's weathered face was bright red, her sweat-beaded forehead matted with wavy brown hair. She held a huge carved mug that was now empty, but which could hold more ale than some drank in an evening.

Larin smiled and rubbed his shoulder, enjoying the warm glow that Trana radiated like hot coals. "Ho, Trana, it's really good to see you. Hope you warned the alehouse you were coming, so they could buy up all the hops from the Hennat Valley."

Trana cackled and slammed her mug to the bar, crinkled eyes giving him the once over. "New shirt, new breeches, shoes with no holes in them. Did I wake up in some neverland where Larin actually cares about his appearance? Or, more likely, you found a woman to whip you into shape."

"Well, Onie helped me pick out the breeches. And she bought me the tunic at Westmarket." He nodded at Trana's giant mug, eager to change the subject. "That's a good start to the night. No reason to go in small."

She snorted. "Young'un, I've been sitting here an hour while you've had your nose buried in that book like a sow digging for mushrooms. This is my third."

Larin scanned the bar as Trana pulled out an empty stool, realizing that while he'd searched the main alehouse, he'd never once looked to see who sat at the bar. To his left was Ruldir, reading some religious text, and next to him sat Dame Elena, sipping her wine and talking to a strapping lad twenty years her junior. Further back, Larin was surprised to see the temple's dour High Priest Tierre, next to a very drunk priest Kedrick. Tierre was a rare sight in the alehouse, for unlike his clergy, he wasn't much given to anything that smacked of enjoyment. Priest Roald, running the bar until Akul's shift, slammed a mug down between the two men in a drunken misdirection, mumbled something, and staggered into the kitchen.

Trana wiped her mouth with her sleeve. "Now if these were Blueflower ales instead of this donkey water they give everyone else, I might actually be drunk by now. You'd think I'd get *some* reward for cleaning that mess in the alehouse last time."

Larin squinted. "You mean the time you helped clear those two drunk fighting Yuls out of the alehouse?"

"It was a gang of Yuls, young sir, and I did more than clear them. I knocked them down and hauled them out to the street."

"That's a black eye of a story."

Trana paused her ale halfway to her mouth.

"Gets better with time."

She issued a short bark of a laugh, and Ruldir smiled weakly. "There's that damn smart mouth I remember," she said. "Forsaken young men, spouting whatever comes to their mind." She tousled his hair, but ended it with a short clip to his right ear.

Larin laughed, covering his ear. "It really is good to see you again, Trana. Emja, it's been six months. Where did you go this time?"

"And you, young'un," she said. "They made me guard commander, protecting a food caravan to the believers in Faustus. Gave me only a week to pull my team together, and I got nothing but misfits and inexperienced boys. No offense, of course."

"None taken," Larin said, unsure whether to take offense for all boys or all misfits. "Though maybe I'll hitch a ride next time. The Wormpile's getting too unhealthy for me."

Trana gave him that blank look that always forced him to keep talking.

"It's gotten worse, Trana. If I'm lucky I can sneak out of these four blocks in one piece, but if one of Oarl's rats is in the wrong place at the wrong time, I get beaten like an old carpet after a dust storm."

She drummed her fingers against the bar. "Young'un, your uncle is the most amazing swordsman I've ever known. Doesn't he teach you his art?"

"He tries. We practice, and I've gotten better with a blade. I might be able to beat some of Oarl's gang one-on-one, but they don't fight that way. Anyway, even if I had eight more hands, I'd never be able to fight like Akul."

Trana nodded. "Well, these caravans are no picnic either, Larin. Too many ways to die, especially as we get close to the disputed region. I lost two of my crew to a brigand's arrows."

"Having my throat ripped out by an arrow actually sounds better than being beaten three times a week. One day Akul will be gone, and Oarl will get to try his blade collection on me. Or maybe he'll prefer hanging—"

"Larin, enough!" Trana said, aghast. "That's one thing that hasn't changed; your morbid imagination is like eating poisoned soup. Things have a way of turning for the better, just give it time."

Larin nodded, suddenly eager to change the subject. "So, tell me about your trip."

Trana's eyes became distant. "The war is taking its toll on the disputed region, Larin. There's no law to speak of, save the law of the street."

She fell silent, and after a moment waiting for her to continue, Larin's eyes wandered the bar. High above were Akul's seventeen mugs, each with some Turmanian or Oestigan moniker; names like "Ausgard" and "Vinelhalm." Akul had received no end of ribbing on this from the regulars, with the prevailing theory that they were Turmanian wenches he'd bedded in his youth. On that subject, as on any other having to do with his previous life, Akul kept silent.

From across the bar, Tierre's beady eyes passed over Larin with only the briefest scowl. Instead, he reserved a much longer and more contemptuous look for Trana, who ignored him completely. It wasn't the first time Larin noticed no love lost between those two.

Larin turned away from Tierre. "But the city of Faustus is ours now, right?"

She sighed. "Aye, Larin, Tanbar owns it now, but it was Seridor's six months ago, and changed hands twice before that. The fields are burnt plains, and the good countryfolk have fled, leaving naught but outlaws." She sipped her ale slowly. "Do you know much about the City of Kaman?"

"Kaman? You mean the capital of Seridor?" Larin drew himself up, pulling facts from his endless reading. "Of course. Three hundred thousand people, and the biggest city in the southern reaches. It's a holy city for Eldegod worshippers and has a temple to Morphat bigger than Aldive's entire Imperial District—"

Trana waved a hand and he trailed off, embarrassed. "I was in Kaman once," she said. "I've never seen an uglier city. The city folk don't look up, nor have I ever seen one smile."

"Right. A city of sleepwalkers."

She raised an eyebrow, and he realized she was serious. He leaned forward. "So how does a city end up that way?"

"Fear, Larin. First there's the semiannual sacrifice, drawn from hundreds of innocent townsfolk. The Old One's bloodlust must be satisfied. Plus, spies are everywhere. The Eldegod priesthoods crawl through the city, sniffing for hints of weakness. Then there are press gangs, for slavery is well-practiced in that horrible town." She sipped her drink. "Don't fall asleep in an alley after a good night drinking; you'll wake in the salt mines of Seridor, chained to a rock for the rest of your life—"

"I wonder if there're any dirty tables out there," a booming voice called from the kitchen. They both stopped short.

"I'd guess Akul's started his shift," Trana said, just as Akul barged into the bar area with a half-cocked expression, craning his neck sideways to scan the alehouse.

Larin smiled weakly as he watched Akul pace the bar in an exaggerated hunt for dirty tables, but resentment kept the smile from reaching his eyes. He couldn't forget Akul's morning post-khald rage, an all too common fury of self-hatred that had subjected him to an earful of abuse. It didn't matter that his uncle meant none of what he said, nor that the afternoon's sullen face was the closest Akul ever came to an apology. Nor did it matter that Akul's rage was mostly directed within.

"Hmmm, one, two, three tables," Akul counted, pointing into the main room.

"Last I looked, there were only two," Larin said wanly. He instantly regretted it.

Akul's eyes narrowed, veins throbbing in that bald dome. "You walked right by two dirty tables and sat at the bar?"

Larin winced and turned to Trana. "Guess I better get going."

"Aye, young'un."

Trana turned back to the bar, slapping the dark oak. "About time you arrived, Akul. I'm dying of thirst. How about a Blueflower, and leave off the boy. He tried to get away, but I forced him to listen to my ramblings."

Akul snorted. "Larin tried to get back to work while you were spinning war stories?" He grabbed Trana's mug, put it beneath the spout, and pulled back the lever. "That's about as likely as flowers sprouting from my rear end."

Trana issued her famous stone-shaking laugh, and Larin smiled, grateful to escape Akul's irritation. He walked into the kitchen to get a rag, but as he emerged, the sight of Onie's hooded, bundled figure at the entrance chased away all thoughts of work. He threw the rag on a table, walking quickly toward her.

Yet as he approached, he knew something was very wrong. Hints of a bruise peeked from under her hood, and she stood in a small, vulnerable way that froze his blood.

"Onie . . ." he said softly.

She didn't look at him. "Let's go to the storeroom."

He glanced at Akul, who was studiously ignoring Onie's entrance, then back at her bruised cheek, just beneath her left eye. He felt the beginnings of a powerful rage. Not trusting himself to speak, he took her hand and they walked silently out of the alehouse, up the stairs, and into the first-floor storeroom.

Larin closed the door, and Onie threw back her hood, falling into his arms. He held her tightly, breathing in the faint scent of rose water, bunching that blonde hair under his hands. Finally she pulled away, left cheek red and inflamed.

"I can't see you for a while." Her nose was bunched in determination, and Larin's heart tightened. He knew why, but also knew if he opened his mouth now, it would spew only venom.

"Larin, I wouldn't care if Oarl beat me senseless. But when he struck my father—oh, my father . . ." Her voice cracked, and Larin wanted to say a thousand things: to remind her they'd vowed not to let Oarl's miserable cockroaches split them up, to ask what would become of their Wormpile escape plans, to ask when he'd see her again. Yet one question burned like hot coals in his throat.

"How many times has Oarl hit you?"

"It doesn't matter . . ."

"How many?" Larin hissed.

Her lip quivered. "He's known I've been coming here for a month—someone in the alehouse must've told him. First they threatened me. Then two weeks ago, Oarl slapped me a few times. Today, he had Utra use his fist. Then they went to my house, threw my father to the floor, and kicked him in front of my brother." She struggled to contain herself. "Not my father, Larin. I can't do that to him." She looked into his eyes, imploring him to understand.

"I know . . ." His voice drifted from a fog. Then, the image of Utra's fat fists on his beautiful Onie sent raw hatred cascading through him like a summer flood. In another instant, the familiar heat awakened behind his forehead, and for a moment, he thought he'd suffer his first true outburst in over a year. The charm fought it off, though barely, it seemed.

"Are you all right?" Onie asked, searching his eyes.

Black winds swirled inside. "I'll kill him."

"No!" Onie shouted, grabbing his tunic. "Don't you see, that's exactly what they want! Stupid men, always thinking the answer is a fight. What good would it do me for you to commit suicide in some hopeless battle?"

Larin looked at her, trying to quell his rage.

She pressed against him. "It's not forever, I promise. Let it play out; let them forget. One day we'll run away, so don't you leave me alone in this scorpion cage. Promise me you'll do nothing."

Larin swallowed a cold lump of despair. Next month was his seventeenth birthday, one year since Onie had first visited him here. Now, that would be the day he returned to his miserable, lonely life.

"I promise." He slowly unclenched his fists. "What am I going to do without you, Onie?"

"You're going to wait for me." She leaned back and smiled, dimpling her right cheek. "Now, all my work making you presentable will fly into the sea. When I see you next, you'll probably be wearing your stained tunic and moth-eaten shoes. Emja knows, with Akul and Candro as your role models, I'm lucky you're not dressed in cleaning rags."

Larin brushed a blonde bang from her forehead, trying to ignore the swelling beneath her left eye. "No, Onie, I'll still be wearing the tunic you gave me. It's the only thing I'll have from you, other than your carving." He looked around the musty storeroom, which was about to become the pit of loneliness it'd always been. "Besides, the tunic's red will hide my bloodstains nicely, and—"

"Enough with your stupid morbid jokes!" Onie shouted. Her lower lip was trembling, and suddenly Larin felt like a monster. What to him was a grim joke was terrifying to her.

"I'm sorry, Onie," he whispered. "I'm going to miss you so much."

They both fell silent, and after a moment, she fell into his arms again. He held her close, her wet hood pressed against his face as he buried his nose in her neck. They kissed briefly, but with the passion replaced by worry, they soon stepped away from each other.

Larin sighed. "I guess we should get you out of here before Oarl's eye reports you again."

Onie looked away. "Yes."

Stone-faced, Larin escorted her out of the storeroom and to the temple entrance, where the last rays of the sun peeked through dark clouds to reveal a blanket of white over the Wormpile's rooftops. He watched her don her hood, feeling like his insides were being ripped from his body. He wondered how long it'd be before she found someone who was a lot less trouble.

She stepped through the temple archway, turning wet eyes on him. "Larin—" Yet there was really nothing to say. Head downcast, she stepped into the snowy courtyard and out of his life.

Larin stumbled back down the steps and into the alehouse, to the table where he'd left the rag. He picked it up, feeling a terrible nausea, a return of the stomach-clenching loneliness he knew so well. He wanted to run after her, steal her away from the Wormpile this very night.

"It happened again? When?" The loud voice came from behind, and Larin swung around. Two Wormpile residents he barely recognized sat with Leyalas, a one-eyed stonecutter Larin thought had disappeared years ago. Leyalas was gesticulating wildly, red-faced with anger.

"Just last night," came a call from another table. "They swept into Westmarket and grabbed eight men and boys. Not that *these* priests will do anything about it." This came from another man Larin barely remembered, a bitter, ruddy-faced baker who'd once owned a bread shop on the Wormpile's north side before it'd been trashed by Oarl's gang. Yet another man he thought had disappeared. He narrowed his eyes as the loud cacophony of alehouse conversations lowered to a dull roar. Something was going on here.

Ropalek stood, long black hair falling about his face like an angry storm. Brooding eyes once continually twisted by rage now held a sharp focus. Larin was struck by how the giant man had changed in the past years—his shoulders had widened, and tattoos ran from his cheeks down a neck bulging with taut veins. He was leaner and more muscular in every way, as if he'd spent years training with arms.

"Quite right, these priests will do nothing," Ropalek said, his voice smooth as silk on a dagger. "Emja continues his idle games while the poor die to fight his wars." He glanced contemptuously at unconscious priest Kedrick, whose face was planted on the bar. "These useless priests from a useless god will gorge on ale, while the Imperial Compound raids you to fight a useless war."

The room was silent as death, as it became clear to even the most inebriated that trouble was brewing. Larin's gaze shot to the bar and then to the door, but Akul was gone, likely to change connections on the giant ale vats two floors up. A cold chill wormed up his spine.

Ropalek began wandering the tables, catching the gaze of every Wormpile resident in the room. "From his khald stupor, the king sends his thugs among the poor, dragging boys from their homes and throwing them on the field against Seridor—a pointless bloodbath in an endless, murderous war. And why? Because the day that Seridor brings Morphat and the true gods to this land is the day the king and his temples will be cast aside like garbage. And while Maldovin raids us for taxes and steals our brethren, he provides no protection against Oarl and his like. Remain sheep, my friends, for the royals depend on your apathy." He swept the alehouse with his proud gaze, and everyone stared back in rapt attention.

Dame Elena, sitting next to her wide-eyed youth, folded her arms. "Morphat's in no position to do anything about it. The Port District temple holds no power."

Ropalek's fiery stare settled on her. "That's where you're wrong. You people in this alehouse have been blinded by Emja's ale bribes. In the rest of the Wormpile, Morphat helps the people resist Maldovin's bloody boot. While Emja's priests feed on your offerings like parasites, Morphat protects his worshippers with dignity and arms. The Wormpile is rising up, and this decaying pit is the last remnant of our shame."

Larin scanned the sea of rapt faces with interest. He thought that while Ropalek had failed everything he'd tried, he'd found his calling as Morphat's orator.

Seeing them in his thrall, the giant man searched their eyes again. "Now, I ask you all—shall we continue fighting this pointless war, watching our brothers and fathers die? Or shall we end this murder and reclaim our dignity?"

"Whatever the king's faults, this war is far from pointless," Trana cut in. She stood at the bar, watching Ropalek with hard eyes. "Tell me—do you truly know what life is like under Seridor's gods, or are you blowing the winds of fools?"

Ropalek walked to Trana, wearing a sickly sweet expression. "I'll tell you what it's like: criminals punished and honest people living without fear. Wars fought by professional soldiers instead of poor, ill-trained peasants dragged from their homes and handed a sword they can't use. Order on the streets, the god's love in the temples."

Trana snorted. "The only thing the Eldegod love is to enslave their people. Ropalek, you truly don't know, do you? Have you even heard of Hessal's ceremony—"

Ropalek slapped Trana hard. "Silence, lying priestess of a useless god!"

Trana shot for the sword rack, but several of the new men sprang to their feet, blocking her path. Larin counted thirteen, all with the warriors' heavy muscle. Trana didn't stand a chance. With that, Larin suddenly realized why he hadn't seen these men in years. They'd been training at arms. For only years of sword practice could give the fat baker the muscle he saw now.

Larin swallowed as he watched Trana back away. Ropalek smiled. "We don't need your lies, or those of your vermin priests. The Morphasti will return discipline to the Wormpile." With that, all thirteen man pulled red-black armbands from their pockets and began tying them around their arms.

"You're all together!" exclaimed High Priest Tierre, and Trana shot him a disgusted look.

Ropalek laughed, walked behind the bar, and began throwing ceramic plates to the floor. "This den of impurity will be cleansed."

"Stop it!" Tierre cried. "Those cost two coppers apiece!"

The angry soldier Kelenas shot his fist into Tierre's stomach, and the High Priest collapsed like a deflated pillow. Ropalek watched Tierre's writhing body for a moment, then turned to survey the gaping faces. "You see what finally causes your priests to speak up? The cost of their pottery. Let's see if they care about anything more important." With that, he walked to the statue of Emja and tipped it over.

To Larin, the statue's fall came in a dream. With surreal slowness, he watched Emja's face hit a table and break, while the rest of the statue smacked the hard-packed dirt floor and shattered into a dozen pieces. As shards of the god scattered across the alehouse, he felt like the world had shifted one foot to the left. He couldn't explain why, but he was certain that right now, at this place, Emja's power was drawing to a close.

"No!" Ruldir shouted, shooting off his stool. Morphasti warriors stepped into his path, and he stopped, his face twisted with rage. The alehouse was deathly silent now, with only the small pops and cracks from the fireplace punctuating the still air. Trana and Ruldir stared at the small army before them, chests heaving. The group of rusted hooks pounded into the alehouse's west wall was the center of attention, though no one looked at the sword rack directly.

"What have you done?" Naela suddenly screamed from the center of the alehouse. "Who are you to do this thing? Go back to your six-legged temples and leave us be!"

"Silence!" Ropalek barked, and strode to Naela with a raised hand. She didn't flinch as he approached, but his open-handed slap brought her to her knees. "Emja's whore!" he cried. "Your impurity has brought us all low—a true god would never suffer harlots in his temple!" He began striking Naela repeatedly, and Trana gave a shout of frustration from behind the wall of warriors.

"Idiot! She's not even what you think she is!"

It didn't matter. Ropalek was lost in a frenzy of beating, striking Naela repeatedly about the shoulders as she crouched on the floor. Larin looked desperately at the back door.

Where was Akul?

As it became clear the beating would not stop, Larin's blood boiled. In his mind, Ropalek's face overlaid with Utra's and Naela became Onie, as the unspeakable image of Utra's fist on Onie's delicate cheek turned the room black. He was one of only a few people who could fight this travesty, since as an official alehouse employee, he was exempted from the warder gargoyle's magic damping. Unbidden, a recently learned three-word dweomer sprang into his mind, one of the minimalist class of first-rank Influence spells. He put a table between himself and the Morphasti and shouted the three Lyrashi words of a fire-eye spell.

His magic was always hit or miss, but for whatever reason, this time it hit. Ropalek cried out in pain and rubbed his eyes, all violent thoughts forgotten. Naela scrambled away, and every single Morphasti turned their gaze on Larin.

Larin swallowed slowly.

Kelenas wore a hard look as he began casting his own spell. Larin shot a glance toward the lunchtime prayer room door and with relief saw a blue glow in the warder gargoyle's eyes—Kelenas's magic would be blocked. Yet relief was short-lived. Ropalek had recovered and, with a snarl of hatred, shot toward Larin like a charging khula.

Larin raced backward, trying to keep several tables between them, but three Morphasti moved to cut him off. In desperation, he whirled around with dagger in hand, just in time to watch an ale mug slam into Ropalek's head and send him sprawling to the floor.

All motion froze at that point, as Trana wiped wet hands on her shirt. "Ayn's ghost. What a waste of good ale."

And that's when it all started.

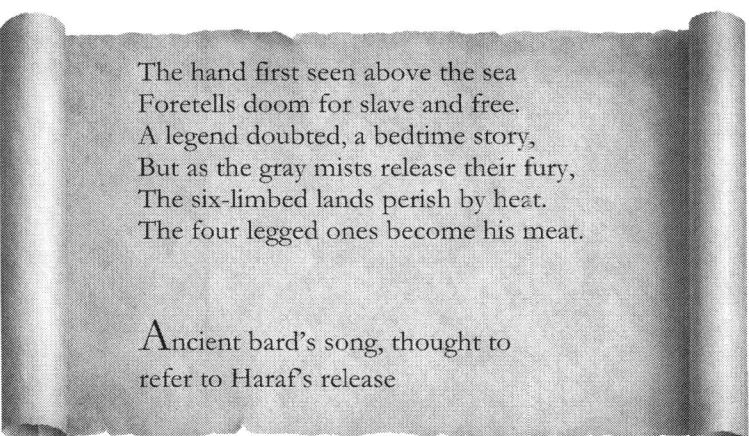

The hand first seen above the sea
Foretells doom for slave and free.
A legend doubted, a bedtime story,
But as the gray mists release their fury,
The six-limbed lands perish by heat.
The four legged ones become his meat.

Ancient bard's song, thought to
refer to Haraf's release

XI

The alehouse froze, then everyone dove for the sword rack at once. Trana was saved by the Morphasti's distraction, for they leapt a second too late. She reached her sword in time to thrust an elbow into Kelenas's face, knocking him backward, as Ruldir's meaty fist slammed another man down before he reached the rack. Trana grabbed a barstool with one hand and shoved it into the crowd of Morphasti, allowing precious seconds for Ruldir to grab his sword. She hurled giant mugs at her attackers as Ruldir vaulted over the bar, then threw the barstool and vaulted over herself. The sound of clanging metal reverberated across the alehouse, as Trana and Ruldir fought the Morphasti onslaught from behind the bar.

Ropalek stirred and Larin grabbed a chair, swinging at the man's head with every ounce of strength. A broken chair leg flew across the room as Ropalek collapsed back to the floor.

Larin watched desperately as the last Morphasti retrieved his sword. The twelve-to-two odds would have been impossible for Trana and Ruldir, had it not been for the close quarters and the wide bar separating the two sides. Yet Ruldir's face already sported a long gash, and he knew the end was near. Swallowing his fear, he drew his dagger and ran forward, just in time to see Akul's sword flying through the melee.

Emja, it's about time.

With the rush of alehouse patrons trying to escape through either door, all Larin could see was the top of Akul's bald head as it pushed through the melee and the blur of metal as he knocked aside flying blades. Wherever the bald dome went, men were spat from the fray like seeds from a farmer's mouth.

The Morphasti turned all attention toward this new threat, but to no avail. They swirled around the bald dome like a twisting storm, only to be hurled away moments later, some spinning violently before crashing onto nearby tables. Then Akul emerged from the mayhem, and Larin saw his uncle's swordplay for only the third time in his life.

With fascination, he watched Akul's sword twirl and arc in a fury of metal, the fireplace's glow flashing from his blade in a dozen places as his enemies flew to the floor. Leyalas aimed a vicious swipe at Akul's neck, but it bounced off an invisible wall, with only a thin blur to indicate Akul's blade had ever been there. The air glinted again in two places, and two of the six remaining men twisted and fell. Dull sounds told Larin that Akul was using the flat of his sword, and he saw that the small amount of blood was from cuts and swipes, rather than the full gushing of opened guts.

Awestruck, Larin watched as Akul blocked a thrust from Leyalas while simultaneously slamming his fist into the nose of the Morphasti on his left. Stepping backward, he let a blade pass inches from his chest and then suddenly ducked and twirled. The air glinted twice again and two more Morphasti went down, one crashing into a nearby table and another landing over the bar, where Ruldir slammed his fist into the man's mouth.

Now only Leyalas remained, and much to Larin's surprise, he remained standing through Akul's barrage of metal. It seemed as though Akul had suddenly lost his aim—the sword slid around Leyalas without finding purchase. Larin stared at the gold disk around his neck.

"Akul, he's got a warder charm!" Larin shouted.

Akul didn't turn his head, but suddenly his strokes became a blur, and Leyalas's smug expression disappeared as he was pressed back.

While the alehouse fixated on this final exchange, Larin heard heavy footsteps and turned a second too late to avoid Ropalek, who grabbed his arm and pulled him toward a table. Larin aimed a fist at the man's nose, but Ropalek caught it, shoving his elbow into Larin's chin. He grinned at Larin's stunned look and twisted Larin's arm back violently, seeking to snap it.

Familiar heat awoke behind Larin's forehead. It became an overwhelming rush, and he knew that this time, his charm would be utterly powerless. Yet the outburst also gave him strength, and Ropalek's face strained as Larin resisted his downward push. Blood boiling behind his forehead, he watched Akul's fury of sword strokes throw Leyalas to the floor, just as the first word of the Phrase bellowed from his lungs.

Everyone noticed their battle for the first time then. Chest heaving, Akul stared at them for a split second, then sprinted over the downed

Morphasti, trying to reach Ropalek before Larin's arm snapped.

As Larin shouted the Phrase's last word, the brown-robed man in the corner shot to his feet, his arms upraised. Larin cursed through his pain, knowing the next moment was critical—Akul had to focus on Ropalek if Larin was to keep his right arm. Yet his gut told him that this man wielded power that could render the warder gargoyle into useless stone, and the threat of a high-rank sorcerer in the alehouse was too high to ignore.

"Akul—" His voice escaped in painful gasps. He nodded at the brown robed man, and Akul swung around, staring. The man's face had vanished inside his hood, as if the robe were worn by an empty shell. A second later, a loud crack issued from across the room, as the warder gargoyle split down the center.

Fortunately, Ropalek was also captivated by this sight, and the pressure on Larin's arm eased. For a long moment, the only sounds in the alehouse were the small pops from the fireplace and the soft moans of injured Morphasti.

Under the stares of fifty alehouse patrons, the hooded man's cheeks and forehead reappeared slowly. His eyes materialized a second later, and he blinked into the surrounding war zone, as if he'd forgotten where he was. Then he pulled back his chair and sat quietly, a statue of calmness in a field of chairs and overturned tables.

The pressure on Larin's arm resumed, just as a sword point slid across his vision and came to rest in the fleshy coating of Ropalek's neck.

"If you break his arm, it will be your last action in this world."

Ropalek tore his gaze off Larin to consider Akul, beads of sweat dripping down tattooed cheeks. "How much do you want for him? I have gold."

The sword point pressed into Ropalek's neck, and blood trickled down his Adam's apple. "Right now, you bargain only for your life."

Ropalek spat but let go of Larin's arm, and Larin scrambled back. "Very well. My life for his."

Akul lowered his sword an inch, contempt etched into his features. "What about your men?"

Ropalek's face was solemn. "The Morphasti are not afraid to die to bring truth to the unbelievers. It is what separates us from you."

Akul wrinkled his nose, turning to the prone Morphasti. "All except their leader, it appears, who clearly chooses not to die. Do you hear that, you misguided fools? Your vile god abandons you, and your commander condemns you to death without thinking twice." He wiped his blade across Ropalek's tunic, turning the long-haired man's face cloudy with anger. Akul nodded toward Ruldir and Trana, who hovered over the Morphasti. "There's rope in the storeroom. Tie their hands and escort them from the Wormpile." He turned to the crowd by the door. "For all who want to stay, the next three rounds are from the temple's Blueflower stock!"

This comment was greeted with cheers, as well as an influx of Wormpile residents returning to their chairs.

Akul watched the parade of returnees, then considered Larin with hard eyes. "Why do I know this all started with you?"

Larin said nothing, and Akul's jaw clenched. "Larin, follow me."

Akul marched into the kitchen, and Larin followed, too relieved at his deliverance to care about the verbal thrashing he was about to get. He passed Trana, kneeling to tie the angry baker's hands behind him.

"Thanks, Trana."

Trana nodded. "Any time, young'un. I only wish it'd been a dagger instead of an ale mug." The lines of worry across her forehead belied her brave words and stopped Larin's smile cold. He read fear in her eyes, and felt it crawl up his own spine. For today, they had crossed a god unknown for mercy.

"Larin, get in here now!"

He smiled weakly, then turned to follow Akul.

Penter and Ula, the two street urchins the temple hired to wash dishes, looked up with saucer-wide eyes as Akul and Larin entered the back room.

"Scram," Akul said, and they fell over each other racing for the exit.

Larin walked to the wall and leaned back, his heart pounding. Akul closed the door, then turned to stare at him. "So what in Emja's name happened?"

Larin breathed deeply. "Ropalek—he hit Naela. And you weren't around, and she couldn't get away, and he broke Emja's statue, so I cast a fire-eye spell, and then—"

"And for that you almost got us all killed?" Akul shouted. "Emja forsake it, Larin, you couldn't have waited two minutes for me to come back?"

"But he was hitting her, and—"

"For all the Demons' sakes, boy, you have a goat's common sense! Naela deals with rough men sometimes—she could've managed a little while longer. Your stupid honor has wrecked the alehouse and almost gotten you killed!" He lowered his voice "*And* you just bellowed your outburst in front of the temple's High Priest. Pray to Emja he wasn't listening!"

Larin was silent. There was really nothing to say.

Akul sighed, rubbing the back of his head. "Look, it's probably best if you head home. I'm going to close after the three rounds anyway."

Larin looked up sharply. "That will just tell everyone I'm no longer welcome at the alehouse. No one speaks to me anyway; now they'll have another reason."

Akul's features softened. "Larin, it's just for tonight. I don't want that walking tagalanth excrement to come back for you this evening."

Larin knew Akul was right, but it didn't ease the sting. Without another word, he pushed himself off the wall.

"I'm not through yet. I saw what you did in there."

Larin turned around.

"Ropalek was going to break your arm, and the only person close enough to stop him was me. But you still pointed me to the real threat. That mage in the brown robe could've destroyed the entire temple."

Larin nodded. "Something about him bothered me. I thought he had more power than the usual magickers we get around here."

"The point is that action could've cost you your arm." Akul's forehead became a shriveled prune, the way it did at any display of emotion. "You did the right thing, and I'm, uh. Proud of you."

Larin stared stupidly. Such comments were completely unheard of after what he'd just done. Lowering his eyes, he turned to the door. "Fine."

Penter and Ula scrambled away from their listening posts as the door opened, and Larin smiled weakly. "What, you couldn't hear him from across the Wormpile?"

He exited the back room just as Ruldir and a few alehouse regulars were escorting the Morphasti out. Glancing at the table with the brown-robed mage, he saw it was now empty. He reached up to grab his coat.

"You!"

The voice echoed across the alehouse with the booming sureness of the God's Word. Larin turned around, shrinking inside as he saw Tierre staring directly at him.

"The enemy within our midst!" Tierre cried. "Demon spawn, assassin from the Gray Lands—thank Emja we now see who you are!"

"Now wait a minute—" Akul started.

"From the earliest writings, Emja has spoken of your kind!" the High Priest barked. His fat face was red with righteous fury, his massive arm shaking as he pointed at Larin. "He warned us there would be those who seek to release Haraf from his cage, told us they must be fought at all costs. For those who've ever doubted Emja's word, cast your eyes ahead—our enemy travels among us." He looked at Trana. "By every oath you have sworn, detain him!"

Larin wanted to crawl into the deepest hole. He looked around the alehouse, seeing mixed expressions of horror, surprise and revulsion; if he'd thought being ignored was bad, this was far worse. His heart stopped in its tracks as he turned to Trana, whose face was as conflicted as he'd ever seen. She remained silent for several seconds. Finally, she breathed deeply and turned to Tierre.

"What are you talking about, old man?"

Tierre gasped. "You heard his words! You are a priestess of Emja; you cannot shirk this duty!"

"I heard something," Trana said, "but it was drowned out by blubbering from the corner, so I couldn't make it out." Her eyebrows lifted. "Wait—weren't _you_ prone in the corner?"

Tierre paled. "You have seen the enemy, and you refuse to act?"

Trana gritted her jaw. "Stupid old man, your enemy was here a moment ago, destroying the god's statue while you cowered. Only those whose blood adorns the gargoyle's horn can cast magic in this place, and with Akul gone, that list included only you, Kedrick, Naela, and Larin. You are High Priest; the power of the god is strong within you—you could've destroyed their leader with a few words. Then why was it only your so-called enemy had the courage to defend the god's honor?" The alehouse had been riveted by this exchange, and now there were a few low murmurs of assent.

Righteous fury painted an ominous cloud across Tierre's face. "You call yourself priestess, but you forget your first lessons. These men were naught but thugs. The God deals with such rabble over time; they are less than dirt beneath our feet. In every age there are those who answer directly to the minions from the Gray Lands, individuals who seek to bring that storm crashing about this world." Tierre turned to Larin again, a look of loathing on his face. "Haraf lives within this boy, awaiting a time to loose his hellions upon us. This danger is true—next to that, a few unschooled ruffians from the Port District's Marble Temple are nothing."

Larin waited for Trana to respond, his heart falling further every second she remained silent. She looked at her feet, solid neck clenched tight as she fought some internal battle. Yet while she didn't respond, neither did she move to collect Larin.

Tierre's eyes turned to steel. "Very well. We are not a fighting order, but we can call on the god's paladins when needed. We'll have this boy tried, whether our priests of the Atlaran order choose to follow their duty or not."

"How do you propose to call anyone with my sword point sticking out of your back?" Akul growled, stomping toward a wide-eyed Tierre. "For have no doubt, if he's harmed in any way, I'll come directly for your miserable fat neck."

Tierre's mouth opened and closed as he stared into Akul's heaving chest. Akul's facial scar was glowing as red as Larin had ever seen it.

"I'll make you a one-time offer," Akul hissed. "My boy and I will leave this temple, never to return. And you will forget this incident ever happened."

"Akul, no," Larin said softly, and all eyes in the alehouse turned to him. He struggled to control his voice. "You—we need the money. I'll leave. There's no reason for you to go, too."

"I will speak to Emja and ask for guidance," Tierre cut in, before Akul could respond. Two inches from Akul's snarling face, he had gone completely white. "Perhaps Emja will see mercy upon your demon child, if he refuses to follow his instincts. In the meantime, the boy is expelled, and you will continue your duties at the temple."

Akul curled his lip. "You mean, as long as I continue to keep these four blocks clear of Oarl's rats and tell the shop owners to donate one-fourth of Oarl's protection money to the temple, you'll leave my boy alone."

If Tierre saw any hypocrisy in this, he hid it well. "Right," he snapped. "And you'll continue your duties in the alehouse."

Akul stared at Tierre.

"Take it," Larin whispered.

Akul looked like he'd just eaten rotten fish. "Very well." He stabbed a giant finger into Tierre's chest. "You stay out of the alehouse when I am in it."

Tierre's eyes narrowed, and he pointed to Larin. "He leaves now."

Larin turned away from Akul's sorrowful look, grabbed his coat, and walked to the door, ignoring fifty pairs of eyes on his back. With a deep breath, he tried to capture this last image of the alehouse. Despite all its warts, the temple had been his second home, a place he'd spent most of his waking moments. A last refuge away from Oarl, one where some few would still talk to him. Now, it was gone forever. He struggled to absorb the enormity of this.

A pair of female arms slipped smoothly around his waist, and a soft kiss planted itself just below his right ear. The kiss was long and sweet, and he felt the blood rush to his face. Head spinning, he turned to see Naela smiling down at him.

"Thank you." Her hair was disheveled, a bruise marked her chin, and she held a bloody towel she'd been using to wipe the floor. Still, she looked more beautiful than ever.

Larin struggled to speak but suddenly found no voice. He looked around the alehouse and saw every man watching him, envious.

Tierre cast an imperious stare from across the room. "Do not touch that one!"

Naela's face was defiant, and she didn't look at the High Priest. "I won't forget it, Larin," she whispered.

Larin smiled and nodded. "I'd do it all over again," he said.

As he exited the temple into the falling curtain of white, the distant alehouse voices followed him like a mocking school child. He stopped, shin-deep in the snow, listening to the low whistle of the wind and feeling the cold pinpricks melt on his neck. The street was dark and empty, its white blanket tinged with Spellgiver's faint blue glow.

He drew his dagger and placed the cold steel against his neck. Onie was gone, he'd never step foot in the temple again, and he'd just made an enemy out of the Morphasti, the fastest growing power in the Wormpile. His isolation was deepening, a well of blackness from which he'd never escape. He concentrated on the icy blade lying flat against his Adam's apple, imagining bleeding his life into the snow. After a long moment, he returned the dagger to its sheath. He stumbled into a deserted alleyway toward home, its second-floor windows dark as his soul.

He turned a corner and there, at the end of an alley, was the brown-robed man from the alehouse. Larin stood in numb shock for a split second, then whirled around.

"Stop and turn around," the man barked, in an accent Larin couldn't place.

Larin halted and turned slowly around, like a marionette in a corner puppet show. His arms were pinned to his sides, and his toes seemed to sprout roots that burrowed deep into the earth.

The man considered him a moment, face dark under his hood. He limped toward Larin through the snow, and Larin's eyes widened—*that limp* . . .

The brown-robed man stopped three feet away, pulling back his hood to reveal a grim expression. Brown hair curled over a thin, pockmarked face angling toward a cleft chin. He was definitely not Tanbari, though Larin couldn't place his origins.

Despite raw fear, Larin couldn't stop the words from escaping. "Well, now I've met two of them."

Stony eyes bored into him. "What nonsense do you speak?"

"You're Haraf's servant, right? The one with King Galin's disease? I've met one of the other personas, and I've seen a third." Larin struggled to move his arms to no avail, feeling the cold seep into his bones. He swallowed slowly as the man approached him.

"What do you know of Haraf?" Something in his tone promised imminent danger, and Larin's budding request for release died on his lips. He forced himself to breathe.

"I know that Haraf said three words before he was banished to the Gray Lands. I know I've been spouting those words all my life. And I know that you're Haraf's servant, and you have King Galin's disease."

The man circled around him, features cast in blue shadows from Spellgiver's light. If it was possible to read surprise on that impassive face, Larin thought he saw it. The silence stretched forever, and Larin ventured more, trying to keep any part of his body moving.

"I don't understand what possible use Haraf could have with me. This curse has brought me only pain. What could I ever do for the Demon Lord?"

The man watched him somberly, and Larin had the surreal feeling he wasn't wholly present, as if part of him occupied another existence. "Yet, surely Haraf has picked you. I've been searching long for the one who will fight this war. I've felt a force emanating from this part of the city, this temple. It wasn't until I heard those words that I knew who it was."

"I'm not going to fight any war."

"You will. You've started that very war tonight."

Larin's eyes began to tear. "Look, can you at least let me move my arms? I'm going to freeze to death."

The man waved a hand, and Larin's arms came unglued.

Grateful for sudden freedom, Larin wiped his frozen face with his coat sleeve. "How do you do that?" He sniffed. "I mean, work magic without saying a single Lyrashi word. Not even violet-sash mages do that . . ."

"The magic of the Masters needs no help from the language of the six-legged ones."

Larin squinted, trying to read his wooden face. "Six-legged ones? You mean the Old Gods? That makes no sense. Lyrashi comes from the Carvers, not the Eldegod."

The man remained motionless, and a freezing wind rippled through his hair. "Ignorant boy from an ignorant land. The language you twist to your own ends comes from the race that spawned the Old Gods. The Masters work their power in different ways."

"The Masters . . ."

"You call them Demons. It is for them you fight."

Larin looked up defiantly. "I fight for no one."

"You will fight. You cannot avoid your fate."

"Fate? So you're saying I can't choose for myself?"

His eyes gleamed. "I'd forgotten the straight-line thinking so popular in this corner of the world." He donned his hood again, throwing his face into darkness. "Fate and free will are no enemies. They are two halves of the same circle."

"And if I choose to resist fate?"

"You will choose, of your own free will, to follow your fate. Man's free will becomes his destiny."

Larin shook his head, trying to clear it from this strange logic. "I'd be pretty useless to your master. I'm almost magicless; I can barely light a candle at five paces on Apex Day."

"Your Seeker will guide you. She will develop your skills."

"She? How will I find her?"

The man said nothing, and Larin breathed deeply, searching for a new tack. "Listen—"

"B'neikarian."

"Listen, B'neikarian, even if I could help, I think Haraf's made a mistake. I'm not really that evil."

Dark eyes stared from beneath the hood. "Haraf requires no such thing. Evil flows from the Old Gods."

"But Demons are no light fairies either," Larin said, shivering from the cold. "Sometimes they possess the souls of their summoners and other times spark wars for their own amusement. I think that qualifies."

The man leaned back, his face hidden. "What you see today was not always so. The race from which the Old Gods sprang once ruled this place with a power beyond anything you can comprehend. They moved worlds, bound together existences that were never meant to touch each other. In so doing, they came across others and destroyed them."

"Like the Demons?"

"If you are to serve the Masters, you must learn their true name. Avillian. And the race that once ruled this world, they who birthed the Old Gods, was called the Hwenaris in their time."

Larin stared. "The Carvers . . ." His mouth opened, then shut, realizing he was learning history that had stumped scholars since the birth of man. No one knew whether any relationship existed between the Carvers and the Eldegod; it was a point of debate that stretched back into the mists of creation. Silence filled the alley, broken only by the sound of a small creature scrabbling up a wall into a warm attic.

The brown-robed man watched him carefully. "To serve their purposes, this offshoot of the Carvers—they whom you call *Eldegod*—banished the Avillian to an existence with no material essence, no energy from the creator, no matter to manipulate. Nothing."

"The Gray Lands . . ."

"Yes. The Masters have existed in the Gray Lands for millennia with nothing material to feed their senses. They have become insane. This is what you perceive as evil."

Larin stared. "Innocent or not, why release an insane godlike race who'll wreak havoc on the world?"

"When one puts a lid on a boiling kettle, one can imagine the water no longer boils. Yet still it does, and if the lid is not removed, the water will rise up and scald. So it is with an injustice of this magnitude. The rage of a race of immortals confined to such hell leaks out into the world we know. It feeds the Old Gods, moves dark tribes across the vast plains to the east, destroys empires. The energy of fury flows into the world of men, enabling Morphat and its ilk to infect your societies like a cancer. The water is boiling over."

Larin breathed deeply. "Morphat hasn't gotten too far yet. Just a few mouth breathers tipping over a statue." But he knew it for a lie as it escaped his lips. Something had changed tonight.

The man leaned forward. "For two thousand years, Tanbar has been the most powerful empire in the human lands. It has resisted the Lidath in the north, Seridor in the south, and the fire-magic tribes of the east, all of whom worship the Eldegod. But Tanbar's time of greatness is ending. This end is something you will see in your lifetime."

Nervous fear crawled up Larin's spine, but none of this made him any more prone to release Haraf from his gray prison. "From everything I've read, freeing Haraf will bring forth an age of chaos and destruction."

"After what happened tonight, you still believe your temple teachings?"

Larin gritted his teeth in anger as he remembered his night. "No. But don't think that makes me Haraf's puppet. I'm not some dizzy-eyed acolyte, I've studied history outside of the temple's books. The earliest Lyrashi carvings describe how the world will be destroyed when Haraf is set free."

The man's hood shifted, revealing a stony face tinged by the moon's blue light. "It is unclear what will happen once Haraf is free," he whispered. "But it is an absolute certainty that if the six-legged ones triumph, mankind will suffer a slavery so horrible, the very stones will cry out from the earth."

"Neither slavery nor death sound good to me. At least Morphat will let us live."

A light wind whistled through the alley, causing a shutter in an abandoned second-story window to bang against the stone wall. Larin suddenly felt the cold penetrate to his bones and desperately longed to be home.

"Naive child, there are some things far worse than death," the man hissed. Without warning, he seized Larin's shoulders and spoke a Word, one unlike any Lyrashi word Larin had ever heard. Larin felt a strange shift, followed by a sick feeling in his stomach.

"You will know your enemy," B'neikarian whispered.

Larin struggled against the violent nausea, then looked up with fury. "Your other persona is a lover of children!"

The man stared, and Larin felt an unrelenting, excruciating pain in every part of his body. His knees buckled, and he fell to the snow, wanting to scream, but biting his lip as hard as he could. He wouldn't give this creature the pleasure. He gasped as the pain faded, and he tried to move his feet with no success.

Larin spat, and the spittle landed a few inches from the feet of the brown-robed man. He braced himself for another wave of pain, but the man only nodded, as if in approval.

"It's said Haraf's servants are bold." He limped backward, never taking his eyes off Larin. "Pleasant dreams." With that, he turned the corner, and Larin felt the paralysis leave his legs. Larin sprang to his feet and ran to the corner but was not surprised when the alley turned up empty, save for a few drifting flakes of snow and two rows of dark windows. He looked down and saw that the footprints in the snow disappeared immediately after the corner's turn.

In numb shock, Larin stood there a full minute, watching his breath rise in clouds. In all the legends, the line between hero and villain was clearly drawn, a wide boulevard separating good and evil. Yet this war sprang from an ancient enmity between two evils, both of which regarded humanity as mere pawns. Somehow, he was supposed to fight for one side—he, a Wormpile street urchin who couldn't even defeat a group of street thugs, let alone a malevolent six-legged god.

Finally, the cold got the better of him, and Larin turned away. He tromped through the thick snow, wondering, as he never had before, who he really was.

XII

For the first time in days, Meidan forgot his fear. Something was watching him, and curiosity focused his attention inward, away from the obsessive dread that had been his companion in this pit of blackness. He wasn't sure how he knew, yet it was certain as the damp air he breathed. Whiffs of a foreign thought here, hints of strange feelings there, a certainty that the input of his senses traveled to two observers. He cradled his head, causing thick metal wristbands to rub his raw skin. He tried to touch the presence in his mind. Was it a casual observer, interested in a dispassionate account of what was to come? Or a mind of darkness, eagerly anticipating the sweet sickness in his future? Inward reflection made his head throb, forcing a reluctant return to the present. The unimaginable present.

He shifted position on the cold stones, feeling a wetness from he knew not what. It seeped into his cloth pants, raising an unbidden delirium that he'd be in for a scolding from Malassa. He started to laugh, but it was a laugh of madness, and he stopped himself.

The stone pit stank. It stank of feces, urine, but most of all it stank of the fear that brought them forth. Quiet sobbing echoed from various directions in this cavernous shaft, accompanied by the occasional rustle of chains and low murmur of hopeless prayer. The sounds drifted bodiless from the ether—darkness was almost absolute, with the only faint light streaming from cruel windows near the ceiling, over fifty feet up. The one clearly visible object was the platform that had brought them here, now suspended by chains at the top of the shaft, cold metal gleaming in the upper window's faint light. Suspended and awaiting descent to the stone floor, from where it would send them to destiny.

The thought of mounting the platform brought a return of stomach-churning fear, and Meidan desperately searched for his watcher. *Can you save me? Oh for all the gods' sakes, please save me* . . . The plea burned in his mind, and he felt his stomach rise into his gorge. He was met only with the silence of his own terror, and he heard himself sob. He bit his lip before it became uncontrollable, trying to focus upon the final glory. For whatever happened, he'd be the god's chosen—at his side forever.

Love drove the rituals, or so it was said. When humans first formed on the earth, the Eldegod, native spirits of the land, saw that they were good and gave them fruit from the trees, meat from the forests. Yet the creation of humanity had been two-fold—from the descending fire also came the Aevnari, the New Gods, commanded by Emja, evil spirits whose lifeblood was power and greed, and who took humanity's form. Despite all the Eldegod had done, the new race worshipped the Aevnari, for the Eldegod could not pretend to be human, and humanity could not abide by monstrous gods. Thus, humanity turned away from their protectors, rejecting the Eldegod to worship the cruel, cunning beings who assumed their own forms. The Eldegod host had become so distraught by humanity's betrayal that they retreated to live in the skies, far from the race they had nurtured.

The lessons spoke of what came after: over time, some humans saw the good in the Eldegod, seeking to regain their favor. Yet the Eldegod king Morphat required surety before his host offered their hearts again. He devised the rituals, that those who would accept his love could prove their devotion and pay for their people's past sins. The chosen were fortunate, for they would stand by Morphat's side forevermore.

Yet Meidan could not fathom why he was here. He was no unbeliever—the rituals were for the conquered races, not for such as him. Many among the early Chandor had been graced long ago, that their descendants might bask in the Eldegod's love forever. Yet rededication should be unnecessary now, after the early submission of his people. Then why him? His vision swam with Malassa's stricken expression as the red acolytes first entered his chamber, and he gripped his chains so hard his hands turned white.

A few minutes of calm, slow breathing exercises stilled his panic, and with slow resolve, he focused inward again. His only possible salvation would come from the Watcher, whomever it was. It was imperative he find out more.

Ignoring the sobs and stink of his prison, he began probing his mind's inner reaches, looking for clues from his observer. It was like chasing a rabbit through a forest—hints of movement here, evidence of its passing there, but when he looked directly, it was gone. Yet as he probed further, he became certain the observer wasn't hiding from him. It seemed—confused somehow, as if it didn't know why it was here. His spirits fell; the remote chance his watcher might be a purposeful savior had faded into the blackness of his prison. Still he probed, for he'd nothing better to do in this place.

He breathed deeply, drifting to an earlier time. A time when those of his class had no fear of their own leaders, when only the conquered ones could be chosen. Then he searched his mind further and chose a specific memory, as if plucking a cherry from his garden tree. It was a sweet memory of family and comfort, his daughter turning in eager anticipation of Malassa's approval before jumping into the lake by their home. The image brought him his first smile in days, though it froze as he detected the Watcher at the periphery of his soul.

He continued dwelling on the peaceful memory, probing the Watcher with a more subtle touch, yet without turning direct attention its way. He sensed innocence, almost—youth. He also sensed foreignness, as if the Watcher spoke a different language, came from elsewhere. Most of all, he detected curiosity and dread—dread that was a reflection of his own.

The mirror image of his fear again brought the rising panic, and he struggled to maintain the long-gone image in his mind. Don't go away, Watcher.

Why was it acceptable when the conquered were chosen?

Surprise and shock made him start, losing his image, and with it, all contact with the Watcher. He cursed, clenching his wrist chains in frustration—his first direct communication with the Watcher, ruined. He tried to still his beating heart, looking up at the narrow rays of light streaming from the upper windows. After a moment, he closed his eyes, placing hands on his lap as he willed himself to resummon the happy image. Slowly, he felt the calm return and, eventually, the barest hint of the Watcher.

A deep-throated roar from the windows above shook the pit to its foundations and broke his concentration. It was a roar that could only come from a hundred thousand throats, the primal sound of a giant bloodthirsty beast. It had begun.

Around him, moans and high-pitched jabbering greeted the crowd's roar, and from somewhere a dripping sound, as another wretch soiled himself. He struggled to keep his own fear in check, willing his heart rate to slow.

A harsh light on the ceiling above indicated that the door at the top of the shaft was opening, and he looked up to see four silhouetted figures mount the platform. Something was odd about them—as if deformed—but the glare stifled his vision. Then the door closed and sounds of grinding metal echoed from stone walls, greeted by moans from the blackness—the platform had begun its descent. He turned his gaze upward, squinting against the harsh light of the windows.

The platform descended on thick chains, sounds of sliding metal and grinding gears filling the cavern. As it passed through the window's light, he saw four guards in Morphat's red and black standing at each corner, watching their descent behind horned metal masks. They faded into blackness as the platform descended below the window's light, and a few moments later he heard clanging of metal against the stone floor. A sharp crack of boots on stones immediately followed as the guards stepped off the platform.

"*Ahsun ifkar!*" One shouted, as he yanked someone's chains in the darkness. Meidan scowled; how things had changed. The tongue of the minority Parbani had become the language of the rituals, but how this had happened was beyond him. Somehow, this dirty, illiterate tribe had infested the priesthood while they all slept. Where was the flowing Chandor of the true conquerors? He felt the Watcher react to this thought, and he started.

What do you say, Watcher? What is your game?

Soft clinks of metal and quiet sobbing drifted through the cavern as the guards unchained prisoners from the wall, then rechained them on the unseen platform. He steeled himself, but eventually the noises stopped, and after a moment, the cavern again echoed with the sound of sliding chains as the platform began its ascent. Relief warred with disappointment—a few more hours alone with his thoughts.

He watched the small visible section of coiling chains, and eventually the platform reached the first light, long shadows giving way to gray silhouettes as it came under the window's direct glare. The heavy door opened, flooding the platform with light, and Meidan squinted as the troop of prisoners marched through the doorway to oblivion. The rear guard pulled the heavy door shut, and the top of the cavern was thrust back into semidarkness. Meidan turned his gaze away.

He tried to calm himself again, focusing inward to reach his Watcher, but it proved more difficult than before. His nerves were shot, and the roar of the crowd as the prisoners mounted the central stage ruined any last attempt to relax.

The next hours were difficult. The ritual chanting of the crowd as each prisoner mounted the final steps brought memories of his time as an observer in the Apex festivities. What had been his thoughts, so long ago? Had he considered the unfortunate wretches who'd been chosen? A moment of honest introspection told him no—the Chosen were honored by the gods' love, the select few who'd stand by their side forevermore. Anyway, in earlier years, only the captured Kulathi had been chosen. The gods had provided Seridor with victory after victory against the tribes of the east, and the ritual honors were critical to ensure an unbroken string of conquest that brought Seridor's might to the edges of the eastern deserts. Those newly conquered tribes must offer themselves up to the rituals, that their people eventually bask in the gods' love. Thus, he had shouted, "*Aoord!*" with the crowd, the word that in the gods' language meant "pain."

In later years, he had seen some members of the less recently conquered tribes in the ranks of the Chosen, those that had thought themselves integrated into the body politic of Seridor. Still he'd explained it away; there were some who couldn't bring themselves to worship the true gods, and only the rituals could bring them peace. Yet this year they had taken him, from the people of Chandor. One of the three tribes of the conquerors. How had it happened? For the thousandth time since he'd arrived in this pit, Meidan racked his brain for what he might have said, done, to gain notice by the priesthood.

After two hours of ritual chanting, cheers, and the distant shouts of the priests, the noise streaming from the upper windows died away, and he knew Morphat had received his gift. The priesthood would alternate now, after a short break while the crowd bought honey treats and spiced meat, or attended one of the festive magic displays so easy on this Apex day. He felt stupid, delirious envy; he was not even honored enough to be chosen by Morphat, king of gods. Instead, he would serve a lesser god.

The door at the top of the shaft opened again, flooding the platform with light. Moans issued from the blackness as the platform descended, though fewer than before. Despite his resolve, Meidan felt a rush of terror at the sight of the horned, masked guards, now in Bekath's yellow and black, as they passed through the window's light. At the clang of metal on stone, an involuntary sob escaped his lips, though he choked it off. Dignity. He must maintain dignity.

Sounds of prisoners being unshackled from their wall chains drifted out of the darkness. He felt a presence above, though he saw nothing but a silhouette of curving horns as they blocked the upper window's faint light. His chains were unfastened from the wall, and with a sudden motion that jarred his bones, he was yanked to his feet. Wordlessly, the guard pulled him through darkness to the platform, and the clink of his chains as they were fastened to the prisoner in front sent another rush of fear through his core. He had no idea how the guards could see well enough to perform these tasks, but he assumed it was a simple magic for the priesthood.

The sounds of other prisoners being similarly chained continued for a few minutes, before grinding metal and an upward jerk indicated that the platform had begun its ascent. *Watcher, now is the time. Oh gods, please help me.* He felt a hint of some emotion from the Watcher—was it sympathy? Yet it was a helpless feeling, and with a sinking heart, Meidan knew the Watcher could do nothing.

As the platform reached the window's light, he saw he was third in line and, based on previous witnessed rituals, tried to calculate how long he'd have to stand on the central stage before his turn.

The platform ground to a halt, and he caught a glimpse of crowds and blue skies through the small windows before the metal door swung open. The blast of light was overwhelming after two days of darkness, and he clenched his eyes shut. They stepped off the platform into a narrow hallway painted with graphic images of the rituals, as if any of them could be unaware of what was to come.

After a moment they reached another door, and though it was windowless, he knew that beyond it lay his destiny. *Watcher, watch well. Observe and record what you see today.*

The door swung open, and the full daylight and roar of the crowd slammed into him like a hurricane. Deep-throated chants of "*Aoord!*" warred with thundering vibrations of steel drums and high-pitched bloodlust screams from the front rows, creating a wall of force that almost knocked him backward. The terror almost buckled his knees as they shuffled onto a stage shaking with fury, and he looked upward to avoid heaving the minute contents of his stomach.

In the sky hung the giant blue moon Spellgiver in all its glory, today at its zenith. He fixated on its blue oceans and the rivers traversing its landmasses like giant veins, trying to quiet his stomach. Spellgiver was enormous, and if there were any doubt that this was Apex day, the moon's proximity would have put it to rest. It was the day the powers of men, and gods would be at their peak.

Bringer of magic, can you save me? he pleaded silently to Spellgiver, as the crowd began ritual chanting. Yet he knew he'd find no help from the sky— as with human magic, the nearness of the moon brought the gods' power to a crescendo, the very power which brought them their gift today.

Bekath's High Priest climbed the platform to wild cheers from the crowd, and Meidan turned away from his contemplation of the skies. They'd done a good job cleaning the dais, and new cloths had been spread out over the entire surface. Even the metal frame on the dais had been wiped clean. Its four hanging manacles gleamed in the sun, providing no hint of the past two hours' activities. At the edges of the platform, four brightly garbed blood-clowns danced and levitated gold balls, to great delight from the children in the crowd. High-pitched laughter accompanied their every motion, as parents lifted their children high on their shoulders to catch a clown's pointing finger.

The priest ascended the dais and stared outward at the sea of humanity. He raised his hands, and the tempo of the steel drums slowed. The crowd quieted, and the blood-clowns ceased their antics, stepping back from the platform's edge.

"You in the front rows, examine your hearts!" the priest yelled. "Bekath hears your enthusiastic screams, but not your respect for the Chosen. My children, be not malicious, but envious, for Bekath's chosen stand by his side for eternity."

Duly chastened, a few murmurs swept the crowds, and they bowed their heads. Within moments, a chorus from the Chant of Gifting rose up with one voice, as the city sought to bathe in his presence. Bekath's priest hung his head low at their song and, after a minute, held up his hand.

"Bekath holds you in his claw and judges your worth!" he yelled into the crowd in Chandor.

From the multitudes came the answer: "We serve him, we obey."

"Bekath's summons the unbeliever to feel his love!"

"Only his love can save them," the throngs returned.

"Bekath protects us through time!"

"We are his servants. The unbeliever is cleansed," came the crowd's roar.

"Before you are Bekath's chosen. They will stand by his side in eternity!"

The crowd dutifully began chanting "Aoord!" to the rising tempo of the steel drums.

Then the priest began ritual chanting in Parbani, and Meidan finally tore his eyes away from the ceremony, casting a desperate gaze at the city he thought he knew. Buildings shimmered in his vision like a horrible dream as he stared through the double vision of wet eyes.

Kaman was a city of temples. Everywhere, their stone towers and pointed roofs rose above the surrounding clay structures like cliffs over anthills. Nearest was Hashinne's temple, its smooth walls lined with dark windows that punctuated the monotony of the yellow sandstone. Further out was the temple of Neelzib, and further still the temples of Bekath, Agurat, and many others, towers and giant walls clearly visible against the squalid cityscape. By far the largest was the house of Morphat. The temple's distant spires and pointed roofs rose high above the rest of Kaman, a statue of the six-legged god at its apex, gazing outward with an incomprehensible expression. By contrast, Meidan could not even see the king's palace, which was hidden behind taller buildings. The flat-roofed houses of the people flowed between the magnificent temples like a river of mud and clay, narrow alleys bisecting the sea of straight rooflines to converge on the boulevards connecting the temples. Colors of clay and sandstone pervaded all, materials dredged by eastern slaves from the nearby foothills to construct every part of the city.

Between the stage and the temple of Hashinne, a hundred thousand people now stood in the hot sun, trying to catch a glimpse of the rituals. Food vendor carts weaved through the crowd, and colorful tents poked above the throngs, some housing magic shows, as magicians displayed their enhanced magical abilities on this Apex day. Throughout the crowd, he saw adults with children on their shoulders and wondered that the horror of this had never struck him. Out among the throngs, he knew there were others like him—those who'd never completely accepted the rituals, even if they believed them necessary. Yet the gods demanded obedience, and sympathy was a trait of the weak. The weak would be the Chosen.

In the front twenty rows stood the Henerami, extended families of the various priestly castes and the true power in Kaman. Some eyed the prisoners with malevolent glee, but most closed their eyes as they chanted along with the Bekath's priest. They swayed and sang, a few with hands in the air, as the steel drums thundered a slow rhythm. Some waved the metal pokers of the rituals as they swayed in closed-eye abandon, while others held their hands open to the skies, supplicating Bekath to touch their flesh.

The drums abruptly stopped, and Meidan felt blood drain from his face. It would begin now. The priest of Bekath turned to the first prisoner in line and spoke a word of ugliness in the Parbani language. Several helmeted guards left the side of the stage, and one approached the man. Wordlessly, he unlocked the prisoner from the chain and pushed him forward.

As the chanting stopped, the blood-clowns sprang into action again, and one cartwheeled to the prisoner as he shuffled to the dais, rubbing his painted eyes with great abandon. When the prisoner stumbled on the first step, the clown twisted his own foot and spun around wildly. This provoked scattered youthful laughter within the crowds, though barely audible above the screams of their elders.

The prisoner was shackled arm and leg into the metal frame on the dais, and the frame was tilted upward so that he faced the sky at an angle, arms and legs stretched out. The High Priest of Bekath spoke a word of power, and Meidan saw sudden smoke from the other side of the frame. The fire's container wasn't visible, but he knew exactly what it was.

The priest turned to the crowd. "The soul of the unbeliever must pass through the gate," he yelled, now again in Chandor.

"Those who cannot see him must not see," chanted the crowd.

"His sight will be filled with Bekath's glory. Before you the unbeliever!" The priest pointed at the manacled prisoner in the tilted frame.

"*Aoord!*" screamed the crowd.

With that, the priest pulled the hot poker from the fire and plunged it into the prisoner's left eye. The man jerked in his chairs and screamed, a primal bloodcurdling sound of pain and desolation, rising above the delighted yells of the Henerami in the front rows. One of the blood-clowns mimicked popping his eye out of its socket, and the strange stew of children's laughter mixed with the prisoner's screams spun Meidan's head wildly. In sick terror, he cast his eyes downward, but horrified fascination returned his gaze to the nightmare above.

When the priest shoved the hot poker into the prisoner's other eye, the woman in front of him collapsed, and Meidan struggled to remain standing as tugging arm chains pulled him downward. The nearest guard pulled her head up by the hair and administered a tonic. Within seconds her eyes were open, and she slowly rose as the guard moved back into position. Meidan stepped back in a daze, trying to avoid a blood-clown who had collapsed beside him, to great amusement of the crowd.

With a final flourish, the High Priest of Bekath spoke a Parbani word, then slit the throat of the prisoner with a knife he'd pulled from the other side of the frame. Blood spurted for several feet, and the man shook uncontrollably as the priest bent to retrieve the vial of Temrissan. He poured the green liquid into the gash at the man's throat and stepped back.

Temrissan was that most cruel of magic tonics. Poured into a bleeding wound, it replaced the blood while simultaneously enhancing the sensation of pain. It eventually killed its victim, as the organs were eaten away. Yet it also prolonged life long beyond its normal expiration, forcing a slow painful death as the liquid circulated through the body, replacing blood and stimulating nerve endings. From previous rituals, Meidan knew it would take twenty minutes for the man to die now, even with a slit throat. Twenty minutes of excruciating pain.

As he watched the prisoner's agonizing death, he felt a touch of foreignness in his mind. He searched within himself. *Watcher?* Yet the Watcher was curled into a tiny ball in his mind's corner, and he knew this new entity was something else entirely. It carried a slow simmer of malevolence, an ancient evil seeking to bathe in juices of fear. Then he saw it in his mind's eye, and his knees buckled.

The god. Bekath.

It infused his mind, touching here, probing there, enjoying the heightened state of panic its presence induced. It pulled at the levers of his memories, bringing forth images of pain and death even as he tried to ignore the slow expiration of the man on the dais. *Great one, tell me I'll live by your side for eternity,* he whimpered silently. With a sinking heart, Meidan felt its indifference to his beliefs and loyalty.

In that moment, he knew it had all been a lie.

His childhood lessons—myths fed a gullible nation to justify their deity's malicious pleasures. For only pain and fear fed the gods. He swirled into an endless pit of hopelessness, the horror before him wavering in and out of his vision.

His death, his pain.

Meaningless.

From somewhere, the beginnings of anger rose from the Watcher. Where Bekath had opened a memory of death, the Watcher closed it. Where he felt panic, the Watcher calmed him, slowing his heart. The Watcher had learned to traverse his mind's pathways, and with its assistance, Meidan felt a slow hardening of resolve. Fear was what Bekath craved—with the Watcher's help, he would deny the god its pleasures.

As Meidan's determination strengthened, the god was pushed back, and with rising hope, he felt its workings blocked at every turn. With sweet relief, the god's manipulations finally halted, and Meidan staggered forward, exhaling loudly. He peered inward, seeing that Bekath had shifted its attention to the Watcher and was now studying it with intense curiosity.

As he joined forces with the Watcher, his mind filled with fury: fury at the gods for their cruelty, fury at the crowds for their blindness. It was a fury that left no room for fear or doubt, and with a giant explosion of anger, they flung Bekath from Meidan's mind as if it were an old piece of clothing. Shocked, Meidan's face cracked into a rare smile, one of liberation, and for the first time in days, pride.

Thank you, Watcher. Thank you.

The Watcher said nothing, yet he felt its presence as it continued to create a shield around his spirit. From that point forward, his fear was muted, and he faced the coming horror with a resolute anger that strengthened his spine.

The man on the dais eventually, mercifully, died, and the High Priest turned his attentions to the next prisoner. Meidan stepped to the front as the woman was unfastened and led away, staring at Bekath's priest. Did they know it was all a sham?

Screams of joy from the front rows mingled with screams of pain from the new prisoner as the tortures of the rituals were administered again. The dancing of the blood-clowns intertwined with the heavy beat of steel drums to create a spinning, surreal kaleidoscope of horror. The priest's robe was covered in blood, and it dripped down the steps of the dais and pooled in the clear space between the stage and the crowd. When the woman died twenty minutes later, Meidan faced his own death with a proud anger, shaking off the guard's grip as he mounted the stairs to the dais. He climbed slowly to avoid slipping on blood.

As he was manacled into the frame, Bekath's High Priest peered at him with a bored expression. Blood spattered the priest's black beard, dripping from the dozens of metal squares piercing his cheeks. His helmet's yellow and black jewels glinted in the bright sun, and through the fog of disbelief, Meidan wondered if those streaks of sunlight would be his last sight.

The blood-speckled beard twisted slightly as Meidan's manacles snapped into place. "Travel by his side in eternity," the priest said flatly. Meidan saw it on his face, the final, horrible confirmation: the priests believed none of it. They tortured only for the gods' pleasure.

Meidan spat, and it landed in the priest's beard. "Your god was defeated by a child and a terrified prisoner!"

The priest's eyes widened, and he slowly wiped away the spittle. The ritual had started, and he reluctantly broke his stare to face the crowd. Was it Meidan's imagination, or did the man's voice break midway through the Chant of Gifting?

The pain as his left eye was seared by fire was intense, but with the Watcher's help, the worst of it was shunted away behind a cold wall of fury. He managed to swallow his scream: his only small victory.

"Your god was discarded like dung!" Meidan yelled loudly, just before his right eye crackled and sizzled under the hot poker's touch. He hoped those in the front row could hear—they expected screaming, yet he gave them defiant curses. A grim satisfaction took root behind the delirious and rapidly spinning darkness of his new blindness. Agony coursed through his being, but the Watcher helped him deflect the major load of pain to another corner of his mind. *Bekath, you have me twenty more minutes. You'll not have me in death.* Whether his defiance arose from the Watcher or from his own mind was unclear, but it was liberating. In a perverse way, wracked by pain and eyes seared into scarred flesh, he felt better than he had in days.

When they cut his throat, he could no longer utter defiant curses, or anything. Yet it was a blessing in disguise, for when they administered the Temrissan he wanted to scream but could not. As he hung from manacles, wracked by pain, kept artificially alive by a magic elixir of highest evil, he felt the Watcher with him, guiding him.

You can go now, Watcher. Don't die with me.

But the Watcher stayed, shunting away the worst of the pain, and he was grateful. He tried to hasten his expiration, but the Temrissan would not let him, the very action that stimulated his nerves also keeping him conscious.

After a moment, he once again felt the presence of Bekath, probing, as Meidan now realized it must do with all dying prisoners, seeking its pleasures in a mind wracked by agony. Together with the Watcher, he created a sphere of resolve, upon which Bekath could find no purchase. After a moment, the god faded away.

He slipped to near unconsciousness many times, but each time, the

Temrissan brought him back to bask in pain, though muted by the Watcher. Myriad images cascaded through his shock and delirium, mostly of Malassa and the children. As the Temrissan faded, and as he felt final, merciful darkness creep through his veins, the last of his mind's light illuminated the Watcher's only question:

Why was it acceptable when the conquered were chosen?

With a great feat of will, he pushed back the darkness a second, struggling to answer this one question. A last, dying gasp of gratitude to the Watcher.

It was never acceptable, Watcher. Oh gods, it was never acceptable. He struggled hard against death, pulling together his mind's loosening strands for one final effort. *Whoever you are, end this madness.*

Then he relaxed and let blackness course through his body.

Yet screaming continued to pierce the darkness, and he moaned in agony. Gods, when would death come? Still, the screaming would not stop. In a distant land, a door burst open.

Larin shot forward in bed, eyes wide open as Akul stood at the now dented door.

"What in Emja's name . . . ?" Akul quickly scanned the room, then stared at Larin.

"It—I—" Sheets soaking, body bathed in cold sweat, Larin struggled to speak, blackest terror gripping his soul. His voice was hoarse, and he knew he'd been screaming at the top of his lungs.

"A nightmare?" Akul wore a disgusted look and his shoulders relaxed. He took another look about the room. "Larin, you're not two anymore."

"Temrissan," Larin whispered.

Akul froze, and even in the somber shades of night, Larin could see his uncle's face had gone pale. From the street below came the low chirping of crickets. "What do you know of Temrissan?" Akul said softly.

"And Bekath." Larin shook with emotion, and he stared straight forward at some distant vista of horror. "I touched Bekath."

Akul stood for a moment without speaking, then walked to the main living area, dragged in a chair, and sat down. He mumbled a quick lighting spell, and the oil lantern next to Larin's bed flickered and lit, throwing long shadows about the room.

"Tell me everything. Leave nothing out."

Voice shaking, Larin relayed the full contents of his dream, describing Kaman and the rituals in great detail, including his host's attempts to communicate. Akul forced him to repeat his battle with Bekath, but otherwise let him finish without interruption. When Larin was done, he sat back in silence, hard face cast in the lantern's flickering light.

Larin exhaled loudly. "Remember I told you about my conversation with the brown-robed man in the alley? B'neikarian? His last words to me:

'You will know your enemy' and 'Pleasant dreams.'"

Akul rubbed his head. "Aye, this was no dream—your description of Kaman is true, and your memory of the rituals is . . . accurate." His face appeared stricken behind the shadows.

Despite fading shock, Larin had the presence of mind to wonder at this statement. "How would you know?"

"Someday, Larin. Not tonight."

Larin nodded, satisfied. Akul's response was his first admission that he owed Larin a description of his prior life someday. Yet tonight he was too shaken to dwell on this tear in Akul's cloak, and he voiced the question burning in his mind.

"In my dream, it was Apex day, yet Apex is still three months away. But I communicated with Meidan as if he were right beside me . . ."

Akul looked deeply disturbed. "I think it was a time-flow binding."

Larin had heard about time-flow magic, one of the more bizarre subcategories of the discipline of binding, but it'd never made sense to him. If it were truly a time binding, Meidan's life could have been in the past, or yet to come. Of all magical disciplines, it required the most power. Just who was B'neikarian?

"I don't understand. If the dream is in the future, what if I change something now so it never happens?"

"Questions like that will make your head hurt. Ask a mage." Akul looked down at a paper seal of khald in his left hand, and Larin realized what he'd been doing when the screams started. He let it pass; the horror was too fresh in his mind.

"The man—Meidan—he called me 'Watcher.' But I didn't know I wasn't part of him, at least not at first. I really thought I would die." Larin took in a deep breath. "I feel like I did die. I felt my mind go black."

Akul's eyes were sympathetic, but he stayed silent.

"And Meidan seemed like a normal fellow, someone you'd see at the alehouse pounding ales with Ruldir. But he hated the other races, and he'd watched the rituals himself. He thought nothing of watching the torture-killing as long as it was someone from another tribe."

Akul said nothing for a minute. He dabbed his finger into the khald and touched his tongue. Finally he looked up, the bags beneath his eyes visible even in the low light.

"You're still young, Larin, but I think you grew a little tonight. Listen well: all it takes for men to perform evil is to convince themselves others are worthy of their hatred." Akul shook the paper seal and emptied the contents onto his fingertips. "Next time you're at the market, see if you can find a Seridorian history book. You'll find it—enlightening."

"I don't want to know any more," Larin said, biting his lip.

"You'd do well to learn more. Learn how Morphat's priesthood drove wedges between the Seridor's conquering races until they had the tribes at each other's throats. Learn how they created a kingdom based on race hatred, forever at the edge of civil war. How they use terror and betrayal to prune Seridor's power structure until it became filled with sadistic monsters at every level."

Larin said nothing, and Akul shook his head. "Larin, we both know your outbursts have marked you for something. I don't know why Haraf has chosen you, but this night I have much greater certainty that the Old Gods are indeed your enemies. As they are mine." Akul rose, favoring him with an inexplicable expression. "Life is wasted without a battle to fight, something to believe in." His eyes flicked to the empty paper khald seal in his left hand, and suddenly it seemed he talked to the demon inside. The desolation of Akul's long battle with the drug hit Larin then, the rage of a once-incomparable warrior brought low by a thimbleful of red powder.

Akul walked to the door, then turned around. "I don't want to scare you, but don't enter Bekath's shrine or talk with any priest of Bekath. You might be recognized."

Larin nodded silently. He hadn't cried in front of Akul since he was three, when, after a nasty fall, Akul had said, "A man's tears fall from joy or sadness, but never pain." Still, tonight his spirit filled with incomprehensible horror, and it was all he could do to fight back the torrents.

It had been no dream. Emja, it had been no dream.

Memories of a terror unlike any he had ever known, screams of pain and desolation from the prisoners, the sick evil of the crowds as they brought their children to laugh at clowns' antics while their neighbors lay dying in agony; all of these shook Larin's soul to its core. He stared straight ahead, not facing Akul, struggling to hold back tears until the door closed.

Akul hesitated, cheek shivering with khald tremors. "Larin—" He began walking to Larin's side, but stopped. "It—it will be all right." His forehead was wrinkled into a tight knot, an image of awkwardness Larin almost never saw. Akul was far from home when it came to offering comfort.

"I'll be fine."

"Don't forget there is good in this world as well." With that, Akul turned and left, closing the door behind him.

Hand trembling, Larin reached out to snuff the lantern. For several minutes he lay on his side, curled into a ball. Once, he heard Akul approach his door, but it stayed unopened, and after a moment the footsteps departed.

Eventually, wiping his eyes, he turned to lie flat on his back, reflecting that the desire to experience life outside the Wormpile had lost all its charm overnight.

Sleep eluded him until morning.

XIII

The scowl of Maldovin IV had become a terrible thing to behold. Having waited a year for this afternoon's misery, he found his torture extended beyond reason by his staff's excruciating slowness. They lifted and heaved the heavy chairs on the dais, trying to follow the queen's darting finger as she argued with Panjus and made instant decisions about each seat's location.

"Finalize those chairs now or I'll smash them over your heads!" Maldovin roared. This sent the already frantic servants into an apoplectic frenzy of bowing and lifting, slowing progress further. Maldovin grimaced and cradled his head, trying to avoid a splitting headache. After a few moments, he dabbed a pinch of khald on his tongue, willing the day to end.

Queen Relena glared at him briefly before returning to her spirited discussion with Panjus. It was a discussion over the location of each lord's seat on the dais, an intricate debate involving royal favor, provincial power, and shifting friendships. A debate Maldovin would once have considered ten steps beyond pointless.

Yet long experience had taught him otherwise. Petty schemes birthed and died in the palace like fish in a fetid pond, and Maldovin had learned such subtleties as seating arrangements were useful to keep his busy courtiers off-balance. Even the timing of this flurry of indecision had its purpose. The hasty preparations for this Council of Lords was a carefully chosen sign of the crown's apathy.

Pinching more khald from a fold in his robe, Maldovin watched his wife and royal councilor debate each other like cackling peasant grandmothers. He leaned back in the throne, reflecting that the Great Hall had been

113

beautified in preparation for a thing absent a shred of beauty—like wearing gilded cufflinks to a swine mating. Still, he enjoyed the finery: the royal platform had been draped by soft furs lined with charging green dragons, and small rubies had been embedded into the railings. Eighty-five shields lined the Great Hall, and beneath them, the walls were festooned with colorful provincial banners, as if Maldovin truly welcomed these provincial toads into his palace. The pointed ceilings rose high enough to shroud the rafters in shadow, with billowing tarps hanging far above, displaying the charging royal green dragon. As always, beautiful arched windows sent shafts of sunlight streaming across the dark wood, now polished and scented with lavender.

Panjus's argument getting nowhere, the royal councilor pounded up the stairs to the dais, pushed servants from his path, and strode forcefully to the chair of Aimes. He faced the royal platform, shifting sideways until his chest glowed with an intense shaft of sunlight streaming from one window. His bearded face twisted in calculation, then he pointed to a spot on the dais.

Maldovin blinked, then burst into laughter. Panjus was a gem. Duke Selton of Aimes would have the prominent seat, but no one said it couldn't be the most uncomfortable spot in the Great Hall.

"Make it so!" Maldovin said gleefully.

Queen Relena's glare could have melted metal, but she wouldn't publicly argue. The servants moved Aimes's seat to the designated spot and began shifting all other chairs to align with it. Sounds of scraping filled the Great Hall, as the queen glided to the royal platform and climbed the stairs. Maldovin winced under her cold gaze, vowing to have the chefs craft her favorite yellow-pepper soup tonight.

When the chairs were arranged, he fitted his crown, watching as the red glow of *Hrenatan* swept the Great Hall with every head movement. He gazed across the polished oak to the end of the Great Hall.

"Open!" he commanded, and the guards swung the doors inward to reveal the mass of waiting lords and dignitaries on the other side. Their annoyed looks quickly faded to mild neutrality as the large group shuffled into the hall, squinting into the crown jewel's red light.

Maldovin sucked a deep breath, forcing a pleasant expression onto his face as Duke Selton of Aimes approached the throne. The man's foppish wide-brimmed hat and self-important swagger turned this serious event into theater, no doubt exactly as calculated. Oh, how he'd love to crumple the Treaty of Gifain into a tiny ball and cram it down the duke's throat until he stopped breathing.

Khald's first glow bathed Maldovin in sweet pleasure just as Selton halted before the royal platform and removed his hat. Maldovin watched Selton's bow with spreading euphoria, suddenly unbothered by the farce created by the duke's shallow dip and cynical smirk.

Selton's hawkish face slipped from disdain to puzzlement as the emperor smiled, for they were far from friends. His puzzlement slowly turned to anger as the king remained still, unwilling to ruin the sweet rush of ecstasy with words. Finally, Maldovin forced himself back to drab reality, nodding almost imperceptibly at the waiting duke.

"Lord Selton. Thank you for coming."

"Your Majesty," Selton said flatly. He backed away, watching the throne suspiciously.

The remaining lords approached individually, each bowing and exchanging respects before mounting the dais to stand by their chairs. Despite his earlier pique, Maldovin wasn't entirely unhappy to renew old acquaintances, for he and Relena did have some friends among the provincial lords. He greeted the Dukes of Entridge and Anacoine with genuine warmth, and the Dukes of Haques, Filstire, and Njordslein with cordial respect. The Duke of Dragonfjord received a casual nod, for though he was friendly to the throne, the gutting of his own treasury had left his southern border defenseless against the strange creatures of the Shernock swamps.

By contrast, the Dukes of Chainston, Mourgleine, Kaelinborg, Ulstice, and especially Shernock—Duke Selton's remarkably unintelligent lackey—received taciturn greetings and eyes of steel, for their support of slavery left deep suspicions over the raids that occasionally crossed into the kingdom proper.

When the Dukes all stood by their chairs, Maldovin looked down gravely, enjoying his one opportunity to command these haughty lords without debate.

"Be seated."

Maldovin motioned his cabinet forward as the dukes took their chairs.

Yalinus and Hekrian came first, and Maldovin pointed his brother to a spot on the royal platform, refusing to acknowledge Hekrian's existence. Next came Talin, and after him the four royal advisors, each from a conquered tribe of the lower valleys. Maldovin motioned them to their spots on the royal platform, then turned to the next member of his council.

Emderian, Tanbar's diminutive High Wizard bowed before the royal platform, his mismatched tunic and breeches barely suitable for the royal court, his ever-present white gloves glaringly outlandish. Leader of the Council of Twelve, worshipper of Morphat, and likely the strongest wizard in a hundred generations, he resembled an abandoned boy, bewildered in the court of his betters. Maldovin had never understood why his wife distrusted this man; all he detected was awkwardness—a trait wholly out of place with the man's explosive power.

"Approach, High Wizard," Maldovin said.

Next came Royal Advisor Panjus, who bowed, then without prompting climbed the steps to stand between Hekrian and the king.

Good man.

Maldovin turned to the Council of Lords, hiding a smile as he watched Duke Selton squint into the bright glare.

"Lords, members of the royal council, thank you for coming," he said loudly. "As you know, events on the empire's borders have brought this Council of Lords upon us. Next year, we will see full-scale war on both northern and southern fronts, something we've not experienced in a generation. Do not imagine these battles will be like our previous campaigns, for today, the empire stands under true threat." He watched his lords' faces carefully, trying to determine who stood with him. Most listened dispassionately, but he noted skeptical looks on the usual faces: Aimes, Shernock, Chainston, Mourgleine, a few others. "I'll now turn it over to Talin to provide details."

Talin left Maldovin's side and approached the royal platform's wooden stand, his purple cape flowing behind him. He stopped and unrolled a large parchment map. "Good day, lords. I hope you're comfortable, for we've weighty matters to discuss, and you will be here a while."

Maldovin shifted positions, gazing out an arched window. He'd heard Talin's official report, and the smooth flow of khald through his veins distracted him, pulling his attention to the beauty below.

From the top of the royal tower, the entire western portion of the city was visible, a panorama of hillsides and tiled rooftops. The stone walls and towers of the Imperial Compound sloped gently down, turning into the Imperial District's keeps and mansions just over the compound walls. From there, the stately residences of Aldive's nobility flowed down the Mount of Empire to the shores of the Tanbar River, which twisted across the city like a beautiful blue serpent. Far in the distance, the squalid buildings of the Wormpile and Port District clustered like ant mounds, busy narrow streets racing across the hills to stop at the vast expanse of blue that was the Kanic.

How Maldovin longed to dip his toes in those waters. The runes that walled this place from magic were both blessing and curse—they kept him safe, but the threat of magical assassination outside the Imperial Compound made it too dangerous to leave. He wondered if the cretins in the Port District knew how often their king gazed down upon them, wishing he were in their place.

"As you all know," Talin was saying, "it's been six years since the last Lidathi assault, and twenty-one years since any real threat. In the North we've enjoyed peace, and the army has fattened." Maldovin smiled at his general's choice of words, implying royal sovereignty over the provincial militias.

"Whereas most years see a few skirmishes along the Avensai passes, these past six low seasons have brought complete quiet. Our spies have spotted movements of great hordes of Lidath in the forests north of the Great Chasm, yet they do not battle each other, nor do they attempt to cross Avensai." Talin scanned the dukes as he talked, his voice low in the silence of the Great Hall.

"Well, peace is deceptive!" he boomed, causing more than one lord to jump in his velvet chair. "If you know the lizards like I do, you'll know they live for battle. What are they doing in those cold forests, and why are they so quiet? Have you ever seen such large numbers of Lidath coexisting peacefully for so long?" Several lords shook their heads solemnly, their attention riveted on the charismatic general. Maldovin glanced at Selton, who was blinking furiously and trying to shift away from the intense shaft of sunlight pointed at his chair.

"Indeed, the reason is clear," Talin said, gripping the platform railing with white knuckles. "My lords, for the first time in history, every Lidathi chieftain within a thousand miles of the Great Chasm has been united under a single banner. Whispers speak of the return of the great Lidathi commander Kemharak, who has risen from his destruction at Commander Lukas's hands to defeat every tribe of his people and form them into a massive army." Talin swept his gaze across the rows of seated lords. "The empire will feel the full might of Kemharak's warhammer next low season."

The fat Duke of Shernock sat forward. "Unite the lizards? Impossible. What you've seen is likely just migrating tribes. Perhaps the Imperial spies need to spend less time behind an ale mug." His high-pitched, reedy voice grated on Maldovin's ears like dry rags on glass.

The queen coughed with displeasure, and Maldovin almost missed the angry glare Duke Selton shot his lackey. Maldovin noted this with interest. Duke Valni's bluster seemed in character, for one would think that Shernock and Aimes, two southernmost provinces, would be the least interested in providing levies to meet a Lidathi assault from the north. Yet somehow Selton had no objections to Talin's speech. What was he up to?

Talin turned ice-blue eyes on the Duke of Shernock. "I suppose they could be migrating tribes. Then the war chariots, thrukk, and wagons behind their lines must be migrating as well."

Valni's face turned bright red, and there were a few chuckles among the seated lords.

"And what are your sources for this incredible claim?" asked the heavy-browed Duke of Chainston.

"A combination of spies and observation, magical devices, and ordinary looking glasses," Talin replied. "With the Council of Twelve's help, I've seen with my own eyes the vast ocean of tents that fill the forests north of the Great Chasm."

Talin unrolled the map further, revealing the empire's Southern border.

"We'll discuss the Lidath in more detail later, but for now, please direct your attention to the South. Here we have a different problem, but one no less dangerous." He pointed to the disputed southern reaches, an area which included Faustus, Loyum, and other smaller towns. "In its effort to harass our Southern border, Seridor has used a new tactic of late. Instead of defending their gains, they've been capturing towns, building a few marble temples, and then departing. They leave in their wake a changed city—the leaders have converted to Eldegod worship, though we don't know why. Even after we reconquer, the town leadership remains loyal to Seridor's gods, though they'll not officially claim allegiance to that kingdom. We've executed some for treason, yet others replace them, as if the entire city has been eaten from within. This is strong magic that we cannot yet counter."

"An impossible magic, I'd say," Duke Selton remarked, to a few murmurs of assent. "How can any magical corps, even Morphat's priesthood, permanently change an entire town?"

"We don't know," Talin admitted. "The local councils officially swear allegiance to Tanbar, yet refuse to destroy the temples. More strangely, the government has changed: hangings, torture, and terror are used to keep order, as if a bit of Seridor remains behind."

"And what of it?" Selton snapped. "So the towns have turned to Eldegod worship and decided to enforce a little discipline. You've said yourself they maintain their allegiance to Tanbar."

"This allegiance is a lie. We've intercepted documents between some of these leaders and sources in Kaman, indicating they are receiving orders directly from Seridor's capital. It's also true that six months ago, Seridor took Loyum without a single battle; the Imperial garrison collapsed like a castle of sand. Though we retook the town, we fear the new garrison has become similarly corrupted. Lords, this is a danger that is growing. We believe by next year over thirty towns will have fallen under this spell, and Seridor will sweep through the southern reaches like a knife through soft butter."

The Duke of Anacoine spoke up. "The answer is obvious: the cities must be cleared of Eldegod temples. The Old Gods bring nothing but pestilence. Remove this curse, and you'll solve your problem."

Maldovin couldn't agree more. He glanced at Emderian, and the Duke's eyes widened as he followed the king's gaze.

"No offense meant, High Wizard," the Duke stammered. "Not all worshippers of the Old Gods are so corrupted. But here, Eldegod temples are being used as a weapon of war, and they should be destroyed where so used. I do not advocate smashing temples in Aldive, or anywhere far from Seridor's border."

"No offense taken, good duke," Emderian said gently. "You are merely proposing what you believe best for the kingdom."

The duke beamed, happy to be understood and, Maldovin guessed, relieved that he had given the High Wizard no offense.

"These towns should be able to worship whoever they choose," Duke Selton interjected, squinting into the window's glare. A few of his allies nodded with him. "Leave the temples alone, and you'll have peace. Destroy them, and you'll get war."

Maldovin was incredulous. "Duke Selton, do you claim Seridor will refrain from invasion if we forgo destroying their temples? Our battles with Seridor are centuries old!"

Selton sniffed, as if responding to the king was a dirty task to which he condescended reluctantly. "And for centuries we've oppressed Eldegod adherents, destroying their temples and casting aspersions on their worship."

Duke Kergven of Ulstice spoke up. "Perhaps if we sued for peace, Seridor would desist. Leave them Faustus and Loyum, if they want them so badly. Anything is better than today's constant warfare."

Maldovin closed his eyes at such idiocy. The kings of old had never suffered the indignity of having to listen to weak-spined, sheltered fools like the Duke of Ulstice. Only his grandfather's folly had brought that.

"Duke Kergven," Maldovin said softly. "If we form the habit of vacating large swaths of our territory whenever Seridor sends a squad against us, how long do you believe it will be before we're all speaking Chandor?"

The duke smirked with self-righteous surety. "Seridor cares only about the disputed region, not the rest of Tanbar. Good riddance, I say, for all the lives we've lost defending it."

Maldovin bit his lip, struggling to avoid leaping off the royal platform to seize Duke Kergven by the throat. Not trusting himself to speak, he turned his gaze out to the Great Hall, where it settled on the shield of Maldovin II.

Thanks, Grandpap.

The Duke of Entridge gasped. "How can you say this, Duke Kergven? Do you care nothing that the citizens of these towns are under our protection and would be subject to the vilest atrocities?"

Duke Selton shook his head. "The people of Faustus and Loyum wouldn't suffer—only criminals need worry. Seridor wants naught but to be left alone and to ensure the safety of its worshippers in our lands."

Maldovin slammed his fist down on the throne so hard, it sent tiny jewels flying in every direction. "They raid our cities and abduct our citizens, murdering them by the hundreds in horrible, excruciating ceremonies!" he fumed. "Still we allow their vile temples to flourish, to placate the few. Not a single temple of Emja can be found in Seridor!" His anger was so great, he cared not a whit about offending his High Wizard.

"These raids are myths," Selton said. "Aimes shares a border with

Seridor, and we've never seen such activity. Perhaps reasoning instead of warfare would allow the rest of the empire to enjoy the fruits of peace also."

"That's a very interesting fact, and one I'd like to discuss," Panjus interjected, nipping Maldovin's gathering tirade in the bud. Panjus froze, realizing the grave offense he had just given. He turned a questioning look on Maldovin, and scowling, the king motioned him to continue.

Panjus turned back around. "Just why *is* it that Seridor loves Aimes so, while the rest of our empire suffers only their mailed fist?" Panjus left his spot beside Maldovin, strolling to the platform railing to gaze down at Selton. "Could it be related to the fact that three new Eldegod temples were constructed in Glenschire last year? What about the numerous state visits from the princes of Seridor to the Selton manse? And for what reason does Aimes not post defenses along its southern border?"

Selton's face flashed fear, and Maldovin stared. Why had Panjus never told him any of this?

"Your rudeness and vile accusations are unworthy of response," Selton spat, sitting up in his chair. "I did not travel from Glenschire to be subjected to these insults."

"If insults they are, then please explain what a contingent from Aimes was doing in Kaman three weeks ago. I believe it consisted of your son and two generals, who I'm told received a specially scheduled viewing of Seridor's heartwarming rituals. Quite an honor, since the torture-murder ceremonies are normally performed only at Apex and during the feast of Hessal."

The color drained from Selton's face, and Maldovin gripped the arms of his throne with white knuckles. Now, everything made sense: Selton wouldn't argue against levies to fight the Lidath in the north because that would weaken the empire against the upcoming invasion from the South. An invasion Aimes was working with Seridor to bring about.

"Enough!" Maldovin boomed, shooting to his feet. He turned to the guards at the giant oak doors, pointing at Selton. "Arrest this traitor!"

The royal council erupted into pandemonium, as every lord shouted at once. Maldovin ignored most of them, focusing on his closest allies, the Dukes of Entridge and Anacoine.

Face stricken, the Duke of Entridge looked up at Maldovin. The vast gap between king and subject stretched before them now, a gap no personal warmth could bridge. "My liege, I beg you, do not do this thing. It will mean civil war."

Maldovin's tight glare softened as he considered his old friend, and he looked across the gulf with sadness. "Duke Jenterau, what I do here, I do for us all. I believe the Treaty of Gifain still gives me right to hang traitors in times of war."

The Great Hall fell silent as the guards approached the Duke of Aimes. For a moment, the only sounds were the sliding of chains across the wood floor and the soft metal click of the manacles snapping around Selton's wrists.

Maldovin surveyed the assembled lords, his eyes burning with emotion. "Lords, are we still a single land, or naught but a collection of states? Surely, this thing we call Empire is no fiction. If it is not, how can we refuse to defend it from treachery?"

The dukes were silent, and now Maldovin swept his gaze across the allies of Selton: Mourgleine, Chainston, Shernock, Ulstice, a few others. They waited, crossing furtive glances and trying to predict the wind's direction. Maldovin glanced at the Duke Valni of Shernock, but the fat duke's gaze darted between the chained Selton and the other lords, trying to determine which position would bring the most gain.

Finally, the Duke of Mourgleine spoke up. "Your Majesty, with due deference, we've only your man's word. Will we allow such a gross violation of Gifain's autonomy provisions, solely based on the word of a palace servant?"

Panjus looked at Maldovin, and Maldovin motioned him to speak.

"Duke Hiltos, I have witnesses and one intercepted document sealed with the wax of Aimes that will prove everything I say. I'll bring them forth at your desire."

"Excellent," Maldovin said. "We'll hold a trial so that all may see that we do not seek to undermine Gifain. I trust this will end the matter—"

Hekrian's small gesture caught Maldovin's eye, and he twisted around. Panjus had left his spot between them, and the king faced Hekrian directly, puzzled by the light of triumph in the man's eyes. Then Maldovin's first muscles gave way, and all feeling left his extremities. After a breathless moment, he collapsed to the royal platform's soft furs amid the stunned silence of the royal court.

"My love!" the queen cried, flying off her throne. Panjus and Talin rushed to his side as well, just as his last muscles stiffened. The shouts of the royal court were like the distant roar of a river, as all feeling left his body. Queen Relena knelt and cupped his face, then twisted around with wild eyes. "He lives! But he cannot move!"

Horrified, Panjus frantically checked Maldovin's heartbeat. "My king, I left your side!" His voice choked. "I left your side . . ."

Talin swung around to face Emderian. "Do something!"

Emderian's face was concerned. He glanced toward the runes flowing across the rafters of the Great Hall, then back at Maldovin helplessly. "My general, I cannot. This palace is dead to me. Perhaps we can move him outside the compound?"

"No!" the queen shouted, staring furiously at Emderian's mild expression. "We'll not expose him to Morphat's vile magic!" With that, she flew down the royal platform steps to call a contingent of guards.

Panjus stared at the Queen's retreating back, then looked desperately at the assembled lords. "I declare for Olivan, king's nephew!"

"We all know Olivan's guardian must declare for him," Hekrian said. "Yet I don't see Duke Eregar anywhere in these chambers. Perhaps we could wait until the day is out . . ."

"Traitor, you know very well Duke Eregar is smitten with fevers!"

Hekrian ignored this, looking out at the royal court. "My lords! We pray for the king's recovery, but until Maldovin recovers, the rules of succession apply. Yalinus will be king."

Only the sound of a fly buzzing in the high rafters could be heard in the Great Hall's silence. Yalinus, hearing his name, removed his finger from his nose and stared stupidly as, in the distance, the sounds of running boots on hard wood became audible.

Groans issued from the royal council. "Emja save us—we'll be ruled by an idiot while the empire is crushed," shouted the Duke of Flerrindor.

Panjus stared at Hekrian in fury. "Servant of the traitor, I know this is your doing. When I prove it, you will die a horrible death."

Perhaps realizing the true power behind the new king, the guards unlocked Selton's manacles, watching Hekrian nervously.

"Release Duke Selton at once!" the duke of Shernock cried, prompting a disgusted look from the Duke of Aimes.

"My lords!" Talin pleaded. "Surely we cannot allow an idiot to rule the empire in its moment of dire need?" He pointed toward the great oak doors where the queen had exited in search of aid, a task they'd all been too frozen to accomplish. "Our queen is a true monarch, smarter than all of us, willing to lead. Will we be governed by an imbecile while the most capable among us is denied?"

The dukes shuffled uncomfortably, many turning their faces away. The kingdom had never been, could never be ruled by a woman. "General, the laws of succession are clear," mumbled the Duke of Mourgleine. With that, Hekrian bent to retrieve the crown where it had fallen. That gesture froze the court anew, for the red glow of *Hrenatan* in Hekrian's hands brought chilling finality to the day's events.

The pounding of boots on wood grew louder, and the Great Hall's doors burst open to admit a platoon of guards. They raced across the Great Hall toward the royal platform, followed by the queen.

"Place Maldovin where we can pay our respects," Selton commanded them, as if he were king in law, as well as practice. "He may yet be curable, and we must be able to attend to him."

Choking back a sob, Queen Relena whirled to face Selton. "We'll do no such thing!"

Maldovin stared straight upward in his paralysis, grateful for his wife's good sense. Selton's only plan was to put him in a place where he could be easily killed. He tried in vain to move a muscle, any muscle, but found the only thing he could do was blink his eyes and purse his lips. He'd be able to eat, then—though only through a straw.

The guards laid Maldovin carefully onto the stretcher, hoisted it onto their shoulders, and then left the Great Hall with the queen, Panjus, and Talin in tow. They were followed by the silent stares of the royal court.

After turning two corners, they were met by Commander Giorlan with another contingent of guards carrying a second stretcher with pillows. Giorlan was a long-trusted servant, handpicked long ago by Queen Relena for his loyalty and competence.

"Your highness," he said to the queen. He turned to his men, pointing to four of them. "You four: guard the exit to the Great Hall, and make sure none try to follow." He pointed at the guards holding the empty stretcher, lined with pillows and hidden by a blanket. "You men: take this to the royal chambers, and make no attempt to be quiet." He looked at the queen, then Panjus. "May Emja guide your path."

Panjus nodded, and stood at one end of the stretcher bearing Maldovin, while Talin took the opposite end. Panjus looked at Giorlan. "It's better for all if you do not see where we go." Giorlan nodded and turned to guard the hallway as the stretcher was carried away.

Maldovin knew what Panjus was doing and again gave thanks for loyal and competent servants. He was carried across a maze of hallways, past giant pantries, and through vast palace storage chambers, places where none would visit for days. A few more turns brought them to a large room filled with discarded clothing. Panjus and Talin lowered the stretcher and began throwing clothes from one wall. Finally, a low door was revealed, and they all entered the hidden chamber. It was dank and dark, and yet it was the closest thing to safety Maldovin would now enjoy. In his straight upward gaze, he saw the queen, Panjus, and Talin look down at him with sadness and indecision. He blinked and pursed his lips, his vision clouding with tears. He'd felt imprisoned before, but it was now about to get worse.

A lot worse.

Emderian entered the fur-lined study where Duke Selton sat, scribbling on parchment. The other lords had retired to their suites in preparation for the long journey home, but Duke Selton had many things to finish before returning to Aimes. He looked up at Emderian's entrance, a feeling of disquiet rising within him.

Emderian stopped and hung his head, his white-gloved hands clasped before him. It was a typically humble gesture Selton had always found odd coming from this man. The High Wizard's small face and narrow shoulders were the picture of meekness, as if to mask the volcanic force lying within.

"Congratulations, Lord Selton."

Selton's eyes grew hard. "No congratulations are in order, High Wizard. The king's tragedy is a tragedy for us all."

"I meant no offense, Duke," Emderian said, his eyes downcast. "But surely your path from imminent death to the new king's puppeteer must provide some relief."

Selton stared coldly, refusing to play this man's game. "I'd have been exonerated at trial. I seek only to clear my name and return to Glenschire so I can be free of these political shenanigans." He stood up. "Is there anything else?"

Now Emderian shot his head up, black eyes boring into Selton. "Let's be done with these games, Duke Selton. Perhaps you forget who I am. Magic has been my life's study, and I have some idea what Hekrian did. What I don't know is how, given that our palace is dead to power."

Selton mulled this, trying to read this small, strange man. Was he as loyal to the crown as he'd always appeared, or did he want something for himself? Selton decided to play it safe.

"I really don't know what you mean. If Hekrian played any role in this crime, it is unknown to me. Am I to be accused yet again?"

"You misunderstand me," Emderian said, smiling. "I care nothing about your motives. Ruling the empire is a very large task, and I come to offer my help."

Selton narrowed his eyes, nodding slightly. At last he had the true measure of this man. "Why should you have any more say with the new king than you did with the old? Your job is leader of the Council of Twelve: you go where the king commands you, and you fight who he tells you. You are a servant to the crown, nothing more."

Emderian's face broke into a terrible smile, his eyes becoming wells of blackness that sucked the breath from Selton's lungs. Selton saw horror in those eyes, for suddenly, he could imagine them dancing with laughter at the vilest rituals of his god. As he was drawn into the void of Emderian's soul, Selton became certain that the gentle High Wizard known to all was but a creature of fiction.

"My good duke," Emderian whispered, his voice a twisting knife. "The castles of the provincial lords do not enjoy the same magical immunity as our Imperial Compound. Are you willing to remain in this palace the rest of your days, trapped like our good king?"

Selton struggled to control the shivering that had taken him. They stared at each other another moment before the Duke of Aimes lowered his eyes.

"What do you want?"

"Just a few decrees here and there, most of which will affect only the capital."

"For example?"

"I'll eliminate the Law of Marble, which limits the size and numbers of Eldegod temples. I only want to guard against the oppression so long visited upon our worship, as you quite eloquently argued before the king."

Duke Selton shivered.

"I'll also have a few decrees concerning the more unruly tribes of the lower valleys. Nothing that should concern you overmuch."

Selton nodded slowly. "And I'll continue to direct the army's movements, as well as pass laws concerning the wider kingdom."

Emderian smiled at the conversation's new direction. "Absolutely."

Selton drew a deep breath. "Very well." He watched Emderian nod pleasantly, marveling at the High Wizard's humble earnestness—an earnestness he now knew was nothing of the kind. "You know, I've always suspected you weren't who you seemed. No one with your power could be so agreeable."

Emderian grinned, and now Selton saw the pure emptiness in those eyes. "I am exactly who I seem. It's just that no one looks hard enough." With that, he spun around and strode from the room.

Duke Selton sank forcefully into his pillows, mind swimming. His arrangement with Seridor was drawing him in, deeper than he'd ever meant to go. Yet what choice did he have; what other path could place the house of Aimes on the throne where it belonged? Selton stared at the door for several long minutes, wondering from where the image of Emderian as High Priest had sprung and whether Emderian truly had some power in this place.

His spine tingled late into the night.

"From each academy shall come three, the brightest lights of their order."

Emperor Faulivius IV, decree forming the Council of Twelve

XIV

Larin slapped a mosquito for the hundredth time, grimacing as his hand came away wet with blood and sweat. Cursing, he wiped it on a nearby shingle, wondering what had moved him to climb this rooftop today. The heat was unrelenting. It matted his hair, stuck his shirt to his back, and sent a constant salty drip into his eyes.

Hugging the crumbling chimney with one arm, he peered four stories down to the crowds below. He snapped his head up immediately, trying to let his stomach settle.

To his right, Candro danced wildly on the sloped rooftop, pretending to vault over the roof's edge, then leaning back in mock horror.

"Village idiot," Larin growled.

"What's the matter, Wiz? A little on edge today?" Candro's cheeriness turned to abject terror as his feet began sliding. He stopped his descent at the last minute, eyes thick with feigned relief.

"Just wait until we're on the ground. I'll be wiping that smirk off your face."

Candro swung around the chimney to land on the other side of Larin. "I guess I'll *have* to wait. You're clearly useless up here."

Annoyed, Larin threw a broken shingle at him and Candro ducked, his bony cheeks clenched into a scowl that made his face an irritated triangle. Everything about Candro was sharp: shrewd eyes, pointed chin, thin lips twisted into a permanent smirk. Short, skinny, and fast, he was the perfect thief—a profession that held no interest for Larin.

Except, maybe, for today.

"I still don't know why we're here," Larin complained. "The only ones getting rich up here are the mosquitoes."

"We've been over this," Candro said slowly, as if speaking to a dim-witted child. "The best place to scout the crowds is from a rooftop. See over there." He pointed at the wall of pikes separating the masses from the fine inhabitants of Aldive's twenty noble houses. "If a Wormpile street urchin such as yourself—"

"Or yourself."

Candro sniffed. "Or myself even glanced in that direction for a second, said urchin would have his head mounted on a pike by sundown."

"I could've figured that out from street level. Just admit it: the real reason we're up here is so you can watch the Apex contest."

"Guilty. But you have to agree, this is the best view we'll get this side of the queen's dress." Candro pantomimed lifting the queen's dress, and Larin burst into laughter.

"Anyway, Wiz, we're here, why not enjoy it?" Candro fished a paper bundle from his pouch, which he opened to reveal a crumbly mess. "Want some honeycake?"

Larin grudgingly scooped some of the mixture, knowing he'd just been manipulated into remaining on this forsaken rooftop for half the show. In the five years they'd been best friends, he'd been lured into countless acts of stupidity by Candro's silver tongue; by now he'd learned to accept the inevitable.

Some of his irritation came from lack of sleep. Since that awful night two months ago, he'd continued to dream—dreams of slavery, murder, betrayal. All dreams of Seridor. Fortunately, those dreams were nothing like that first soul-shattering nightmare, but they were real enough to wake him in a cold sweat nearly every night, real enough to portray a horrifying image of the kingdom to the South. Alone with his terror, he'd been inventing excuses to stay awake. It was a habit that was starting to take a serious toll.

"Let's see," Candro said, mercifully interrupting Larin's thoughts. "Who'll be paying for Liander's gift today?" He swept his index finger across the sea of humanity, as if to pick some unfortunate target at random.

"You're playing with fire, trying to steal Oarl's girlfriend. You might want to take up something safer, like reading."

Candro wiped oily fingers on his torn breeches. "She's not Oarl's girlfriend. I just think the prettiest girl in the Wormpile should end up with the wittiest man in the Wormpile. Oarl's got nothing to say to her, except maybe to describe how he just laced his boots for the first time, or can finally remember the names of all three of his lieutenants. "

"Right. She'll see through Oarl eventually."

Candro smiled wistfully. "Don't blow smoke at me, Wiz; your face gets greasier than a Westmarket horse trader. You're probably right. It's an impossible dream." Larin was about to deny the obvious when Candro broke in. "So who are you after these days? Two months ago I heard nonstop blathering about Onie, but now it's utter silence."

Larin froze. *Onie* . . . How he'd missed that shy smile as she stole through the alehouse entrance, the electric attraction of their storeroom kisses. Now, the temple and Onie were gone, though only Onie mattered.

He'd heard nothing from her since the night of the alehouse fight.

"She's done with me," he said flatly. "I'm too unhealthy for her."

Candro picked at his toe where it stuck through his shoe. "Someone's got to do something about Oarl."

Larin nodded, tight-lipped. They both fell silent then, listening as the shouts and dull roar of the crowds warred with the high-pitched whine of mosquitoes swooping in for their feast.

Below them, Aldive spread out like some vast, multicolored map. Splitting the city into North and South was the mighty Tanbar River, draining from the eastern Linesai Mountains to pour into the city, where it twisted between rows of mansions and plazas. Today, the river's sparkling waters were crowded with the flat-bottomed leisure boats of the wealthy, tall masts and colorful sails blocking the view from the river's north side. To the east, the Imperial District spires rose high above the city upon the Mount of the Empire, cast in shadow by the massive walls of the Imperial Compound at its summit. To the northwest, the squat structures of the Wormpile and Port District were barely visible behind the sprawling mansions of the Flerrindor District.

Following the river, the Royal Boulevard was heavy with the black boots of Tanbari infantry, beginning their march to the Avensai passes to fight the Lidath. Thousands of people thronged the southward side of the boulevard, watching the marching troops and waiting for the day's *real* festivities to begin—the Council of Twelve's Apex magic duel. Food carts threaded through the masses, bringing the faint scents of roasting meats, flamed nuts, and rose-tinted incense.

Visible across the entire city, the royal platform jutted from the clock tower in the Plaza of Trade, its metal railings glowing in Spellgiver's blue light, high floors draped with the charging green dragon of Maldovin IV. Men and women in the blue and gold robes of the Council of Twelve milled about on that dais, conversing amongst themselves with animated gestures. On the side of the platform, twenty men and women contest judges sat in high gilded chairs, each of them lord over one of Aldive's noble houses.

Above everything, two great gods battled—only fifteen days from Apex, the moon hung in the heavens like some vast celestial kingdom, its rivers and oceans shining blue beneath the white funnels of massive storms. This close to its zenith, Spellgiver was bigger than a wagon wheel at five paces, already much larger than the sun. It approached its nemesis with slow patience, preparing to fight for dominance of the sky.

A wild cheer from below yanked Larin's attention to the royal boulevard, where, rounding a turn, fully plated men astride terrifyingly large, spike-headed beasts swung into view. The cheers grew louder as the lead knights raised their lances.

"Khula knights," Candro whispered unnecessarily.

Larin always found it hard to believe that his depressive and drug-addled uncle had been one of these elite monsters, though Akul's sword work certainly qualified him. Surely they'd have drummed any soldier with a khald problem out of the unit—though in fact, maybe that's what had happened. He leaned back and squinted, trying to resolve every detail.

The knights rode five abreast, raised lances forming a row of pointed death that along with horned helmets, lent them a vaguely demonic appearance. But it was their mounts that always drew his stares. The indigen six-legged khula had an oblong, plated head studded by sharp horns that formed a cage around four red glowing orbs. They had bony plates across their flanks and vestigial wings that allowed them quick bursts of flight just above the ground, turning them into a massive armored missile in combat. Khula knight battlefield charges were said to be the only tactic capable of routing the Lidathi.

"I think that's my spot," Candro said suddenly, biting into his honeycake. He pointed to an area near the Royal Boulevard, where the tents of gold merchants rose above the throngs like towers of cloth. "There's enough gold there to keep even Liander happy."

Larin tore his gaze from the khula knights to consider his friend. "Sure. I'll visit you in the salt mines, and you can tell me how it went." He counted the shiny helmets of Imperial Guards near the tents. "One guard, two, three, many. But who knows, maybe none of them will notice a scrappy street urchin lurking around the gold vendors like a cat in a kitchen."

"Mmm. Good point."

Larin pointed to an area near the vegetable stalls. "I think I'll be heading there. I see a few opportunities, and no Imperial Guardsmen."

Candro's face was blank. "Good idea, Wiz, but don't stop at tomatoes. You should think bigger, like oranges or bananas. Me, I'll stick to gold."

"Imbecile, I'm not robbing the food vendors. I just think money will be handy in that part of the crowd."

Candro grimaced. "Look, the only people who buy tomatoes at the Apex show are the poor. The rich are eating cakes, laughing at the people buying the tomatoes. Didn't you get droopy-eyed when I suggested this, wanting to make sure you didn't rob someone who needed the money? Well, those people"—Candro pointed to the long row of vegetable stalls—"need the money. Stick to the merchant section, Wiz. Better results, and less guilt."

Larin nodded reluctantly, and it sunk home just how unsuited he was for Candro's life. How many real thieves cared about their victims' financial status?

Yet something had to change. Banned from Emja's temple, his days were filled with endless reading as Trana stole the occasional tome from the temple library to pass to Akul. There was nowhere else for him now. He'd angered Morphat's temple, which now rivaled Oarl for control of the neighborhood, buying all the food from the markets to give to their favored. Surrounded by two enemies, he was mostly stuck in his four-block zone, relying on Akul's largesse for every copper. It was unbearable, and he'd redoubled his magical studies in the past months, trying to learn enough to make a living. Power wasn't everything, and he knew there were others like him, small talents with enough smarts to earn a few coins selling charms to the upper classes. All he needed was formal lessons. Yet the magickers in the city's Lyrasa District charged a lot for tutors, and Akul would only pay for half.

The other half would have to come from the streets below.

Larin watched the throngs swarm the wooden stalls, waving shiny coins and trying to grab the attention of the harried vendors. Then he imagined returning with someone else's food money, and the whole idea lost its appeal. Anyway, he knew what would happen the minute he stepped into the Wormpile.

"Yes. Well, I wouldn't want to disappoint Oarl. He's counting on me to provide for his crew."

Candro's raised eyebrow became lost in his bangs. "Doesn't have to be that way. I'll show you a secret way into the Wormpile."

"I know all the secret ways. You can thank the thief god that Oarl ignores you, but the god of rejects is apparently too busy to look after me. Oarl's got some fixation with my outbursts—he'd rather shake me down for a copper than anyone else for a gold."

Candro scowled. "You want pity, try sleeping in the Netrina one of these days, instead of in a house with someone who marginally cares whether you live or die. Till then, don't talk to me about favor from the gods."

Larin nodded and said nothing.

"Anyway, Wiz, you have it all wrong," Candro said in a softer tone. "Oarl doesn't hate your outbursts; he hates you because you fight back." He waved three grimy fingers in the air. "Wormpile youth fall into three categories. One: those who run fast enough not to get caught. That would be me."

"You've been caught before."

Candro ignored this, bending his third finger down to leave two in the air. "Two, almost everyone else. They're so afraid of Oarl's crew, they let him do anything: take their money, slap them around, whatever." He brushed thick bangs from his eyes, lowered a finger, and pointed the remaining one at Larin. "Then there's you. You don't run fast enough to escape, but you don't give your gold away without a price. Have you ever just handed Oarl your money?"

Larin grinned fiercely, remembering countless fists on flesh as he connected with the first of Oarl's gang brave enough to grab his bag.

"Never."

"There you have it. Oarl hates you because he can't control you."

Larin sighed. "You're right. I should just hand over my money and avoid the beatings. One day, Oarl's going to do something permanent." He rubbed his crooked nose, broken once and now sporting a permanent bump.

Candro looked at him sharply. "No, that's not what I'm saying at all. Listen to me: the Wormpile youth respect you, whether they admit it or not. You show them what it's like to have pride. Stupidity too, sure, but also pride."

"So you're saying I'm the leader of a gang that refuses to fight?"

"I'm saying that with you out there, Oarl doesn't look so tough, and *that's* why he hates you. Don't stop fighting. You're the only one we can even remotely look up to."

Larin glanced at Candro sideways. It wasn't often he got anything but good-natured insults from his friend. He was about to reply when the day suddenly dimmed, as if someone had thrown a blanket over the sun. Cheering rose from the masses below, and Larin looked up to see Spellgiver's disk slip over the sun, marking the start of the Apex festivities. The cheers turned into a roar as the sun fell completely behind Spellgiver, bathing the city in an eerie blue glow. Soon, the Song of Magictide drifted up from the crowd, a multi-throated chant that shook the city walls.

They looked expectantly at the royal platform, but Larin noticed something amiss. The council was furiously debating something, waving their hands excitedly. Emderian's white gloves could be seen even at this distance, pointing into the crowd. Larin squinted, counting the men and women in the blue and gold robes.

"There are only eleven . . ."

Candro nodded. "I bet it's Laniette who's missing. First her husband, now her . . ."

Larin considered this. Laniette's husband, Theralle, had been the empire's High Wizard for fifteen years before Emderian had supplanted him. Theralle had been the Apex festivity favorite, creating flamboyant displays that always drew the most cheers, but last year he'd gone missing. Laniette, a rising violet-sash mage herself, had been picked to replace him in the council. Unlike ten of the other council, whose faces were plastered in paintings across the city, Laniette was a mystery, for this was her first year in the festivities. That was also true for Kedrick, the other new mage on the council this year.

As Larin watched, the High Wizard Emderian began shouting from the royal platform, and suddenly his voice echoed throughout the city:

"Laniette! Your city awaits you!"

The strength of the magic was such that Emderian's voice seemed to echo from every stone of the capital. Surprised, the crowds gasped, then gave polite scattered applause. Soon, the song of Magictide turned into good-natured chanting, calling for the twelfth wizard to present herself.

"Laniette! Laniette!"

The roar of the crowd died away after a few minutes, as Emderian spoke to the other members of the council. He turned back to the crowds.

"We'll delay this no further," he boomed. "Let the contest begin!" With that, one of the dots in blue and gold walked somberly to the front of the platform. This was Hielanak, who vied for Theralle's old title as the empire's second most powerful mage. Hielanak raised his arms, and suddenly a darkness descended upon the city.

"In the earliest days of the empire, the fate of men was uncertain . . ." The voice glided through the city, an ominous whisper echoing throughout every street and alleyway. The crowd gave a loud "ooh" as the moon's light faded, casting the city in darkness.

Suddenly, the blue light was back, and the city looked very different. Larin realized he was looking at Aldive as it existed three thousand years ago, and his breath caught. The illusion was very well done—while the faint outlines of modern buildings were still visible if one looked carefully, a more casual view revealed a town whose walls were much shorter, concentrated in about one-tenth its current size.

Without warning, Lidathi warriors streamed over those short walls, overwhelming a ragged band of human defenders. They swarmed the stone defenses, running into the city and opening the gates as the crowds screamed in excited pleasure. Shortly, a line of Lidathi on shaggy, six-legged thrukk charged through the open gates, slaughtering the human soldiers and setting fire to everything in their path. The fires raged at the city outskirts, and the image was so real, Larin imagined he felt a warm glow on his face. Just as the Lidathi seemed poised to reach the city center, a man stepped from the fires wearing a golden crown. Larin knew this was Jathan, the most powerful wizard in history—the one who'd eventually gouge the Great Chasm.

Jathan raised his arms, and great beasts descended from the skies onto the charging Lidathi, ripping them to shreds. The Lizards fought bravely, but within minutes, the battle was done, and the streets were thick with scaly corpses. As the Lidathi were chased from the walls, the people swarmed out to cheer their victory.

The moon's light darkened and brightened again, and the city was back to normal.

After a surprised pause, the crowds erupted into wild cheers, and Hielanak bowed, a lone figure bathed in blue light. The judges scanned the crowds and wrote into their ledgers, and after a minute, he stepped back.

The wizardress named Kuylanne waited for the last applause to wane before stepping forward. Her voice was tiny in the distance, but the effect was large. Within seconds, the sky became thick with white doves, swarming through the city streets and flocking around the buildings in a mass of white feathers. They formed into spirals, patterns with a snowflake's complexity, then swooped through the city's streets and alleyways, the sounds of their flapping overwhelming the excited squeals of the crowd. Finally, the doves flew to the northeast toward the Imperial Compound, and all necks craned to follow their path. The white mass of birds, now tiny in the distance, swirled around the base of the palace like a twisting wind, giving the illusion that the Imperial Compound floated on a white cloud. The flock then broke apart and flew into the distance, and the crowd roared its approval.

However, Kuylanne was not done. The sky flashed, and a mass of white objects rained down upon the city. At first Larin thought it was snow, but as they plopped all over their rooftop, he realized the sky was raining fragrant white flowers. He picked up a white rose, watching in amazement as it dissolved into water on his hand. He gave a cheer, then turned to Candro.

"That was great!"

Candro stuffed a clump of honeycake in his mouth. "The first one was better."

Larin waved a hand in dismissal. "Hielanak's display was only an illusion. Kuylanne's was true transmutation, which takes a binding of three different disciplines. That's a lot harder."

Candro scowled. "Have I told you that you read too much?"

"All the time."

The crowds seemed to agree with Candro, for their cheers seemed slightly less enthusiastic than for Hielanak's more dramatic display. The judges furiously scribbled in their books.

Kuylanne finally stepped back, and the demonologist named Kedrick walked forward. Though Kedrick was newly ascended to the Council of Twelve, Larin had followed his rise closely, for he'd never seen a demonologist among the council ranks. He watched in fascination as the mage began his chant.

The demon took shape from every direction at once. Its form didn't so much appear as assemble, as the air condensed to form the creature's various parts: a greenish hand covered with ridges, glowing orbs vaguely resembling eyes, a leg knotted like an ancient oak. Unnerved, Larin watched pieces of the apparition materialize above the platform, condensing into this bizarre monstrosity. Over twenty feet high, the demon wore a man's face over a ridged body, a giant knot of scar tissue that writhed furiously beneath ebony-black skin. Small pustules covered its twisted extremities, spewing plumes of smoke that swirled in the turbulence of flapping orange wings. With unexplainable insight, Larin knew this couldn't be the creature's true form.

Candro yelled with excitement, just as the Demon's ear-piercing shriek sundered the air. It began flying above the city, heavy beat of its wings intertwining with excited and disgusted shouts from the crowds below. As the creature's shadow cooled their rooftop, Larin leaned back to stare in fascination.

And the world became, suddenly, forever different.

He lay transfixed, staring at the Demon's humanlike face. Its mouth was twisted by unearthly emotions, its glowing yellow eyes wild with eternal chaos. Yet with unwanted clarity, Larin saw something far different from the evil visage provoking the crowd's screams: he saw the face of unimaginable madness. Insanity borne of an immortal race condemned to an eternity without sensation.

Vivid images raced through his thoughts then: beings of light desperately trying to communicate with each other through an impenetrable fog, floating lonely and confused in the perpetual mist. Swirls of energy as once joyous creatures spun wildly in an effort to feel the smallest sensation, frantically attempting to punctuate the nothingness. Creeping madness as the centuries passed with no break in the endless gray, save for the occasional summons into the world of men for a minute of beautiful sensation before being forced screaming back into their hell. Larin knew that whatever horrors the Old Gods had perpetrated upon humanity, they were as nothing beside the monstrous crime they had visited upon this race.

Haraf, please stop, he begged, trying desperately to keep his stomach from rising into his mouth. The demon passed, and he found himself barely able to maintain his composure.

But normality had not returned. He saw things now he'd never seen— the demon was surrounded by a red haze which had nothing to do with the steaming pustules on its skin, a red haze of rage and helplessness. He swept the city and saw that the same haze covered everything; it sat upon the city like a heavy blanket. To the right, a dense red plume issued from the Port District's south end, just where Morphat's temple should be.

B'neikarian's words crept through Larin's mind then: *The rage of a race of immortals confined to such hell leaks into the world of men, allowing Morphat and his ilk to infect your societies like a cancer.*

Suddenly, everything became clear: such misery was the lifeblood of the six-legged ones. They drew sustenance from the Demons' desperation, fed on their agony. And Larin knew one thing for certain: the Eldegod would never be defeated until the Avillian had been given their freedom.

Without warning, the demon began flailing its misshapen arms wildly.

With a loud shriek, the creature fell to the earth, crushing several people below.

"Emja's butt cheeks!" Candro shouted, scrambling to his feet.

The crowd's fascinated yells turned into true screams of terror, as the demon launched off the ground with a terrifying flap of its wings. As it lifted from the ground, it shot a fist down upon Kedrick with a sickening crunch, sending a spray of blood across the royal platform. The screams of the crowd were everywhere as people tried to escape the carnage. Larin watched numbly as the demon flapped above the royal platform, its orange wings blowing Maldovin IV's green dragon banners backward.

Candro looked at Larin wildly. "What in all the gods' names is going on?"

Larin said nothing, transfixed by the scene below.

The judges scrambled off the platform into the clock tower, as the remaining council banded together, hands held high, amid high-pitched screams from below. The Demon was pushed back temporarily, but this lasted seconds. It began to dart forward in short bursts. reaching a pustule filled hand toward the council, who were now united in a chain, holding hands high in the air. Great winds swirled around the platform, flapping cloaks and blowing clouds of dust over the railings.

With a terrifying screech, the Demon became sucked into one of these vortexes, bringing him close enough to the council to slam an enormous hand over a dark-haired wizard in the center. The crush of bones could be heard from the rooftop, and as the demon was blown back, the man jerked, stood up, and collapsed to the platform in a pool of blood.

This gap in the chain spelled the council's doom. The two halves of the chain tried to link hands again, but the Demon darted forward, crushing Kuylanne. It then began sweeping forward regularly, slamming a pustule-covered fist onto a new council member with every foray.

Eventually, only Emderian was left. As the last of his compatriots died, Emderian reeled backward, his tiny Lyrashi shouts audible even through the crowd's roar. The bodies of the council lay scattered about the royal platform, and the blood streaming over the platform's edge brought Larin a horrible memory of Kaman's rituals.

The demon and Emderian seemed to lock forces for a long minute of stalemate while the crowds below shouted and trampled the less fortunate underfoot. Several standing banners and vendor booths went down beneath the sea of moving heads.

Eventually, Emderian gained the upper hand. He began twisting the Demon's figure with every wave of his white glove, and the creature's face crunched in great agony, its form becoming transparent.

Larin caught a glimpse of the Demon's face just before it left the world of man—a face ravaged by desperation to see light and color just a moment longer. Its lips parted; its glowing yellow eyes were unfocused and turned upward. The look of utter hopelessness as it faded filled Larin with an intense, unexplainable sadness, one that clashed with the crowd's wild cheers:

"Emderian! Emderian! Emderian!"

"Did you see that?" Candro shouted over the roar of the crowds. "Wiz, we've witnessed history today! Almost the entire council slaughtered at the Apex festivities. Thank Emja that Emderian was there!"

Larin nodded. He considered telling Candro that Demons weren't supposed to last in this plane even one second after their summoner had died, that sixteen days before Apex, the Council of Twelve should surely have defeated a single grade-three Demon without loss of life. Yet he himself didn't know how it all added up. He looked down at the crowds, still cheering Emderian's name.

"I guess we should stay up here until the madness below dissipates."

Candro stared as if Larin had just sprouted horns. "You're kidding, right? With all those people panicking and trying to get away, no one will be watching their purses. This is the best time to get to work!"

As he said this, the first rays of the sun peeked from behind Spellgiver's disk, as if formally announcing an end to the killing. Within seconds, the brilliant yellow of full daylight again bathed the Aldivian stone.

Candro breathed deeply. "And if that's not a sign, I don't know what is."

Larin nodded, though his desire to try Candro's profession had faded with the day's events. He wouldn't be stealing anything.

"Lead the way." With that, they climbed off the rooftop and swung around the ledge to the dusty, abandoned apartment below.

The noise, heat, and smell of the crowds hit them like a wave as they exited into the street. Tall heads blocked their view, and Larin immediately pressed against a building, as the mass of jabbering people flowed by. He watched the violent jostling of the crowd with distaste, but one look at Candro told him his friend saw it differently. Candro's eyes darted right and left.

Larin smiled weakly. "If you licked your lips, it would be perfect."

Candro grinned. "So much gold, it's hard to know where to start." He disappeared into the crowd for a moment and returned with a small pouch. He tossed it to Larin.

"Here you go."

Larin held up his hand. "Candro, no—" But Candro had already become swallowed by the tight mass of moving people. Larin twisted around, but finding the owner of this small velvet sack would have been impossible.

Shaking his head, he let himself flow into the crowds toward home.

XV

Deep in thought, Larin flowed with the crowds onto the Flerrindor Bridge, its gray stone traversed by viney tendrils. On the bridge's east railing, the three gargoyles of Tanbar raised eight-pronged claws and hissed toward the north and east, from where ancient enemies had once threatened. They were smaller replicas of the monstrous beasts atop the Imperial Compound walls: Hesiteth, guardian against the Old Gods, Etureth, guardian against the Demons, and Kekureth, guardian against the Lizards.

The babble of a hundred voices replayed the day's events as Larin ascended the last stair. Determined to escape that cacophony, he shoved his way to the bridge's eastern wall and placed a hand against Etureth, breathing deeply and letting the river's rush fill his thoughts. He tried not to smile at the irony inherent in Haraf's servant leaning against this particular gargoyle.

To the east, the Tanbar River snaked through Aldive, a shimmering ribbon of blue girded by a thousand stone walls and red rooftops, the chaos of ten centuries of stonemasonry along every inch of the river's length. In the distance, that blue ribbon wrapped around the base of the Mount of the Empire, twisting past the ornate buildings of the Golden Promenade. The grandest of these was the Imperial Playhouse, its two arched windows staring across the river like the eyes of some old madam. From the river's edge, the Mount of the Empire rose sharply upward, a sprawling mass of keeps, spires, and wide boulevards, its summit topped by the massive walls of the Imperial Compound.

Everywhere, Larin saw the red mist. It grew fainter now, but still it was there. The thickest fog came from the southwest, just where Morphat's Port District temple should be. Another plume came from the northeast, near the Kesserat District, where he knew a much smaller Eldegod temple existed.

A red mist of desperation and misery.

He listened to the river for some time, watching the redness slowly disappear. After half an hour, he pushed himself away from the view and headed home along a much emptier bridge. On the far side of the river, he turned west toward the Port District, trying to find a little-used entryway into the Wormpile by skirting the Port District's upper hills.

This close to Apex, the fish market was long gone. That area was now filled by the sea, which flowed through the forest of pillars supporting the district's houses. It was high tide, but today the ocean rose only halfway to the bottom floors. In sixteen days, the high tide waters would lap against the base of the buildings and would have crept up the stone ramp, a few blocks from the Wormpile's border. Giant nets now hung between the pillared buildings, waiting to catch hundreds of fish as the waters receded.

Beyond the high tide point, the Port District lost its barnacled pillars. Larin found a cramped alleyway behind the fish-packing house and headed east, hoping to slip into the Wormpile unseen. Yet as he turned a corner, the sight at the end of the street brought him to a halt. Near the Wormpile's boundary, several men in red and black jerkins had halted a tagalanth-driven cart, apparently extracting some sort of tax.

His face hardened as he watched a Morphasti bang the cart with his fist. In the past two months, he'd watched Morphat's influence creep through the Wormpile's alleyways like the rot plague, desperately hoping it'd trigger a war with Oarl. So far, nothing. The Marble Temple had flexed its claws everywhere except Akul's four-block zone, always first by offering food to the poor, then by offering training with arms. Yet it didn't take long for most to realize that all food dangled from Morphat's circular mouth. In exchange for sustenance, Morphasti priests demanded obedience: regular temple attendance, strict discipline, willingness to monitor neighbors for signs of dissent. Rumors that the Morphasti gave smaller portions to Hemeks became prevalent, though nothing could be proven. Meanwhile, Emja's temple continued to brew ale for an ever-dwindling supply of worshippers as its priests played their silly games behind jade walls.

Larin squinted thoughtfully as the cart driver handed two coins to the highway robbers in red and black. Collecting entrance taxes was a bold new step for the Morphasti, a step that would place them squarely on Oarl's turf. For a brief moment, Larin's mood brightened, and he turned away with a hopeful smile.

He headed east, where the Port District's large warehouses turned into overhung timber frame buildings, their upper windows so close, the cross-street neighbors might shake hands. Even the bottom floors were an arm-span apart, giving rise to the Wormpile's hallmark narrow alleyways. He slipped into one of these, passing dirty walls plastered with Eldegod propaganda: images of Morphasti priests standing tall, while Emjaian clerics cowered beneath. Scowling, he drew his dagger and began slashing these as he walked, leaving giant tears that sent the bottoms dangling in the light breeze.

He replaced his dagger before stepping into Westmarket plaza, where the shopkeepers were packing their stalls for the evening. Backing against the clock tower, he scanned the few clusters of people still left in the marketplace, looking for Oarl's crew. Instead, he saw a sight that stole his breath: his beautiful Onie walking toward him, carrying a basket of vegetables.

Heart beating wildly, he opened his mouth to say something, but her eyes were down, studying the cobblestones. He shook his head—surely, she just hadn't seen him.

"Onie!" he called, not too loudly. Yet she continued walking, turning slightly left to enter another alley. Larin stared after her, his stomach churning. "Onie . . . ?"

He wanted to die where he stood. Loneliness flowed through him in waves, closed his throat tight. There was nothing for him now, not here, not anywhere. He stood with a hollow chest for a long moment, fighting back desperation.

Knowing he had to move his feet, he turned away, but the sense of being watched caused him to whirl around. There he saw Seishan, an informer for Oarl's gang, staring at him coolly from across the plaza.

His heart skipped a beat. Was that why she'd ignored him? Had she known Seishan was there? He shook his head, knowing he was being foolish—Onie was a beautiful girl who could have her pick of Wormpile boys. Wiping wet eyes, he shuffled into another alley.

His mind boiled with blackness as he stumbled home. Dark thoughts raced through his head: images of Onie kissing another while Oarl surrounded their building with steel. Images of the Morphasti dragging both he and Akul into the Marble Temple, to feed the god's pleasures in one of Morphat's horrible rituals. So thick was the evil brew swirling through his thoughts that he forgot his usual practice of peering around corners before turning, a precaution he'd developed for good reason. He rounded a corner and almost bumped into Kaligh's deep chest.

"Ho, Larin," Kaligh said, in his nasal twang. "We were getting worried about you."

Larin whipped around, but the silhouettes of two others stepped out of the side alley, and into his path.

Heart sinking, Larin watched six more of Oarl's crew amble from the shadows, the Wormpile's purest concentration of bullies and sadists. Now that group had one new member: a stocky man in red and black, sporting arched eyebrows and a face that looked like it'd be happiest pulling wings from insects. The wide forehead typical of Seridor's Parbani tribes was wrinkled in amused curiosity as he watched Larin blanch.

What was a Parbani doing in Oarl's gang?

As always, last to arrive was Oarl, a lanky brooder with pitch-black hair and a jutting chin that reminded Larin of a clenched fist. Oarl's face was all hard edges, an effect that created a strangely sculpted expression, a statue come to life. It was a face that somehow attracted pretty women, though when Larin looked, he saw only cruelty and spite. Oarl's smile always meant something mean or petty, his eyes permanently unbothered by laugh lines or any other sign of humanity.

Larin backed against the wall, gaze shifting nervously.

"Ah, Larin." Oarl stopped just out of Larin's reach, watching him through heavily lidded eyes. "That's quite a big pouch for someone of your strength. Let me take it off your hands."

Larin glanced at his pouch; he'd almost forgotten it.

"If you come get it yourself. Or is someone else going to do your job?"

Oarl ignored this, searching the alley with an exaggerated expression. "Where is your wife, Candro? Or are you the wife? I never can get it right."

Small, high-pitched titters escaped from Oarl's gang, and Larin scanned them desperately, waiting for the first to make his move.

Oarl grinned at Larin's frantic look. "Maybe if you can still walk after our games here, I'll have you fetch Candro for me. He and I need to have a discussion."

"Just listen for your mother's moans of pleasure; you'll find him."

Sharp laughter echoed from the alley walls, and Larin glanced up to see the darting movements of small heads as his observers hid behind the rooftop ledge. He almost smiled, remembering Candro's insistence that some misguided Wormpile youth actually looked up to him. It was strangely comforting, though it helped not a bit.

Oarl's eyes flicked upward at the unexpected laughter, but he gave no other sign he'd heard. "You have a smart mouth. One day, you'll wish you'd kept it shut." He stretched out his right hand, revealing a ring of red and black on his middle finger. "Morphat's temple is training me to be a priest. And I plan to rise far."

Larin's stomach dropped to his knees, and he fought surging panic. His worst nightmare had come to pass—all his enemies had joined forces. Even Akul wouldn't be able to stand against both Oarl and Morphat. He forced himself to look into Oarl's eyes.

"That role fits you perfectly."

Oarl smiled and leaned forward, early evening light casting shadows across the gaunt hollows in his cheeks. "When I'm a priest, the temple's full might will be behind me. I'll do whatever I want with you—your khald-addled old man can't take revenge on Morphat's entire army."

"He won't need to. He'll just come for you."

Oarl frowned and turned to the Parbani. "This conversation is over."

The Parbani smiled, a strange pointed smirk that almost matched the shape of his arched eyebrows. He began speaking Lyrashi words, and Larin's panic rose as he stared at the green-sash around the man's arm. Now he knew why the Parbani was here: the Marble Temple had given Oarl a Seridorian green-sash mage to help enforce Eldegod law in the Wormpile.

With helpless dread, Larin watched the Parbani begin his magic, realizing he'd be denied the dignity of landing a single blow on his tormentors. Soon, he recognized the spell: a green-ranked curse of gut-wrenching pain, one that'd shoot bursts of misery through his body for days. Yet his familiarity offered no advantage, for he'd as much hope of countering green-sash magic as he did flying out of this alley. Knowing it was hopeless, he put the pouch over one ear and a hand over the other and shouted the word of negation, preparing for horrible pain.

It never came. With shock, he felt himself bathed by the coolness of dissipating magic, and realized his anteword had actually worked. The mirror image of his surprise slowly dawned upon the mage's face, and for a frozen moment neither of them moved.

Larin recovered first. He whipped the pouch like a club, smashing the mage's nose and sending him sprawling in a spray of blood. Cheers rang out from his rooftop observers as he shot from the alley and Oarl's gang stumbled over the mage to tear after Larin.

He raced into the deserted street, sounds of pounding footsteps and bloodthirsty shouts close behind. He felt the sudden blow of a slingstone on his back, and he lurched forward, barely keeping his footing. Shouts of pleasure and laughter accompanied the impact, and wetness sprang to his eyes at the sharp pain.

Then he saw a sight that dropped his jaw.

Watching the entire chase from a courtyard was a slender, straight-backed woman in an explosion of red curls. She wore a silk dress draped by a purple mantle of nobility, sporting so many golden neck chains her throat appeared armored. While those chains dipped deep into her bodice, Larin knew they each ended in a charm—for he'd seen this woman before.

His enchantress.

He gaped and she squinted back at him, as if trying to read tiny letters on his forehead. Then she disappeared into a nearby alleyway, and without hesitation, Larin changed course and shot for the alleyway. For whoever she was, whatever she wanted, she was his only hope against the bloodthirsty horde behind him.

Larin whipped around the corner, half-expecting to see the damp brick wall of a dead end. Yet she was still there, studying him with those ice-blue eyes as he raced toward her. He pounded to a stop and tried to say something, but it escaped in unintelligible gasps. In any case, her attention had shifted to the alleyway entrance, where Enatt had just swung around the corner. He was followed closely by the others, who collected near the mouth of the alleyway, breathing hard and fixing their stares on the enchantress. The Parbani mage arrived last, rubbing his bloody nose and staring at Larin with hatred.

From the surrounding buildings, Larin heard the muffled stomping of dozens of small feet, and he realized his silent, supportive audience was racing up the stairs to view the confrontation from the windows above.

Oarl parted his gang and stepped to the front with his sword out. "You—out," he said to the enchantress, flipping his sword toward the alley entrance.

She tossed back a cascade of red hair, a gesture that Larin found strangely attractive. "I have business here." Her words were shaped by the clipped vowels of high nobility. "Begone."

Oarl smiled, and his eyes flicked over her haughty frame. "In other circumstances, I'd be more interested in pleasure than pain. But today, I'm in a hurry." He looked at his Parbani mage, who stepped out of the group and began shouting Lyrashi words as Oarl's gang began advancing. The enchantress watched them coolly, then began her own incantation. Larin recognized the Parbani's spell and scrambled away from her.

Without warning, a burst of flame shot from the Parbani's fingertips, enveloping the enchantress and coming close enough to Larin to bathe his face in a hot glow. A cloud of dust whipped into the air behind the Parbani and Oarl's gang, who hunched over as if freezing.

As the flames dissipated, the enchantress still stood, none the worse for wear. Fascinated, Larin noticed a dull glow from below her mantle and knew she'd been protected by one of her charms.

Then it was her turn. She finished her spell, and a sudden loud clanging filled the alley, as every member of Oarl's gang dropped their swords and fell to the ground, scratching themselves uncontrollably.

Sounds of amazement issued from the windows above, and Larin stared openmouthed as Oarl's gang twisted on the floor in a seizure of itching. He looked at the enchantress in wonder.

"I could watch that again and again."

She turned her piercing eyes his way, as if examining some strange sea creature just tossed onto the docks. Despite that cold stare, to Larin she was nothing but beautiful. Perhaps her lips were a little thin, and maybe her face could've been less stark, but those Nydyn high cheekbones, red curls, and pale blue eyes gave her an otherworldly beauty. To Larin, she held the visage of some spirit ice queen.

"Who are you, really?" she demanded.

His fascinated stare turned into a scowl. "Duke of Haques. You?"

Her blue eyes flashed, and Larin realized insulting a high-rank mage wasn't the smartest thing he could be doing. He swallowed. "Larin. Remember me?

"Of course I remember you! Do you think I'm an imbecile?" She waved her hand for silence, then uttered what Larin recognized as a privacy spell. She finished and looked up to the rooftops above, as if convincing herself their audience would hear nothing. Then she turned that hawklike gaze back on Larin.

"I've no time for games," she snapped. "Last night, I dreamt that I should avoid the Apex festivities and dreamt again that in the Wormpile, I'd find one who could defeat this black creature they call High Wizard. The first dream was exactly right, and I think you're the subject of the second, or I'd not step foot in this absolutely foul neighborhood. So I ask you again: who are you, really?"

Larin breathed deeply. "Apparently, I'm Haraf's servant."

She squinted, as if confirming a suspicion, and the import of her words dawned on Larin.

"Avoid the Apex festivities . . . and just who are *you?*"

"Laniette."

Larin stared, aghast. "*The* Laniette? From the Council of Twelve?"

"More like the Council of Two, now. But yes."

Larin was speechless. Somewhere in the distance, a shutter banged against the wall, accompanied by the gravelly shouts of a man yelling at his wife. "When we met before, you said you were green-sash," Larin said, finally. "Yet only violet-sash mages sit on the council. Were you lying then, or are you lying now?"

"You seem different from the sweet boy I remember—"

She was interrupted by the wet smack of a chamber pot being dumped from a window in a nearby alley, followed by a loud trickling that temporarily covered the shouts from the building on the other side.

Laniette's lip curled. "The people here are beasts."

"You don't much like Tanbari commoners, do you?"

Her face softened, but she ignored his comment. "I wasn't lying, then or now. It's possible for magical strength to grow even into the thirties. The day we met, I was probably already blue-sash strength, but didn't yet know. My husband Theralle recognized my blossoming talent and trained me to walk the final steps to full power. By last year, I was made violet-sash and was picked to replace him in the council."

"And what happened to Theralle?"

Her expression became stormy. "He was betrayed as he sat to talk peace with the Lizards. Betrayed by the same one who murdered the rest of the council today."

"Murdered? It was Kedrick's demon that—"

"Don't be ignorant!" she snapped. "Emderian planned that whole slaughter today—anyone with an ounce of magical knowledge can see that!"

Larin breathed deeply, knowing she was right. It explained everything, for no grade-three Demon should have been able to wipe out ten violet-sash mages. He looked into Laniette's pained eyes.

"So, Theralle's dead?"

"Long dead, Larin. We have only you and me to fight this monster they call High Wizard."

"I don't see how I'm going to help that fight, unless you physically throw me at him. I've been studying violet-sash spells, but my power is almost zero. Though Haraf seems to think otherwise."

Her mouth turned down. "Haraf. In every age, the Demon Lord chooses a servant, but they're usually men of high power and high evil. You seem as unlikely a choice as a newborn kitten. Perhaps you suffer delusions of grandeur."

"Then why are you here?" Larin snapped. "Take your Nydyn hauteur back to the Imperial District. I'm sure you've better things to do than grouse with a Wormpile street urchin."

"You do have spirit. Tell me, what makes you think you're Haraf's servant?"

"My Phrase: it means 'The lord escapes his prison.' Haraf's last words before being banished to the Gray Lands. I've talked to another of Haraf's servants twice now, a wizard with King Galin's disease named B'neikarian. And he gave me dreams—"

Laniette's face went pale. "B'neikarian . . . a being to be fought, not consorted with."

"So you believe me?"

She looked away and nodded, exposing a smooth, slender neck. "No matter. I'd ally with Haraf himself if it helped dispatch the monster who sent my husband to his death."

"*Tra* Laniette, this war isn't just about Emderian," Larin said, using the female honorific for nobility. "My puppet master wants me to release his host from the Gray Lands, and that will change the world. Are you sure this is your fight?"

She was silent a long moment. From the windows above came a few hushed rustling sounds, as their observers watched the silent conversation in awe.

Finally, she straightened, throwing red curls about her cheeks. "In my dream, Emja warned me to avoid the Apex festivities. Then he told me to come here, to the Wormpile, and I suspected it was you I sought, though he didn't show me your face. In my dream, Emja gave me visions of the Hunter—a tall man with a longbow. The very image the ancients used to depict Haraf." She breathed deeply, and Larin tried not to let his gaze wander down to that heaving chest. "It's true that in every book, in all the histories, Emja and Haraf are enemies. But now, Emja seems to be telling me to ally with the Demon Lord."

Larin shook his head; a world in which those two were allies was a strange one indeed. "There remains the small fact that I have zero magical talent. I am good with words, though. Maybe Emja thinks I can lower

Morphat's morale with a few insults."

She smiled, pushing a curly red lock behind her ear. "I find it hard to believe Haraf would pick an ordinary street urchin for a task he hasn't accomplished in thousands of years." She hesitated a moment, then seemed to come to a decision. "Come to the Kielenas mansion in the Imperial District on Apex day. I'll test you."

"I've been tested for magical power before . . ."

"By a violet-sash mage?"

"Well, no—"

"The Kielenas keep is on the east end of the Imperial District, recognizable for the yellow tiles on the main tower rooftop. Ask the servant at the gate to lead you to the dungeon."

Larin stared at her a moment.

"Go now. You have ten minutes till the spell wears off." Laniette waved toward Oarl's gang, twitching uncontrollably throughout the alley.

Larin nodded. His back aflame from the slingstone's blow, he retrieved his pouch and stepped over the jerking bodies until he reached Oarl, lying closest to the alley's entrance. He bent to retrieve Oarl's sword, triggering a wide-eyed look from his helpless enemy. For the first time in his life, Larin saw terror on Oarl's face.

Larin stood frozen, struggling with a flood of emotions as Candro's words swirled through his thoughts:

Someone's got to do something about Oarl.

Now was his chance. A simple downward cut, and a lifetime of pain and misery would be avenged. He felt the heady thrill of the possibility: two of Oarl's three lieutenants were here—he could take out Oarl and those two, then run back to Akul, and Akul would race out to dispatch the third lieutenant, Utra. The man who'd dared lay a fist on Onie's beautiful cheek. With Oarl and his three lieutenants gone, the gang would dissolve forever, like blood in the ocean.

He looked at Laniette and knew she wouldn't stop him. He scanned the windows above the alley and saw the faces of Penter, Lani, Yuok, and a dozen others, his silent audience, the ones who'd cheered him before. Yuok made violent throat-slitting motions, but the rest remained completely still, staring into the alley with wide eyes.

Everyone was watching him, and he had no idea what to do.

He looked down at Oarl, and memories from Morphat's temple sprang into his mind—Oarl manacled to a wooden structure that Larin now recognized as Seridor's ritual torture frame, the frame upon which Meidan had breathed his last agonizing breaths. His hand began shaking as he imagined slicing Oarl's throat as he lay helpless.

He threw the sword down, disgusted with himself. Oarl's eyes widened into relief, and Larin spat. "You're lucky I'm not like you." He looked at

Laniette, who watched him impassively, then shook his head and stepped out of the alley. He stumbled toward the temple, feeling a sudden urgency to warn Akul about Oarl's new alliance with Morphat.

Yet after another block, he slipped into an empty alleyway and leaned against the wall. For a long moment, he listened to the sounds of his own breathing, feeling the press of cold stone against his hands. Two memories filled his thoughts: the slingstone plowing into his back as Oarl's crew laughed at his pain, and Onie's face as she avoided his eyes.

The loneliness of his Wormpile life was absolute. He had no more friends, except Candro—all scared off by Oarl, as had been his beautiful, sweet Onie. The temple, the place he'd spent all his boyhood hours, the only place where some few would talk to him, had rejected him forever. The circle of isolation was tightening; it felt like the entire Wormpile was falling in on him. With all that, he couldn't kill Oarl, even after being given the only chance he'd get in this lifetime. He struggled to contain his emotions, staring straight ahead and forcing his eyes to remain dry.

Loud ringing interrupted his thoughts, and he pushed off the wall, listening to the hollow clanging echo from every part of the city. Within seconds, the sound of bells was joined with the cacophony of a thousand voices, as Wormpile residents streamed from their houses to meet on the street, talking loudly over each other. Though Larin had never heard those bells in his lifetime, everyone in Aldive knew what they meant.

Tanbar had a new king.

He raced out of the alley, into a street packed with people.

"Maldovin is dead!" someone shouted.

"No, not dead. I hear he's unconscious!"

"Who's the new king—Selton?"

"Idiot! Selton can't ascend the throne—it's Maldovin's brother, Yalinus."

"But they can't let an imbecile rule the empire! Where is Olivan's guardian?"

"Just watch—Aimes will govern through Yalinus."

With that, Larin felt suddenly sick. For no reason he could name, he knew Akul would take this news hard. He spun around and raced for Emja's temple. He darted around the milling crowds, twisted through several alleyways, and ran through the jade arches, not caring that Tierre had banned him from the temple on pain of death. He ran through the empty alehouse and up to Ruldir, who stood behind the bar.

Larin placed his hands on the counter, breathing hard, as Ruldir looked at him with a worried expression. The fact that Larin wasn't supposed to be here seemed the farthest thing from his mind.

"Where's Akul?" Larin gasped.

"I don't know. A man came in and gave him a sealed scroll and a wad of woman's clothes, including a wig uglier than a dead octopus. Akul opened the scroll, told me to run the bar, and then raced out. And then the bells started ringing." Ruldir glanced nervously at the door. "Larin, I think everything's about to change."

Larin nodded, then began racing out.

"Oh, Larin—"

Larin turned around, and Ruldir pulled at his black beard. "Onie was here for you; she didn't know you'd been banished. Said something about it being too dangerous earlier, and she'll meet you outside the temple gate tomorrow."

Larin gaped, staring at Ruldir. "Right," was all he managed to say.

He turned around, his back sore as a raging fire, entering a Wormpile now even more under control of his enemy. He knew he should be terrified.

Yet he walked the entire way home without touching feet to the ground a single time.

"The khulas shot from the trees all along the southern flank, ripping units apart and sending General Hamitor's army into panic. They rode in twos and threes, each beast and rider cutting through a platoon before disappearing back into the forest. When Hamitor's army swung around to reinforce its southern flank, hundreds more knights stormed into the weakened northern defenses, slaying General Hamitor and his commanders. Then, the army scattered like mice, discarding weapons and insignia."

Eyewitness account of the slaughter of Seridor's fifteen-thousand-man sixth division by Commander Lukas and five hundred knights. The final battle of the Swamp Wars, Seridor soon sued for peace along its entire northern frontier. This capped a string of victories that resulted in Lukas's ascendance to the royal council, only the second non-Nydyn so honored since the birth of the Maldovin dynasty.

Tanbari history and modern legends, edition thirteen.

XVI

The palace cleaning servant was broad-shouldered, her face hard. Her body moved woodenly under the simple dress as she stomped through the empty hallways of the Imperial Compound's storage rooms, continually brushing woven hair from her eyes. The new shoes made her gait wobbly, and she'd twisted her ankle twice already. It was far from pleasant, but this mission was too important for niceties like personal comfort.

She entered a room filled with old clothes and out-of-date palace uniforms. Closing the door, she sifted through discarded leggings and coats, as if to wash every piece in the room. Yet she had no intent to scrub a single stocking. Eventually, she found that the bottom mound of clothing was stitched together, formed into a rope that disappeared into the wall. After a second glance, it was clear the wall was nothing of the kind. With a satisfied grunt, the maid yanked open the hidden door.

The queen, Panjus, and a second man stared as she crawled through the entranceway, wincing at the very unladylike curses issuing from an unladylike throat. Finally, the maid stood and threw the black wig to the floor, exposing a head balder than a polished apple.

"You wore it well," Panjus quipped.

"Stow it," the maid growled, then immediately kneeled as the queen stepped forward. "Your Highness."

"Lukas," she whispered, eyes wet. "Thank you for visiting us in these difficult times."

"My liege, I rushed here at all speed."

The queen nodded, her diamond dragon earrings glinting in the room's low light. Her hair was tightly braided and coiled behind her head several times, creating a gray pinnacle to offset her short stature. She wore a fur-lined red gown, laced in front and embroidered with charging green dragons that matched the emeralds in her golden headband.

Lukas watched the creased face of this remarkably intelligent woman, a face that, when he'd last seen it eighteen years ago, had contained not a single wrinkle. Back then, her hair had been pure black, the source of a secret bond neither had ever acknowledged. For they were the only two black-hairs in the king's close council, two ebony dots among a sea of flame-headed Nydyns.

She touched his shoulder lightly. "My dear Lukas. Rise."

Lukas rose, his eyes widening as he took in the second man. "Korrin . . ."

Korrin smiled broadly. "Well, after eighteen years I expected to see an old man, but I must say, that dress does give you a certain glow."

Lukas laughed, and the two men hugged tightly, pounding each other on the back. "For all the gods, I never thought I'd see you again, you old tagalanth," Lukas said, pulling away. He held Korrin at arm's length, staring at the red beard now flecked with gray and strands of silver-red hair falling about that flat, wagon wheel of a face. "You, on the other hand, have definitely gotten older."

"Heartwarming," Panjus said. "Now may we begin?"

They both stopped, and Lukas nodded coolly. "Aye." He turned to the queen. "My liege, by what trickery does Yalinus claim the throne? Olivan's guardian Duke Eregar should possess *Hrenetan* until the king's nephew turns fifteen. The rules of succession are clear—idiocy disqualifies ascension if a royal family member is present."

She sighed, twiddling a silver lock that had escaped those massive braids. "Actually, it's more complicated, Lukas. The guardian must declare for his ward on the very day the king cannot rule. Duke Eregar was incapacitated by severe fevers and has been absent from the court for months."

Lukas shot Panjus a hard look. "Isn't it the royal advisor's job to ensure the ward's representation in court?"

Panjus's face was dark. "Duke Eregar was in no state to pick a successor, yet it's true I didn't push as I should have." He closed his eyes and breathed deeply. "Lukas, I know we've had our differences. But we must bury them now, for too much is at stake." He held out his hand.

Lukas glanced at Panjus's hand as if it were a cluster of poison needles. "Differences? By all the Demons, you bearded possum, you sent me fleeing for my life over a love that was no crime!"

Panjus stiffened. "Just as I remember you, Lukas—a hothead with a remarkably poor understanding of politics. Do you think our royal court is some nursery, where only the rock-throwing child is punished? Keeping our fractious provinces from civil war is a monumental task, one far surpassing your stupid notions of justice."

Lukas's face reddened. "And you have no concept of honor! Your contempt for justice confirms everything—"

"Enough!"

Queen Relena glided across the room to stare unflinchingly into Lukas's eyes. Her golden headband glinted dully, its dragon emeralds a sad reminder of a royal house brought low. "Our empire is in far too dire peril for old enmities," she said softly. "My loyal servants, everything depends on you. You *will* shelve this vitriol."

Lukas bowed his head. "Yes, Highness. Forgive me."

"And me," Panjus said.

Lukas turned to Panjus, taking his newly offered hand without enthusiasm. "Aye, Panjus, let us bury the past. We've more important things to worry about now." He sighed, then searched the room. "Can I see him?"

Panjus nodded, and Lukas followed him to a corner in the low-ceilinged room. There, on an unassuming cot in the corner was the Emperor of Tanbar, a man Lukas had grown to love. On the table next to him was a stewed bowl of oats and a reed straw, which Lukas assumed was the only way to feed the most powerful man in the world. The king was lying face upward, blinking furiously. That was all.

Lukas knelt, touching his bald head to the cot's edge. "My king. Whatever is required, this tragedy will be undone."

Maldovin blinked, and his eyes became wet. *Luka, you were ever my loyal servant*, he thought. *I sought to smooth political feathers, and in the process I wronged a great man. You were the best—the khula knight brigades excelled under your command, as they have not since.*

He could say none of it. His eyes became wetter, the pure frustration of being unable to apologize to the man whose punishment haunted him often.

Lukas rose, his face visibly upset. He looked at the queen.

"Command me."

Queen Relena nodded slightly. "Panjus has uncovered some information about the king's condition. There is hope, but only the slimmest. Panjus, please explain."

Panjus sat wearily, stroking his beard. "Korrin, what of your family?"

If Korrin were surprised by this, he hid it well. "My wife is long dead from the rotting disease. My two sons are in the army, traveling to Avensai as we speak. Only my mother still lives, in the Uvalan valley."

Panjus nodded, then looked at Lukas.

"I have only a son, who lives with me," Lukas said. "My nephew, really, but a son to me."

"Will you leave him now, to serve your empire?"

Lukas rubbed his bald head. "I—I cannot leave him to face Morphat's horrors alone. We hang by a thread in the Wormpile; once I'm known to be gone, he won't last a day. Unless the palace can order action against the Wormpile gangs and Eldegod stain blotting our Port District?"

Queen Relena shook her head reluctantly. "We believe our illustrious High Wizard is in league with Hekrian's treachery. Just minutes ago, we received word Emderian plans to revoke the law of marble, the law that limits Eldegod temples in the empire. We've no doubt Yalinus will do as he's told."

Lukas grimaced and flopped into a chair. "Then Eldegod temples will sprout everywhere. All of Aldive will know the Wormpile's terror." He put his face in his hands, and the room remained silent a moment.

"Your son," Panjus said with a subdued voice. "Will you leave him to serve your king?"

Lukas lifted a red face. "We must protect him first. Perhaps we can move him outside the city?"

Korrin nodded. "My mother lives in a house near the Uvalan Falls, a hundred miles from the city walls. He can stay there."

"Good," Panjus said. "We may have other uses for that house."

Lukas's face hardened. "Panjus, stop dancing around the fire. Tell us why we're here."

Panjus rose from his chair. "Then listen well. As you all know, the Imperial Compound is dead to magic, other than that of passive devices like warder charms. The empire's magicians have accomplished this feat over a hundred years, through countless warding spells that are woven through every stone of our compound."

"Does this civics lesson go on much longer?"

"We'll keep a gracious tongue in this room," the queen snapped.

Lukas hung his head. "Pardon, Highness."

Panjus smiled tightly. "As I was saying, our compound has been hardened against human magic—that is, anything based on the Lyrashi language." He began pacing the room. "Yet, in the Shernock swamps, there exists life not so polite as to follow human magical laws. *Indigen* life that has existed for millennia before humans first came to this land, life that moves and breathes to Spellgiver's phases. The plants and creatures of those dark swamps know nothing of Lyrashi, yet radiate intense magical power, of a type we know little about. It was one of these plants that Hekrian used to incapacitate the king." Panjus stopped his pacing and looked at Korrin and Lukas. "Qunaserre."

They stared back blankly.

Panjus began pacing again. "A plant with three sexes, which emits flying seeds that look very much like insects. When two seeds from the same plant meet, they fight to the death and sometimes exude toxins. Only the survivor flies off to form a new plant."

Korrin's round face elongated slightly. "Toxins . . ."

"Yes. Toxins that, when ingested, can shut down most muscle function in the body."

The room was silent a moment. Then Lukas shuddered, making the sign of the hermit god across his forehead. "Rakva . . ."

Panjus nodded. "It was a perfect crime. The toxin is of a magical nature and triggers upon force of will. In the swamps, nearby plants magically influence battles between seeds, to surround themselves with plants of the opposite two sexes. The Qunaserre plants can force alternate sexed seeds to emit the toxins, thereby killing seeds of the same sex."

Korrin gaped. "This is all very complicated."

"That it is," Panjus said, wearily. "Shernock is strange beyond imagining. The point is Hekrian could have slipped the seed into the king's food any time. It would lie dormant until a small force of will from Hekrian released the toxins, one requiring no Lyrashi words. Our warding spells would have been—were—useless."

The queen nodded. "It is no accident that the king's condition occurred while arresting Selton. Hekrian timed it well."

"This is almost beyond belief," Lukas said. "So then, what? I assume all isn't lost, else our trip here is in vain."

"We've one chance to save him," Panjus said. "The seeds germinate under the branches of the Yirikan fan. It's the only place they can grow, for as seeds dissolve, their own toxins kill any new sprouts. Only Yirikan fan leaves absorb the toxins and allow the seed to grow."

Lukas folded his arms. "Then we're after the Yirikan leaves. Or are you holding back yet one more twist to this story to drag it out further?"

The queen straightened, and Lukas continued quickly. "Pardon again, Highness."

Relena's smile was brief. "Gathering Yirikan leaves is no small feat, Lukas. The Shernock swamps teem with dangerous plants and creatures about which we know little. It is said in the high season, the swamps radiate so much magic that no non-indigen creature can survive long." She breathed deeply. "Yet, if you do not go, he will die. What we ask of you is to assume grave danger for your empire—there is no shame if you cannot."

Lukas and Korrin both knelt then. "My queen, I offer my sweat and tears," Lukas said. "Once we move my boy outside the city walls, I am ready."

"I am yours to command, Your Highness," said Korrin.

"Good," Panjus said gravely. "We'll make arrangements to spirit away Lukas's nephew, and you'll both leave in two days."

Korrin rose, round face wrinkled with strain. "It—It may be more than two days. My queen, as difficult as this is to say, other tasks await us, equally as important as saving the king."

The queen's eyes widened, and Panjus gasped. "Korrin!"

Korrin's expression was pained. "Emja speaks to me in these dark times and has told me much. This whole treachery"—he waved his hand around the room—"is but a small battle in a much wider war. There are great forces at work, forces we can barely perceive."

Panjus rolled his eyes. "Korrin, as Emja's High Priest in the empire, your dedication to our god is without question. But this is no time for fearful prattle. Emja helps those who help themselves."

Lukas turned to Korrin. "Do you find him as annoying as I do?"

The queen searched Korrin's eyes. "Korrin, if we lose the king, we have lost all. A traitor's servant whispers into Yalinus's left ear, and a devotee of Morphat whispers into his right. Surely this cannot serve Emja's purpose?"

"No," Korrin admitted. "I don't expect to be believed, but at least hear me out. Emja speaks to me in dreams—"

Panjus snorted, and now the queen turned that cold gaze on the royal advisor.

"Please continue," Panjus said, his eyes merry.

"We think we see simple treachery," Korrin said, "but it is much more. As you all know, the Old Gods, Human Gods, and the horrors from the Gray Lands—Demons—have fought a three-way war since the time's beginning. Both the Old Gods and Demons are forces of evil, but fortunately they despise each other even more than they do the Human Gods. Yet what has always been may not always be so. The Eldegod begin to gain the upper claw, for Seridor conquers tribe after tribe of the southern deserts, converting them to their cause. We in Tanbar do not make enough new adherents for the Human Gods—and while this was true long before my birth, as Emja's prime servant in this age, I accept my share of blame." Korrin clenched his fists. "We now find ourselves at the cusp of history—the victories of Morphat and his host are about to snowball into full-blown disaster."

Panjus scowled. "If Emja is so concerned, why doesn't he just smite Seridor's armies when they attack us?"

"It's not nearly so simple, Panjus. The gods don't directly operate in our plane, yet their influence is unquestionable." He looked at the queen and Lukas for support. "The Eldegod are winning. The Lidath in the north, Seridor in the south, and the cannibal tribes to the east all worship the six-legged gods, and they prepare to descend upon us without mercy. Emja tells me this mission to save the king is critical—if he lives, we have some chance to turn Morphat's army. If he dies, nothing can save us."

"Then, all the more reason to make haste," the queen said softly. Her eyes bored into Korrin, pleading for action.

"My queen, Emja has imparted something else to me, something remarkable. The Human Gods have realized that Morphat stands on victory's ridge. For the first time in history, they've sought alliance with *them*. Demons." He spat the word, as if to remove it from his tongue immediately. "Haraf and Emja are joining forces to stave off defeat."

Lukas rubbed his head nervously. Panjus's eyes shifted between the queen and Korrin.

"Then, what? Why should we delay this journey?"

"Because our party isn't yet complete. Lukas will serve as the empire's champion, I as Emja's servant. But two others will come. I am horrified by this, but we must travel with Haraf's minion, and also his 'Seeker.'" Deep distaste played across Korrin's round face. "As loathe as I am to truck with the Lord of Demons, our journey is doomed otherwise."

"Korrin," said the queen. "Shall we risk the king's life based on a dream? And how will we find Haraf's servant? While you are Emja's greatest champion, could your dream be but the workings of your own soul?"

"Er—my queen." Lukas stammered. The scar running from nose to ear was throbbing. "Eh, my boy. He—he may be the one of which Korrin speaks. I think he's Haraf's servant."

Korrin paled. "You have such a monster living with you?"

Lukas shut his eyes. "Korrin, we've saved each other's life more times than I can count, and we are closer than brothers. Only for this do I not wring your neck."

Korrin stepped back, though not from fear. "Describe him."

"My boy is a good lad. He has a smart mouth and makes a few unwise choices now and again, but he's kept his sanity in a neighborhood of horror."

"I'm sorry, Lukas. I cannot reconcile serving Haraf with being a 'good lad.' Does he pray to Haraf? Sacrifice small animals in his name? Swear death to servants of the Human Gods? What makes him Haraf's servant?"

The veins in Lukas's endless forehead popped to the surface, but he kept his cool. "Since he was a tyke, he's shouted the same three words: 'Kinech Aklad Vahrusen.' It means—"

"The Lord Escapes His Prison," Korrin interjected, eyes hard. "Go on."

"He spouted that phrase randomly until two years ago, when we bought a charm to ward it off. Since then, he's been free of the curse."

Panjus scowled. "Well, I'm not sure that—"

"There's more," Lukas said. "A year ago, he met a high-rank wizard who serves Haraf and who bespelled him with horrible dreams. The man swears my boy will fight Haraf's war against Morphat. This wizard is strange; he has multiple personas, which appear at different times in the guise of different people . . ."

Korrin made a choking noise, furiously tracing Emja's glyph across his forehead. "B'neikarian . . . The multifaced one . . ." He staggered to a chair and sat down, swallowing slowly. "There's no doubt then. Your boy indeed serves Haraf."

Lukas sighed. "I'm almost afraid to ask: who is this man?"

"B'neikarian is no man. He's a creature that has existed since the beginning of time. He assumes a man's body, changing form to match his personas. The personas themselves change over time, and some say they're real people who've lived and died. But the dark spirit that is B'neikarian never dies. He only guides Haraf's minions down the path of evil."

"Larin doesn't have an evil hair on his head; I don't care what you say."

"So you may think, Lukas. It's clear to me there are things about your boy you don't know. Haraf's servants cannot escape the malevolence of their master. The phrase he shouts—it means he is chosen to release Haraf from the Gray Lands. That in itself is an evil act, for it will bring our world to ruin." Korrin stood, placing his hand on Lukas's shoulder. "As you said, Lukas, we're brothers, but I tell you now that I'll not allow your boy to loose that group of horrors upon us. I'll not allow the Demons to escape their world and end ours."

The room was filled with heavy breathing, and Lukas found his own chair, suddenly overwhelmed by the day's events.

The queen looked uncertainly at all three men, suddenly seeming very small. "My—my apologies for doubting you, Korrin. It appears your dreams had some truth."

Korrin nodded graciously. "My queen, it is nothing, but I worry about this Seeker. Lukas, do you know who that might be?"

Lukas shook his head. "Of that, I know nothing."

Panjus shifted his gaze between Korrin and Lukas. "Then where does that leave us? Does Emja insist we wait for this Seeker?"

Korrin nodded. "This journey will not be successful otherwise."

Panjus looked annoyed, and Korrin scowled at Panjus's impatient expression. "Panjus, you clearly misunderstand the game we play. Saving the king is critical, but only one skirmish in an enormous war. The gods have been aligning their champions on this Thirazi board for years, and if we engage without all the pieces, we will fail."

Panjus sighed, knowing he was defeated. "I'm still skeptical, Korrin, but everything we hold dear, we may have no choice. We are in Emja's hands." He looked at Lukas, whose head was hung in deep thought.

"And apparently, Haraf's."

<hr />

"Here we are." Emderian beamed, as he inserted another sweet into Yalinus's open mouth. They'd made it a game—Yalinus would close his eyes and try to guess what flavor taffy rested on his tongue.

"Berry!" came Yalinus's muffled voice, as he chewed through the sticky mouthful.

"Very good!" Emderian said, smiling. "You're most certainly the world's taffy expert." He pulled out two scrolls, unrolling one of them with two white-gloved hands. "And now, we just have to do two tiny things before we can get back to our taffy. My plan is for us to eat everything in that bowl before we go to bed tonight."

Yalinus clapped his hands. "I'll get all the berry taffies—those are good!"

"Very well." Emderian sighed, as if sorely disappointed. He placed the scroll before Yalinus. "You remember how to mark your name?"

"Of course," Yalinus said, scowling. "I can make big letters, watch." He signed the scroll with big looping letters, and Emderian's eyebrows lifted in appreciation.

"Those are big letters indeed. Can you make even bigger letters on this next scroll?"

Yalinus proved that he could, and Emderian beamed. "That is excellent! You did such a good job, you should eat all the rest of the taffies!"

Yalinus gave a small squeal of pleasure and began digging into the bowl.

Hekrian scowled. "Thus are laws fashioned in the Empire's capital in these times."

Emderian's pale cheeks stretched into a sardonic grin. "I suspect you'll have a few laws of your own."

"At least I'll explain what he signs so he has some understanding."

The High Wizard nodded earnestly. "Excellent. Please do invite me when you describe how you'll allocate smaller provincial tax collection percentages based on the mean number of contributed infantry divided by the provincial estimated assets."

Hekrian stared with distaste at this diminutive, falsely humble man, an annoyance who'd inserted himself into Hekrian's machinations like a persistent shrew. A man who, without his power, would've been but a small-time clerk in the office of his betters. Emderian was short, balding, and cursed by a small, recessed chin that gave him a deceptively weak demeanor. He dressed in funny ways, as only a lifelong bachelor could—brightly dyed leather shoes contrasting with too-short breeches, a thin silk tunic that might've looked acceptable on a sturdier man, and those cursed bright white gloves, permanent as skin.

Hekrian opened his mouth to reply but stopped as he saw Yalinus watching them without comprehension.

"Your Majesty, there are some new toys waiting in your chambers. There is a bird-kite, and a wagon, and in the stables a tagalanth to pull it."

"I want to see them!"

Hekrian snapped his fingers, and the king's butler left the group at the base of the royal platform. Yalinus flew down the steps first, and the man whirled around to follow the king. Silently, Hekrian and Emderian watched Yalinus skip down the length of the Great Hall, his entourage shuffling somberly behind.

"He's probably the happiest monarch to sit in this hall," Emderian remarked pleasantly.

Hekrian's eyebrows furrowed, then he stooped to pick up the signed scrolls. "Let's have a look at these. Yes, this one revokes the law of marble, as we agreed. What is this one?" He read the second scroll a minute, then looked at Emderian. "Why in Emja's name would you decree that all Hemeks turn in their weapons?"

"Emja has nothing to do with it," Emderian said, eyes twinkling.

"Bah—" Hekrian exclaimed in disgust. He threw the scrolls back at Emderian. "Your laws are temporary. When Selton is anointed, Morphat's temples will be banned altogether. No more half-hearted decrees like the Law of Marble. Maldovin might tolerate a few Eldegod cesspools, but we will not."

Emderian shrugged mildly. "Funny, I've heard our temples are sprouting throughout Aimes like mushrooms after a rain."

"That is temporary also. We've a few accommodations with Seridor. But when the house of Selton alights that throne, be sure things will change."

"Yes, of course," Emderian said, wringing his gloved hands in consternation. He looked at the throne. "Still, after Selton is lifted to that seat by Seridor's might, I wonder if our duke will have much to bargain with."

Hekrian sneered. "You seem to have mastered the art of hiding your sharp tongue behind a pleasant demeanor, High Wizard. Well, I'm not taken in, though I see how you've kept your true nature from Maldovin all those years."

"Honored Royal Advisor, I am merely pointing out a subtle flaw in your excellent plan."

"Do you think us fools? We have a balance of power between Aimes and Seridor. The army of Aimes will wait patiently, poised at Seridor's throat while its armies rampage through the lower valleys. If Seridor refuses to withdraw, it is but a short three-day march to Kaman for us." Hekrian folded his arms. "We both get what we want—Seridor keeps the disputed region, and Selton gains the throne."

Emderian bowed deeply. "As I said, a most excellent plan."

Hekrian squinted. "I cannot make sense of you. I assume with these two laws, you're finished? I'll be needing the king's full attention for the next several days."

"I'll have some additional decrees regarding our Hemek population, but those can wait a few weeks. Other than that, I have one small trifle, which doesn't require the king's attention. It could be handled directly by his advisor."

Hekrian lifted an eyebrow.

"I have a secret mission for Lieutenant Beurak of the palace guards. If you could send him to my chambers at his earliest convenience, I'll have everything I need for now."

"Secret mission?"

"Well, that's what we'll tell him."

A mild look of disgust crossed Hekrian's face. "Lieutenant Beurak is married."

Emderian exploded into laughter, a sight Hekrian had never seen on this strange, mild-mannered High Wizard. "Oh, my royal advisor, don't ever lose your innocence," he wheezed, trying to catch his breath. "Yes, let's pretend I want him for my bed."

Hekrian drew his cloak tight around his body, suddenly aware that they were totally alone in the Great Hall. "I never believed the rumors that your chambers were specially constructed to muffle screams," he whispered. "Or the stories of palace staff who disappeared forever into your chambers. Surely these are lies."

"Of course they're lies," Emderian said, winking. "Morphat's service may require sacrifice, but it is done for love and only to the willing, that they might stand by his side in the afterlife."

Hekrian spat. "Do you think I'm some ignorant Seridorian peasant? Don't feed me that swill. I know what Morphat's worship entails. Love has no part of it."

Emderian's mouth twitched. "Well, the god does have to feed."

"Why Lieutenant Beurak?" Hekrian searched Emderian's pale eyes for understanding. "He's a good man, well-loved by his troops. He has a wife, children. He is a good father . . ."

"Interesting thing about fathers. Mine smashed me to a pulp on a regular basis, then locked me in a cage for years." Emderian shrugged, as if describing a childhood lake visit. "Some fathers teach their children letters, and others beat them until they cannot walk. Each to his own, eh?"

Hekrian stared. "Your father had no right to do what he did. But that doesn't change—"

"Oh, he had every right," Emderian snapped. "Those who have power use it. Those who lack power take what they are given. At that time, he had power, and he did as he pleased."

Hekrian looked sick. "What kind of man are you?"

Emderian smiled a small, triangular smile that hinted at something severely broken deep beneath. "I'll tell you, my good advisor, though I don't think you really want to know. Let's just say that, as a child, I alternated my time between hiding from my father's rampages and capturing small animals in a nearby forest, where I proved that I, too, had power—the power to take their lives. At first, I merely killed them. Later I drew it out, seeing how much of their bodies I could destroy while still observing breath in their lungs."

Hekrian watched Emderian in silent horror.

Emderian smiled a sickly smile. Then he removed his right-hand glove, revealing five blackened stubs where once had been fingers. Hekrian backed away, feeling his stomach rise. "My father gave me a special gift, once. I opened the box eagerly, caring less about the present than the fact my father was showing me love for the first time. The box contained a manacle. When I looked at him curiously, he took the manacle, chained my hand over the hearth, and burned my fingers to stubs. For you see, I'd touched his whiskey flask the night before."

Hekrian gasped. "High Wizard, I'm sorry."

Emderian replaced the glove, then turned to lean over the platform railing, gazing out at the Great Hall. "My mother, bless her, fought to stop my father's torture, but she had no power. She was beaten as regularly as me, and we became partners in victimhood. At twelve, my father locked me in a cage in the basement, telling me he'd killed my mother. I spent two years unable to stand, fed hard bread and water, forever stunting my growth to this small frame you secretly scoff at."

Hekrian closed his eyes, not trusting himself to say anything.

"My mother found me, finally. She'd stunned my father with a lantern, and we escaped. But it was only after my magical training in the city of Floire, where I learned I had spectacular talent, that I began to feel truly powerful." He twisted backward to look at Hekrian. "Can you guess the first thing I did after leaving Floire as a violet-sash mage?"

Hekrian's face was stormy. "I would have killed my father."

Emderian beamed. "Splendid! Quite right. He was my first human kill, and I made a mess of it. Intestines on the floor, blood everywhere, a mess. I've become much better at invoking pain while keeping the floor clean." He chuckled.

"But after you killed your father, what need have you for these atrocities? You proved you were more powerful than he."

"My dear royal advisor, do you think such power cravings can be awakened by an entire lifetime, then turned off so readily? I assure you, it isn't so. With my skills at magic, I found myself easily able to move from animals to people. Yet, in the end, even one of my magical talents cannot kill forever and remain in polite society."

"For all the gods, no," Hekrian said, shivering. "People like you must be stopped."

"Yes, perhaps. Yet with the popularity of Morphat, I've found another way. Morphat's temple allows me—nay, *requires* me—to continue my hobby while still allowing me to appear respectable. We both win."

"B-but surely in this world someone loves you. Your mother—she cared for you, rescued you. Can you perform such acts knowing what she would think?"

"I gave my mother an even more excruciating death than the one I gave my father."

Hekrian's jaw dropped, and he began to shiver uncontrollably.

"Serving Morphat requires severing the bonds that tie us to this world. Only by taking the people we love most and feeding them to the god can we truly give ourselves over to him. This is the purest act of devotion." A brief crack in Emderian's pleasant tone showed a hint of remorse, but it was gone as soon as it appeared.

The Great Hall was silent then, as Hekrian struggled to control his stomach, and Emderian watched him coolly. Finally, the High Wizard's mouth turned downward.

"Oh, don't look so appalled. That land to the south you're so cozy with—its government is filled with men like me. Did you think you were signing your treaties with wood sprites?"

Hekrian's face turned scarlet. "Whereas you are a monster, we merely use the monsters to achieve our goals. In the end, we'll banish your kind from everywhere in the kingdom."

Emderian turned around again, gazing at the streams of light playing across the wooden floor. For a long moment, the only sound in the Great Hall was that of a bird flapping high in the rafters. "If you're planning to kill me, it's ill-advised. I'm wearing very powerful warder charms, and as you know, those function perfectly in our compound." He straightened, keeping his small back to Hekrian. "Unless, of course, you have some of whatever you gave the king."

Gritting his teeth, Hekrian removed his hand from his dagger. Suddenly desperate to escape this monster, he whirled around and raced for the stairway. He hesitated at the top stair. "So, in the end, why Lieutenant Beurak? You are High Wizard—you've no need to show your power over a lowly palace guard."

There was a moment of utter stillness. The sunlight streaming from the great arched windows glinted in a thousand places from the rows of hanging shields. Hekrian watched Emderian's narrow back as he stared outward, wondering if the High Wizard had heard his question and whether a crossbow bolt could find its way through his defenses.

Finally Emderian sighed. "Because he is a good father. Because he has people who love him." He twisted around to peer into Hekrian's eyes. "It's not urgent. You can send him to my chambers tomorrow after dinner."

"I'll see to it," Hekrian mumbled, flying down the steps.

Emderian smiled, watching Hekrian stride the length of the great hall. When the royal advisor had almost reached the massive doors, Emderian called out: "You know, it's all the same in the end." The words echoed through the rafters, bouncing off the rows of shields lining the great hall. Hekrian halted, but did not turn around.

"Whereas I admit this is about my own personal power, you claim a higher cause. Otherwise, I think we're not so different."

Hekrian's fists clenched. Finally, without turning around, he resumed his march, opened the massive door, and stepped out.

Emderian watched him leave with a melancholy smile.

"The Lizards will never win, for one simple reason: they care nothing about the future, about strategy, about tactics. They live only for battle. Even victory is nothing to them next to the violent throes of combat. My lords and ladies, theirs is a threat we need not fear."

General Uthan the Great, to the royal court under Maldovin II, after clearing the Avensai passes of Lidathi forces for a hundred miles.

XVII

The constant sway of the thrukk had turned Kemharak's lower appendages numb. He wasn't often sick, but the endless journey atop this lumbering, rocking monster was driving him close. He placed his lower arms on the creature's back, trying to avoid watching his beast's six furry legs shuffle in hypnotic rhythm across the hard ice.

Days ago, they'd exited the forests onto the frozen wasteland of this immense sloping ice sheet. The jagged peaks above were lost in clouds, and the wind whipped down the field of ice like an angry god. Before them, mountains stretched outward in every direction, their sides hugged by ageless ice that ran through the valleys, disappearing into unseen depths. Kemharak marveled that they'd traveled so long on this sideways tundra, struggling with their footing lest they roll down the slope to their frozen deaths. Yet such was the terrain here at the top of the world; the mountains proclaimed their power proudly. Only by descending and admitting defeat could one be free of the ice.

Kemharak reduced exposure to the swaying thrukk in front by shifting emphasis from vision to hearing, focusing what little sight remained on the backs of his elite guard. No more than twenty rode before him, protecting him from surprise attack. It was formality only; the chances that any band of humans would brave the ice to engage this immense army were remote. The bulk of his forces lay behind—they stretched forever, a multiheaded beast slithering its way across the mountainside. Yet for all its might, his army was but a trail of ants across the vast expanse of white.

Below him, the human struggled to keep pace, its arms chained to

Kemharak's saddle, staggering forward step after endless step. It was wrapped in an old thrukk-fur coat, the two lower sleeves cut away. At first, Kemharak had watched it try to maintain balance on the steep ice, attempting to keep pace with the thrukk. In the last day or so, he'd seen it slowly surrender to circumstance, allowing the thrukk to drag it for miles across the frozen landscape. Only when the pain in its arms became unbearable did it try to right itself, staggering forward for another hour until it surrendered again.

Kemharak looked at the riderless thrukk beside him, carrying his personal belongings, then at the beast ahead. "Guard!"

The guard's rear vision pods flipped open, but then he twisted on his beast to face his commander. "Revered one."

"I would converse with the human. Rearrange my belongings and mount it upon this thrukk." He pointed with his upper left claw at the beast beside him.

The guard's vision pods tinged red for the briefest instant, but Kemharak ignored it. To do otherwise would mandate this soldier's immediate death.

"Yes, revered one," the guard said, halting his thrukk. Up-thrust claws and sharp-pitched whistles traveled down the line of troops, as the head of the army slowed to a stop.

Manek pulled his thrukk beside Kemharak. His pods were pink, and the scales about his feeding orifice were pulled back. "This is wrong. The human will ride the thrukk, while most of our soldiers walk."

Kemharak swept his gaze across the ice field, lidding his pods against the sharp wind. "It shall be as I say." He turned to the guard, busy disconnecting the human from its chain. "Take care to leave the arm chains—they have etchings that bind its power."

Manek watched him, head ridge hardened, barely keeping red from his pods. Kemharak turned back to the guard. "Shackle its arms tightly in front of it. If it is to sit upon the thrukk, it must feel pain."

Manek's pods returned to neutral gray, and he kicked his thrukk forward.

The guard lowered the rope ladder from the thrukk's back, and the army's front guard watched silently while the human climbed, barely able to use its tightly bound arms. Halfway up, it missed a rung and fell to the ice with a hard smack. The guard kicked it twice, and Kemharak did not interfere. It curled into a ball, then when the kicks had stopped, rose and tried again. Eventually, it alighted the thrukk's back, and the guard returned to his beast. Within moments, whistles and outstretched claws rippled down the line of soldiers, indicating progress was to resume.

The army lurched forward, as lumbering and plodding as the thrukk, which were its lifeblood. Kemharak spared a glance at the human, but its head was bent into the wind, face twisted against the pain caused by its arms' unnatural position. He drew the furs about himself.

"Human, we ride to battle your wizards."

It shifted its arms, trying unsuccessfully to relieve the pain. "Yes," it said, voice barely audible against the wind's howl.

Kemharak looked to the rolling sky above, where the edge of the Spellgiver's giant disk poked through the fast-moving clouds. "Never before have we attacked when the moon is near. Your wizards' power will be high."

The human said nothing. They rode for a silent moment, the dull thud of the thrukk's six massive feet echoing faintly over the wind. Far downslope, a herd of denarin buried their bowl-shaped heads into the snow, their six legs rigid in the slanted ice as they searched for allimoss.

"You will tell me what I must do to be successful."

The human finally lifted its head. Its face was scarred against the cold, and its vision pods seemed dead to Kemharak. "No."

Kemharak's head scales hardened, and he struggled to contain fury mixed with fascination, for this creature seemed not to care that its life was in his claws. Kemharak pulled his face back, exposing a round orifice of sharp teeth.

"Human, I can make your death very painful. I ask again. What advice do you give for the coming battle?"

The human turned away and hung its head.

Kemharak moved his thrukk beside the human and struck it. "You will do as I say! Answer me now!" His voice was loud for all to hear, as he struck the creature again with an upper arm while his lower arms loosened its chains with small, hidden movements. He delivered another blow, then moved his thrukk away.

The human pulled its arms apart in new freedom. It turned wide vision pods on Kemharak, the motion of small muscles on its face inscrutable.

"Why do you do this?"

"It will be easier for you to talk without pain." Kemharak sensed there were deeper reasons as well, but they were not to be examined.

The human turned away. "I still will tell you nothing."

Kemharak's claws extended, but he maintained calm. "You think not to help me, but you are too late. Your description of human"—he looked for the word—"formations has helped me conquer a hundred tribes of my people and create this army."

"Lidathi formations are a poor imitation of what we achieve," the human said. "They may work against your own people; they will not work against human armies."

Kemharak turned to the creature, knowing his vision pods were bright red. He wondered if the human understood his people well enough to read danger there. Yet he swallowed anger, for this was precisely the honesty he sought.

"Tell me why you say this."

"Your commanders direct their troops to guard each other, to move as a unit. But it's a sham—your people form no bonds; they have no friendships, no loyalty. They feel only anger and duty to follow orders. Your formations rest on sand."

Kemharak did not understand "sand," nor several other words in the human's speech. Yet he caught the creature's tone, and he wanted— needed—to understand more.

"Yet the end result is no different," he said. "I have seen that the fighting prowess of human units is much greater than the individual humans within. From you I learn how these units work. We have now accomplished this feat ourselves."

The human turned its strange white and blue vision pods upon him. "And what happens when the unit's commander dies? Or when the unit is ambushed? Will your troops truly fight as a team, or will they break into a collection of individual warriors, to be mowed down by a disciplined human platoon? Lidathi fight as individuals, and nothing will change that."

Kemharak considered this, restraining his anger at this creature's impudence. He'd long known human successes came from their capacity to bond with each other, but this human was mistaken—his people had the same capacity. It was but a matter of learning to do it as effectively as their enemies.

"Then tell me about the human bonding that makes their formations superior."

The human sheathed its vision pods. "Humans bond with each other in ways your people do not. The soldiers form friendships, become like brothers. These ties can become so strong that they'll sacrifice themselves to save a friend, perform impossible feats to keep their brothers safe. Units held together by such glue are strong far beyond their numbers, far beyond what your commanders can order."

Kemharak clenched four claws in frustration, knowing the creature was right. He would understand this concept, or his cause was doomed. He swallowed bitter pride at asking the human to teach him, as if he were a new guardian at the birthing dens. He stared straight ahead.

"How do humans become friends?"

The human also stared straight ahead. "It starts when two people enjoy talking to each other. They may spend more time together. They learn about each other's lives, feel empathy for each other's misfortunes, and experience joy at their successes."

Kemharak rode in silence another minute, considering this. "I sometimes find your conversation tolerable, and I spend more time with you than Manek. Does that make us friends?"

The human's vision pods widened, a reaction Kemharak associated with surprise. "I don't think so . . . Friends don't hold absolute power over each other. Friends know something about each other beyond the necessities of war. And your plan to kill me makes you more of an enemy." It paused, one corner of its feeding orifice turned upward. "But something in you makes you different from the rest of your people. I, too, sometimes enjoy our conversations."

"What do your people call you?" Kemharak asked.

"I am Theralle," it said softly.

"What rank did you enjoy among your people?"

Theralle moved its head up and down, but Kemharak did not quite understand this gesture. "Yes, this is how humans become friends. I am—was—a wizard in the Council of Twelve. I'm a violet-sash mage, the second most powerful mage in Tanbar before I was betrayed and given to you. By the same one who now delivers our magical strength on a platter." Theralle looked up. "Your two alternate sexes—I don't know what the Created Ones call them—what are their names?"

Kemharak's pride welled up, suddenly disgusted with himself for conversing with this creature as if with a person. It didn't know that discussing seconds and thirds was taboo; it could never understand the ways of the Created Ones. His anger rose, and he longed to strike it down from the thrukk.

Just then, the wind's howl was broken by a low rumble from the surrounding valleys, soon becoming a deafening roar. The army's front ground to a halt as it watched the mass of snow blanket the next mountainside, sliding down the ice in a roaring wave of white. The avalanche's fury echoed from the jagged peaks and shook the ground even where they stood, turning Kemharak's pods green with fear. It was an emotion to which he was unaccustomed.

"Human, can your Twelve-Council bring the ice down upon this army?"

The human thought a moment. "We are two days from Apex. At such time, even green- and blue-sash mages—like the ones you'll soon battle—have the power to bring the ice down upon us from a safe distance. The violet-sash mages in the Council of Twelve could do so from several valleys away."

Kemharak raised his pods to the giant white block hanging above them—a ridge of snow more than enough to bury his army, as it had done to the next valley over. Suddenly, the ice was no longer merely a barrier, but a bitter enemy. His claws extended, and he kicked his thrukk forward. "Move!" He whistled sharply to the front guards.

The army lurched forward, and he was seized by dark thoughts. He became consumed with eliminating the human's magical threat; until it was done, he'd have no rest.

"Human, what do you think of my plan to attack the wizards near Apex?" he said through bared teeth. "My commanders think me mad. They come near to revolt."

Theralle rode silently for several moments, as if pondering whether its answer was unacceptable betrayal. Finally it spoke, voice barely audible above the wind.

"I think it's brilliant. They'll never expect it."

Despite the occasional red tinge in his troops' pods, Kemharak allowed the human to ride its thrukk until they reentered the forests. He was glad none asked why, for he had no answer.

He stood near Manek, watching the small dots in the clearing below. It was night, but Spellgiver hung in the heavens like a vast blue god, its blue glow bathing the forest. Kemharak saw the clearing without difficulty—the gold-embroidered tents dotting the snowy meadow were probably the luxurious abodes of the human high-rank wizards. Surrounding each grand tent were several shanties, housing the entourage accompanying each of the human powers. Kemharak counted over seventy of the larger tents and was forced to conclude he'd not been betrayed. As far as he knew, the primary human magical strength outside of the Twelve-Council was gathered before him.

A few human soldiers were awake, supposedly guarding the encampment against just such an attack as was about to occur. They lounged and conversed about a fire, and occasional low laughter drifted through the woods. Kemharak had learned laughter's meaning, and he wondered if the guards below were friends. If so, it seemed the concept had inefficiencies—these troops were far from alert.

Manek broke the silence. "It is not too late. We can still stop this madness." Even in Spellgiver's low light, Kemharak could see the tightened scales at the top of Manek's head. Not enough to negate his submissive stance, but almost enough to challenge. Almost.

Kemharak said nothing.

Manek's neck flaps opened and closed unevenly. "Revered one, yesterday was the moon's zenith. Those below us will be unstoppable. They will flatten the mountains beneath our feet and destroy this army."

Kemharak kept his gaze on the encampment below. "The Creator will be even stronger."

"We will be destroyed long before we complete the summoning. By all the ancestors, let us wait until the moon has receded."

Now Kemharak turned to face his high commander. "As we always do?"

And how often have we succeeded by this path?"

Manek was silent, his pods' orange glow indicating he was carefully considering Kemharak's words. Kemharak watched him warily, looking for any hint of red that might presage mutiny.

"Revered one," Manek said finally, "you have provided a lifetime's learning on the ways of war. None can equal your skill. Yet I do not grasp that attacking the humans at their power's height will give this battle to us."

Kemharak faced the encampment, convinced Manek would not challenge. "If indeed I've taught you well, recite the first lesson of war."

"A fully thought-out plan," Manek said immediately.

"Then think through your plan, Manek. Describe how this encampment will look at Nadir."

Manek turned to face the clearing, remaining silent for a long minute. "Most of the human army will have arrived. Instead of three awake guards, there will be hundreds. Three to four wizards will be awake in shifts, in case of attack. Tents will be scattered throughout the forest instead of bunched into a clearing so they cannot be destroyed in one blow." Manek faced him now, pods white with submission. "The opportunity will be gone," he said softly.

Kemharak splayed a claw in the sign of agreement. He enhanced hearing at the expense of vision, listening to the small sounds of preparation from the forests above. His troops were digging snow banks to guard against walls of fire, and his archers were spreading about the hills.

"Ready the troops—at the fire arrow, the attack begins."

Manek disappeared into the dark forest without another word.

The sound of humming was audible to Kemharak long before the alcohol-addled humans below registered any noise beyond their own raucous laughter. That was good, for every second was vital. The feeding orifices of the summoning victims had been bound tightly, lest their screams start the battle prematurely. An unpleasant detail, yet the Creator would not come without pain.

The humming wound its way through the trees, and Kemharak clenched his claws with tension. Was there a shimmer in the air to his right? No, not yet. He opened rear vision pods, and the image of the archer superimposed over the encampment below. The soldier held a torch in his lower right claw, the great bow pulled back in his upper two claws.

"On my order only."

Finally, a human guard rose by the fire, looking into the hills. The other two stood up also, nervously peering around. Kemharak waited as the three guards considered the dark forests, debating whether to awaken an angry wizard. Yet as the humming grew louder, the humans could no longer imagine they were listening to wind.

Kemharak sucked freezing air through his neck flaps. *It begins.*

He gave the order to fire a mere second before the first human bellowed its warning. The flaming shaft shot into the sky, just as the other two guards turned and raced for the tents.

The arrows fell like rain throughout the encampment, taking down all three guards and piercing tents all over the clearing. Kemharak lidded his pods in relief—as he'd hoped, the human magicians hadn't even bothered to set guarding wards. The deadly shafts sailed into the encampment without difficulty, and Kemharak was sure some of the human wizards would never emerge from their arrow-riddled tents.

Yet many did, far too many. Distant shouts in the god's language could be heard as the wizards raced from their tents, and within an instant, arrows began bouncing from the surrounding air. The rain of arrows was so thick, Kemharak could see the shape of the half-dome of power now surrounding the human camp, walling it from the flying death. Still his archers did not cease. As he'd instructed their commanders, human magic was finite— every arrow that struck their protections drained them of power. The hail of arrows would continue until battle's end.

The human wizards gathered in a line beneath that half-dome of protection, several using wizard's sight to find the direction of the summoning. Then, walls of flame shot through the woods to light the night sky, and the hiss of boiling water drifted over the trees.

His troops' humming had grown to a full-throated roar, and Kemharak scanned the dark tree line for some sign of what was to come. He saw nothing, his claws clenching as the flames inched toward the mass of his army. The fire spread across the hills, scarring the forest to cinders and sending steam clouds rising into the night sky. Rivers of melted snow gushed down the slopes toward the encampment, but the human wizards continued their magic, undeterred. Eventually, the red fury of their fire-magic reached the snowbanks that were his army's first line of protection. Kemharak watched with dread as two human wizards broke ranks and shouted new words into the sky. Wind suddenly howled through the forest, bending trees, sending snow flying from their branches. Kemharak hugged a tree trunk as the snow banks blew apart, the boulders behind them slowly beginning to lift.

As intense wind pushed that wall of flames upslope, Kemharak witnessed his first glimmer of hope. A six-legged shape shimmered above the treetops, in dark outline against Spellgiver's blue glow. Its elongated body was larger than two thrukk, its six giant claws crackling with energy. The ridged head was concave, shaped like a shallow bowl, and encircled by eight black orbs. It was a creature that bore far more resemblance to his people than the humans below, though it clearly differed from either. Despite his elation, Kemharak couldn't deny his thick fear as the god took shape, a primal terror having no relation to rational thought. His people had no defenses against this one, no path other than absolute, complete submission to its will.

The Creator.

Kemharak knew it would take several minutes before the god fully entered this plane of existence. As the first licks of fire reached his chanting troops, it was clear there wasn't enough time. His initial hope turned to sinking dread as he watched his army waver under the heat. Some broke off their chanting and ran toward the encampment, shrieking in bloodlust. Arrows flew from the surrounding hills and brought them down, as Kemharak had instructed. As those who broke formation were slaughtered, the chanting army wavered but held fast, and Kemharak's thin hope returned.

Yet the wizards' rain of fire and wind had finally destroyed the last barrier. He cast his gaze to the god, saw it was still semitransparent, and knew he was out of time. The fire swept through the front ranks now, cutting them down by the hundreds. Reserve troops raced from the forest to continue the chant, only to die moments later. Kemharak watched the god's image waver in and out, as his army struggled to maintain the summoning's continuity. How he wished he could have called the god from the other side of the mountains, away from the wizards' power. Yet he knew it was impossible—once summoned, the Creator had only a few minutes in this world. It could never traverse this mountain and dispatch the humans in time.

And so, he watched his dreams unravel before him. The fire scorched the forest floor and enveloped his troops so rapidly they could do nothing but burn. The last of the water in the trees had boiled away, and now raging fires swept through the forests, bathing the snowy hillsides in an intense reddish glow. With sinking hopelessness, he watched his army's front ranks disappear into flames, as they struggled to maintain their chant. A strange feeling welled inside him as their song drifted over the trees, even while they burned alive.

Soon, the walls of fire reached the army's center. The mass of troops broke formation and began running in all directions, as the Creator's outline shimmered. For all their pain, his troops continued to chant as they ran, and it was only this that kept the outlines visible. Yet it was clear the intense prayer required to summon the Creator was undone. The god's outlines began to fade, and Kemharak knew the thick despair of defeat. Swallowing his shame, he prepared to call the retreat.

Then came the event that changed everything.

A squad of archers had slipped around the encampment and let loose a rain of arrows from behind, beyond the magical barrier. One wizard fell, and the humans who maintained the half-dome hurriedly extended their protection to the rear, forming a full dome. Surprised at this assault, several fire wizards sent walls of flame toward the forest behind them, and the sudden removal of pressure from the main army gave Kemharak's troops the crucial time they needed. The army reassembled and strengthened their chant, the Creator's outlines solidified, and by the time the wizards turned back around, the god had blown apart a ring of trees and descended to the earth.

In that moment, Kemharak knew he'd won.

The god let out a piercing shriek, and both armies fell silent, watching the apparition in horror. For a moment, the only sounds were the raging fires crackling through the forest and the hiss of rising steam, as the god focused eight pods on the encampment below. Then the Creator began scrambling through the river of downed trees, following that burnt path directly to the human army. Kemharak felt a rare moment of empathy for his human foes as they watched this ancient monstrosity scramble toward them on six scaled legs.

Trails of flames shot from the encampment, buffeting the god in a raging ball of fire as it descended the hill. It stopped in the face of the furious onslaught, but then produced another shriek, and the human encampment was suddenly bathed in a furious yellow glow. As one, the human wizards fell to the snow, writhing in agony. The trail of flames died, and the god descended to the clearing.

Kemharak's army watched in fascinated horror as the Creator scurried through the camp, seeking its pleasures among the fallen. Wherever it went, the human spasms became more violent, their cries of pain flying above the trees. Kemharak averted his gaze, knowing their agony would last for days, and the Guardians would forbid his army to dispatch them. He counted time, hoping the god would spend its remaining moments in this world rampaging through the human camp.

To his horror, the sounds silenced. He braved a downward glance to behold the god's shape bunching together, turning into the swirling cloud Kemharak had always thought was its true essence. He was sure its physical body was an ancient form worn only to terrify its enemies, while its real existence was pure energy. Now, that swirling cloud was drifting away from the encampment, heading up the charred hillside.

Directly toward him.

Kemharak was slammed to the snow as the swirling cloud approached, forced to all six legs, as if no more than a simple forest animal. The god enjoyed such displays, a demonstration that even Kemharak was as nothing before it. At such times, his people were merely the burrowing field creatures the Creators had found millennia ago, before bestowing the power of speech upon them. Such as he could only stare upward in uncomprehending awe, as had their ancestors when the Creators first collected them and brought them to their lairs.

When the pain wracked his core, Kemharak knew the god was nigh. He unlidded one pod and saw a swirling cloud of chaos. Colored streaks flashed like lightning in that maelstrom, and crackling energy throbbed in time with the agonizing pulses shooting through his body.

You please me, Kemharak, came its thought, and he knew that it was so. For his pain could have been worse—he felt only the agony that naturally accompanied the god's presence, not punishment.

I serve you as always, Creator.

Their pain was beautiful to me. Now, you will descend upon their kingdom and bring me more.

Kemharak struggled not to dwell on this war's true purpose—to recover the stolen lands. Despite the god's wishes, pain was to be avoided, if possible. These thoughts he pushed hard from his mind, lest the god see his untruth.

Yes, Creator.

Yet I do not detect your essence at the rituals, Kemharak. To be of me, you must learn to give pain, to see the beauty of agony through my pods.

Kemharak struggled for calm, trying not to focus on the pulsating cloud keeping time with spasms of sickness racking his core.

Yes, Creator.

The cloud began fading, but as Kemharak hopefully gazed upward, misery returned, and he lidded his pods against the crackling energy surrounding him anew.

Your human wizard. It was powerful in its empire, and I will welcome its suffering. You will subject it to the rituals.

Kemharak's scales hardened with fear at what he was about to do.

My Creator, it yet provides useful information and helped us to win this battle. I beg for more time with it.

He gasped with pain as the god's energy brightened in fury. The torture was unbearable, and he fell to his side, twitching violently as his open feeding orifice filled with dirt and snow. Why had he questioned the Creator on this? Had he gone mad? The agony lasted a lifetime, an agony he had not thought possible.

You will extract what you need, then subject it to the rituals, said the god. With that final permission, the pain left him suddenly, and Kemharak gasped animal sounds, struggling to stay conscious and stop the liquids draining from his feeding orifice. His face was planted in the snow, and he lifted his head with untold agony, seeing with relief that the Creator had returned to its plane. He struggled to stand, but lost his balance and fell hard to the snow. His troops were beginning to rise from their prostrations, and seeing the Creator gone, they rushed to his aid.

Manek and Pourak pulled Kemharak up as he tried to focus his blurry vision. Manek looked into his pods, then spun around to face the waiting army.

"He lives!"

"He lives!" came the echoing shouts, and the cry traveled through the forest to every part of his army. A low rumble rippled through the trees then, and from everywhere on those snowy hills came the cry: "Kemharak! Kemharak!"

Kemharak staggered forward, supported by the two commanders as his troops surrounded him and shouted to the skies, thrusting their swords in the air. The purple in their pods was a rare note of triumph and pride, one Kemharak had never seen in any battle with a human foe. He stumbled past the chained human wizard, glancing at it.

"Is this the loyalty we must learn from you?"

Its vision pods were wide, and Kemharak turned to face his troops. He drew his sword, holding it high in the air, and the fires from the surrounding mountainside glinted red on his steel. "To Tanbar!" he shouted.

"Kemharak! Kemharak! Kemharak!" they shouted, and the cry came from every hill, every patch of forest, as far as the eye could see.

The mountains shook with his name until the first sunlight bathed the snowy peaks.

> *Word of Negation (formal: Anteword):* A Lyrashi utterance
> which, when spoken, negates the spell's magic. Specific
> words are mated to specific spells, and effective negation
> requires matching tone and timbre with that of the
> summoner, in order to create a wave of Lyrani threads that
> negatively crests with the spoken spell. However, if the
> power of the negater is very strong, the negation may be
> effective regardless of verbal nuance.
>
> Complete Magical Theory, 11th edition, working text of
> the Elduvian Magical Academy.

XVIII

From his first waking second, Larin knew it wouldn't be a good morning. Candro had thrown one pebble too many, and a spiderweb pattern had spread through his window. His head hurt from reading too late the night before, and the sharp crack of another rock broke through his fog like a smack to the forehead. Gritting his teeth, he pressed his scowling face against the glass. In the dark street below, Candro lowered his arm, mouthing words Larin couldn't hear and couldn't care less about.

Worst of all, Onie wasn't beside him—she'd said she might not make it, but disappointment was still dagger-sharp. He'd seen her just once since her foray to the temple last week, and that was brief, just enough to plan their next meeting. A meeting that was to have been today, attending Alack's ceremony in the Plaza of Exchange, where they'd watch Emja's ghostly outlines appear from the city's prayers. It was a day lovers traditionally expressed their feelings for each other, and now he'd be watching it with Candro.

Akul's sour look as Larin left his room didn't help either. The black rings around his eyes, inflamed scar, and dark expression were all the signs of a post-khald binge morning. The big man cradled his head at the front room's only table, his steaming cup of Kurra bean untouched.

Larin walked to the door but knew it was too much to ask.

"Where are you sneaking off to, without even a nod?" Akul grumbled.

Larin paused without turning around. "Well, it's Alack's day, and there's a tiny ceremony they perform around this time of year. You know, the one involving every temple in the city?"

"Don't use that tone with me," Akul snapped. "Try earning money for once, instead of spending all day watching others."

Larin whirled around. "You ordered me to spend my time within the zone, for my own safety! How can I make money living my entire life in four blocks?"

"Well, I'm as sure as Emja's next wine bottle you'll earn no gold sitting in Lockya's Smokehouse all day!" Akul yelled. "You're a shame to your father—at least he made something of himself!"

Larin's eyes narrowed in hatred, but something in Akul's expression stopped his retort. Pain and self-loathing stared back from beneath that bald fury, and with sudden insight, Larin knew Akul's comments were really directed within. The pure sadness in his uncle's eyes was all too familiar, the misery of a once-mighty warrior trapped in poverty, enslaved by red powder. Larin swallowed the venom on his tongue.

"Akul, get some rest."

He slammed the door and stomped down the stairway, but when he exited to the street, all was forgotten. For standing next to Candro was a very wide-eyed Onie.

"You made it!" Larin said, beaming.

"Emja, you could hear his tirade from here," Candro said, looking nervously toward their apartment.

"He has to throw his problems onto me!" Larin hissed, turning to Candro. "Why can't he sleep through it, instead of sitting in the main room and making my life miserable?"

"Well, he has to leave his room sometime."

Larin faced Onie. "I'm really glad you made it."

She smiled, her nose freckles bunching in the way he remembered so well. Her blonde bangs were wet, matted to her forehead, and for the first time, Larin noticed it was raining. The drizzle shrouded the sleeping Wormpile's dark streets, its constant beat echoing from the surrounding alleys. Spellgiver's light barely penetrated the clouds, creating a blue haze as it reflected from the curtain of rain.

She stepped forward, and suddenly she was in his arms, oblivious to the wet sheets enveloping them. "I missed you so much, Larin. I had to lie low so Oarl would forget."

"I thought you'd found someone better looking and less trouble." Larin tried to keep his tone light, but to him it seemed to emit all his desperate loneliness in a single burst.

"That wouldn't be difficult," Candro mumbled.

"Larin, I'm far too snared by you to let that happen. I just couldn't involve my father in this madness. But maybe Oarl doesn't matter anymore . . . ?" She let the words hang in the damp air, and Larin looked away. Since the incident with the mysterious red-haired enchantress last week, news of Oarl's humiliation had spread through the Wormpile like weeds after a summer flood. Everyone'd heard about the powerful mage who'd dropped Oarl's gang with a few words, and rumors abounded that it was Laniette, the no-show wizardress from the Apex festivities. Candro had been trying almost nonstop to wring the information from Larin, but somehow, the story felt too private to disgorge just yet.

"Onie, I—"

"Larin," interrupted Akul's gruff voice, "I need to show you something." They all turned to see Akul standing before the doorway, his grim face dripping wet. He'd donned leather armor, and his bald head glinted dully in the moon's blue light.

Larin disengaged from Onie and stared at his uncle. He glanced at his friends, who both nodded, then back at Akul, wondering if this was Akul's twisted version of an apology. Yet those khald-wrinkled eyes held a steely grimness indicating there was more to it.

He nodded, and Akul stomped away.

The cobblestones were slippery with wet moss, and Larin concentrated on his balance as he struggled to follow Akul's long stride. Candro and Onie walked several paces behind, trying to stay outside Akul's field of vision. Like most in the Wormpile, they regarded the cantankerous warrior at the neighborhood's heart with a mixture of nervousness and reverence— tiptoeing around his mood swings, but grateful for the single force in the neighborhood willing to resist Oarl.

They turned onto Wide Street, the Wormpile's only main thoroughfare outside their four-block zone. Larin barely had time to wonder at this, as he tried to keep up with Akul and avoid the streams of water rolling off the awning edges. Akul rarely showed his face here.

A few shop owners were out, hunching against the rain as they unlocked their stores. Their eyes grew wide as Akul swung into view—surprise temporarily supplanting the fear that these days seemed to blanket the Wormpile like a thick fog. Larin watched their expressions grow hopeful as Akul approached, for he was the only force capable of challenging Morphat's temple, and his confident stride into the central Wormpile meant something was going to happen. Yet Akul didn't meet their eyes.

"Akul—" Larin started.

"I know," Akul growled. "They're looking for a savior, but he doesn't exist. Despite what they think, I can do nothing for them."

They remained silent for another few minutes, Larin following in wet misery as Akul twisted and turned through the Wormpile's alleyways. Finally, they entered Westmarket Plaza, where a few brave souls moved goods from tagalanth and horse-pulled carts into the wooden stalls of the market. Dark shadows stretched from the side of one building, and Larin squinted through the drizzle, trying to make them out.

Akul walked toward the shapes, and Larin felt his stomach rise as they came closer. Long dead, three men hung by their necks from metal poles bolted to a second-story balcony, their bodies swaying in the light wind. Water ran down the corpses to create puddles below, and the blue in their faces couldn't be resolved between Spellgiver's glow and the constriction of death.

Larin grimly watched the rain wash over the twisting bodies. Peering into their faces, he recognized one of the men—a farmer from outside the city walls who occasionally traveled to the Wormpile to sell his goods. The other two were unknown. Onie and Candro caught up to them and stared solemnly for a moment, no one saying a word.

Larin turned to Akul. "Why?"

"Rumors are these men moved food into the Wormpile, bypassing the Marble Temple," Akul said. "Those rumors are lies. The real reason is something else entirely."

"That would be?"

Akul faced him, rivulets of water running down his cheeks. "Look carefully at these men. What do you notice about all three?"

Larin looked but saw nothing in particular. They were all dressed shabbily, but no differently from everyone else around here. Their features were dark and barely visible in the Spellgiver's faint light.

"They're all Hemeks," Candro whispered, then looked at Akul nervously.

"Aye."

Larin squinted, and saw that they were right. All three had the wide-set eyes and broad cheeks of the Hemek peoples, and the men were stocky, as was typical of that desert tribe. He couldn't see why that should make any difference at all.

"So . . . ?"

Akul's scar throbbed. "Have your dreams taught you nothing? When the Eldegod assume power, they begin by setting the races upon each other's throats. They always offer good reasons—they'll claim one tribe is stealing from the others or trying to assume power. So easy to buy the silence of those who should know better." He looked back at the dangling bodies. "Eventually, it'll be clear Morphat cares nothing for whose blood feeds him. By then it'll be too late."

Larin remembered Meidan's surprise that he, a member of the Chandor tribe, could be chosen for the rituals, and shuddered. He looked away to see Akul's wide back disappearing into the downpour.

"Is that all you wanted to show me?" he called, but Akul didn't turn around.

They turned back to the twisting bodies, listening to low sounds of merchants unpacking their carts amid heavy gush of water from the surrounding buildings. For a moment Onie looked sick, but the expression was soon replaced by anger. She whirled around, and with one grim look at the gallows, they followed her through the plaza.

Candro glanced at Larin as they walked. "Dreams? Do those dreams have anything to do with your mysterious wizardress?"

"I think he has to tell us now," Onie said over her shoulder. Her light tone sounded forced, and Larin guessed the sight of the executions had shaken her. Finally, she turned and let them catch up. "Larin, you know the entire Wormpile is talking about Oarl's humiliation, and no one's seen him since then."

"Oarl's probably still cleaning his breeches," Candro said fiercely.

Larin sighed, trying to overcome deep reluctance to reveal any part of that day. For there was much more to the story than Laniette, and there was no way to tell only a portion of it.

"Let's leave this public space first," he said. They entered an alleyway lined with wooden crates, stepping into the shelter of a roof overhang. Larin looked down the alley in both directions, then back at them. "Yes, the dreams are related to the wizardress. But only indirectly . . ."

He held back nothing. He told them what his outbursts really meant, about his supposed servitude to Haraf. He described his conversations with B'neikarian, the horror of his Seridor nightmares, ending with the day he'd met Laniette. They listened with wide eyes as the sound of pouring water echoed throughout the narrow alley.

When he was finished, the three of them remained silent for a long minute, no one looking at each other. The shouts of Westmarket vendors were barely audible over the patter of rain, now coming down harder.

"Where will you go to—"

"Is he going to help you fight this—"

Onie and Candro both stopped. "You first," Candro said.

Onie brushed wet bangs from her forehead. "And where do you go to free the Lord of Demons? Wherever it is, I'll follow . . ."

Larin felt a bittersweet rush, but he shook his head. "I'll have no part of freeing Haraf. I just want a normal life, far away from all of this."

"You can't avoid it, Wiz," Candro said. His eyes widened. "To think all these years I've called you 'Wiz' because you can't pronounce a Lyrashi word to save your life. Now, your name could be written into one of the magical legends they inscribe in the book of Immortals."

"It won't happen, Candro. Haraf can find someone else to fight his battles."

Candro shook his head. "Listen to me. We're a couple of street rats. We get nothing but a mouthful of fist in the Wormpile, and sneers from our betters when we leave it. Do you know what I'd give for a chance like this? To believe that somewhere, there's a master plan with my name on it? Wiz, you can't avoid what you've been given—it's fate, and no one avoids fate."

"He's right," Onie whispered. "I want that normal life with you, but I don't think that's your place."

Larin stepped back, trying to quench the hollow feeling in his stomach. "Fate doesn't exist. I can choose any path I want, and no one can tell me otherwise, not even a violet-sash mage."

Onie wiped a wet sleeve across her face. "And what if only you can fix everything? What if you choose not to fight, and Morphat wins?"

Larin remained silent, having no answer to this. Candro and Onie stared at him without a word, trying to reconcile his bizarre story with the boy they thought they knew. As he looked into their intent faces, he knew why he'd been so reluctant to tell his story.

It was to avoid the return of loneliness.

He knew that whatever they claimed, they'd never see him the same way. Now he was Haraf's servant, the one who appeared in every age, proscribed by all the legends. He could well release mayhem into the world, ending everything they knew. He was no longer just their friend. He was Other.

He turned around so they couldn't see his face. "We better hurry to the Plaza of Exchange. It's getting late."

<hr />

The next two weeks were a blur, as Morphat tightened his grip throughout the Wormpile. Rumors that the Marble Temple gave smaller portions to Hemeks became more widespread, and Hemek families began venturing outside the Wormpile to fill their evening tables. However, the Morphasti controlled most of the Wormpile entranceways, and any Hemeks returning with food were taxed heavily. It was a situation that could only end in disaster.

The explosion was brief and bloody. Angry Hemeks staged a massive food riot just outside Morphat's temple, a riot violently smashed by the Morphasti. The next day, Westmarket saw eight new bodies dangling beneath the makeshift gallows, all of them with gaping holes where eyes had once been. By evening, the Wormpile was covered with edicts warning residents against Hemek agitators and offering rewards for information. Some took the offers, though the Morphasti did little to verify the truth of their accusations. As neighbor turned against neighbor, a toxic cloud of fear blanketed the neighborhood, one far more insidious and chilling than anything Oarl had ever created.

Akul and Larin watched this horror unfold from their four-block zone, which for some reason remained unviolated by the Morphasti. Many fled to Lokya's Smokehouse, a narrow café within the zone, for the latest information. After Emja's alehouse became off-limits to Larin, Akul had relaxed his prohibition on entering Lockya's establishment. Since then, Larin had spent most afternoons there, reading books until his eyes grew too red from the smoke. In those few weeks, many came from throughout the Wormpile to enjoy a brief respite from Morphat's watchful eye. Several of these quizzed Larin relentlessly, desperate to know if Akul or his mysterious wizardress would become the Wormpile's savior.

It was in this cloud of fear and uncertainty that Apex day dawned, an explosion of sunny brilliance that was soon shrouded by the moon's shadow. Larin greeted the day with anticipation, unsure what to expect from Laniette's testing. He spent the afternoon walking, and as the sun escaped Spellgiver's disk for those few brief hours before disappearing for the night, Larin found himself standing in the middle of a dungeon.

His trip to the Imperial District had been uneventful, his worries about being tossed out of that wealthy enclave by the king's guard unfounded. The district was thick with servants and the lower born like him, all of whom served the city's noble families in the immense stone keeps of their betters.

The guard at the wooden gate had curled his lip in disgust and led him down a series of stone steps to a metal door, which opened to reveal a fat Yulish merchant. The man licked his lips when he saw Larin, and the guard's look of disgust became more acute. Larin looked after the guard with alarm.

"Wait, there's been a mistake!" he called, but the Yul yanked him inside the dungeon and slammed the door.

"What the—" Larin started, but within a second, the Yul became his enchantress, wearing a man's breeches, red hair bunched over her head. Her frame was cast in silhouette in the room's low light.

"No one knows who I am here, and that's the way I like it," she said softly. "To them, I'm just a Yul merchant who rents out the dungeon and does Emja knows what down here. They don't ask questions, as long as the money's good."

Larin looked around, uneasy. Braziers were mounted in the wall, two of them lit, casting the dank stone room in shadows. The acrid smell of burning coal mixed with a humid stink, likely from a few different unsavory sources. The room had once been a true dungeon, for chains were mounted on the walls, and manacles hung from the ceiling, though aside from few wooden tables, the room was empty. From somewhere, the hollow dripping of water echoed off the stone.

"What is this place?" he murmured.

"One of my three lovely homes," she said. "Theralle and I once had a castle only four blocks away, with private gardens and a lovely view of the river. Since my husband was betrayed, I haven't set foot in it. Our High Wizard would love me to show my face there."

Larin walked to a wooden table, arrayed with a man's collection—Theralle's things. A too-big tunic, a shaving knife, other small mementos impossible to make out. Suddenly, the image of his confident, cool goddess dissolved into something more real. He now saw a woman racked by lonely fear, beset by powerful enemies. A woman who'd lost the only thing in life that had ever mattered to her.

He tried to read her expression in the low light. "But why this dungeon?"

"Dungeons allow me to set my wards without notice, to prevent Emderian's roving eye. He's been searching for me over a year; I only appear in the presence of the rest of the council. This is one of three dungeons I've rented throughout the Imperial District." She sighed and sat wearily on a stone step, wrapping her arms around her knees. "Once, my husband and I spent our evenings dining with the royal family, invited to the castles of Aldive's nobility. Now I'm reduced to eating stale bread in an old torture chamber."

"You're violet-sash. Can't you just teleport, or fly out of the city?"

She looked dismayed. "I see your lessons will be a long, uphill path. "Do you know what a binding is?"

"I—I thought so . . ."

"Emderian has bound himself to all council members. Each binding continuously saps his strength but also alerts him when any of us uses true power, and any trans-dimensional spell like teleportation will bring me instant death. He's the most powerful wizard in generations, Larin. Even my husband could not approach his strength." She leaned back. "Now, there's you. Someone who knows nothing of magic, yet who for some reason I dreamed would be the answer to Emderian's power. Perhaps I should eat less starch before bedtime."

"If he knows whenever you use magic, why didn't he blast you after you wiped the ground with Oarl's gang?"

She smiled. "One thing we learn in the academies is to use as little power as possible to accomplish any magical feat. Dropping that rabble took nothing more than a simple influence itching spell—not nearly enough to trigger Emderian's binding." Her face became suddenly weary. "Hard to believe I'm going to have to teach you such basics."

"I know something of magic; I just have no power. I've actually been reading spells of all levels for years, even violet-sash. I remember everything I've read."

"That sounds dangerous. I suppose we should try a Kriani spell so we can put this question to rest." At Larin's blank look, she sighed. "Can you name the levels of magic, from least to most powerful?"

Larin nodded. "White, red, orange, yellow, green, blue, violet."

"Tell me why the different colors translate to magical power levels."

Larin said nothing.

She rubbed her forehead. "The colors represent energy, Larin. White is a combination of the other colors and means the mage can't even create a coherent pattern—thus, it is the lowest level. Red light has the lowest energy, and violet the highest. Think of the colors of a rainbow."

Larin's eyebrows raised. "Ah. So how does that—"

"The Kriani spell allows me to see which part of that spectrum you manipulate." She turned around and walked to the end of the room, where a candle was mounted on a small table. "Stand two paces forward, let me finish the Kriani spell, then cast an aura of lighting."

Scowling, Larin walked to the designated spot. The aura of lighting was the first spell any child learned, useful for lighting lanterns from a distance. He'd only ever been able to cast it the two weeks before and after Apex day.

He waited for her to finish the Kriani spell. Then he mumbled the Lyrashi words, trying to ignore her pained grimace. After a moment, the candle flickered, and a small flame crept up its wick.

Laniette stared, open-mouthed. "Amazing! Your pronunciation is like listening to cats mate in a windstorm, yet still the candle lights. You do know that you didn't pronounce a single intelligible Lyrashi word?"

Larin's face was dark. "This is where you try to make me say individual Lyrashi words one by one, to see if that helps. I'll save us a lot of time by telling you how it ends—I'll pronounce them in a way that sounds perfect to me, but will sound completely wrong to you."

"There is something here. I feel it. Pronounce the first word again."

"Suraina."

They tried several more passes, sounding out each syllable. As he knew would happen, Larin pronounced each syllable correctly, but stringing them together was spectacularly unsuccessful. After ten minutes of this, he spun around and stomped toward the door.

"Where are you going?" Laniette snapped.

Larin turned around. "I've had enough. Akul will be worried, and this is getting us nowhere."

Laniette's regal frame was a dark statue in the basement's eternal dusk. Strands of hair fell from her bun, giving her a strangely vulnerable demeanor. "After searching for your Seeker, is this how it all ends? You have talent, Larin—I can't measure it, but I can feel it bubbling below the surface. This war is too important for childish tantrums."

"Childish? No more childish than going through the same catastrophe again and again."

Laniette began barking Lyrashi words, and Larin recognized a spell of captivity he'd studied one day in Lockya's Smokehouse. Red-faced, he placed hands over his ears and shouted the word of negation, knowing it'd be useless. But to his utter amazement, the coolness of dissipating magic bathed his forehead. With numb shock, he knew the impossible had happened.

He'd negated magic from one of the Council of Twelve.

Laniette's jaw dropped. "A boy who's not even familiar with Kriani somehow knows the anteword to blue-sash Influence binding spell. And more amazingly, can successfully negate it."

Wide-eyed, Larin said nothing.

"Let's try it again."

Twice more she uttered the spell, and each time, Larin's anteword was successful. Head swimming, he felt a strange internal glow, knowing he was at the cusp of something immense. He'd never had power, never thought it was possible—it was just part of who he was. So what was he doing dispelling the workings of Aldive's second most powerful mage?

Laniette began snapping her fingers. "You know, your pronunciation of antewords is almost correct. Why do you always cover your ears when you speak the word?"

Larin watched her intently. "Well, it's hard to concentrate on saying the word when I'm listening to your spell."

"Interesting. I am going to try something; come here a minute."

Larin hesitated, but now he was intrigued. He walked to a spot eight paces from the candle.

"My theory is that your own hearing twists the words, causing mispronunciation. The hands over your ears was a clue. I've actually heard of this before. Sometimes traumatic childhood magical experiences can cause the mind to seek backhanded ways to avoid wielding Lyrani threads."

Larin shook his head. "I don't remember any traumatic experiences."

"I could ask you to place hands over your ears and cast the aura of lighting again, but I suspect it will work only marginally better than before. So I'm going to cast a spell of deafness—don't be alarmed. I'll remove it when this is over. After I'm done with that and the Kriani color spell, I want you to try the aura of lighting again. Yes?" She squinted at him as if at a wild animal about to bolt.

Larin nodded.

Laniette stood near the candle and cast her deafness spell. After the last word, the world went strangely silent. Though he'd expected it, the absolute lack of sound was disconcerting, and it took a minute to get his bearings. Laniette mouthed the Kriani color spell, then turned to him expectantly.

He faced the candle, took a deep breath, and began casting the aura of lighting.

Something felt different this time. Power began building inside, an overflowing river of charge that cascaded through him like the Apex day tides. The surge touched every nerve ending, every limb. Laniette's mouth opened, and as he uttered the final power word, she began racing toward him.

Then the room exploded.

They both flew in different directions, and all the dungeon's high windows were blown outward, revealing the blue shades of a high season evening. As Larin flew backward, he wondered how in Emja's name he'd ever doubted he had power.

It was his last thought before the darkness descended.

"They crept through the city with torches lit,
In darkened alleys, their brows knit,
Men without conscience, men not at all
Gods, oh gods, I fear your downfall."

"Night the Darkness Came" snippet, by Eshan Karlia

XIX

He opened his eyes to silent confusion. Laniette's illusory Yul was yelling soundlessly, the wooden tables had been blown to shards, and the braziers had been extinguished. The room's only real light came from Laniette's wizard fire, flickering above the Yul's head. Everything was utterly silent.

Larin scrambled to his feet, and Laniette yanked him forward so hard he thought his arm would leave its socket. They flew into the cobbled avenues of the Imperial District, taking an immediate right on a narrow street beneath a stone bridge. A few couples strolled lazily on that blue-tinged evening, glancing curiously at Laniette's Yul illusion as he dragged Larin behind.

Laniette slowed to a hurried walk as they twisted through hilly cobbled streets up the Mount of the Empire. Spellgiver loomed large in the heavens, casting the district's ancient stone in deep blue and overwhelming the feeble light of dragon-shaped street lanterns. Soon, the Imperial Compound's enormous walls stretched upward in dark splendor, the royal tower a distant shadow against Spellgiver's disk. Laniette pulled him down a narrow staircase between two massive walls, into a small courtyard. Her mouth moved, and sound rushed back like a burst of wind. She spoke more Lyrashi words, and within seconds her Yul illusion had disappeared, replaced by a very worried wizardress.

"Listen," she hissed. "Emderian felt that burst of power. If it had issued from my mouth, we'd both be dead. Fortunately, he has no binding on you, but I feel his dark cloud moving across the city. He knows something's amiss, and he's searching."

Yet she might have spoken Chandor for all Larin heard. His eyes were wide with wonder. "I have power. I really, really have power."

Laniette grabbed his head, forcing him to meet her hard glare. "Listen to me, naive boy! Yes, you have power, far more than I can even measure using a standard dweomer like Kriani. Right now, that power is more likely than not to get us both killed. The fact that you've spent years learning spells far beyond your knowledge is more dangerous even than Emderian at the moment. Do you understand?"

Larin nodded, then shook his head. "Not really. If I remember a spell, why can't I use it?"

"Your power is a large formless thing. You have no idea how to channel it, and you have no concept of kickback." At Larin's blank expression, Laniette sighed. "The laws of physics govern magic no differently than anything else. For small magic, their effects are invisible, but for powerful spells, those effects can kill. Have you ever stood behind someone casting a fire spell?"

Larin thought back to the Parbani mage's spell. "Well, not actually *behind*."

"The area around the magician becomes frigid. It's said when Jathan the Great cast his immense firestorm at the retreating Lidath, the snows fell for two weeks afterward—and that was in the middle of the summer. That's conservation of energy. We don't create the energy for our fire spells; we simply move it from one place to another."

Larin nodded, recalling how Oarl's gang hunched against the cold as the Parbani's fire spell kicked up dust. "I can remember that rule."

She closed tired eyes. "Don't you see? There are a thousand such rules, and I can't teach them all to you now. We spend years at the academy learning the side effects of our spells. Only then do we gain enough confidence to cast violet-sash spells. Do you understand now?"

Larin nodded, not meeting her hard stare.

"Good. Now listen well: we must flee this city. Emderian's searching for us, and believe me, he'll find us."

Larin scowled. "I'm not leaving Akul, Candro, or Onie in this snake pit, especially not with the Old Gods gaining control. I've seen what happens when the Eldegod seize a city, and it's not pretty."

Her expression grew fierce, but then her gaze drifted. "Yes. I—I think my dreams indicated the same. Somehow it feels like this party needs more people. Listen: I have another hiding place underneath the Henefraus castle—gather everyone you need, and meet me in the Henefraus dungeon. Go through the west basement door, the way my illusory Nydyn flower merchant usually enters." She tucked a red lock into her bun, her eyes gleaming. "Just ask your 'Akul' how to get there. I think he's quite familiar with the Imperial District."

Larin froze. "Why would you think that?"

She smiled, for once erasing the worry lines about her eyes. "I remembered who he was after I left your house. If I'm not mistaken, your uncle is Commander Lukas."

Larin made choking noises. It wasn't possible. Lukas was a name from the legends—a commander who, with a few hundred men, had broken Seridor's back multiple times. He'd been the stuff of bard's tales, even during his lifetime, before his death by wizard's fire.

"But Lukas is dead!"

"Apparently not. Anyway—" She yanked him against the wall, and Larin followed her gaze upward, where a bizarre, six-legged flying indigen creature circled high above the city.

"Listen!" she whispered. "That's Emderian's terret! He searches for me, and for whatever just released that large burst of magical energy. That would be you." She looked nervously to the sky, as the monstrosity passed across Spellgiver's disk. "You have to hurry; we have little time. Whatever you do, don't cast your eyes upward; his terrets will remember you. To form a binding, all Emderian needs is an image of your face."

Larin nodded, suddenly frightened. He turned to go, but Laniette touched his shoulder. "One more thing. I know I told you to avoid casting your memorized spells, but if your life's in danger, you'll have no other choice. Until I find a permanent fix, the only way to use your full power is to make yourself deaf. Let me teach you the spell, quickly."

Larin shook his head. "I remember it. I always remember."

"Fine. The anteword is 'Yuhala.' Now go!"

Larin whirled around and hurried into the quiet streets of the Imperial District. He hugged the sides of the buildings, trying to avoid unwanted attention from the Imperial Guard. He passed the occasional carriage bumping home along the cobblestones, a few strolling couples enjoying the city's romantic blue glow, and several stragglers in servants garb. A quick look at the stragglers' somber faces told him they were Hemeks, most carrying sacks on their backs. As he twisted down the Mount toward the Tanbar River, he found out why. Affixed to a post along the Avenue of the Empire, a royal edict spelled it out in no uncertain terms:

"Due to agitation among Hemek tribes of the lower valleys, the presence of Hemeks anywhere in the Imperial District shall henceforth be considered a threat to the empire. All Hemeks are commanded to vacate the district by midnight on Apex eve."

Larin's face hardened, but he didn't stay long. He followed the promenade for several minutes, feeling relief wash through him as he stepped into the Porcelain District. As his tension loosened, he allowed his mind to wander between the two subjects consuming him—his own power and Akul's history.

Laniette had deflated his initial excitement, but the possibility he might one day tie a violet-sash around his waist filled him with heady visions. He imagined splitting the earth beneath Oarl's miserable gang, burning them with fire.

Then he returned to reality. He knew that with great power would come great expectations. Would he be strong enough to defeat Emderian? Morphat? The prospect of confronting the six-legged god filled him with dread and turned him toward the other subject burning in his thoughts:

Akul—Lukas.

Growing up, he'd spent hours in Emja's temple library, poring over tomes on magic and history. Studying the empire's recent past, the exploits of one man had popped up again and again—the only name from this century to appear in the Ballads of Tanbar, some chanted in the temple alehouse while Akul served drinks.

Lukas.

Larin had read how, with a few hundred knights, Commander Lukas had repeatedly defeated Seridor's thousands-strong army, while the empire's attentions were focused on the North. After their fourth catastrophe, Seridor had sued for peace, unwilling to confront the horned demons of Lukas's unit. For this, the king had raised Lukas to supreme commander over the empire's five-thousand-strong khula knight cavalry, a title that elevated him to Peer of the Realm, equivalent to any provincial duke. A secret pleasure for Tanbaris, who weren't used to seeing a brown face among the pale Nydyn elite of the kingdom's inner circle.

The histories didn't stop there. With command of the empire's khula knights, Lukas had transferred his attentions to the North, where the Lidathi had burst out of the Avensai passes to seize the Neteilland baronies. In a series of attacks, Lukas had decimated the Lizards so thoroughly, they'd left the empire alone for a decade, an eternity for foes who normally attacked every few years. He'd then swept through the inner kingdoms of Turmania and Oestiga, finally quelling the revolts in those mist-shrouded lands, bringing them again into the fold of the empire. Legend said that Lukas had finally been killed nineteen years ago, after Turmanian wizards banded together to destroy him.

Larin frowned. Laniette had to be wrong. He knew Akul had been a khula knight, but the ballads always described Lukas with flowing black hair, and anyway, he couldn't imagine a khald-addled Commander Lukas. Yet . . . though hard to square his cantankerous uncle with the godlike figure of legend, he had to admit, it would dispel several mysteries. The name for one: he'd always wondered about Akul's strange moniker, one he'd never heard anywhere else. Plus, Akul did have mysterious connections to the palace . . .

Lost in thought, Larin stopped at the Porcelain District's western edge, where dozens of men in red and black patrolled the Wormpile's eastern border. Dismayed, he watched for a moment as they milled about in the blue light of evening. Feeling uneasy, he backtracked to the Haques Bridge, where he crossed to the Tanbar's south side. He strolled through the quiet streets of the Flerrindor District, then crossed the Flerrindor Bridge, intending to enter the Wormpile from the Port District.

His stomach sank as he passed the high-tide railings. Thirty or forty Morphasti filled the Port District's eastern edge, their low voices and the clink of arms drifting through the quiet evening.

That night, Larin used every trick he had to avoid Morphat's army. He descended stairways into abandoned buildings, ascending on the far side only to see more red and black uniforms. He inched through side alleys, using every bit of Wormpile knowledge to stay within the least-known paths. He avoided Westmarket, which would be crawling with Morphat's troops, and listened for voices before turning every corner. After an eternity, he finally saw Emja's temple spires poking above the stone walls, the anchor point of Akul's four-block zone. He peered into the wide promenade bordering the temple, relieved to see that no Morphasti had yet dared to cross that street. Heart racing, he ran all the way home, pounding up the stairs to their fourth-floor apartment and bursting through the door.

"Akul—" he started, but stopped in his tracks. A red-haired giant sat beside Akul, his enormous frame swallowing the chair. His hair was partially braided, falling about a circular face that was a rarity among the high-cheekboned Nydyns. Covered head-to-toe in leather armor, a fearsome horned helm sat by his booted feet, etched with Emja's runes. A red beard cascaded down his cuirass, lying flat on the table.

At the moment, that great bearded face was staring at Larin in horror. "Is this him?" His voice was a thunderclap, every bit what Larin would have expected.

Akul rubbed his head, looking warily between them. "Larin, this is Korrin. Korrin the Defender. Leader of the Atlaran order of Emja's fighting monks."

Larin was about to proffer his hand, but one look at Korrin's scowl stopped him short.

"Well, he looks normal enough," Korrin growled, watching Larin like a venomous spider. "But with Haraf's servants, one must always be careful."

Akul stood up, pushing his chair behind him. "Korrin, this is my boy, and anything you say to him, you say to me."

Larin's rage spilled out. "Who are you to come into *my* house and insult me? Take your Nydyn arrogance and—"

"Larin, enough!" Akul shouted. Now Korrin stood as well, and Larin looked up an impossible distance to the giant's stormy face.

Akul exhaled loudly. "Larin, Korrin is Emja's chief fighting priest in the empire, and he'll need time to accept he must deal with Haraf. You remember Tierre's feelings on this. Now multiply that a hundred times."

"He can take his 'feelings' and shove them deep into—"

"Larin, enough!" Akul shouted again. Korrin's hand hovered over his sword's hilt, and Akul gave him a brief warning glare. "We have far more important things to worry about than either of your egos. Like it or not, you two are allies."

"That's hard to imagine, Akul. Or is it 'Lukas'?"

Akul's brief flash of guilt told Larin everything he needed to know.

"So it's true. It's really true . . ."

An unexpected bellow of laughter erupted from Korrin, a shaking force of nature that Larin could have sworn made the walls tremble. "You haven't told him? Of all the secrets to keep . . ."

Akul ignored him, watching Larin with pleading eyes. "Sprite, it was for your own good. Too many want to see me dead."

Larin shook his head, still reeling from the impact. He realized that even after Laniette's revelation, he hadn't truly believed it. Akul—Lukas. The world had turned upside down.

"But the legends say you died, and—"

At that moment, the door flew open, and Trana, Ruldir, and Candro rushed in. Ruldir's eyes were as wide as Larin had ever seen. "The Morphasti are on the march," he said, wheezing. "They descend upon Emja's temple, and likely this place, too!"

"They've arrested Loupanis, the only priest who lives outside the temple," Trana said, breathing hard. "Your Grace," she whispered suddenly, as she saw Korrin.

Candro stepped in. "I saw them by the Netrina, and I rushed here to tell you. I think this is the end game!"

Akul flew into action. "I've been planning for this day!" He yanked downward on the roof trapdoor rope, which opened the door and allowed a rope ladder to cascade down to the floor. "To the roof!"

"Wait!" Korrin yelled, and they all stopped their mad rush to the ladder. "Where do we go? This one"—nose wrinkled, he gestured at Larin—"must find his Seeker, or some such. Without that, we simply flee."

Everyone looked at Larin, and he swallowed slowly. "I met her. Laniette, from the Council of Twelve. We're all to meet in the dungeon underneath the Henefraus castle."

Akul and Korrin looked at each other, nodded, then motioned for everyone to climb the ladder. Larin ascended first, and as soon as he'd reached the top, he ran to the edge of the flat roof, where he saw something that sent deep chills through his spine: trails of torches inching their way through the Wormpile's alleyways. On the other side of the river, several fires burned brightly, accompanied by distant screams. With that, he knew tonight's action wasn't confined to the Wormpile—this Apex evening, Morphat consolidated his power throughout the capital. He felt a sudden panic for Onie and twisted wildly to look to the east. He saw with relief that so far, the Porcelain District was untouched. He returned his attention to the torches twisting through the Wormpile's maze. A stream of bright dots moved toward Emja's temple, but by far the largest trail of lights was heading for a point due south of there.

Directly toward them.

Korrin's wide frame squeezed through the door to the roof, and Akul turned to all of them. "Follow me and stay close. Do exactly as I say." He turned and ran across the rooftop. They reached the edge of the building, and Larin saw several wooden planks stacked neatly on the side, dimly glowing in Spellgiver's blue light. A sack lay next to the wood, presumably filled with supplies.

"Help me," Akul said, and Larin rushed to help Akul position a plank. They stretched it out over the alleyway below so that it anchored to the roof of the next building. Larin nodded. "Now I know why you were spending so much time with those woodcutters a few years ago. You've planned this escape for a while."

Akul grunted, then turned to Candro. "You're the lightest. You go first, then anchor the beam from the other side." Candro's face was pale in the blue shadows, but he nodded and began crawling across the beam. He reached the other side, then Akul motioned for Larin to cross.

Swallowing quickly, Larin got on hands and knees and scrambled along the beam as quickly as he could, feeling sick as the wood bowed in the middle. How in Emja's name would Korrin get across?

He reached the other side, grateful for the central Wormpile's narrow alleyways and identical buildings—this escape would never be possible elsewhere in the city. He helped Candro brace the wood as Trana crossed next, followed by Ruldir, Akul, and finally Korrin. Korrin placed a large stone on the wood before he mounted, and Larin was sure Akul had stored it there. The giant man was surprisingly agile as he crawled carefully over the plank, his helm attached to a strap and balanced on his back. Though the plank bowed dangerously, it did not break.

As soon as Korrin was across, they ran to the other side of the rooftop. There, another stack of wood was stored, and they went through the procedure again. After Larin had crossed again, he looked south to see how many alleys they could traverse before reaching a wider street. With relief, he saw they'd be able to make the river's edge. From there, it was a quick jaunt to the Flerrindor Bridge, and they'd be out of the Wormpile.

As Trana crossed, bloodthirsty shouts issued from the direction of their apartment, and Larin's heart stopped. The Morphasti knew. The crack of boots on cobblestone echoed in the distance, and Larin gritted his teeth as he watched a grim-faced Korrin make the final slow crossing, his fearsome helm dangling from a strap over his side.

They ran to the rooftop's other edge, and Akul looked over his shoulder. "Last crossing," he hissed.

They almost made it. Korrin was two-thirds across when a sharp yell turned their heads to the street below. A man in red and black was pointing at the beam, shouting to his comrades a block away.

"Demons take it!" Akul spat, yanking Korrin off the plank as soon as he was within reach. He whirled to face them. "We're doomed if we become trapped on this rooftop. Korrin and I first—we'll clear the stairwell. Everyone else stay close behind!" With that, he ran to the roof's edge and vaulted to the balcony of a top floor apartment. He disappeared inside, then Korrin went next, followed by Trana, Ruldir, Larin, and Candro. Larin almost gagged at the room's musty darkness, and he needed no light to know it'd long been abandoned.

He kept his eye on Ruldir's back as they raced through the apartment door and pounded down the stairway. Shouts of surprise and fury issued from the bottom floor, and as Larin raced down the steps, he stared death in the face. Men in red and black uniforms were spilling through the front door, running toward the stairs, and it was clear they'd all be trapped on this confined stairway. Slaughtered one by one.

Yet Akul's speed never ceased to amaze him. Akul threw himself headfirst into battle, sailing half a flight to plunge his short-sword into the lead Morphasti's chest before the man could raise his blade. The force of his leap pushed the thicket of charging men down several steps, and Akul bounced backward to land on his feet. Before Larin had time to absorb this, Akul's short-sword had already slid in and out of the next Morphasti's stomach as the man tried to regain his balance. Snarling, Akul kicked the screaming man hard in the chest, pushing the stunned group down another step amid a spray of blood.

A thick hand reached from behind the bloody man to hurl the dead Morphasti away, and Larin stared at Ropalek's dark face, a commander's insignia on his uniform. Akul's sword licked in and out of Ropalek's guard like a snake's tongue, and Ropalek dropped his sword, red gushing from his neck. With a savage punch, Akul struck the dying man with his other hand, knocking him back into his compatriots, then unexpectedly pressed himself flat to the wall. Like two actors in a finely rehearsed play, a be-helmed Korrin roared headfirst past Akul, into the temporarily stunned crowd of Morphasti on the bottom step, scattering them like chaff. Larin saw that what he'd thought were horns atop Korrin's helmet were in fact daggers, for Korrin's head blades rammed straight through a Morphasti's chest.

Korrin's charge cleared the stairway, and Akul, Trana, and Ruldir raced down, Akul drawing his broadsword as they left the confined space.

Larin began to follow, but Akul's voice rang out: "Stop!" he shouted, as he blocked a blow and decapitated another man in a single motion. Larin stopped, frightened, and turned to Candro, whose face had gone completely white.

Frozen, Larin watched the ensuing fight with a dropped jaw, not sure he breathed even once. For though he'd never seen anyone as good with a sword as Akul, today he had to give Korrin that honor. Akul and Korrin fought furiously to gain the doorway, and bleeding Morphasti flew away from those deadly windmills with stunning speed. With a blade in each hand, Akul ducked beneath his enemy's swipes, then rose again in a furious leap that embedded metal into two enemy chests at once. One fell twisting to the floor, and the other Akul swung to his front, still impaled on his broadsword, then kicked the man forward into the crowd of Morphasti. He used this temporary surprise to twist around and finish off two men behind him, then back to those in front, one of which received a short-sword in the neck.

Korrin's fighting style was all about momentum. He charged into groups of pale-faced Morphasti, decapitating two men with a single blow as he sent his fist into the face of another. Trana and Ruldir guarded the rear, taking cover in the fury of Akul and Korrin's blur of steel, lunging out to strike any enemy who came too close.

Larin watched this with utter shock, sure it couldn't continue any longer. Just as Ruldir sprouted a red gash across his chest and stumbled forward, it became clear their furious charge had broken the enemy's morale. Two Morphasti turned and fled, and within seconds, it was a rout, with some Morphasti trying to surrender, others fleeing in terror.

"Forward!" Akul yelled, and the group raced for the door, Korrin's blade felling every surrendering Morphasti in their path. As they reached the entrance, Larin watched a familiar blond man turn away, just before Korrin's sword plunged deep into his back.

Nitalen collapsed and turned to stare with incomprehension as Korrin stepped over him, blood spreading quickly over his uniform. Larin stared at Korrin in horror, heart twisting at the brutality—Nitalen had only wanted protection from Oarl. Then they were through the door, into the beautiful sweetness of an Apex evening, and Larin had no more time to think.

Only a few Morphasti stared after them as they raced away, unwilling to engage that fearsome party. They turned left onto Wide Street, then right into another alleyway. Larin's hope rose as they raced toward the river promenade, the street that would take them to the Haques Bridge and out of the Wormpile. As they swung the corner, Larin's heart froze at the sight ahead. The entire group stopped, as if they'd hit a brick wall.

Before them, a dozen Morphasti surrounded the giant statue of Jathan the Great. Atop the statue's base, two Morphat priests stood with hands upraised. If the color of the priests' green-sashes matched those of the magical academies, they were all doomed. Several Morphasti moved to block the alley entrance from which they'd come.

Akul and Korrin turned to look behind them, for once unsure. They could run alongside the river in the other direction, which was now unguarded, but that would expose everyone to whatever deadly magic the priests were assembling.

Then, the Eldegod priests began shouting Lyrashi words, and Akul decided. He raced toward the statue, followed closely by Trana and a limping Ruldir, while Korrin hung back and shouted Lyrashi words of his own.

The air between Korrin and the Morphasti priests began shimmering, as sounds of clashing metal filled the promenade. Numbly, he and Candro watched Akul fell two Morphasti with lightning-fast strokes, as Trana and Ruldir guarded his rear. Yet without Korrin, their charge ground to a halt, and the Morphasti surrounded them in a fury of swordplay. Korrin hung back a hundred yards from the fight, face straining as he repeatedly chanted the same words.

The air between Korrin and the Morphasti priests became black with storm clouds, roiling in pitched fury, punctuated by the occasional flash of light. Sharp cracks of thunder overwhelmed the shouting priests and clang of metal. Within seconds, a black, eight-pronged claw appeared in the maelstrom, only to disappear again. Then, the outlines of *something* became visible, a shape that steadily became more solid as the Morphasti priests continued their chants.

Within seconds, Larin's knees turned to water as he stared at the enemy for the first time.

Morphat.

Though it resembled the statue atop the Port District's Marble Temple, that carving did nothing to prepare for the true horror of the god's presence. Morphat's head was concave, slightly bowl-shaped, and ringed with eight black orbs that rotated wildly from side to side. Its body was the size of two khulas, adorned with black wings, and supported by six scaly legs ending in eight-pronged claws. As it materialized, those orbs stopped rotating, several of them becoming fixed on the apparition ahead—a formless gray cloud that was clearly Korrin's doing. However, as Morphat concentrated most of its attention on Korrin's summoning, one orb spun around with blinding speed to focus on Larin.

Larin almost vomited from fear. Morphat knew who he was.

The six-legged god dove into the gray cloud, screeching a horrible sound evoking images of eternal pain. As the gray cloud surrounded Morphat, Larin knew what it was: despite the temple's depictions of a human god, the cloud was Emja himself. Mouth open, Larin watched the being he'd prayed to since boyhood engage combat with the enemy he'd been warned about for just as long. Trying to escape Morphat's gaze, Larin ran left, but the single orb followed him, even as its other orbs concentrated on the battle ahead.

Larin knew they couldn't win. Morphat's wings beat in a frenzy as it inched closer to Korrin, pushing against a cloud so thick, it looked like it would condense from the air. Morphat extended its front claws within two feet of Korrin's straining face, as the gray cloud swirled around its orbs. It would be a minute's time before Morphat encircled Korrin's head with that black talon—and when that happened, Emja's summoning would be gone.

Desperately, Larin shouted Laniette's deafness spell, noticing Morphat's gaze sharpening as he spoke the Lyrashi words.

It didn't work.

Panicking, he put his hands over ears and shouted the spell again. This time it was partially effective, for the fight's din and Morphat's screeches lowered in volume. Then he tried a third time, placing his hands over his ears again. This time, the combination of partial deafness and hands over ears worked—all sound immediately evaporated. The scene became even more surreal as he watched Akul, Trana, and Ruldir battle the Morphasti in silence, while above raged an utterly quiet battle of impossible power, against the backdrop of a giant blue moon.

Staring at the Morphasti priests, he forced panic down and began mouthing a violet-sash spell of opening, a spell Jathan had once used to split the earth beneath the Lidathi. He felt Morphat sharpen its focus, and he darted his gaze leftward to see two orbs now watching him. Swallowing terror, he focused on the Morphasti priests as the Lyrashi words spilled from his mouth. Akul battled two Morphasti who obviously wore warder charms, for his sword beat down furiously yet didn't touch them. Ruldir and Trana barely held off the others, and all had sustained several cuts.

Larin watched it numbly, feeling his veins crackle with electricity as the Lyrashi words left his tongue. He knew raw force a hundred times greater than anything he'd ever felt, an energy he thought might split him apart. Feeling he'd become a god himself, he mouthed the final power word, watching the priests in anticipation.

Then, everything changed. Morphat's claw was inches from Korrin when both Morphat and Emja disappeared in a sudden yellow burst. A rush of air pushed his flesh inward, an explosion he thought might've punctured his eardrums if he hadn't been deaf.

That same deafness stopped him from noticing the descending building until it was too late. The stone structure across the street crumbled as if made of sand, and giant, partially decomposed stone blocks bounced off the promenade cobblestones.

The fight stopped as everyone tried to dodge the collapsing building, and Larin watched, horrified, as stones rained everywhere. One slab landed on two Morphasti, but a rock also struck Akul in the chest, knocking him down. Another slab landed on Ruldir as he turned to flee, flinging a bloody spray across the cobblestones. Screaming, Larin ran toward Akul, jumping over fallen Morphasti in his haste, while Trana scrambled to rise. Akul stirred, and with immense relief, Larin grabbed his arm and hauled him to his feet. The three remaining Morphasti rose, too, looking stunned. Larin shot a glance toward Ruldir's position, and the bloody arm dangling from beneath a giant block told him everything he needed to know. Spine cold, he turned to the statue and felt an even greater chill.

The two Morphasti priests were untouched and had been using the time well. Their robes glowed in the blue light, one of them staring at Akul and Larin as he mouthed Lyrashi words. Akul started rushing toward him, but still dazed, he stumbled and almost fell. Larin suddenly noticed Akul was covered in blood, and he doubted it was all Morphasti. In bitter defeat, Larin watched the mage's eyes light in triumph as he spoke the power word.

Nothing happened.

Surprise crossed the mage's face, and the other mage began a new spell.

Apparently recovered, Akul flew into action. He leapt toward the three Morphasti and brought two down in two strokes, before stopping a moment, surprised. They'd been wearing warder charms, and up to now, Akul's sword had bounced off them as if from metal armor. Snapping out of his shock, Akul turned toward the other Morphasti, who threw his sword down and ran away. Akul looked upward, just as the second Morphasti mage mouthed the final power word.

It, too, was ineffective. With grim determination, Akul ran toward the first mage. Panicked, the man jumped off the statue, but Akul's sword brought him down after two steps.

Larin shouted his deafness spell's anteword, wincing as sound roared back. He turned to see Korrin racing down the street to intercept the last mage, who was almost comical as he tried to escape in his long robes. Korrin slammed him to the ground, drew his dagger, mumbled a prayer to Emja, then pulled the man's head back and sliced his throat.

Larin turned away, disgusted, and noticed Candro, who'd been watching the whole fight completely frozen. Larin wiped his brow and walked toward him, wanting to make sure his friend was unhurt. As he approached, the faint smell of urine assaulted his senses, and he sniffed suspiciously.

Candro trembled. "When I saw Morphat, I—" He stopped, swallowing. "Wiz, if you ever tell anyone, I'll kill you."

Larin looked away to see Korrin stomping toward him, face twisted with fury.

"Monster!" he cried, pointing his sword at Larin.

Larin reddened. "I saved you! I don't know how, but my spell negated

Morphat's summoning!"

Korrin's eyes narrowed with hatred. "Your spell has killed dozens of innocents!"

Larin turned toward the rubble, and his heart sank. Several bodies lay throughout the ruins—on one side, a small baby was twisted into a strange shape, like a stuffed toy. On another side he heard loud shrieks as a woman sifted through the rubble, finding the body of a husband or son.

He faced Korrin, unable to speak.

"Thus we witness Haraf's true nature," Korrin spat. "Ever has it been so—Haraf assists his minions only when he can amuse himself with murder." Larin stared, unable to quench the horrible, hollow feeling in his core. Korrin's reddish mane and beard ruffled in the light wind, giving him the countenance of Emja's avenging angel. Larin was sure the giant was a hair's breadth from slicing his throat, as he'd done the Morphasti mage.

"It's not what I meant to do . . ." Larin whispered.

"Enough!" Akul shouted, holding Trana's arm for support as he stumbled toward them. The sight of his uncle covered in blood pulled Larin's thoughts away from the horror he'd just created. He ran to support him, but Akul waved him away.

"Listen," Akul said fiercely. "There are Morphasti everywhere tonight. We'll split up. Korrin, Trana, and Candro in one group, Larin and I in the other group. Both Korrin and I know where the Henefraus dungeon is. For all the gods' sakes, keep quiet as you traverse the city streets tonight, and make sure no one follows. Go!"

Korrin nodded and shot Larin a last glare before sheathing his sword and turning away. He, Trana, and Candro ran down the street as Akul and Larin watched. Akul turned to him, his face pained.

"Let's go."

They walked-ran in silence down the promenade, encountering no more Morphasti. They passed into the Porcelain District and crossed the Haques Bridge, keeping their heads low. Distant sounds of screaming and the crackle of fire drifted across the city, but they kept to quiet streets, staying close to the walls. Larin's mind churned with the image of bodies lying amid rubble, and Ruldir's bloody arm sticking out from under a giant stone.

As they reached the Imperial District, Akul slowed noticeably, and Larin draped his uncle's arm around his shoulders as they ascended the Mount of the Empire. It was a measure of Akul's true state that he accepted the help. Akul gave him one-word instructions as they traversed the Mount, and once, as they passed two Imperial Guardsmen, Akul began singing as if he were drunk.

Eventually they reached a giant keep only one block from the Imperial Compound walls, the moon's blue light glowing from the gray stones. Larin felt more of Akul's weight on him, and it was all he could do to open the heavy stone door.

Laniette, Korrin, Trana, and Candro stared as they entered, and Akul's head slumped forward.

"He needs help," Larin said, gasping.

He sighed with relief as Korrin took Akul's weight off his shoulders. Laniette immediately began hovering over Akul, murmuring Lyrashi words. Larin scanned the new dungeon, a dark stone room split into individual jail cells, with a common guard's area in front lit by three braziers. Everyone had congregated in the common area. From a bloody, scarred face, Trana eyed him with compassion and fear, and Candro stared as if he was some strange plant from the Shernock swamps.

Larin unbuckled his sheath, flashing a sudden fear that Onie had been caught in this madness. Still, she now lived in the Porcelain District, and they'd passed through without seeing any action. The Wormpile would've been the hardest hit.

Larin walked to an empty cell and sighed, staring at the benches along the walls and latrine hole in the middle. As long as he could convince himself Onie was safe, he could tolerate anything fate threw his way.

Anyway, he didn't have much choice. This would be home for a while.

Shattered Mage Effect: the theory that some very powerful wizards gain their power through extreme life events, usually negative. These events are said to "shatter" the future wizard, releasing raw force that would otherwise be trapped within. This concept is unproven, despite a few real-world anecdotes.

Complete Magical Theory, 11th edition, working text of the Elduvian magical academy

XX

Giorlan knocked loudly, soldier's stoicism masking his fear. "You asked to see me, High Wizard?" he called.

The door opened to reveal Emderian, his boyish chin twisted into a grin. A strange brew of colors as usual, the High Wizard's red doublet and white gloves seemed overly formal next to his faded yellow breeches, as if he'd made some half-hearted attempt to dress for the occasion. Mousy features added another dimension of strangeness, and not for the first time, Giorlan thought a mustache might add dignity to that small face. Though this one needed no gimmicks to command respect.

"Please do come in, Captain Dekaust," Emderian said pleasantly. He turned and walked into an adjacent room. "Tea?"

Giorlan stepped into the room, staring at the assortment of vases, urns, and statuettes lining Emderian's shelves. In the corner, an unobtrusive Morphat figurine stood on two scaly legs, waving four in the air. Smells of lime soap pervaded all, leaving hints of some unidentifiable odor underneath. Not what Giorlan had expected from the High Wizard's den, but he supposed books were kept in other rooms. However, some palace rumors suggested darker possibilities—if true, Giorlan fervently hoped never to see those chambers.

Emderian frowned as he entered the main room with two cups of tea.

"Oh please, Captain Dekaust, sit. We're not barbarians here." At Giorlan's hard face, he sighed. "I suppose you've heard the servants' gossip.

Perhaps you think I'll feast on your flesh later, or feed you to the god?"

"Are they true? The rumors."

"Please don't listen to such nonsense. The Eldegod brook so much misunderstanding among the uninitiated." Emderian's earnest expression put Giorlan at ease somewhat. "I beg you, sit. Let us converse as civilized folks." He handed Giorlan the cup of tea, and Giorlan sat stiffly on the divan by the door.

Emderian sat on a gold-inlaid chair, crossing his legs. He sipped from his cup, small white-gloved finger jutting outward, and Giorlan watched, stone-faced, as Emderian closed his eyes. "This tea was imported from Kuraneth, one of the inner kingdoms. It's by far the best I've had." He looked askance at Giorlan, who hadn't touched his cup. "But of course, you're not here to discuss tea." He placed his cup on a cherrywood stand, then leaned forward.

"Captain Dekaust—and I think I'll call you Giorlan—I must beg your assistance on a particular matter. Perhaps you already know?"

Giorlan debated affecting ignorance, but he sensed acute danger in any path but pure honesty.

He put his tea down, untouched. "You have an agreement with Duke Selton to share access to the king. But you command no loyalty in the palace. You've only your Huja guards, who must watch their backs lest they grow a dagger in the spine."

"Ah, but those Huja guards have the strength of ten men. They come from the elite fighting ranks of Trastore."

"Yes, but they don't know the palace, and they're lost here. You have enough of them to stop open revolt among the palace guard, but they cannot control the entire compound. You've replaced palace functionaries with Morphat worshippers, but they know little, and can't function without support of the wider staff. And though that staff officially answers to Yalinus, Queen Relena commands their loyalty. You can do nothing without her blessing, and she detests you."

Emderian smiled sadly, and Giorlan sensed he'd passed some sort of test. "Alas, what you say is true. I admire your soldier's candor, despite all the awful rumors you've heard about me." He rested his chin on his fist, looking absently at the Morphat figurine. "Yet, I want only what's best for the kingdom, Giorlan. I need truly loyal troops, those who share my goals."

"High Wizard, I serve the king. If your orders issue from his mouth, I will obey."

Emderian's black eyes were unreadable. "Yet I think you have no loyalty to our imbecile king. Literal obedience is no boon to me, my good captain, if your heart lies elsewhere."

"Perhaps if you explain what you want."

Emderian smiled warmly. "Yes, I see no amount of gold will buy your loyalty, though I assure you I've plenty of that." Emderian stood and faced his shelves, arms behind his back. "My goal is nothing more than to prevent Tanbar's destruction. Seridor masses its army along the southern border, poised to attack next low season. Aimes, our largest province, shares a border with Seridor longer than the empire's own, but has made a traitor's alliance. Our wily Duke Selton will watch from Glenschire as Seridor's cavalry thrusts like a dagger into our heartland. The Lidath in the north have assembled their greatest army in history and will fall upon us at Nadir. We shall be sorely tried in the next year, Captain Dekaust." Emderian turned back to Giorlan, eyes imploring him to understand.

Giorlan wrinkled his nose. "You worship Seridor's gods—surely Seridor's victory wouldn't displease you. This is why you command no loyalty here; everyone suspects you are in league with Kaman."

"My dear captain, you must not count yourself among the ignorant. Think clearly: should my worship truly affect my loyalty to king and state?" Emderian's small mouth was pursed with tight displeasure. "Several of the inner kingdoms worship the Human Gods, like Tanbar. Do they open their mountain castle gates whenever Tanbar's army storms the passes, simply because they share the same priesthood? Clearly not."

Giorlan considered this. "Then I don't understand what you want. Perhaps instead of whispering in the king's ear, you should be at Avensai, preparing to face the Lidath."

Emderian's eyes flashed, and Giorlan suddenly wondered if he'd carried the honesty strategy too far. Yet the High Wizard's tone was even. "Captain, I assure you, I've no desire to wander the palace hallways where my power is castrated. I yearn to be free of these walls, yet I do important work here that cannot be done elsewhere." He extracted a small cloth and dabbed his forehead. "Tanbar's pending demise is quite related to its choice of gods, my good captain. Emja, Rakva, An-Dhura, and all of your other self-absorbed deities play silly games while those you call the Old Gods bear down on our empire with a fury you can't imagine." He strode to Morphat's statuette, grasping it by the legs. "What I am about is providing our empire a chance to survive. If we turn toward Morphat, he'll abate his fury, and the coming storm will become naught but a battle of armies. Yet if not, we'll fight a battle of gods. If that happens, there is no hope."

"So, your only goal is to increase Eldegod worship in Tanbar?"

"Yes. But for that, I need the throne."

Giorlan sat straight. "You want someone to kill Yalinus?"

"No, no, Giorlan. Nothing so crude. The king will collapse of his own weight. All that is necessary is for me to do good deeds, and the empire will soon tire of their idiot monarch. With the unfortunate demise of our Council of Twelve, I'm all that's left to counter the might of the Lidath and Seridor. If I can do that, the path to the throne will follow."

Giorlan tried to hide a small tremor as he brought the teacup to his mouth. "So if I agree with your path, then can I assume some reward when you become king?"

Emderian nodded earnestly. "Of course. He who risks much, gains much. Would the Duchy of Aimes interest you? I believe it will need a new duke, when this is all over."

Giorlan almost dropped the cup. He gaped at Emderian.

Emderian smiled. "You're one of the four highest-ranking officers in the palace, and I know you have the queen's absolute trust. Loyal servitude will make you quite valuable to me. And I assure you, I reward valuable servants."

Giorlan lowered his cup and stood. He was a foot taller than the High Wizard, but he felt no advantage of height as he looked down into Emderian's mild expression. It was rather more like a mouse watching a cat from the ledge above.

"High Wizard, why me? There are two other captains in the palace guard."

A half-smile touched Emderian's lips. "I recognize a kindred soul, Captain Dekaust. I watched you on the sparring field last week. I saw how after you beat your opponent, you thrashed him until he could barely move. Some might see this as unnecessary, but not you and I. We understand that to dispatch an enemy requires ruthlessness. Mercy off the battlefield may be virtuous, but on the battlefield, it is certain defeat."

Giorlan grinned. "Pelaran had it coming to him. He stole my woman two years ago, and I'll not let him forget it." He looked at Emderian thoughtfully. "If I agree to serve you, will you place him under my command? Presently he's under Captain Tuethan, and I must wait for events like sparring contests to have at him."

Emderian beamed. "As I said, Giorlan, we're kindred spirits. Tomorrow, I'll talk to Hekrian about shifting Pelaran's command chain. Consider it my gift to you, whatever your decision."

Giorlan nodded. "I'll consider your offer." He turned to go, but a flash of pure gold stopped him short. It came from a smaller, golden Morphat figurine he'd missed before, standing on six razor-sharp legs. Yet it wasn't the brilliant gold shine that seized his attention, but a brown crust on two of the legs and a piece of *something* hanging from the rear right leg.

He turned uncertainly toward Emderian. "That's an interesting statuette. There's something about it . . ."

Emderian smiled, his recessed chin clenched in a way that bathed Giorlan's heart in icy water. "Yes, pretty, isn't it? That one catches many a person's eye." Emderian winked, and Giorlan walked out, hearing the door latch behind him.

Giorlan strode the hallway from the High Wizard's isolated chambers, knowing with chilling certainty that the brown crust was blood, and the detritus hanging from the rear right leg was skin. Or . . .

That one catches many a person's eye.

Shuddering, Giorlan quickened his pace.

Giorlan stepped tentatively into the queen's chambers, feeling at once privileged and ashamed. Queen Relena's back was toward him as she surveyed the city's panorama from the royal tower's arched window, which spread golden rays across the oak floors. Her hair was in a coif, and her purple dress draped to the floor, its edges sewn with charging green dragons.

"Your Highness," Giorlan said, head bowed.

"Captain."

She didn't turn around, and without moving, Giorlan darted a quick glance about the chambers. Bursts of finery filled his vision: a bed frame of solid gold, diamond window knobs, royal purple tapestries depicting victorious armies in the north. Smells of rare incense and scented oils mixed with hints of vanilla-infused tallow. Once again he marveled that he'd been allowed in this place, a place rightfully only entered by the royals and their servants. Yet the queen had insisted they could talk freely only here, and his curiosity burned to see these chambers. That she allowed him here showed how far they'd fallen.

She turned away from the window. "Well, Captain?"

"Your Highness, I believe all went to plan."

Her face brightened, and she glided toward him. That brown face was a rarity among the royals, for Maldovin had been the first of his line to wed outside the Nydyn race. She'd once been a great beauty, a desert child bride from the inner kingdom of Clarinor, betrothed to a young Maldovin IV in return for Clarinor's incorporation into the empire. Now, gray hair framed that regal face, topped by brown eyes Giorlan thought too trusting to belong to the woman who'd spent thirty years manipulating the royal court.

He met her gaze directly, for she brooked no groveling.

"Tell me," she said.

"He truly wants my help. I think he knows he has no real command here, save for his Huja warriors and the palace guard's grudging obedience when the order comes from the king's pen. He thinks if he has me in his pocket, he'll have true sway in the palace."

She smiled so widely, the gold band on her forehead lifted. "Excellent job, Captain Dekaust. You must continue to earn his trust; do nothing to lose it."

Giorlan nodded, trying to mask his awe. He'd aced every test in the officer's academy, knew his numbers better than most, read the ancient scholars. Yet there were rare times where he knew he'd encountered a light so bright, it dwarfed his intellect as the sun dwarfs a candle. The queen was such a one.

"Your highness, the success is yours. How did you know my beating of Pelaran would attract his attention?"

Her mouth set in disgust. "I know his type. They're all the same, those who rise high in Morphat's service. They thrill in pain and bullying of every stripe. I've seen him watch the sparring matches, and I know what he's about."

"And—and you've surrounded yourself with Tanbari officers who have Hemek wives. They'll fight him at every turn, yet he'll never know without seeing their families, who reside outside the Imperial Compound. How did you think of this?"

The queen smiled. "I watched the hatred in their faces after he enacted his latest edicts against our Hemek population. From this I see who'll never stand with him, no matter what he offers. What better justice than to turn his evil back upon himself?"

Giorlan breathed deeply. "My queen, I am grateful you are not my enemy."

"See it continues," she snapped. At Giorlan's bowed head, she softened immediately. "Our apologies, Captain Dekaust. I have very few friends these days. Panjus will be gone soon, then I shall be fighting this battle alone. And I'm sure Emderian has offered you much."

"The Duchy of Aimes."

She gasped, her face registering the first hint of fear he'd ever seen.

"My queen," he said, quickly raising his eyes to hers. "It means nothing. Even were I not loyal to you, could I live in a world where my wife and children are degraded, simply because they have Hemek blood? Never."

She eased somewhat, eyes pleading. "I pray it is so, Captain, because only you do I trust absolutely. The others I keep close, but not too close. One betrays me, and I'll find out who."

Giorlan read worry on that regal face, and something else besides: desperation and sick doubt. Once a sheltered desert king's daughter, she'd become Maldovin's most competent steward of empire—no naive girl, now. Yet though Giorlan knew Emderian was outclassed in every way, she was only one woman. One without any official power, other than the tenuous strands of loyalty.

"Your Highness, let us be done with him. He has no power in this place, I can kill him with a single blow."

Her eyes widened. "You must not, Captain Dekaust. Our compound walls stop only spoken spells, not warder charms. He's the most powerful wizard in three hundred years; his warders will be undefeatable. Your sword would slide past him with every thrust, while he throttles you at leisure. In any case, we need him."

"Your Highness?"

"I believe in his own twisted way, Emderian desires the empire's victory, for his power play means nothing if we are overrun. We must spend his strength on our enemies and wait for our day to wrest power."

She glanced toward the door, then stepped close. Giorlan didn't flinch. "Captain, as a measure of my trust in you, I will tell you something known only by the inner royal circle: this battle reaches far beyond our conflict with the High Wizard, and even beyond the upcoming war with Seridor and the Lidath. Emja is fighting for his own existence, and that of our gods. The events you see before you were arranged long ago, pieces arranged on the Thirazi board by the gods in a pattern far beyond our ability to understand. To defeat Morphat's ilk, our gods have aligned with Haraf."

Giorlan stared. Haraf was a creature used to scare children at bedtime, not a being with which one made alliances. "Haraf? Such a monster is real?"

"Oh yes, Captain. And in that long game of Thirazi, Emja has imparted two things we must do to defeat our enemies: one, we must get the king out of the city and to safety. Two, we must send our boldest on a quest to find his cure, for our only path to victory is through his survival. While it may seem I only champion my own personal desires, I assure you there are reasons why I fight for my husband's life beyond my torn heart."

Giorlan looked into her pleading brown eyes, intensity and worry etched into her face as if by chisel. "I believe you, Highness," he said truthfully.

She relaxed a little. "Good. For the second of those, I have no idea how we can help. The city is closed off, with guards at every gate. I don't know how we'll get a large party out, though I will seek your help when the time comes. But for the first, getting the king to safety, I have a plan. Listen closely."

She told him what she wanted to do, and Giorlan stood back, staring.

"Are you sure?" he asked, surprise temporarily overwhelming protocol.

"Yes." She stepped back, smoothing a wrinkle in her voluminous purple dress. Then she looked at Giorlan with a sad expression. "And Captain, please give our apologies to Pelaran for his injuries. When this is over, he'll be rewarded."

Giorlan's back stiffened. "Your Highness, Pelaran wrestled the rest of his platoon for the honor. He *won*."

She stared, her expression unreadable.

"My queen, all of us would gladly die for you. Next to that, a few blows are nothing."

Giorlan caught a flash of wetness in her eyes, before she turned her gaze to the velvet tapestry on the far wall. She nodded, remaining silent for a long moment. "You are dismissed, Captain Dekaust."

He bowed and exited the royal chambers.

"This seems a strange, obscure path, good captain."

Giorlan nodded, but didn't slow his pace. "High Wizard, as you yourself have said, we must take care none see me with you—the queen mustn't suspect I'm in your employ."

Emderian panted as he tried to match Giorlan's long strides, though the sound was overwhelmed by the heavy stomping of the four Huja warriors behind them.

"Quite right," Emderian gasped. "Though if you've truly found the king's hiding chamber, perhaps naught else matters. Once Maldovin is dead, she has no prospect for resuming the throne, and men tend to abandon paths with no hope of eventual gain."

Giorlan said nothing, and they continued marching along the Imperial Compound's dark storage chamber hallways for several minutes.

"Tell me again, Captain Dekaust. How did you come by this information?"

Sensing importance behind the question, Giorlan slowed to look at Emderian. "High Wizard, I'm the only one the queen trusts. I've worked carefully to nurture that, and she has few others to turn to. Someone must bring Maldovin his soft foods, and Panjus is too well-known. She has only me. I came to you as soon as she told me where he was."

Emderian shrugged, his expression mild. "Very good then."

They continued for several more minutes until Giorlan stopped at one obscure door in a long line of such. Emderian lifted his eyebrows, and Giorlan opened the door. They stepped into a room filled with clothing, and Emderian frowned slightly.

"No sign anyone's ever lived here, Captain."

Giorlan grimaced and began throwing clothes away from the wall furiously. Emderian turned to his Huja guards. "Help him." They fell to with a will, and after another minute, a small handle and the outlines of a door became visible.

Giorlan turned to Emderian in triumph, then pulled the handle. All six men crawled through the small passageway, Huja warriors first, in case battle was necessary. They reached the hidden chamber and stood, Emderian palpably disappointed as they searched the empty room. It'd clearly been evacuated in haste, and there was no doubt it'd once served as living quarters for several people. A well-padded cot lay at one corner, as if to cushion one who would spend a lot of time there.

Emderian's mouth pursed. "Perhaps there's a wee chance she trusts you less than you think." He turned and began perusing the room, while

Giorlan and the Huja warriors frantically moved furniture, looking for clues.

Giorlan looked up, his face sour. "She trusts me, High Wizard. She mentioned another she thought was betraying her. Perhaps she thought it better to be safe."

Emderian said nothing, but bent to examine something on the floor. He picked it up, examining it with interest. He walked to Giorlan and dangled a green cloth under his nose.

"Do you know what this is?"

Giorlan shook his head.

"This is a piece from one of the cloth sacs they use to throw out the garbage. It appears our good former emperor is escaping via one of the trash chutes." Emderian tucked the piece under Giorlan's leather breastplate, as if to ensure he wouldn't lose it. He then turned a horrible stare on Giorlan that sucked the breath from his lungs.

"Find him."

Giorlan gulped and backed away, whirling around to face the Huja warriors. "The closest chutes are the North and East. The West chute is over one hundred feet above the courtyard, and he'd never survive the fall. You and you—to the North chute. The rest of us to the East." He fairly ran from the room and did not once turn to face the High Wizard.

———

Funny how one never really noticed ceilings, until one was forced to stare at them for hours. Maldovin had seen whole worlds on those high landscapes: spiders amid veritable cities of webbing, moths, and once a bat. When this was over, he'd order the immediate cleaning of every palace ceiling. Of course, Panjus's concerned face now filled his vision, giving him a welcome reprieve from his usual fare. Still, he suspected he'd soon long for the sight of another ceiling.

"Your Majesty, at any other time, I'd drink poison before doing this," Panjus whispered. "But—it is our only path. Please forgive me, my king; by tomorrow, you'll be safe beyond the city walls, where we can await a cure." Panjus left Maldovin's vision, returning shortly with a scoop of chicken guts, meat shards, and bones. He sprinkled them over Maldovin, and Maldovin closed his eyes and pursed his mouth, his only possible response.

He opened them again, and Panjus's beard filled his vision. "Your Majesty, this is necessary to throw off the scent hounds. I've taken us to the West chute, for it is the least used. The drop will be over a hundred feet, but I've placed warder charms about both of our necks to cushion our fall. These were magicked just yesterday by green-sash mages. We still have friends in the city." Panjus looked uncertain, as if trying to think of something else to justify his actions. Finally, his face withdrew, just out of Maldovin's sight. "I'll be with you the entire way, Your Majesty."

Panjus returned with more trash that he sprinkled over Maldovin, until the smell of it would have made him vomit, were that an option. As it was, Maldovin closed his eyes, and his last sight was Panjus sewing the bag around him in wide loops. When the bag closed around his eyes, Maldovin wanted to scream but could not. Tiny holes in the cloth allowed him to breathe, but barely, and the stench threatened to overwhelm him.

Panjus, I'll have your head for this.

Then his feet tilted downward, and he felt the rushing fear of free fall. He closed his eyes and waited for impact.

Once Umraut stood, strong and proud
On Elesh Mountain, above the clouds.
But the Duke of Olakor dreamed a dream
Of the Hunter awake, his arrows agleam.
He searched for gray mists, mind astew,
Travelled the world as evil winds blew,
Returned home, shouting aloud,
Madness now, love disavowed.
Yet when fires leapt high, he cried aloud
For his burnt city, above the clouds.

Legend of Umraut, Bard's song

XXI

That first night, Larin was too tired to care he'd be sleeping in a jail. He picked the furthest cell, sniffing unhappily as he saw the floor-hole latrine. He knew this entire dungeon would reek after a day. Leaving the heavy door open, he curled on the hard bench, lulled to sleep by Laniette's low murmur as she chanted over Akul.

A cacophony of voices woke him just as a brief burst of daylight flooded the room. He left his cell in time to see Candro stepping out of the dungeon, giant sack slung over his shoulder. Larin returned to his cell, grabbed his sheath belt, and strode toward the dungeon door.

"Where do you think you're going?" Akul growled from the guardroom, where he stood with Trana and Korrin over a city map.

Larin smiled. "Glad you're feeling better."

"Aye, thanks to her." Akul nodded at Laniette, who was hunched over several metal disks, whispering Lyrashi words to herself like some crazy mountain witch.

"I'm going to see Onie. She'll be worried sick."

Korrin frowned. "Apparently Haraf has a whole brood."

Akul shook his head. "Not a chance. Aldive is nothing but a city of shards now, and Morphat's strengthening his grip. Morphasti are out everywhere, and the Imperial Guard is helping them. No one leaves until this settles down—it'll probably be several days."

"I just saw Candro walk out!"

"Someone has to get us supplies, otherwise I'd keep him in, too."

Larin stood unhappily, dying to see Onie. Akul returned to his debate with Korrin and Trana over exit strategies from the city, and Larin shuffled back to his cell, throwing his sheath belt to the floor. He stood for another moment, then walked back out of his cell toward Laniette.

Laniette's reddish hair was wild, much of it having escaped its bun. Her gray bliaut was smudged with dungeon dirt, eyes bleary as she murmured Lyrashi words over several Kulden disks scattered on a ledge. For some unexplainable reason, her unkempt, vulnerable look made her more attractive than ever. Larin shook his head, banishing the thought. That was one distraction he didn't need.

As he waited for a break in the endless chanting, something made him turn around. There he saw Korrin staring at Laniette unabashedly, his wrinkled eyes intense. Larin turned away, realizing he wasn't the only one who noticed the wizardress's charms.

"Laniette, I—I have to know what went wrong," Larin said, unwilling to wait any longer. "Whenever I close my eyes, I see dead bodies and Ruldir's bloody arm. I can't banish the images . . ."

She broke off her chant and turned red uncomprehending eyes on him. Larin withered. "Or, I can come back another time."

"Larin," she rasped. "For enchanters, the two weeks around Apex are the most important of the entire year. Whatever power we invoke when the charm is fashioned is the power it will hold forevermore. The longer I wait after Apex, the weaker the charms will be."

"I'm sorry . . ."

She brushed a tired strand of red hair from her eyes. "I'm trying to fashion protection charms for everyone in this party. I spent half last night healing your uncle, and every minute I talk with you steals precious time from my task." She grabbed a small knife from the ledge, held his arm, and scraped skin from his wrist. "Speaking of charms, hand me yours—the one I made for you two years ago. I'm going to add some protections."

Brows furrowed, Larin unfastened his charm and gave it to her. "Doesn't that contradict what you just said about the charm locking in its power?"

"I'm not adding more *power*; I'm adding different facets of protection. The power absorbed from Spellgiver on this day is as much as it will ever have." She touched his shoulder, and now it seemed her eyes had returned to something resembling human. "We'll have plenty of opportunity to go over the basics of magic later. All right?"

Larin nodded tightly, and Laniette's Lyrashi murmurs resumed before he'd turned around. Sighing, he ambled to the other side of the guardroom, where Akul, Trana, and Korrin stood over a city map.

"Rakva's gate has the least experienced guards," Trana was saying. "It leads only to the small villages on the peninsula, and no threat ever comes from there."

Akul shook his head. "It's what Emderian will expect. I'd wager the queen's gold band that plain clothes Morphasti lurk near the Rakva gate as we speak."

Korrin nodded. "The An-Dhura gate opens to the farming villages of the south Hennat valley. Though it's well-guarded, there are opportunities to hide in the thousands of food carts that pass out the city every day."

Larin moved to stand next to the map, but Korrin's wide back seemed to move with him, as if trying to block his view.

"An old trick," Akul said, unaware of the strange maneuvering to his side. "We need something the Morphasti won't expect."

Larin finally shoved around Korrin's side to stand next to the map. "Maybe we should consider the Dalik gate," he said. "It's the busiest entrance, so we'll have good opportunities to hide in the crowds. Unlike the other gates, there aren't any wide streets leading up to it—we can get lost between buildings."

Korrin scowled. "Yes, maybe Haraf can collapse all the structures and murder enough people for us to escape in the shuffle."

Akul glared at Korrin. "Do you ever stop?"

Larin whirled to face the red-haired giant, but his retort died stillborn. Memories of the child's body swam through his vision, a twisted rag doll in the rubble. The shrieks of the bereaved woman filled his ears again, as it had since yesterday. As impotent anger suffused him, the familiar heat rose behind his forehead. He ignored it, as he'd done so often in the past two years. Yet the heat refused to dissipate, and with a sinking heart, he remembered he'd given Laniette his charm.

Humiliation was boundless as he lost control, passing through every stage of outburst before the whole group. He stomped his feet, raised his fist in the air, and shouted the Phrase, to stunned looks from Trana, Korrin, and Laniette, who'd stopped her chant and turned around. Both Korrin and Trana reflexively traced Emja's glyph, though Trana dropped her hand as she looked into Larin's pained eyes.

In black despair, Larin whirled around and stormed back to his cell. Trying to choke back his embarrassment, he sat in the corner of the room, listening to the abject silence in the rest of the dungeon, willing the conversation to resume with all his might.

Instead, that silence was punctuated by loud footsteps, growing louder until Akul pushed the stone door open wide. Akul's endless forehead was wrinkled like a bunched-up cloth, the way it always did when he had to express his feelings.

"Larin, Korrin's just spouting dogma he's heard his whole life," Akul said. "Nothing he says matters; he doesn't know you like I do."

Larin nodded, waiting for Akul to go away.

Akul glanced behind him, then back at Larin. "You'll be all right then?"

Larin nodded, and Akul beamed. "That's a good lad." He whirled around and walked back to the guardroom. As the conversation resumed in low tones, Larin reflected that after years of fatherhood, Akul still didn't understand him in the least. It was amazing that someone who excelled at so many things could be utterly deaf to what mattered.

Larin continued to mope for the next hour, listening to hushed conversations outside his cell and trying to banish the image of bodies in the rubble.

Daylight flooded the dungeon again, and Larin left his cell to see Candro opening a full sack of goods. Akul, Trana, and Korrin approached, and even Laniette broke off her chanting to see what Candro had brought.

"It wasn't easy," Candro said. He sniffed importantly, seeing all attention on him. "Morphasti are still out, and they're watching the whole city. I kept my head low, and they ignored me." He unloaded several skins of water, smoked meat, and two blankets.

Akul narrowed his eyes. "No one saw you enter?"

"I had to walk around a bit until I saw an empty street."

"Good." Akul grabbed a stick of smoked meat and broke off pieces for everyone. Chewing, he returned to the map, followed shortly by Korrin and Trana. Laniette grabbed a blanket, wrapping it around herself. She looked miserably tired as she fished into her bag and gave several gold coins to Candro. "Next time, more blankets."

"All right, who are you, and when is Candro coming back?" Larin said, as Laniette walked away. Candro looked at him blankly.

"The Candro I know doesn't spend all day dragging a full sack around the city, only to donate the contents the end. Doesn't that violate some kind of thief's code?"

Candro smiled weakly. "Don't have much of a choice . . ."

"Well, while you're at it, I'm going to miss all the books I left. Can you grab them next time?"

Candro started. "You want me to return to the most dangerous part of the city and haul a hundred pounds of books—" He stopped as he saw Larin's faltering smile.

"Not you, too," Larin said. "Everyone here acts like I'm a leper, and now even you can't tell when I'm joking."

"Sorry, Wiz. It's just been . . . busy."

Larin stared. "Candro, don't you treat me differently, too. Not you."

Candro pushed black bangs from his eyes, looking down. "Wiz, I'm not trying to. It's just that . . . well, two weeks ago you were just some street urchin who couldn't utter a Lyrashi word to save your life. Now I hear you're the servant to some evil god, and you can collapse buildings with a few words. I—I'm trying to chew that and swallow it down."

Larin nodded coldly. "Right. Well, I better get back to my evil rituals."

"Wiz, just give me some time to get used to it. Nothing's changed."

Mouth tight, Larin walked back to his cell, standing a moment before collapsing onto the cold stone bench. He winced at the brief flash of daylight as Candro left the dungeon again, and he wrapped his arms around his knees. He remained like that for the next hour, trying to banish Ruldir's bloody arms and rag-doll babies from his memory.

After some time, a shadow darkened his doorway. He looked up to see Trana, her face somber in the low light.

"Can I come in?"

Larin nodded, pulling his legs closer to give her room. She flopped on the bench with a heavy sigh, and Larin's eyes widened as he noticed scars on her arm and a deep gash at her neck.

"The Morphasti didn't spare you."

She nodded. Her flat face was tired, pale with exhaustion instead of its usual red, and Larin wondered if he'd ever seen her sober before. They sat without speaking for some time, the silence suiting Larin just fine.

Finally, she turned to him. "You know, Larin, Emja's teachings name Haraf an enemy, no better than Morphat. It'll take some time before Korrin's comfortable with you."

Larin shrugged. "You belong to the same order. Why are you so reasonable?"

"Korrin's faith has ever been stronger than mine."

"You mean he's more close-minded."

Trana patted his knee. "Young'un, I've known you since you were a wee tyke. Haraf or no, I can't spot a drop of evil in you. But Korrin, he doesn't have that. I can't say how I'd feel were the roles reversed."

Larin leaned back, studying the cracked stone at the far side of the cell. His thoughts churned as he listened to the sounds of their breathing, intertwined with Laniette's low murmurs drifting through the doorway.

"Trana, who are the gods? I mean, where do they come from?"

She arched an eyebrow. "That's a question I can't answer. The Tiyani Codex tells us that the New Gods and humanity were born on the same day, but even Emja's verses don't claim he's our creator. That which created us also birthed the gods."

"And Morphat?"

Her nose wrinkled. "Whatever vile sludge disgorged the Old Gods, its origins are unknown. It's obvious the Eldegod are related to the indigen creatures, for they have similar features—six legs, multiple orbs, and so on.

But no one knows much beyond that."

Larin nodded, tracing the cracks in the stone bench with his index finger. "Yesterday I saw Emja and Morphat fight each other. In all the legends I've never heard of a direct battle between the gods."

Trana nodded gravely. "The gods exist on different planes, planes that barely interact with each other. They don't appear unless summoned, and a million summonings may occur before one is successful. That this one worked tells you the enormous stakes we play for."

"If they can't appear until summoned and can't interact with us, then they're not all-powerful."

Trana shrugged. "Some believe that. The gods have a subtle influence, but its effects can be huge. They can modify man's thoughts, ever so slightly, without his awareness. Through dreams and small nudges, the god's will can be multiplied across a kingdom—that will then turns into the movement of armies or the collective decisions of nations."

Larin hugged his knees tighter. "Trana, Emja was no match for Morphat yesterday. Morphat's claw was inches from Korrin when both gods disappeared. I don't know how I caused it, but if I'd waited another ten seconds to cast my spell, we'd all be in the Eldegod's hell. I—I think Emja cannot prevail without help."

Trana's mouth tightened. "Well, young'un, I was busy trying to stay alive, so I didn't see any of it. Surely you can't judge the outcome of such a monstrous battle."

"I know what I saw. Emja will not win without Haraf."

She said nothing for a long minute, and they listened to Laniette's low chanting in silence. Finally she turned to him with hard eyes. "Let me tell you about Haraf. In every age since the birth of man, he's picked a servant to win his release from the Gray Lands. The legends describe them— usually they're corrupt men given great power. Yet, for all their strength, not one has ever succeeded."

Larin shrugged. "I haven't even decided whether to try. So far, all I have are these insane outbursts, and sometimes I know things I shouldn't. But Haraf has never spoken to me."

"When that happens, hold your soul close."

Larin looked at her blankly.

"Lad, this tale always ends the same way—Haraf's evil pervades his servants in the end." She leaned back. "Legends tell of the murderous Duke of Olakor, who lived in the city of Umraut. He awoke one day to find he was Haraf's servant, commanding great power. Haraf repeatedly sent B'neikarian, the multifaced demon to convince the duke of his 'duty.' But he refused every overture, for he wished to use his power to destroy the armies of the neighboring duchies. Finally, Haraf forced himself into the duke's dreams, trying to bend his servant to demonic will." She looked at

Larin, eyes soft. "Legends say he became insane. He left his castle and traveled the breadth of the land, trying to find the gray portal, by which he could release Haraf's host. When he could not, he returned to his city and, in a fit of anger, destroyed it. He killed everyone there, including his entire family and all he once loved."

Larin searched her eyes. "Is it true?"

Trana nodded unhappily. "Yes. To this day, the ruins of Umraut stand in testimony to Haraf's evil." She placed a hand on his shoulder. "Larin, when your master finally commands you to action, something will change inside you. In this, Korrin's fears are well-founded."

"I won't let Haraf change me."

"Change will come, young'un, whether you will it or not. When insanity bathes you, remember who you are. You're the boy who risked his life to tell Luard that Oarl was coming for him. The one who saved old Higlen's shop by giving him every copper you earned for a year. You have a purity I believe has never been seen in the Demon Lord's servants. Haraf will steal some of that, but never lose what is in your core."

Larin swallowed slowly, and Trana stood up with a tired smile. "Well, I suppose that's enough doom talk for now. Care for a game of Thirazi? I found an old board and most of the pieces, used by the guards when this place was still a prison."

Larin shook his head.

She nodded, looking like she'd say something more, but finally turned around and left his cell.

Larin sat unmoving for the next few hours, his brain numb. Daylight flooded the dungeon twice, but he had no interest in what Candro was bringing. Once he heard the door open, but he saw no daylight and knew darkness had come. He curled up on the bench, his mind racing.

He was drifting to sleep when the low whisper of voices lifted him back into consciousness. After a moment he recognized Akul's and Korrin's voices, the hushed tones of men trying not to be heard. His curiosity piqued, Larin got up and quietly opened his door wider. He stepped carefully out of his cell, finding the one spot where their voices bounced off the stone walls and became clearly audible.

"—teachings."

"I don't care about your teachings. I don't care about any of it," Akul hissed. "Korrin, we've fought a hundred battles together, and our friendship is blood-sworn. But the bond with my boy is stronger even than that. When you attack Larin, you attack me."

"What is this talk?" Korrin whispered. "Is he some barmaid who cannot withstand a few spoken barbs? You've not undergone the rites, Lukas; you've not learned the long history of base evil accompanying everything Haraf touches. Next to the thousands already killed, and next to the millions more that will die if your boy releases the Demon Lord from his gray cage, a few insults are nothing."

"Let me tell you something about my boy," Akul snapped. "He's spent his entire life alone, due to this curse. He's been shunned in his own neighborhood by a group of thugs not a tenth the man he's becoming. I will not—" Akul stopped, as if too angry to speak. He continued a moment later, his voice calmer. "Now that he's free from that hell, I will *not* see him shunned again by his own allies."

Korrin was silent, and Larin leaned against the wall, feeling a rare warm glow. Akul understood him after all, understood him only too well. Why did his uncle have such a hard time saying it to his face?

There were rustling sounds, and Larin thought Korrin was getting up. "Lukas, it pains me to see our friendship strained. But I cannot change what I know. On the day Larin completes his transformation, you'll see why I act as I do. On that day, it will give me no pleasure to show you I am right. None at all." Korrin's voice sounded genuinely sad.

"Korrin, our god has made a pact with Haraf. Surely you can do the same."

"My part of that pact is holding off from killing him where he stands. No more can I do." There was further rustling, and Larin darted back into his cell. He curled up under the thin blanket, thinking of what Akul had said. Feeling better than he had all day, he drifted to sleep.

He awoke to a brief burst of daylight and Candro's excited tones. As he exited his cell, he saw a barely conscious Laniette standing next to Candro, while Korrin, Akul, and Trana crowded around from the other side.

"Quiet—the city is completely quiet," Candro said, gasping. "I've been up and down the Imperial District, and the Morphasti have crawled back in their holes, along with everyone else. Only the Imperial Guard is out."

Akul's face was grim. "Then Emderian has completed his consolidation. The city belongs to Morphat now."

Larin breathed deeply. "Since the Morphasti are gone, can I go see Onie? She'll be worried sick."

Akul scowled, but nodded reluctantly. "I'd come with you, but the Morphasti know me too well now. Stay low, and you *cannot* tell her where we are. If she's ever caught and reveals our location, we're done for."

Larin nodded excitedly, dashing into his cell to retrieve his sheath belt. He was running toward the door when a female voice barked behind him.

"Larin!"

He stopped and turned to Laniette. She wavered on her feet as she held out his charm belt and another metal disk hanging from a thin chain.

"Take these," she whispered. "I've added more protections to your charm belt. And this one"—she held out the small golden disk—"will allow you to become deaf, simply by touching it."

Candro raised his eyebrows. "Well, now, *that* sounds useful."

Larin draped the charm around his neck while the rest of the group watched in silence, then touched it with his right hand. Instantly, the low breathing and other small noises in the dungeon ceased. He looked in wonder at Laniette, who motioned him to touch the charm again. He did so, and sound came rushing back.

"That will be quicker than casting the spell," she said.

Candro sniffed. "I need one of those for when Larin tells me about the last book he's read."

Larin snorted, somehow happy Candro was insulting him again.

"Larin—" Laniette said, looking close to death. "Be careful with your magic. Forget your power spells unless your life is in danger."

"I know," Larin said. "Get some sleep." With that, he raced out the door into the eerily quiet streets of the Imperial District.

The day was warm, his excitement at seeing Onie burning bright. Yet it wasn't long before the city's oppressive pall weighed on him. Something felt different, an almost palpable fear seeping from the stones. A few people were shuffling quickly from their houses to the market, but no one lingered, and those he passed kept their gazes to the cobblestones. He shivered, remembering Trana's description of Kaman so many months ago: *The city folk don't look up at you, nor talk to their neighbors.*

At the border with the Porcelain District, a large plaza contained a mass gallows, where over thirty bodies twisted in the light breeze. A sign over one of the bodies labeled them as resistance, those who'd fought the Morphasti's coup.

Face grim, Larin turned into one of the hilly streets of the Porcelain District. On one street, the brick walls were lined with Imperial decrees, and he stopped to read one.

Those who agitate against the god will deny his love to us all. A fifty-crown reward awaits any who can help flush out the undeserving.

He swallowed slowly. This was how it had started in the Wormpile—Morphat turned neighbor against neighbor, until no one could be trusted. He backed away and ran down another street, suddenly even more desperate to see Onie.

Onie's family had moved to the Porcelain District after her father's brush with Oarl, but Larin had never seen their new apartment. Still, she'd told him where it was. For some time, he circled a two-block area, sure he was going crazy. Onie's description had been clear: it was on the Street of Tailors, across from a balconied pink building ready to collapse of its own weight. He stared at a building that had to be it, a small stone flat-roofed structure. Yet he'd traversed its stairway twice, knocking on every door. Everyone was gone. With growing dread, he jogged away, determined to search every street in the Porcelain District.

He was peering down a narrow street when he was assaulted by a pair of arms around his neck, accompanied by a howl of utter desolation. Bowled back by the onslaught, he turned to see a mass of blonde hair shoved into his face as Onie clung tightly to him, sobbing uncontrollably. He barely kept his balance as he grabbed her tight.

"Onie!"

"They killed them, Larin," she wailed. "They killed them. Everyone!" She was gasping so loud Larin pulled back and held her shoulders, wanting to make sure she breathed.

"Who? Who did they kill?" Yet one look into her grief-torn eyes told him everything.

"My parents, my brother, everyone," she gasped. "We—we were in the Emjaian temple in the north end of the district, when the Morphasti came to destroy the temple. All the men, they fought. My father, he pushed me out a side door to save me, and it was the last—" She stopped a moment, her face clouded by horror. "It was the last I saw him. The Morphasti— they burned the temple, and everyone inside. Everyone, Larin."

He held her tight, Onie's horror overwhelming him. A light breeze blew against his neck, rattling the Imperial decrees posted on every wall. He couldn't even imagine her pain.

"I didn't know what to do," she continued, fighting for breath. "I went to the Wormpile to see you, but the Morphasti were crawling through the area, and your building had been destroyed. Emja help me, I thought I'd lost you too . . ."

A movement caught his attention, and he looked up to see curtains parted, eyes peeking at them from an upstairs window. Chills passed through him as he remembered the Imperial decree: *A fifty-crown reward awaits any who can help flush out the undeserving.*

"Onie, listen," he said quickly. "We have to get out of here. I'm leaving the city soon, with Akul, Candro, and a few others. Come with us!"

She nodded, eyes red, but lit with what Larin thought was her first hope in days. "Yes. Take me away from this Eldegod hell."

Without another word, Larin grabbed her arm, and they traveled silently through the Porcelain District and back into the Imperial District. They circled the Henefraus castle two times, making sure no one was out, before they descended the stairway to the heavy stone door.

The dungeon's stink hit him like a wall as they entered, and he realized how accustomed he'd been to the rising stench from the prison's sinkhole latrines. Wrinkling their noses, they stepped inside, watching Akul's momentary surprise turn to anger.

"Akul—" Larin said quickly. "Onie's just lost her family. She's coming with us."

Face stormy, Akul opened his mouth to shout, but stopped himself as he absorbed Onie's stricken face and Larin's determined expression. There were rare times in Larin's life where he knew he'd never budge, no matter what anyone said, and his uncle seemed to realize this was one such time.

Akul exhaled loudly. "Ah, Rakva's balls, what's one more? I'm very sorry, Onie. For whatever it's worth, we won't rest until this Eldegod excrement pay for what they've done."

"Absolutely not!" Korrin boomed, shoving his way in front of Akul. "Emja's instructions are clear about who embarks on this journey. Even that one is too much"—he gestured toward Candro—"yet I sense something about him may be useful. But I'll not accept another member of Haraf's brood in this party."

Larin's eyes were steel. "You have absolutely no choice in the matter. If she doesn't go, I don't go."

Korrin stomped toward Larin, lowering that red-bearded face until his wrinkled eyes were level with Larin's. "Listen to me, Demon's servant: I'm barely able to stomach this 'pact' as it is. Don't think you have any power to influence this journey; I'll gladly leave you in this city to face Morphat's host."

"And defy your god?"

"My god needs no help from the destroyer of Umraut!"

Larin watched Korrin calmly, feeling a surge of power from another place. "Now you listen to me, you close-minded fool. Morphat's claw was an inch from your fat nose when I cast my spell. Faced with Morphat directly, all of Emja's might wasn't enough to protect his highest servant in Tanbar for more than two minutes. If you think your puny god can defeat the Eldegod without Haraf's help, you are the biggest idiot in the long history of idiots who have served Emja."

There was stunned silence in the dungeon, and Trana slowly traced Emja's glyph across her forehead. Larin was as shocked as the rest of them; the words hadn't come from any place he could recognize.

Korrin straightened up, smiling. "Well, at last your master peeks out for a bit of fresh air. As always, Haraf lies as easily as most of us breathe—"

"Enough!"

Everyone looked to Laniette, whose mask of exhaustion had been replaced by righteous fury. She pointed a shaking finger at Korrin. "I am tired of your propaganda, tired of you destroying the cohesion of this party. It's *you* we should leave behind." She gestured at Onie. "She's coming with us."

Korrin stared at Laniette a moment, and something finally gave way. "Insanity!" he barked, but then whirled around and stormed off. Larin stared in amazement at Laniette, for in the few days he'd known Korrin, he'd never once seen him back down. Shaking his head, he walked back to his cell, Onie leaning against him.

"Who was that horrible man?" Onie asked.

"No one of any importance," Larin said loudly, hoping Korrin heard every word.

All that night, Larin held Onie close, while sounds of packing echoed from the rest of the dungeon. He listened with half an ear as Trana, Korrin, and Akul finalized their plans—the next day, they'd leave through the Tu-Nara entrance, a minor gate opening to the north Hennat Valley, which contained sixty miles of farmland before it was swallowed by the lush eastern forests. Tu-Nara was small enough to be lightly guarded, but not small enough to be an obvious choice. Laniette had made illusion charms to hide their appearances, which she'd briefly explained was the only way she could maintain the spell if they lost sight of each other. Larin knew she was done now, for her loud snores swamped the low voices in the rest of the dungeon. He fell asleep sitting on the bench, leaning against Onie.

The next morning, Onie pushed him out of the cell so she could use the latrine, and he wandered to the main guardroom. Laniette, Trana, Korrin, and Akul were discussing last-minute preparations, while Candro watched silently. When Onie came out, Akul motioned all of them to gather around the room's single wooden table, where a ragged map displayed the city.

"Everyone listen," Akul said, pointing to a dot on the city's north wall. "Today, we travel to the Tu-Nara gate, on our way out of Aldive. Many of our faces are well-known in the capital, including mine, Korrin's, and Laniette's. Laniette has made us each a charm to hide our appearance." He nodded at Laniette, who began passing out small disks affixed to thin metal chains.

"These are bound to each of you," she said, "so you won't be able to switch. The illusion works better when it shows the same gender, so each of you will be some version of your current self, but different enough to hide your appearance." She looked at Onie. "I didn't have time to make one for you, but I think it doesn't matter. You'll not be recognized."

Akul waited until everyone had received their charm. "To activate the illusion, you only need to touch the charm. Do it now."

They all touched their charms, falling to utter silence as they stared at one another. Everyone's faces had become squatter, flatter, and darker, the type of face adorning thousands of Hennat Valley farmers. Larin thought it a good choice; they'd be as noticeable as the pigeons roosting all over the capital's red rooftops.

"Now touch the charm again," Akul said, and as everyone did so, their faces returned to normal.

"Each of us will take one of those," Akul continued, pointing to a row of cloth sacks on the floor. "They have our provisions, but they are also stuffed with vegetables, so a simple inspection should reveal only goods that our farmer illusions weren't able to unload. We'll store our weapons in my sack and Korrin's so we can get to them easier."

"What if *we* have to fight?" Candro said, his thin arms folded. He didn't look happy about giving up his dagger.

"Korrin and I can handle anything the Morphasti throw our way."

"Ah, there we have Commander Lukas's famous ego," Laniette said, her upper crust accent making the words sharper than she'd probably intended.

Akul looked at her without a hint of embarrassment. "Wizardress, I am merely stating fact."

"Yes, surely there was never any bravado in your speeches," she said, the gleam in her eyes belying her dismissive tone. Larin stole a glance at Korrin, and the giant's wistful expression told him he'd caught it, too.

Candro's and Trana's mouths had fallen open. Trana swallowed slowly. "Commander Lukas?"

Akul rubbed his forehead, as if forestalling a massive hangover. "A story for another day." He turned to Candro. "Listen carefully. Do you know where the entrance to the Imperial Compound is, at the top of the mount?"

Candro shook his head, gaping at Akul. "No, but I can find it, *Commander Lukas.*"

Akul scowled. "There are three levels of guard posts until you get to the main gate. At the first post, ask to speak privately to a man named Phios, or if he's not there, a woman named Nerallia. One of them will be on duty. To one of them *only*, you'll convey the following message for the queen: 'At all costs, keep our friend within the palace until tomorrow night. Signed: the one who fell over Girenne.' Can you remember that?"

"The qu—queen?"

Akul flashed annoyance. "One of them will convey the message up the chain to the queen. All you need to do is exactly what I've just said. Can you do it?"

Candro nodded silently.

"Good. Meet us back at the south side of the Haques Bridge. We'll wait a few minutes, but if we don't see you, we'll leave without you. Understood?"

Candro nodded and raced out the door.

Sighing, Akul motioned to Korrin, Laniette, Trana, and Onie. "We'll leave in four hours to give the queen time, and to allow Candro to reach the bridge."

While they waited, Laniette approached Larin. "Larin: cast *no* magic unless you're in imminent danger. Your bowl effect will be our death."

"Bowl effect?"

She ran her fingers through tangled red hair, her curls a distant memory.

"Every use of Lyrashi exercises the Lyrani threads in the area. That's called the bowl effect because the dampening of Lyrashi energy spreads out like an inverted bowl. Extremely powerful magic can create a bowl effect that stops all future spells for minutes, within hundreds of feet. It's said after gouging the Great Chasm, Jathan sucked so much Lyrashi energy from the air, no one could cast a spell for two days, up to three miles way."

Larin stared. "So that's why the Eldegod priests were powerless after I cast my spell! And the Morphasti warder charms stopped working!"

"I wasn't there, but I heard about it, and yes, it seems likely that's what happened. If so, your bowl effect is the strongest I've seen, maybe as great as Jathan's. When you cast magic above a certain power level, our illusion charms will die, and it will stop my spells. Understand?"

Larin nodded.

Korrin scowled. "All that power, wasted to help the Demon Lord."

This stopped the conversation dead. Akul rubbed his head silently while Onie held him tight, as if afraid he'd disappear into thin air.

They waited for four hours, with the silence filled only by the occasional tense, hushed tones of those about to risk their lives. Then, touching their illusion charms, they stepped into a city just getting used to its new chains.

222

Wit defeats power, but only if married to patience.

Philosopher Errin Klaide

XXII

Metal glinted through the tall hedges, and Queen Relena turned nervously to her four guards, who trailed at a respectable distance. She motioned them to surround her, then waited patiently for the assailant to show himself. The Imperial Compound was large enough to boast several parks and gardens, some extensive enough to hide a quick murder for days. Especially the murder of a queen who wielded no real power.

Yet the hedges shook with the bustling of one making no attempt to be quiet, and Relena knew quick relief as Captain Dekaust pushed through the thorny bush, looking annoyed as he shoved aside the brambles.

His expression became earnest, and he strode toward her urgently, stopping only when the guards moved to block him. "Your Highness," he said through their pikes. "I must speak with you in private." Relena's heart froze; how well did she really know this man? Yet within seconds, she reached the same conclusion she always came to. Giorlan already knew enough to slay her a hundred-fold. She must trust someone.

"Please let us walk in private," she said to her guards. Eyeing Giorlan suspiciously, they halted and let the queen walk forward. Giorlan moved beside Relena, remaining a deferential half-step behind, but close enough to converse.

"My queen," he whispered. "We have a message from the outside: 'At all costs, keep our friend within the palace until tomorrow night. Signed: the one who fell over Girenne.'"

She stopped, gazing at the rolling meadow, hills of soft grass that beckoned her to lay her head a minute, forget all her terrible worries. One could almost imagine they existed in true countryside, if one could ignore the giant compound walls in the distance. Shaking her head, she turned to Giorlan and moved close to his ears, to keep her words private.

"Captain Dekaust, remember when I told you that our only path to victory requires two things—getting the king to safety and helping our champions leave the city to find his cure?"

Giorlan nodded, staring straight ahead.

"We have embarked on the first, and for this I thank you. Now, we must achieve the second, and *everything* depends on this. I've been planning this for a long while, and all the pieces are in place. Let me tell you what you must do."

She outlined her plan in detail and when she was done, she stepped back from his ear, suddenly conscious of appearances. She searched his face, and he nodded, his eyes glowing with that persistent look of awe he seemed to have whenever she commanded him. With a quick bow, he ran off in the other direction, and the queen looked back at her guards, who watched them from atop the grassy hill.

"Guards," she called. "Please escort me to the main gate."

When the Great Hall's giant doors creaked open, Emderian was busy playing a coloring game with Yalinus, the goal of which was to sign the king's name in a different color for each scroll. Emderian tried to ignore the strengthening sounds of boots on wood, but was finally forced to tear his attention away from the parchment. He squinted into the flood of sunlight streaming through the arched windows and recognized Kopan, one of his few loyal non-Huja palace guards. Kopan halted next to the king's retinue at the bottom of the dais, his arrow-straight posture somehow conveying urgency.

Emderian returned to his game with the king, but Kopan's patient presence at the bottom of the dais was a constant distraction. Sighing, Emderian closed the scroll.

"Your Majesty, I think we have to continue this game some other time," he said. "By your leave?"

Yalinus looked at him, hurt, and Emderian made his best happy face. "We shall continue tomorrow, if it pleases you."

"Oh, all right," the king said petulantly, and Emderian bowed. Then he turned and descended from the dais.

He approached Kopan smiling, placing a hand on his shoulder. For many, that touch was the clasp of doom.

"This had better be very, very important."

Kopan swallowed and lowered his eyes. "High Wizard, I have a message from Goullard, Morphat's chief servant in the city. He says he's detected the presence of Emja's High Priest, and he believes the others are with him. They are on the move."

Emderian pursed his lips. "Well, get back to your duties, then." He walked past a very relieved Kopan and exited the Great Hall.

Queen Relena was watching the Imperial Compound's main gate, so she didn't actually see Emderian enter the front courtyard. Yet she knew all the same—she'd always been able to detect the High Wizard's immense disquiet, a bored cruelty mixed with an underlying anguish she doubted he even knew existed. She moved a little closer to her soldiers, but Emderian and his guards passed her without a glance, striding intently toward the portcullis. He slowed to a stop as he saw busy workmen swarming over the huge gears that moved the gate.

Emderian turned around, noticing the queen for the first time. Smiling pleasantly, he approached, his Huja warriors locking stares with the queen's elite guards.

"Well, my queen, it seems there's a bit of difficulty with the gate," he said, with the even tone of one discussing the weather.

"It would seem so, High Wizard."

Emderian placed a gloved hand on his chin, as if lost in deep thought. "Pray tell, why close the gate in midmorning? Perhaps we are expecting an onslaught of Lidath? Last I heard, the nearest dragon troops are about fifteen hundred miles away."

"I believe the guards were conducting a drill. The gate doesn't close much these days, and they need to move it back and forth every few months to ensure the gears don't stick." She nodded toward the gate. "And 'tis a good thing, for as you see, one of the parts no longer works."

Emderian stared at her intently a moment, then turned back to face the gate. "Ah, too true. Still, there are ways of speeding things along." He turned to a Huja guard. "Run to the smithy that is working on the gear wheel. Tell them if it is not ready within the hour, I will personally invite the entire team to my chambers to explain the problem." The giant Huja nodded silently, then spun around and ran off.

Emderian gave the queen a sideways smile. "If I am to have these awful rumors about me spread throughout the palace, I may as well use them to my advantage occasionally."

Queen Relena said nothing, and they both watched men scramble about the great gate's machinery for some time, loud curses punctuating the air of the Imperial Compound's front courtyard. Within minutes, a group of men ran out of a nearby building with the gear wheel.

Emderian beamed. "There, you see? I'll be on my way in no time."

They watched silently as the men hammered bolts through the gear wheel's lip, into the main shaft. With a nod, the head smith flipped his hand in the air and scrambled back from the gate. The men at the giant handle wheel began to pull down with all their might, and the gate gave a loud groan.

Just as the giant doors began to move, loud sounds of shearing metal screamed through the front courtyard, and men dove for cover. Finally, a sharp crack and plume of smoke made it very clear the gate would not open anytime soon.

The fat smith came running to the queen, his hand atop his hat. "Your Highness!" he said. "Now the smaller gear wheel has snapped as well. Something is preventing the gate from opening. It will take at least until tomorrow to fix."

The queen nodded gravely. "Make haste, smith, for our High Wizard has important business in the city." Her flat tone implied none of the urgency of her words.

Emderian's sour look lasted but an instant before he grinned sheepishly at the queen and gave a deep bow. "Well done!" He began clapping vigorously, the hollow sound of glove on glove echoing across the courtyard. Several workmen shot furtive glances at the exchange, returning quickly to their work.

Relena arched an eyebrow. "I'm at a loss to understand your praise, High Wizard."

Emderian pulled a long white pick from his pocket. "Oh, let us dispense with these games, my good queen," he said, digging between his teeth with the pick. "While I have clearly been outwitted by you this day, please grant that I am not a complete imbecile. I bow before your superior gamesmanship." With that, Emderian removed the pick from his mouth and gave another flourishing bow, to several sideways glances from around the courtyard.

"It shall be fixed by tomorrow night, High Wizard," the queen said. "No need for theatrics."

Emderian's small mouth pursed into a look of mischief. "And long beyond the time it will matter, as you well know. No, no, you shouldn't be so modest." He began picking his teeth again, looking intently at the queen. "You know, for people like us, superior intellect is a double-edged sword. While useful, it is also somewhat lonely. Let me submit you this, my queen: let us have tea together, as worthy adversaries. We could learn much from each other, and quite honestly, I find myself yearning for the challenge of such a conversation."

Queen Relena watched the High Wizard with distaste, suddenly nauseated by the forced politeness of this conversation. Decree by decree, she'd watched this man systematically turn her beloved city into a place of hatred and fear. She turned fiery eyes upon Emderian.

"I'd rather eat my own excrement than sup with you."

Emderian removed the pick from his mouth, turning to one of his Huja guards. "There now. Is a queen allowed to say 'excrement'?" The man remained silent, and Emderian turned back with a mild expression. "You see? I long for intelligent conversation."

Relena scowled. "Next time you seek to make a date for tea, it would be wise to stop picking your teeth like some Filstirian peasant." She whirled around, and her guards closed ranks around her.

"Oh, but how else will I remember the lovely Maera?" Emderian called after her.

Relena's blood froze. She turned around slowly. "Who?"

Emderian lifted an eyebrow, studying his pick. "Surely you remember your servant Maera? She was so sweet."

Relena's breath caught in her throat as waves of sickness engulfed her. Maera. Her most trusted servant, a woman who'd become like a sister, despite the vast gulf of rank. A loyal friend who, with no explanation, had one day simply disappeared. Relena turned her horrified gaze on Emderian's pick, now knowing it for what it was—a filed finger bone. Numb with shock and grief, she allowed her eyes to wander to the High Wizard's horrible smile, a smile speaking of atrocities far beyond those imagined by the palace staff.

She wavered on her feet, knocked backward by the aching gulf of Maera's loss, nearly fainting from Emderian's monstrous expression. She closed her eyes, forcing calmness. Then, fierce rage steadied her balance, and she strode out of her cluster of guards, directly through two surprised Huja guards, to plant her face inches from that of the High Wizard. He was a small man, and her eyes were level with his.

"You think to frighten me with your horrors, you disgusting, miserable man. Instead, you strengthen my resolve. By every ounce of strength left in me, I will defeat you." With that, she whirled around and stomped out of the courtyard, her guards struggling to catch up.

Emderian watched her go, picking his teeth absently. "That one is trouble."

He looked up, scowling at his Huja guard's empty stare. Mood dark, Emderian folded his arms and stared at the broken gate.

Strange are the ways of gods. Like a Port District champion, they play their Thirazi pieces far into the future, and with every bit as little regard to sacrifice.

High Emjaian Priest Korrin Tuarre (diary entry)

XXIII

S acks slung over their shoulders, they crept out of the Imperial District along deathly quiet streets. Walking silently through the Porcelain District, Larin breathed a sigh of relief as they climbed onto the Haques Bridge. He stopped and listened to the river's rush, gazing at the Tanbar's sparkling waters as it twisted through the city. He followed its winding path until it disappeared behind the Mount of the Empire, wondering if the capital's sights would ever fill his vision again. Then Onie turned around with a frantic look, and he hurried to catch up with the group.

They crossed to the river's south side, the street empty save for a few men loading a river barge with cloths and a homely farm boy watching the barge with a dull expression. The boy turned a placid gaze at Akul as he stepped off the bridge, and his stupid stare didn't waver as they approached. Unnerved, Larin looked away, but a soft, familiar voice snapped his head around.

"What an ugly bunch. The one in the back looks like he was run over by an apple cart."

Larin smiled. Candro.

"Your illusion is a vast improvement," Larin whispered.

Candro grunted, then moved to the front of the procession. They walked in nervous silence through the Little Hodjat District, staying close to the walls and trying to look innocuous. They turned left on the Street of Jewelers, keeping their heads down before the fine carriages clattering along its cobblestones.

As they approached the Tu-Nara gate, they saw others like themselves: farmers from outside the city walls carrying sacks or leading tagalanth-pulled carts. Larin marveled anew at Laniette's illusion, for they blended in well with the mass of humanity entering and leaving the city. They funneled into a crowd of people heading toward the gate, Larin's nose wrinkling at the close proximity of unwashed bodies.

Tu-Nara. Goddess of fools and adventurers: this entrance was aptly named for their journey. The gate and city walls loomed large before them, pitted stones green with moss, some stained black from an ancient fire. An upper walkway along the wall allowed men to run its length during siege, firing outward through any of the hundreds of arrow wells carved into the thick stone. But today, the archers along that walkway held their crossbows pointed downward *toward* the city. Eyes alert behind slitted helms, they watched the teeming masses below, waiting for the command to fire into the crowd. Larin's stomach clenched; he doubted this was normal. Someone was looking for them.

Tu-Nara, if ever we needed your help, this is it, he prayed. Yet as they inched closer, a cloth banner strung from a nearby balcony proclaimed the gate's new name: "Bekath's Entrance." Larin felt a chill that belied the sunny day.

As they came closer still, he saw groups of city guards pacing below the walkway, questioning people at random before they passed through the gate. A few guards held metal rods that Larin first thought were strangely shaped swords, but his curiosity deepened as he came closer, for they were like nothing he'd ever seen. Then Laniette whirled around and motioned them all close.

"Listen! Those rectangular poles are dispeller rods, designed to banish any magic they touch—Morphat's priesthood is desperately trying to find us."

Akul's illusory farmer rubbed what looked like a full head of hair, then stopped, confused. "So what do we do?" he asked.

"The rods won't break my illusion—they'd have to be enchanted by a higher-rank magician, and only one of those exists in this city. But they could detect our charms, and if so, we'll be questioned. We can't let that happen!"

Trana's illusion studied the gate a moment as the whole crowd inched forward. "I've been watching them. They're looking for big groups. Three times now, I've seen them stop large families and touch a few people with the rods. They're mostly ignoring families of three or four."

Akul nodded. "We'll split up. Laniette, Candro, and I will stay in one group—that should attract little attention, for we'll look like a simple family. Korrin, Trana, Larin, and Onie will be in the second group. Allow us to move ahead to make sure no one sees us all together."

Korrin and Trana nodded, and the four of them held back a few minutes while Akul, Laniette, and Candro were swallowed by the crowd. Finally, Korrin breathed deeply and motioned them forward. They inched toward the gate in silence, listening to the roar of the throngs, punctuated by sharp barks from the soldiers manning the gate. As they came closer, Larin could see the guards' faces, and knew immediately their normal commanders had been replaced by Morphasti. The three officers wore red and black armbands over their mail, and sour looks from their men told Larin they hadn't been there long. Their commander was a squat, bow-legged man who strutted before the gate, eyeing the crowd hungrily. Occasionally, he moved forward to place his hands on a woman, grinning at the husband or brother as if daring them to object. Larin guessed one did so, for a man was hauled out of the crowd at the commander's order and taken inside a building near the gate.

Not many objected.

The soldiers with the dispeller rods moved separately, occasionally stepping forward to tap someone, then moving back. With a chill, Larin saw that small groups were no guarantee of safety, for several times he saw them approach families of three or four. Yet one thing seemed universally true: whenever their commander took interest in a woman, the soldiers with the rods moved away, as if afraid to come near him.

It was probably what saved Akul, Laniette, and Candro.

He watched Akul and Laniette's illusory forms at the gate, several hundred feet ahead. The commander was leering at Laniette's illusion, and a soldier with a dispeller rod who'd been approaching her stepped away. Larin watched open-mouthed as the commander put his hands all over Laniette's body, reflecting that it was well the man couldn't see her true form, for she'd stand out like a rose among cobblestones. He waited for Laniette to fly into a rage and collapse the stone arch upon the commander's head, or engulf him in flames. She simply bore it. Akul's head was hung low, as if he was the beaten farmer he appeared to be. In that excruciating minute, Larin thought Akul showed the most self-restraint he'd ever seen.

Then the three of them were through the gate, and Trana issued a whooshing exhale.

Nerves on edge, Larin stood close to Onie, not sure what he'd do if the commander noticed her. Her blonde hair and slender frame would catch his attention in a heartbeat. Larin bent down to whisper in Onie's ear.

"Stay between Trana and Korrin. I'll block the rear."

She nodded, frightened, and the crowd moved forward.

They approached within a few feet of the gate, and Larin saw with relief that the commander was focused on a woman behind, while the two soldiers with dispeller rods conversed. Yet just as his hopes rose, one soldier idly turned around, eyeing them. After a moment's hesitation, the man walked forward, and Larin shot a terrified glance at the dozen archers on the walkway above. Most had pointed their crossbows further out, but two were trained directly on their position. He looked toward the gate, where several bored soldiers milled about, eyeing the crowd. Larin's panic rose as he watched the tip of the soldier's dispeller rod begin to glow green, and he shot quick glances at Korrin and Trana, both frozen with indecision. Most of their weapons were on the other side of the city walls, along with Laniette, the only person who could protect them without weaponry.

They were doomed.

Gritting his teeth, Larin was about to touch his deafness charm in preparation for magic when Onie shoved her way out from behind him and strode toward the commander.

"Hello! Over here! Are you blind?"

The soldier with the dispeller rod stopped and stared open-mouthed as Onie strode toward the commander. The squat man turned in surprise, then beamed widely.

"Well, hello, my beautiful yellow flower. How in Morphat's six claws did I miss you?"

"You've paid attention to every other woman here. Am I not good enough?"

Larin's heart broke. "Onie no . . ." he choked.

The commander noticed Larin's anguished expression, and his smile widened. He walked toward them, dragging Onie behind, and the soldier with the dispeller rod turned away.

"What a lovely blossom you have here," the commander said sweetly, as he ran his hands up and down Onie's body. His breath stank of alcohol as he stared intently into Larin's eyes, looking for a hint of defiance. "She really is a treat."

The three of them stood frozen, and Onie struggled to keep the revulsion from her face as the commander lightly kissed her neck. They stared at the commander, muscles tensed.

"Well," the commander said, disappointed at the lack of response, "I think I'll keep this one for myself—she clearly needs a real man." Onie's weak smile melted into unconcealed panic as he hoisted her over his shoulder and began walking away.

Larin's jaw dropped in horror as Onie's hair cascaded downward in blonde streams over the man's shoulder. Her face was wild with desolation, yet girded by determination. She lifted hollow eyes, desperately mouthing the words: "Go, go, go!"

The thought of Onie trapped here with this troll emptied Larin's soul, leaving no room for any other thought. He didn't care how important this war was, who he was supposed to be, or whether the Demons ever escaped their gray prison. Right now, all that mattered was Onie.

"No!" he screamed, and the commander whirled around and dropped her. Larin began running to Onie, when a giant weight hit him in the back of his head and his face landed on the cobblestones.

Brief words traveled through his consciousness for the next few minutes.

". . . he thinks she's his, but she never wanted to come to our farm . . ."

". . . no, Commander, we are your servants . . ."

". . . Morphat's blessing on you, Commander . . ."

Once, he opened his eyes to see the gate's arch a hundred feet away. Confused, he struggled to focus, trying to understand why they were walking *away* from the entrance and why he was traveling on Korrin's shoulder. Then, Onie's face leapt into his consciousness. His eyes flew open, and he twisted out of Korrin's grip to land on hard-packed dirt, staring at the city with raging fire in his gut.

"Onie!" he screamed, and several people on the road started in surprise. He whirled around to look at Trana. "We have to go back!"

"If he doesn't shut up, we're doomed," came Korrin's voice behind him. Then Larin heard footsteps, and he turned to see Korrin holding a giant rock as if about to knock him down again.

"Don't you dare!" Larin hissed, and something came over him then. A raw force that seemed to rise from deep in his soul, magical energy that needed no Lyrashi words. It stopped Korrin cold, despite his attempts to move forward. Several farmers passed them by on the dirt road, staring at the exchange in fear. Korrin stepped back, watching Larin incredulously.

Larin turned back to the city, touched his deafness charm, and brought forth a violet-sash spell of seeing he'd learned six months ago. A spell that focused the water droplets in the air like a giant prism, allowing one to watch events from miles away. Feeling the fast rush of energy through his veins, he concentrated on Onie's face, desperate to see whether she'd escaped the commander. Raging power cascaded through his body as he uttered the Lyrashi words, a power that boiled his blood and seemed to set his skin afire. He shouted the final power word furiously, and felt the sudden chill of energy released.

Korrin and Trana watched helplessly as Larin searched the air for some sign of Onie, exhausted dizziness threatening to bring him down. He touched his charm again, and sound came rushing back.

"By all that's holy, our illusions have failed!" Korrin shouted. "We have to get out of here!"

"We can't leave Larin!" Trana said, at the edge of panic.

Exhaustion overcame him. He fell to his knees, staring at the dark clouds of moisture rising from the sea and spreading over the capital. They formed an ominous arc a thousand feet high, connecting the city and the ocean like some vast celestial bridge. Crestfallen, he searched that moisture for some sign of her, but no visions sprang from those clouds. As before, his magic was powerful but useless.

Devastated, he watched Aldive become swallowed by blackness. The ocean's dark mist surrounded the city, and wild howling could be heard even from a half-mile away, as winds wrapped the city walls like tortured wraiths. Several people stared stupidly at Larin, but his eyes were fixed on the city, ignoring Trana's anxious tugs.

They watched the walls for some time, listening to the howl of winds and the pounding of rain, until that rage reached them where they stood. Buckets of water poured from the sky, and their audience scattered.

"Let's go!" Korrin shouted over the deluge, but Larin remained on his knees, desperately trying to see the gray city walls through the downpour. He heard Trana and Korrin shouting at each other through the roar, and finally, he rose unsteadily to his feet. Trana looked at him with a grim expression, rivers of water washing down her flat face. She mouthed the words: "Let's go."

Larin shot one last glance at the city, enveloped by black clouds no less dark than his soul. Struggling to control his pain and sheer exhaustion, he nodded in dejection.

Hunching against the pounding rain, they ran down the road.

XXIV

Queen Relena smelled the fear from far down the wooden hallway, well before she reached the gold-inlaid door. Captain Giorlan strode swiftly ahead of her and turned the corner into the room. "Attention: the queen!"

She smiled sadly. They both must appear rather ludicrous, demanding respect from their soaked peasants' garb. Yet she'd needed this shawl and drab kirtle, now dripping wet, to slip unnoticed past Emderian's hyenas.

She turned into the doorway to see them all standing there, heads bowed. Twelve men, three women, loyal lords and city functionaries. A sorry collection, but it was from this she'd fashion the resistance. For the first time, she noticed the barely audible low rumble now shaking the Imperial District keep as torrential rain pounded the tower roof.

"Thank you, loyal subjects," she said softly, entering the room. "Please, sit."

They sat, averting their eyes from her wet peasant rags. Queen Relena, a fashion trendsetter throughout the Imperial District and entire city, now garbed like a street beggar. The room smelled of wet mustiness and tea as Lord Ituran, owner of this keep, sipped from a mug that clinked softly from shaking hands. Outside the arched window, a gray curtain of rain obscured the Imperial District, shrouding the nearby towers in dense fog.

She'd prepared a speech, but in this room of packed misery, where the fear was thick enough to spread on stoneloaf, she knew something else was required.

"Speak your thoughts," she said, sitting in the chair reserved for her.

"Highness, we don't know who to trust!" blurted Mattean, ex-commander of the City Guard. "Morphat's spread spies throughout the ranks, and my men won't talk to me, thinking I work for them now. I feel the same way. The price of sedition is torture and hanging!"

Lady Sophie's face had drained of all color. "My guards stopped them from destroying Emja's statue outside my keep," she whispered. "The next day, those guards were hanged outside my walls with their hands and feet missing and eyes gouged out. The fact that I am here today is—is beyond terrifying." She looked wildly around the room.

"They've been interrogating my servants," said Lord Ituran, "asking them to report on any malfeasance I may be planning against the Morphasti. My wife's loyal handmaiden told us in private. One wrong word where the cooks can hear, and we shall be straight on for the gallows."

Queen Relena shot to her feet. "My friends and allies, fear is Morphat's lifeblood," she snapped, interrupting several people about to speak. "They mean to cow us with atrocities while they consolidate their power, but do not let them fool you. Their control is not so great—defiant men and women still resist the Eldegod claw in pockets throughout the city. If we huddle in fear now, this nightmare will swallow us whole, and we will lose all momentum. But if we coordinate our actions while Morphat still struggles for balance, we can keep the fire alive." She stopped, listening to the pounding rain outside. The air was damp and still, and they watched her intently.

She sighed, smoothing her wet kirtle. "The Imperial Compound was designed to withstand indefinite siege. We will be a base for the resistance—we will grow the food that Morphat seeks to control. We have blacksmiths to make armor and weapons with which we'll arm the resistance. We are in stalemate now with the High Wizard's Huja guards, but with another few hundred soldiers on our side, they'll not be able to touch us. I want every one of you to pass the word to your guards and soldiers: any with Hemek blood must come to live within the Compound. They are in danger in the city, and their added loyalty in the compound will keep our backs firm against Emderian's warriors. Can you do it?"

She surveyed the room, feeling a tiny measure of relief at the slow nodding of heads. Not all would be brave enough to help, but some would. Before fear could seize them again, she turned to the tall, gaunt man leaning on the window ledge. As Prelate of the Elduvian Magical Academy, Teigham was now the strongest wizard in the city after Laniette and Emderian.

"Master Teigham, I believe you have some news for us."

Teigham nodded. "Some bad, some good, Highness. The bad: Kemharak's army has destroyed our Wizard's camp just north of the passes."

Relena felt it again like a dagger to her stomach. Everything was collapsing around her. She'd hoped Teigham would temper the news for this audience, given the room's near fear-paralysis. Yet he'd ever been the blunt academic, unable to read a mood. She continued staring out the window toward the Imperial District rooftops, where rivers of rain cascaded to the streets below.

"Yes. I have other sources who say the same."

Teigham must've detected her annoyance, for he continued quickly. "There is good news as well, Highness. The party has successfully left the city—Lukas, Laniette, Korrin, and a few others."

Relena's vast relief came in counterpoint to the palpable disappointment that draped the room like a wet cloth. They'd been hanging on this one positive shred, and it was nothing to them. She faced her assembled lords and ladies.

"It is indeed good news, my loyal subjects. You must understand, our only hope for victory is to find the king's cure. This is not my opinion—it has been stated by Emja himself to his High Priest. The success of this party is our best and only hope."

"Highness, with all due respect, I want to believe but cannot," said Mattean. "Kemharak descends upon us from the north, Seridor from the south, and when they see the noose around our necks, the High Desert tribes from the east will join in as well. With our Council of Twelve gone and Morphat's monster whispering into our king's ear, I do not believe we will be saved by any band of heroes. No matter how mighty they are."

"There is something else," Teigham cut in, as Queen Relena was about to respond.

She looked at him with pleading eyes. *Teigham, say something good now, or all is lost.*

Teigham stopped, looked around the room, then focused on her face. "This rain—it's unnatural."

Relena blinked. "Well, it did come suddenly from blue skies . . . ."

"It is more than that, Highness. There is a bowl effect—a dampening of magical energy—so large, it has encompassed the city for six hours, since the beginning of the rains. No one will be able to cast any significant spell today, not even Emderian. The power behind such a phenomenon is almost too great for words, perhaps larger than the bowl effect created during the gouging of the Great Chasm. In my lifetime, I've never seen anything like it."

The room was still as death, with only the steady drumbeat of rain to pierce the silence. "Could Laniette have worked such magic, to aid in the escape?" Queen Relena asked softly.

Teigham shook his head. "No, certainly not Laniette. Even Emderian is not powerful enough to draw such energy from the Lyrani threads. Remember, he was once leader of the Council of Twelve, and we know well his power. It is enormous, but not this great."

"Then—"

"There is another magical force with them, Highness," Teigham said, looking extremely uncomfortable. "Some say Haraf's minion has joined their ranks."

Queen Relena closed her eyes. Of course, Lukas's nephew. Now, her last chance to sway these people had washed away with the torrential rains. For Haraf was an enemy no better than Morphat; none of them would ally with that monster.

Yet when she opened her eyes, she was surprised to feel the excited tension in the room. Dame Tierrette, once City Treasurer, leaned forward in her chair. "So this party has a wizard even more powerful than Emderian?"

"Well, the magic feels formless, and it's not clear how much training—" Teigham stopped at Queen Relena's intense stare. He swallowed and turned back to Dame Tierrette. "Yes. Yes, the wizard that caused these rains has more raw power than even Emderian. Much more."

They traded glances of hope and fear, and Queen Relena cut in before they could ask questions. "Emja has allied with Haraf against Morphat, giving us a much-needed boost in this war. While none of us countenance the workings of Demons, in this fight for our lives, we will take our allies where we can. This is an alliance between gods, and you must understand that the party that's just left our city is on no ordinary mortal's errand. My loyal subjects, we are very much engaged in battle, and we are by no means defeated." She glanced at each one of them. "Now I ask again: will I have your support in this fight?"

An immense relief washed over her as all the heads nodded, especially when Lord Ituran stood up. As the unofficial leader of this group, Relena knew that he was a man of integrity and that his agreement was a bond of steel.

"Your Highness, we are with you."

Queen Relena nodded, knowing he spoke for them all.

"We will fight the Eldegod, and we will do it with every bit of strength in us. And we will succeed." Lord Ituran placed his teacup on a bureau, and Relena saw that his hands were no longer shaking. "We simply must."

Pity your Lidathi enemy: gifted with speech, yet not with free will. For they are beholden to monstrous gods and base desires that constrain their lives as surely as iron chains.

General Igran Nyales to his soldiers, 7030 CH

XXV

Kemharak burst into the tent, trailed by a guard. His commanders rose, but he ignored them and strode directly to the chained human. The creature was curled into a ball on the ground, the wounds on its body clearly visible.

"Release it from the ground chains at once. Leave its appendages chained."

Low whistles sounded from the back of the tent, but Kemharak kept both frontal pods on the human, watching as it rose unsteadily to its feet. The elastic substance covering its body was marred by several long red streaks, and it bore many dark blotches where its body had been opened. All the result of one commander's rage. Telhasak had almost killed the creature while the other commanders watched, despite Kemharak's clear orders that the human was to be left alone.

Telhasak had been instantly executed of course, for there was no other possible response to this challenge. Yet the fact that his other five commanders had watched this outrage from their seats troubled him. His entire command must be disciplined at once. Any planned mutiny would come today, the Day of Rising.

The human's orifice stretched back to reveal the flat-bottomed fangs of its kind, an expression Kemharak had come to associate with pain. He opened rear pods, letting the images of his commanders superimpose over the human's face. Their pods bore the gray of neutrality; the only contrite cyan came from Manek. Kemharak took what comfort he could from this and closed his rear pods. His commanders' ghostly forms vanished, leaving the human in clear outline.

"Come," he grunted to the human, grabbing its arm. He dragged it behind him, finally stopping at the tent's entrance flap and turning to his waiting commanders.

"Manek, come with me. The rest of you will stand until I return." He watched their pods carefully, searching for a hint of red that could presage a mutiny. Satisfying himself, he whirled around and exited the tent, pulling the human behind.

He strode through the camp, now filled with reenactments of the Day of Rising. Everywhere he went, groups of seconds and thirds danced around the Jehibulleth, waving tree branches to frighten them back and forth across the lair, then shouting words in the gods' tongue and setting them free. The ceremonies inevitably stopped with his approach, as the seconds and thirds crouched in respect. Kemharak ignored them, marching purposely through the camp and dragging the human behind. In its weakened, pain-filled state, the creature was not able to keep up with Kemharak's long stride, and it occasionally lost its balance. Still, it uttered no cries as its lower appendages were pulled across the ice, and Kemharak did not slow until he caught a glimpse of it twisting backward to see the ceremonies.

Kemharak hesitated, suddenly curious to hear this creature's thoughts on today's events. He pulled it to a standing position.

"Watch."

Power was given to the second and third—the other sexes—only one day out of the year, so what was given on that one day must be great. On the Day of Rising, the two other sexes were made into gods, releasing the Jehibulleth just as their ancestors had once been released. Kemharak felt a simmering brew of emotions he would once have ignored, for the ceremonies were normally performed deep within the tribal mountain lairs. Only his war had brought them here, a few miles from the blood-soaked Avensai passes. He peered inward, as he did often lately, knowing an indescribable melancholy that came with being a hundred miles from home.

The human drank it in with unconcealed interest, and Kemharak watched it watching the ceremonies. One by one, the Jehibulleth were released from their cages, to be sent scurrying back and forth by the seconds and thirds standing in a circle, dancing and whistling in the gods' language. Eventually, the creature was allowed to scamper away, to much chanting and singing. Kemharak wondered whether the human considered these ceremonies pitiful, a subject race scrabbling pathetically over the hard ice, trying to emulate its gods. Then anger filled his core, anger at himself for caring what this small, weak-boned creature thought about anything.

He turned around and yanked it behind him, walking so fast, the creature's lower limbs scraped across the ice. Manek followed in silence, and they marched for several more minutes through the camp, the human's lower appendages dragging behind.

It was a measure of his army's size that this vast ice field barely held them all, for most years they fit into a small corner of it. The long walk from his tent through the camp lifted his spirits, swinging his newly overwhelming emotions from black despair to cautious optimism. He cursed the avalanche of inner thoughts that plagued him every day now, a consequence of too much time spent around this human. Yet, he could not pull away from it, as if the creature was the salt rock that had once nourished his tribe.

Eventually, they entered the surrounding forests, and Kemharak dragged the human a little longer before coming to a halt. He considered its ineffectual claws, satisfying himself that they were still manacled by the rune-etched chains, then looked into its beaten face.

"You will follow."

He turned around and let the human walk behind him, Manek bringing up the rear. They began climbing the hill at the base of the Avensai summit, their boots sinking into the thick snow as they weaved through the great pines. The forest was quiet, with only the crunch of snow beneath their feet and the occasional rustle from a nearby bush to indicate that anything other than great trees lived here. The human's heavy breathing sounded behind him, but it seemed to keep pace.

After a few minutes of silent climbing, Manek's voice whistled softly behind him. "Revered one. You drag the human across the camp, yet it walks on its own here."

It was not a question, only a statement. Kemharak stopped and opened his rear pods. "The people do not understand, Manek. The god tells them the human must feel pain."

Manek's throat flaps opened and closed steadily as he considered this. "You do not agree?"

There was danger here. Kemharak turned around to consider Manek with his front pods. The forest was deathly quiet, interrupted only by the sounds of their own breathing and the crackling of distant branches. Manek's question could mean anything. Yet whatever Kemharak told him, Manek might later dream—and dreams were the domain of the gods.

Kemharak considered his words carefully. "Pulling the human up this slope makes no sense. Why should I expend energy bringing it pain for no purpose?"

The yellow-orange of suspicion flashed briefly from Manek's pods, before they returned to neutral gray. "Revered one, is there no other reason?"

Kemharak was consumed by sudden anger, but he quelled it instantly. Manek's directness was exactly why Kemharak had made him High Commander.

"Yes. Giving it pain now will reduce its willingness to tell us more. It is already weak from Telhasak's wounds. If it becomes much more damaged, it will be unable to speak or think clearly."

Manek's pods turned white in submission, an acceptance of Kemharak's argument. Still, without looking again, Kemharak knew those pods still bore the faintest trace of orange-yellow. The creator had designed them well; hiding strong or even moderate emotions was impossible. Kemharak turned around, his anger rising again. His rage came not from Manek's doubts, but from the fact that Manek's suspicion was right. There was another reason.

Kemharak looked down at the creature, who was watching them both with its constant-colored blue and white pods, unable to understand the conversation. Extending his claws, Kemharak looked away and began climbing again. That other reason was not to be explored.

Despite his earlier words, Kemharak had to drag the human for the last several hundred lengths. Its weakened state had brought it down well before reaching the summit, and Kemharak would not carry it—that was going too far. He climbed the last outcropping, sliding the human across the rock as delicately as he could.

He and Manek stood atop the summit, pods half-lidded against the fierce wind that whipped through the crags and slapped at their faces like a bent tree branch. The might of the human army was arrayed below, six endless trails of ants across the vast white sheets. Those trails extended far down the mountain until they were out of sight, a collection of soldiers, thrukk, wagons, and other equipment. At the head of one trail came the only real threat, other than the magical corps—khula knights. He tried to note its direction and calculate where on the plateau the khula would be tethered.

A noise came from below, and Kemharak saw the human trying to rise, its red blood oozing in a few places along its face.

"Stay down," Kemharak said. "Recover your strength." Then he turned to Manek. "I told it that it could stay down. Do not kick it if it cannot rise."

The human ignored Kemharak, reaching a cloth-wrapped, manacled appendage upward to grip a nearby rock. In obvious pain and with its last reserves of energy, it slowly pulled itself upward, gasping as it unbent its damaged body. Finally, it stood straight against the wind, its head fur flying backward.

Manek watched the human closely, the swirling colors in his pods unreadable. Yet Kemharak had known Manek long enough to deduce what emotion danced there: respect.

With his upper right claw, Manek pulled out a Tuana root stuffed with denarin meat, wordlessly holding it out to the human. Both Kemharak and the human stared at Manek in shock, though Kemharak quickly turned away. With side vision, he saw the human tentatively take the offer from Manek's outstretched claw. It studied Manek carefully as it bit into the root, then both of them turned to gaze at the spectacle below.

With the whistling wind as their background, they watched the endless trails of the human army ascend the slopes, a long journey that would end at their vast campsites on the Avensai plateau. Jagged peaks surrounded them in every direction, throwing shadows across the valleys, even as their summits glowed gold from the sun.

The human army was early this year, for the beginning of the war season was usually marked by the Nadir. Kemharak suspected his enemy had been shocked out of their complacency and had finally taken the measure of their foe. This victory would not come easy.

"Human—Theralle," Kemharak said, bracing himself against the wind by holding a bare tree root with his middle claws. "Why do Tanbar's armies come so early this year?"

Theralle shook its head, bowing into the wind. "I do not know."

Kemharak turned away, controlling his anger. Their dance was frustrating, yet somehow fascinating. The human withheld information whenever it could, but Kemharak could sometimes peel away its obfuscation by playing to its strong emotions—humanity's great strength was also its curse. Sometimes, Kemharak talked about his impending victory as if it had already happened, bringing the creature's anxiety to the surface, where true thoughts sometimes escaped. Other times, discussing its enemies at home made it wild with anger, an emotion Kemharak had found often caused humans to say things they wished they hadn't.

One thing he'd learned never worked was threats.

Kemharak stared outward, deciding to try the second strategy. "I do not understand the motives of he who betrayed you. He destroys Tanbar's power by"—Kemharak searched for the human word for subterfuge—"by treachery. Yet then he sends this army against us, the largest human army we have seen in generations."

Theralle turned its beaten, leathery face upon Kemharak. "The one who betrayed me has no control over the army. The king sends the army."

Kemharak splayed his claw in the sign of agreement. "Our spies tell us that the old king is dead. The new king is his litter-mate, whose every action is controlled by your enemy." Kemharak watched, interested, as the human's deadened expression turned to rage. Its face often went red when this happened, and Kemharak used this to know when he was getting close.

"It cannot be," Theralle said fiercely. "The people would never accept Yalinus as king!"

"Yet it is so, human. Your enemy has used his position near the king to bring the gods of my people to your empire."

Theralle made a choking noise and clenched its cloth-wrapped appendages through its manacles. The human's pods were wild, holding back emotions Kemharak could only guess. For a moment the three of them stared outward, watching the human army creep up the Avensai slopes.

"Tell me more about this traitor, Theralle," Kemharak said after a minute. "First he betrays you, the second most powerful mage in Tanbar. Then he gives us information that allowed us to destroy the human midrank wizards. Then he destroys the rest of your Council of Twelve, the most powerful wizards in your land. Now he sends this enormous army against us, but has just given us new information that will allow us to destroy much of it. Does he truly seek our victory?"

Theralle stared at Kemharak, its feeding orifice wide open. "What—what did you say about the Council of Twelve?" Its voice was low, almost inaudible against the wind.

Kemharak studied the human. "Your enemy has destroyed Tanbar's Council of Twelve—except himself, of course."

Slowly, Theralle sank to the snow, making strange, pulsating noises. Kemharak had heard such noises before on humans, just before he killed them. He had thought such behavior was related to fear, but it appeared crying could be caused by other factors.

Manek looked at Kemharak with the amber of confusion, and Kemharak bunched his head ridge with uncertainty. He looked at the human.

"Why do you—cry, human?"

Yet it shook its head, merely repeating the same word over and over again: "Laniette."

Kemharak's anger rose, for he did not like not understanding. "Human. You will explain to me this word you utter. What is Laniette?"

Theralle looked up, its face as red as the berries that poked through the snow in spring.

"Laniette was my wife. She would have been next to ascend to the Council of Twelve after my capture. And that monster"—Theralle hung his head again—"that monster killed her."

Kemharak considered this. He knew the word "wife"; it was the human's other. Humans had only one other, unlike his own people who had a second and third. Yet he could not imagine why the loss of his other would cause such a reaction. He was about to ask this, but stopped as Theralle slowly rose from the snow, its pods wild and its orifice clenched into a tight expression Kemharak had never seen. He thought it was anger.

"I will help you," Theralle whispered. "Anything you ask."

Kemharak stood in shock. He focused all senses on this human, burning to understand its motivations. "In the past, you have refused to give us information against your people," he said. "Yet now that your enemy has killed your other, you will help us?"

Theralle breathed deeply. "It is more than that. My enemy—

Emderian—will bring Seridor's gods to my beautiful Tanbar. I have seen what hell comes from worship of the Eldegod. If Emderian succeeds against you, he will become king, and Tanbar will sink into such depths of despair that it will wish it had been destroyed. If you destroy his plans, he will never gain the throne. Perhaps you would overrun my country, but perhaps also you will be defeated. Even if your armies do reach the capital, I see some hint of reason in you, Kemharak. I think it would be better for Tanbar to take its chances with you than live directly under Morphat's claw."

Kemharak stepped back, surprised by the intensity of the human's passion. He stole a quick glance at Manek, who seemed keenly interested in the conversation, but whose pods were pink with frustration at being unable to understand. Kemharak looked back at the human.

"Then tell me about this Emderian. If he would be king, why does he help us destroy his own empire's might? If we succeed, he will be ruler of nothing."

"You have no idea of this man's power. All of us in the Council of Twelve, we measured our power in units of energy—how much Lyrani heat we can generate at noon on Apex day. As second most powerful mage in the empire, my score was twenty-five." Theralle looked directly into Kemharak's pods. "Emderian's was seven hundred. He will cast lakes of fire upon your entire army, even at Nadir. You cannot prevail against him."

Kemharak tried to keep fear's green from his pods. It would not do for Manek to see his leader afraid. "Even so, human, why would he betray his own army?"

"He needs heroic action to claim the throne. He betrays the army in order to weaken it—Tanbar's salvation must be by his hands, and his alone. He believes he can single-handedly turn the tide of battle, even when the army is on the verge of collapse."

"And do you believe this as well?"

"Yes."

Theralle said nothing else for a long moment, as he gazed into the valleys below. Kemharak let it mull its words, and he was rewarded when it spoke again.

"But he has a weakness," Theralle said finally. "To claim the throne, he'll have to travel back to the capital. There, he will be anointed in the palace, a place immune from magical power. Your army need only survive until he is gone."

Kemharak flared his throat flaps in satisfaction—it was everything he needed. This was the information he'd been seeking for so long; the fact that the human had kept it from him all this time told Kemharak that it was the human who'd really won their game of words. He gazed at the trails of the human army below, thoughts swirling in his head. A plan was beginning to take shape.

They watched the valleys below for some time, Kemharak waiting in vain for the end of the human army to become visible. The wind waxed and waned through the summit rocks, throwing their thrukk-fur coats backward with its force. It became clear that the trails would not come to an end before nightfall, but Kemharak stayed anyway, admiring the beauty of the mountains and thinking through his plan. Eventually, his thoughts turned to the Creator, wondering how he would stave off its bloodlust once his conquest was complete. Considering the Creator brought him back to this day's celebrations.

"Theralle, what did you think of the Day of Rising?"

Theralle had buried its face into the fur coat, but it lifted its head to look at him. The human's face was dead and parched from the freezing wind, but Kemharak saw fascination there.

"I—I've never seen anything like it. I had no idea Lidath—Created Ones—had holy days. The animals were . . ." Its voice trailed off, and Kemharak struggled to keep his pods neutral gray.

"The animals are called Jehibulleth," Kemharak said. "Finish your thought."

Theralle suddenly looked frightened, as if it had said too much. It stole a quick glance back at Manek. "The animals were very vigorous in their escape," it said finally.

Kemharak's head-scales clenched with tension. "That is not your first thought. Say it, human. Say what is in your head."

Theralle swallowed, then looked into Kemharak's pods. "The animals. They are you."

Kemharak turned back to consider the valleys, feeling tension's release. "The Jehibulleth are our ancestors. They are as we would be, if the gods had not brought us high. They scurry on six legs, they have larger guanath sacs at the base of their throats, they burrow into the earth, and they do not speak. But they are us."

Theralle's pods were wide with wonder. Then he turned to Kemharak. "But you don't have any sacs at all in your throat. Unless . . ."

Kemharak struggled to keep red from his pods. "We do, human. We keep them flat, for it is forbidden to use them. They are features of animals, dirty. We will speak no more of guanath."

Theralle considered this, then turned his gaze away. "So the Day of Rising celebrates—"

"The day the gods brought us into their lairs and gave us speech. Today, the seconds and thirds become like the gods, working the creator's magic before releasing the Jehibulleth. Just as we were once released to work the metals from the earth and bring them to the gods' cities.

"The forest was different then, full of singing vines, Henila mounds, and

245

many other plants and creatures which exist no more. You humans have changed everything." Kemharak didn't know why he was telling the human this; he felt some unexplainable need for it to understand their past.

Theralle moved its head up and down. "It is what I always thought. The gods created your people for work, not for pain. It means there are some gods who care more about what you can produce than what misery you can cause."

"Or it means the original gods have become insane over time," Kemharak said. He was very glad Manek could not understand.

Theralle's face became animated, and its deadened face seemed suddenly alive with energy. "I have thought about what you said earlier. How your god comes to you in dreams, making you angry, commanding you to inflict pain upon others. I—I think there is a way out."

Kemharak turned to the human, struggling to keep the amber of confusion from his pods.

"Listen," Theralle continued. "In our magical studies, we often make warder charms to block external influences from Demons, spirits, and even gods. Usually, those are bound to the individual. But we can set magical wards over an entire area as well, charms that can block low-level Influence such as you receive at night. It will be less effective than individually bound charms, but we could set them over your entire tribal lairs . . ." Theralle's face was on fire now, his pods dancing with energy. "Kemharak, we may be able to free your people from the influence of your Creator!"

It happened almost without volition. Kemharak's upper right claw slammed into the human's face, sending it sprawling to the snow in a spray of its red blood. "You presume too much!" he shouted, as Theralle rolled over in the snow. Manek took two steps toward the human, but Kemharak held up his claw.

"It does not concern you."

The human slowly lifted its face, now streaked with red, and considered Kemharak. Its pods had returned to their deadened expression, and Kemharak felt a sudden, overwhelming shame. It was not a common emotion for him, and he struggled to banish it. Never had such an action caused him anything but brief release, especially not when the action was upon the human enemy. Yet the shame consumed him nonetheless. He walked to where Theralle lay in the snow and held out his upper right arm.

"Take it."

The human grabbed his arm, and Kemharak lifted it to a standing position. Manek watched all this, his pods amber with confusion.

"Apology accepted," the human murmured as it tried to stand straight. Kemharak did not know what "apology" meant, but he let it go.

They descended from the summit in silence, the human stumbling between them. Once, it fell to the ground, and Manek did not kick it. They both watched as it struggled to pull itself up, then turned and continued the descent.

A few circles remained in the campground, where seconds and thirds frightened the Jehibulleth back and forth, waving their tree branches with mighty whistles. Yet most of the campsite had gone quiet, for the sun had slipped over the mountains and night's deep freeze was close. Kemharak did not drag the human through the camp, but allowed it to walk behind.

The three of them entered the tent followed by a guard, and Kemharak's throat flaps opened with pleasure, both at the warmth provided by the glowing rocks and by the sight before him. His commanders still stood at their table, and he knew they had not sat once since he'd left them this afternoon. There would be no mutiny.

He motioned the guard to chain the human to the side of the tent and considered his commanders. "Tomorrow, we will discuss the vital information this human has provided today, which will allow us to win this war. Information that all of you would have let die without lifting a claw." He saw the cyan of contrition in their pods, a true cyan, without a hint of pink or red. He'd made his point. "Go back to your tents."

One by one they pressed their four claws together in respect, then left. Kemharak turned to Manek. "You too, Manek."

When the tent was empty save for him and the human, Kemharak walked to a spot near the glowing rocks and sat, letting his mind drift back to his last conversation with Theralle. He struggled to piece together what had led to his rage, an introspection that had become all too common since he'd met this creature. As his mind absorbed the possibility that magical wards could block the god's insane night terrors and return his people to reason, he knew what had caused his outburst. An emotion he'd never known, one he had no right to feel, and one the human had no right to invoke in him. An emotion so removed, he had to struggle to remember its name.

Hope.

THE END

Steve Rodgers

EXPERIENCE THE CONTINUATION OF LARIN'S JOURNEY
IN BOOK 2 OF SPELLGIVER:

IN THE CLAWS OF THE INDIGEN

BOOK3 OF SPELLGIVER:

SECRETS OF THE LAND

TELLS THE STORY OF WHAT CAME AFTERWARD

.

Newsletter Signup and Reviews

I hope you enjoyed this book. A review on Amazon is one of every author's end goals—it allows us to validate our books, and helps readers decide whether spending their hard-earned dinero on this particular novel is worth it. So please consider leaving a review on Amazon for this book, and help make the world a little better!

To receive information about upcoming book releases, bonus content, and other miscellany, please sign up for my mailing list. You can find the signup form on my website at www.steverodgersauthor.com.

Books by Steve Rodgers

- **Spellgiver Book 1: City of Shards** (this book)
  —Available on Amazon

- **Spellgiver Book 2: In the Claws of the Indigen**
  —Available on Amazon

- **Spellgiver Book 3: Secrets of the Land** (Coming February, 2019)

- **Mountain Witch** (in the world of Spellgiver)
  —Available on Amazon

- **Recall**—science fiction novelette (Coming September 2018)

- Science Fiction/Fantasy Short story collections will be out in 2018/2019

Acknowledgements

Writing a book is an enormous undertaking filled with self-doubt and the near certainty that no one will care. In that environment, it seems to me an impossible task without 100% suport from the home front. That I have. My wife Lori provided love and moral support when I was down, allowed me to blather on about my writing plans at dinner, and exhibited superhuman patience as I spent weekends typing away. She was also one of my first beta readers, gave me much useful advice, and her enthusiasm for the books despite never having read epic fantasy provided encouragement on those days when I wondered if anyone would be interested. I really could've never written this without her.

I had many beta readers for this book, and for "In the Claws of the Indigen", all of whom gave useful feedback. Some of the early readers included Kira, Amanda, Faye, Kyle and Fonda Lee, my Viable Paradise XVIII classmate. Fonda's book "Jade City" has just been nominated for the Nebula, and it's well deserved. Pick up her book, you'll be glad you did!

My two friends Dawn and Doug from the Penny Dreadfuls writing group read through every word of these books, and gave me so much useful advice that I can honestly say almost every chapter has been influenced by their comments. These books would be much poorer but for their attentive detail. Doug passed away before he could see these books in print, which was a huge blow. Doug, RIP, and Dawn thanks for all your help!

And finally to my "little brother" Kyle, who despite my predictions that he'd be bored by my writing, kept requesting more pages until I finally had to print both books on my straining laser printer and give it to him. His enthusiasm helped clue me in that I might have something here.

The cover art was produced by the incomprehensibly talented Raoul Vitale. You can see more of his art at: www.raoulvitaleart.com. Those gorgeous maps were created by Cornelia Yoder, at: www.corneliayoder.com.

I was very honored to be able to land a first class editor, and one who's worked on several bestselling fantasy books. This book, and "In the Claws of the Indigen" are edited by Chersti Nieveen, with help from Calisa Cramer.

About the Author

Steve Rodgers has been reading science fiction and fantasy since he was old enough to carry a stack of hard-bound books out of the library. The Spellgiver series started as a fantasy daydream from his teen years, some of which was composed onto paper using an honest-to-god typewriter. The novel was abandoned for decades, during which time those typewritten pages sat in the garage, steadily yellowing inside their clear plastic case. Much later, after many years of moving virtual bits around on a computer, Steve decided that dreaming up alternate worlds was way more fun, and picked the story up again. And then ditched it, rewriting it from scratch. Then he rewrote it again, and then again, into one big book. Which was then broken apart into two and rewritten. After enlisting an army of beta readers and making many more revisions, two books were born: "City of Shards," and "In the Claws of the Indigen." Both of those are now complete, and the third book, "Secrets of the Land" is being written now.

Somewhere in the middle of the endless revising, Steve began writing science fiction and fantasy short stories, and selling them to a variety of on-line and print magazines. To date, he's written 30+ stories, 15 of which have been sold to magazines like Compelling Science Fiction, Perihelion, Metaphorosis, and many others. You can find a full list of publications and a blog at his website: www.steverodgersauthor.com. Many of these will be coming out in forthcoming collections.

Steve Rodgers is an engineer working in security and cryptography. He has over 30 issued patents, with many more pending. He lives in Southern California with his unbelievably accepting wife, and a golden retriever that has turned sleep into an art form.

Made in the USA
Columbia, SC
29 December 2018